Who's to S[ay]
the Wind Will Blow

Part One of the
Who's to Say Trilogy

by

Carol Carpentier

Brighton Publishing LLC
501 W. Ray Road
Suite 4
Chandler, AZ 85225
www.BrightonPublishing.com

Who's to Say Where the Wind Will Blow

Part One of the
Who's to Say Trilogy

Carol Carpentier

Brighton Publishing LLC
501 W. Ray Road, Suite 4
Chandler, AZ 85225
www.BrightonPublishing.com

Copyright © 2012

ISBN13: 978-1-936587-75-9
ISBN10: 1-936587-75-0

First Edition

Printed in the United States of America
Cover Design by Patricia McNaught Foster

⟨Dedication⟩

To my grandson Brent Haskin, who at age ten planted the seed of inspiration for my novel while traveling with us through Ireland.

⟨Acknowledgements⟩

I thank the following people for their invaluable input while on this journey through the lives of Laura and Liam:

Bob, my loving husband, whose encouragement and belief in my story was validated by his devotion to the process of helping me put my thoughts into words.

Lif Strand, my longtime friend and fellow Arabian horse breeder, who traveled many miles to bring skills so vital in transforming my vision into a novel.

Pat and Bob Radmacher, our dear friends and partners in the world of Arabian horses, whose companionship during research in Ireland brought us a wealth of memories.

Susan, Una, Josie and Toppy of the Corcoran family in County Tipperary. By the warmth of their hearth, these Thoroughbred breeders and trainers entertained us with colorful tales of life on the Emerald Isle. Toppy Corcoran, the leading jockey during the period of my story, was an invaluable source of information about the world of Irish horseracing.

⟶ Chapter One ⟵
February 1975

The sleek black Bentley coupe raced through the twilit countryside of the south of Ireland on twisting, narrow back roads. The young woman behind the wheel normally enjoyed the drive home from Cork—but not today. A storm was looming off the Atlantic coast, and it felt to her as though a cloudburst was imminent. But she thought the weather could be a welcome challenge, a diversion from the despair that had plagued her since the death of her father three days before. She switched on the car radio.

"Rather cloudy with spells of rain, heavy at times, especially in the south."

Fey heaved a deep sigh. *Dear God, please let me get safely back to the Manor. I know Laura was upset at being left behind, but I just needed to be alone...*

At times, the country road seemed to be a mere path winding its way through a giant hedge, and Fey was forced to slow her pace. There was barely room for one car, and darkness was quickly closing in. A pair of approaching headlights melded with her own, the oncoming car slowly squeezing past. Rain began to pound across the verdant land.

"Dear God," Fey said out loud. Her heart began beating faster as she slowed her Bentley to a crawl, still forging ahead. Her eyes strained to see the road, but she could only make out distorted images through the fogged windshield.

The squealing tires of a fast approaching-car, its headlights darting across the landscape, struck terror to the very core of Fey's soul. Blinding beams were now directly in her path. There was no room to move over.

Fey clenched the steering wheel in desperation, and in a flash, the treacherous journey came to an end.

With the southwest of Ireland deluged by the Atlantic storm, the fire in the living room of Montrose Manor provided warmth, yet no comfort, as it cast its glow upon the anxious man. Lord Aidan Meegan sat motionless staring into the embers. *Fey should have been home hours ago. I wish she would have let me go with her to Cork...*

The sudden pounding of the heavy brass door knocker jolted him out of his chair.

Captain Flannery of the Garda stood solemnly at the doorway. One look into the captain's eyes and Lord Meegan knew the worst of his fears had been realized. The image of his precious eight-year-old daughter Laura tugged at his heart. With blinding certainty, he knew that without Fey their lives would become as dark and turbulent as the storm now engulfing the estate.

ᴄ✑ *Chapter Two* ᴄ◡ᴅ

Spring 1975

Upon the vast estate of Montrose Manor, night brought a layered darkness which hung over the land like a heavy fog. Laura, at the window seat of her elegant bedroom, looked out over the stillness in anticipation of what tomorrow would bring. She was fearful of any change after the tragedy that had occurred only two months before.

Laura could still see the haunting darkness of her father's grief-stricken eyes as he told her there had been an accident and her mother was never coming home.

The joyous times with her mother were now only fleeting images for Laura, who was pulled further into the void deepened by the absence of their spirited activities.

Like Fey, Laura had inherited a natural musical ability, and the legacy of song and dance had been alive in the Manor from the time she was a toddler. Fey had nurtured Laura's gift, teaching her daughter to play the piano as soon as the child's tiny fingers could reach the keys.

As Laura was her only child, Fey had forgiven the little imperfections that crept into her daughter's behavior as she got older—behavior Aidan said was a regression to the unconventional ways of Laura's gypsy grandmother. His daughter was the quintessential tomboy, with a stubborn preference for wearing jeans instead of dresses. Laura's deep passion for horses usually resulted in her returning from the barn much later than expected.

But Laura, her beauty accented by soft brown eyes, could charm either parent into permissiveness. Any trouble that followed the girl would pale beside the glow of her loving and caring heart.

The devastation of February, however, had been beyond Laura's grasp. Now it seemed there was nothing to look forward to—not even her ninth birthday, just a few weeks away. Laura's darkened heart was filled with emptiness.

Lord Meegan had been married to his beloved Fey for thirteen years and now, for the first time in his life, he was unsure of himself. A handsome man in his late forties, Aidan Meegan was tall, with graying hair and soft brown eyes. A descendant of one of the old titled Gaelic families, Lord Meegan carried himself with a proud, regal presence, even now, despite his unbearable grief.

The fondest memories of his wife were no comfort to Aidan, who was now perpetually shrouded in a cloud of loneliness. He loved his daughter deeply, but Laura, with her long wavy blonde hair, was the mirror image of his Fey, and it was difficult for him to even look at her. Aidan found the need for escape to be compelling. He could not give Laura what she needed most: a strong and comforting father.

The Lord of the Manor would soon be leaving for Dublin to lose himself in his business endeavors and rejoin the racing circuit with his horses.

While no one could ever replace his Fey, Aidan knew he needed to find someone to care for Laura. After several interviews in the village, he hired a family to join the staff at the Manor. Noreen Delaney had excellent references as a nanny, and her husband, Philip, was highly recommended as a gifted horse trainer. The interview with the Delaneys went well, reassuring Aidan that he was doing the right thing. However, his confidence could not offset his concerns about how his daughter would handle the news. He waited until almost the last minute to tell her.

"Laura, dear," he began gently, "tomorrow morning a family will be joining the staff. They will live in one of the cottages by the barn. Mrs. Delaney will be your nanny. Mr. Delaney will be the new horse trainer, and their son, Liam, will be helping with the barn duties. I believe Liam is only a year older than you.

"There is a special task I have given to Mr. Delaney—to find you your very own horse and give you riding lessons."

Laura nodded politely, but only felt a mild stirring of interest.

Now lying down on her window seat, clutching her teddy bear, Laura's anxiety grew. She didn't want a nanny—she wanted her mother. Laura yawned and rubbed her eyes. "Teddy, let's go to bed."

Climbing under the covers, Laura began thinking about her trusted pony, Lilly, who could no longer be ridden after the onset of arthritis. *I hope Lilly won't mind if I get a new horse. And the new boy...I wonder what he's like. It might be nice to have someone to play with. But the nanny...What if she makes me wear dresses? I want my mother!* Laura wept, finally falling into a restless sleep with fear and anticipation bounding in and out of her dreams.

As the old truck entered the estate the next morning, cautiously winding its way along the tree-lined driveway, Noreen Delaney was awestruck by the sight of the enormous castle before them. "This estate is wonderful!"

Noreen was small in stature, but strong. She and Philip had always wanted children, but they had not been blessed with Liam until Noreen was in her mid-thirties. *I hope this job will work out and we will finally have a nice home for Liam,* she thought.

As the driveway turned towards the Manor, Philip Delaney's anticipation deepened as he looked past the river and caught sight of the extensive horse facilities.

"What a grand place this is," he remarked.

Philip Delaney was known as a man close to the souls of the horses he trained. Many said he was part horse himself. Tall and extremely good looking, with a rugged, outdoorsy appeal, his manner was always gentle and patient.

Even for a gifted man like Philip, employment as a horse trainer was seasonal on smaller farms. He had always wanted to work for a world-class barn, and at Montrose, he would have the opportunity to start some of the best bred colts in Ireland—and be employed by Lord Meegan, whose reputation as being fair and generous preceded him.

Young Liam was the only member of the Delaney family who was unimpressed with the estate and the promise of a new life. Once again, he had been uprooted. His family had moved from one place to another, always in hope of finding steady employment and making a permanent home. Liam was going to be ten soon, and in his five years of education he had attended eight different schools. He was not looking forward to starting over yet again.

Being the son of a working man, Liam always seemed out of place around wealthy people. He was shy, soft-spoken, and a deep thinker, often misunderstood to be unfriendly. In truth, Liam had a heart of gold and a soul to match. Like his father, Liam had a natural ability with horses. In fact, he had a way with all animals.

Mrs. Delaney turned to gaze at her son, who had his father's good looks, dark hair, and incredible blue eyes. She was particularly proud of her son's musical ability and gifted voice, although she was frustrated with his unwillingness to share his talents with others. She wondered if he would even try to fit in with these new people. *This is all so excitin'. I only wish Liam wasn't so gloomy.*

Laura was awakened by the sound of the vehicle coming up the driveway. Bolting out of bed, she rushed to the window to see an older pickup truck approaching the Manor. Quickly, she dressed and headed for the stairway. Stopping impulsively in her tracks on the landing, Laura sat down behind the banister. She was not quite ready to meet the new family.

Lord Meegan made a point of personally greeting the Delaneys at the door.

"Welcome to Montrose Manor," he said cheerfully, his hand extended. "Please, come in, and let's have some tea."

"Thank you, Lord Meegan," Philip said as they walked in. Liam followed a few paces behind in an attempt to go unnoticed.

"Please, call me Aidan."

"Thank you, Sir," Philip replied, pleasantly surprised. Aidan gave Noreen a warm smile and shook her hand. She bowed her head slightly before she spoke.

"Thank you so much, Sir, for the opportunity to be a part of this wonderful estate."

As they crossed the marble floor, Noreen was in awe at the grand entry with its crystal chandelier suspended high above. She suddenly turned back to glance at Liam, making sure he wiped his feet at the door. Her son was busy surveying the intimidating surroundings, squirming as he walked. At that moment, his eyes found Laura, who was still sitting on the landing at the top of the stairs as she studied the new people. She, too, was attempting to go unnoticed.

"Oh!" Aidan exclaimed, acknowledging the boy. "My apologies—you must be Liam." Startled, the Delaney boy froze in his steps.

"Liam, say hello to Lord Meegan," Philip prompted.

Liam reluctantly stepped forward and took the man's hand. "Hello, Sir," he said, almost inaudibly. Aidan noticed Liam's distraction and followed the boy's gaze upward to see Laura peering through the railings.

"Laura, dear, please come down and meet the Delaneys."

She hesitated, and then slowly descended the stairway. Liam avoided further eye contact with the girl, as though figuring he'd already done enough damage by drawing attention to where she was hiding.

Aidan gently encouraged his daughter to come closer. "Laura, this is your new nanny, Mrs. Delaney."

The woman met Laura with a hug. "God bless you, child!"

Mr. Delaney gave Laura a big smile. "I promise to find you a grand horse to ride."

Laura was silent until prompted by her father's raised eyebrows.

"Hello, Mr. and Mrs. Delaney," she replied dutifully.

Philip was not pleased to see Liam standing behind his mother. "Liam, come and meet Miss Laura." Suddenly he turned to Aidan. "Or is it—Lady Laura?"

"Just Laura will be fine," Aidan replied. "We no longer stand on the ceremony of traditional title, although the people around here still do call me Lord Meegan out of habit. My family has owned this estate for many generations."

Liam slowly came forward. "Hello," he said, with eyes lowered.

Laura had already decided he was unfriendly, and she only spoke at the prompting of her father.

"Hello, Liam!" she said loudly, in mockery of his shyness.

Aidan intervened. "Liam," he said warmly, "Cook has prepared tea and scones for us. You are welcome to join us in the dining room if you wish."

"No thank you, Sir," he replied quietly. He walked over and sat on the stair.

Aidan turned to his daughter. "How about you, Laura?"

"No thank you, Father." Laura brushed past Liam on her way back up the stairs. She resumed her post on the landing above, looking down on the uncomfortable boy. Liam knew she was there, but wasn't about to acknowledge her presence. He felt a certain advantage in staying right where he was, within earshot of the dining room.

The adults took their seats at the table, and Iris, the downstairs maid, served tea. As Aidan went over details of their employment, the Delaneys responded with sincere enthusiasm. Aidan was increasingly pleased about his decision to hire them, and added some incentives he hoped would make young Liam feel more at ease.

"I would like to have your son tutored here at the Manor with my daughter, if it's all right with you. I'll see he gets a good education. Laura's new tutor starts in two weeks."

"Thank you so much, Sir," Philip said with gratitude. "Liam is a very bright student—eager to learn."

"Also," Aidan continued, "in addition to the horse for Laura, I would like you to find one for Liam. I feel my Thoroughbreds are too large and too spirited for the children. Perhaps you could find a smaller breed, such as the Connemara or the Arabian. I've found Arabians to be very gentle and relaxed around young children."

The last remark struck a chord in Philip. "I have seen that, too, and I think I know just the place to look. I'll make sure to get a gentle horse for your Laura. I know Liam will appreciate this very much—he has a way with them, Sir."

Liam heard this and was momentarily excited. His thoughts quickly darkened. *As soon as I get the horse, we'll probably have to move on.* The adults came back out to the entryway and Liam anxiously stood up.

"Well, Son, did you hear what Lord Meegan said about the tutor and about the horse?" Liam nodded cautiously. "Well, I'd say that's mighty generous!" Philip nudged his son. "What do you say?" Liam straightened up.

"Thank you, Lord Meegan, Sir."

From her post, Laura had also heard everything. She, too, was excited about the horses. She felt having someone to ride with could be fun…maybe. But Liam's apparent lack of enthusiasm was disappointing. *He doesn't want to be my friend—he doesn't even want to be here. Why do I need a nanny anyway? I miss riding with Mother…*At that moment, a deep sadness overwhelmed her.

Fey and Laura had spent countless hours together horseback riding on the lavish 850-acre estate. Galloping in the green fields and trotting through the forest, they had often stopped along the River Maigue to picnic. Laura had ridden her Welsh pony, Lilly, and Fey her Anglo-Arab mare, Velvet.

Laura knew those days were gone, and she felt like her loneliness would never end. With tears in her eyes, she turned and ran down the hall, retreating to her room.

Aidan walked the Delaneys out. "Continue down the road towards the barns, and Mr. Callahan will show you to your cottage. You may begin moving in right away. If you need anything, please let me know."

"Thank you, Sir," Philip replied. "I believe we've got everythin' we need—and thank you again for leavin' the cottage furnished."

After the Delaneys said their goodbyes, Aidan looked around for his daughter. She was nowhere in sight.

⊂✐ *Chapter Three* ✑⊃

A
s an experienced nanny, Noreen Delaney was accustomed
to the challenge of earning a child's trust and knew success
with Laura would begin with finding any activity to divert her away from
grief. Noreen saw her opportunity one morning as she took notice of
Laura's interest while Cook was baking.

"Laura," Noreen asked gently, "if I were to bake some biscuits
and needed a helper, would you be willin'?"

A glimmer came to Laura's eye. "Mother and I used to bake
biscuits and scones together." She began to take a cautious liking to her
new nanny, who made her feel special with words of encouragement and
a smile.

As Laura played the piano one day, Noreen ventured into the
room, softly singing along. Laura was pleased and continued playing. In
the days that followed, their bond strengthened with the music they
shared.

Laura looked for Liam during these moments, but he was never
around. She only saw him at mealtimes, and he never said a word.

One morning, Laura was determined to make a friend out of the
boy.

"Liam, do you want to play? I could show you some fun places."

"No! I don't play with *girls!*" He rushed out the back door and
was out of sight before she could say another word.

Noreen shook her head in dismay. "Child, give him some time.
He's very shy. With movin' around so much, he's had a hard time
makin' friends."

After that, Laura grabbed her riding cape and headed out for the
Delaney cottage. She walked along the river, suddenly stopping as she
noticed some ripples in the water. Liam was skipping stones. Without
hesitation, Laura picked up some rocks of her own and joined in. Having
learned from the gardener, Mr. Callahan, the girl's skill was advanced.

At first Liam pretended he wasn't watching, but he soon saw that
Laura was getting at least a half-dozen skips from each throw. "Not bad

11

for a girl," he said. He let the stones fall from his fingers as he got up and began to walk off.

"Wait!" Laura cried. "I just want to talk to you!"

"Well, you'll have to keep up, little girl." Liam hurried down the path. Laura tried to catch up, but soon lost sight of him.

"Liam, where are you?"

There was no answer—just a rustling noise from a nearby tree. She spotted the boy twenty feet above her. *So, he thinks he thinks he can hide from me up there?*

The challenge of a tree-climb proved to be nothing for the tomboy who was, of course, wearing jeans and not a dress. Within seconds, she was on the branch beside Liam.

"Well, I'm impressed, little girl."

"Well, I'm impressed, too, Monkey Boy!"

They stared at each other until Liam's lips quivered into a smile, and the two children broke into laughter. In that moment, a friendship was born.

ᴄ✐ Chapter Four ᴄ✐

Philip Delaney quickly settled into the routine of the barn, and by the end of the second week, he felt comfortable enough to take a journey away from the estate to find two horses for Laura and Liam. He was headed for the farm of a previous employer, who just might have what Philip was looking for. Although Philip had trained the Thoroughbred racehorses at the farm, he had also schooled two Arabians for the owner's son and daughter, who rode regularly until the day they left for college. Philip knew those gentle horses would be perfect.

Making his way up the drive to Michael O'Leary's farm, Philip recalled pleasant memories of working there. O'Leary was a respected horse breeder, producing some of the best Thoroughbreds in the county. Unfortunately, the market was soft and buyers weren't paying quite as much. Cutting his staff to part-time help was O'Leary's only choice. With a family to support, Philip was forced to move on—much to O'Leary's regret.

O'Leary beamed as he saw Philip step out of the Montrose horse van—*lorry*—and walk in his direction.

"So, Philip, the word around town is that you've got yourself a good spot with a big-time farm."

"It's big enough for us to hold our own and put in a good days' work."

They talked about the latest buzz from the track, and discussed Lord Meegan having two of the best colts in the country entered in the stakes race at Limerick. The conversation shifted to O'Leary's horses. Philip rubbed his chin thoughtfully.

"It's a shame the two Arabians aren't bein' ridden. Perhaps a new home could be found for them."

"Somethin' tells me you've already got a place in mind," Michael quipped, nodding towards the Montrose lorry.

"Now, Michael, you know I'd only want the best for those two—not some public barn where they'd just be a number. It just so happens that Lord Meegan wants a horse for his young daughter—and one for my son, Liam, as well."

At first the man was reluctant. "You know, Philip, those two Arabians are part of the O'Leary family. They've been here longer than most of the Thoroughbreds."

"True enough, but the mare and gelding are now ten and eleven. I'll bet they miss the attention now that your kids are away."

"Well, I guess I can't argue with that."

"Michael, you know the reputation of Montrose. They'll be stabled and cared for together 'til the end of their days—even if *I* don't last 'til the end of their days." The two laughed warmly.

"You'd better stop before you bring a tear to me eye," Michael chuckled, extending his hand. "You've got a deal. Sold!" The handshake became a hug. "Why don't you stay the night so you can get a fresh start in the mornin'? You don't need to be drivin' four hours back to Montrose in the dark."

"Only if we don't lose ourselves in takin' of the drink," Philip laughed.

The next morning at Montrose Manor, Chloe, the upstairs maid and night nanny, came from her room just down the hall to see if Laura was dressed. Chloe was in her late twenties, tall, with a medium frame. She had red hair, bright green eyes, and a warm smile which could light up the room. But on this morning, the true glow came from Laura.

"Chloe! Today my new horse is coming!"

"Good Lord, child, I can see it now—horsehair and dirt everywhere. I'm sure you'll be wearin' dresses to the barn and tearin' hems. I'll be part seamstress along with my other duties…" Chloe busied herself in the room and continued to ramble on while Laura slipped out the door and down the stairs.

Hurrying through breakfast, Laura and Liam chattered excitedly about the new horses. Mrs. Delaney watched, pleased to see their enthusiasm. *Maybe havin' a new horse will help ease Laura's sorrow, and Liam can start to feel like he's got a home.*

The children jumped up from the table, heading for the door, but stopped in their tracks at the sound of Mrs. Delaney clearing her throat.

"Yes, you may be excused," she said wryly. "Just be careful!"

With a dutiful *thank you,* the two youngsters rushed out the back door, running to the barns as fast as they could to wait for the lorry's arrival.

The stately stone barn of Montrose was built with an impressive entrance through twin oversized mahogany doors, the elaborate Meegan Crest hand-carved into each. Built in the round, the barn was set up with twenty-four large horse stalls—box stalls, actually—facing the covered riding arena in the center. At one end of the arena was an open space with a large tack room and washroom, and several cross-ties used for grooming, tacking, or farrier work. The second story was a large capacity hay loft, complete with doors to the hay feeders below.

The facilities were designed for training in all kinds of weather, perfect for the frequent rainfall in Ireland. Lord Meegan stabled his yearling colts here in the main barn until they were ready to start race training as two-year-olds at his other farm in Kildare.

Apart from the main building, there was also a large hay storage barn with a few box stalls in the back for use when there was a temporary overflow of horses. At the front end was a place to park and store carriages.

The morning barn crew had readied the boxes for the new horses in the normal manner, but Laura and Liam insisted on bringing in extra bedding and hay.

"I don't know what else we can do but wait," Liam sighed.

"I do," Laura said, reaching into her pocket. She pulled out a handful of sugar lumps. "I must tell Lilly about the new horse," she said thoughtfully. Liam followed her out to the pasture where they found the Welsh pony grazing. She picked up her head and nickered to Laura, whose face saddened as the pony slowly made her way to the fence. Laura offered Lilly treats as she stroked her neck.

Tears came to Laura's eyes. "Lilly, you know I'll always love you. I hope you understand about the new horse, but you'll always be number one." The pony nuzzled the girl before returning to the other horses grazing in the pasture.

Liam took Laura's hand. "She knows how much you love her, and look—she's happy." Laura gave him a little smile. "I'll bet I can beat you back to the barn," Liam said with a slightly mischievous smile.

15

It took no more than that for Laura to start off at a dead run. Liam followed, but intentionally let her win.

Between gasps—and laughing—Laura pointed up into the barn. "We could wait in the loft. We can see everything from up there!"

Naturally, the waiting period was not wasted. The two children passed the time swinging on a rope and jumping into large piles of hay. They laughed so hard it brought tears to their eyes. It had been a long time since either Laura or Liam had felt so carefree.

Knowing the children would be too excited to come back to the Manor, Noreen decided to bring them a picnic lunch. Approaching the barn, she heard the children's unbridled laughter. *What a wonderful sound it is! I think Liam is finally happy now, and little Laura has the companionship she so desperately needs.*

Noreen called to them as she entered the barn, but they didn't hear her. She climbed the stairs of the loft to find the two children covered in hay.

"Oh, my! It looks like you're havin' fun. Both of you will need a good scrubbin' this afternoon. Laura, your father's invited us all to join him in the dinin' room tonight."

The children dusted off the hay and began to devour their sandwiches and gulp down the cold milk she brought them. Noreen shook her head and smiled as she left to return to the Manor.

A few minutes later the children's faces lit up at the sound of an approaching vehicle.

"Liam, I hear the lorry! The horses are here!" They scampered down the stairway, giggling as they tripped over each other.

The royal-blue horse transporter came into view, barely rolling to a stop by the barn before Laura and Liam were upon it. Philip greeted them with words of caution.

"Now, I know you're both excited, but I want you step back and wait while I unload the horses." They eagerly agreed, and he proceeded to lower the ramp. A soft nicker came from inside.

"That must be my horse saying hello!" Laura exclaimed.

The first horse Philip led from the lorry was a grey Arabian mare with a beautiful mane and long flowing tail. She walked with hesitation

16

down the ramp, pausing to flare her nostrils, taking in the smells of her new surroundings.

"Is this my horse?" Laura cried, barely containing her excitement.

"Yes, Miss Laura, this mare is yours."

"She's the most beautiful horse I've ever seen! Just look at her big, beautiful, brown eyes."

"Indeed she is, Miss Laura. Now, please stay where you are. Liam, I want you to hold the mare while I unload the gelding."

Liam took the lead rope and carefully turned the mare towards the lorry, gently stroking her neck. "Now you can see your friend coming."

Liam waited patiently with the mare, his anticipation growing as his father went back up the ramp. The son of a trainer, Liam had learned to ride at a young age, but always on someone else's horse. *I can't believe Lord Meegan is giving me my own horse.*

At that moment, a proud Arabian gelding, almost black in color, appeared at the top of the ramp and halted. He picked up his head, surveying the new sights and sounds, and then exhaled with a loud snort. The mare answered with a soft nicker, and the gelding stepped boldly down the ramp.

"Father, is that one mine?"

"Yes, my son. I'll lead him in—you take the mare. You've got their boxes ready?"

"Yes, Sir, since this morning."

The gelding pranced, with his neck arched and tail curled up over his back. Liam's attention was drawn to the regal animal, but never strayed from his duty, leading the mare, who followed along quietly.

"Laura, look how proud he is!"

"Look at my mare! She's so dainty when she walks—and her mane and tail are like silk..."

After the new horses settled in their boxes, the children fed them carrots while Philip looked on.

"You know, children, these two have Arabian names—they're a little hard to pronounce. You could give them names of your own choosin' if you like."

17

Liam studied the noble gelding. "I know, Father. I'll call him Desert Sky. Desert because that's where Arabians come from, and Sky because of his almost-black coat—like the night sky. Laura, what are going to name your horse?"

"Mine will be...Desert Rose, because she's so delicate, like a rose."

As the children groomed their horses' coats and fed them more treats, an instant bond was formed.

"Now it's time to let them rest from their long journey," Philip announced. "We'll see about ridin' tomorrow."

All through dinner, the children chattered and laughed. Laura's enthusiasm was boundless, and Aidan was happy to see the spark return to his daughter's eyes.

"Rose eats her carrots like a lady, taking small bites," Laura bragged. "Sky wants to eat the whole carrot all at once. Liam had one in his pocket and Sky helped himself."

Everyone laughed and the children continued with their colorful descriptions.

Aidan thoughtfully studied his daughter while concealing his worry. *I only hope her new horse—and Liam—will somehow make it easier for her when I give her the news...*

"Laura, I want to talk to you before you go to bed tonight."

She smiled. "Father, this has been the most perfect day!"

Laura was ready for bed early and could hardly wait for her father to come to her room. He knocked softly and came in, sitting on the edge of her bed. *I wonder if we're going to talk about my birthday party next week,* she thought.

"Laura, my darling daughter," he began gently. "I'm so pleased you love your new horse. And Liam is going to be a great friend to ride with." His head was lowered, and Laura looked at her father cautiously. "Laura, I must go away tomorrow for a while."

"You'll be back for my party, won't you?"

"No, dear. I have business to take care of. It will be some time before I return."

"Oh, Father, you can't miss my party!"

"Now child, please let me finish—this is already hard enough for me." Tears filled Laura's eyes while she tried to hold back soft whimpers. "After my business, I'll be going with my Thoroughbreds on the race circuit."

"Father, please take me with you! I promise I'll be good!"

"Now, Laura, your tutor starts here next week—you know you can't go with me. You'll be fine. Mrs. Delaney will take good care of you, and Mr. Delaney will give you riding lessons on your new horse. And don't forget, Liam will be here for you to play with."

Aidan searched for a sign of comfort in his daughter, only to find the shadow of uncertainty in her eyes.

As Aidan tucked in his little girl, thoughts of Fey overwhelmed him yet again. Every day, Laura's presence was an increasingly painful reminder of his loss. Aidan could bear it no longer. He had to leave.

Laura awoke suddenly with her heart pounding, the morning light glaring like the reality of her father's words the night before.

Chloe came cautiously into the room. "Now there, child, your father will be home before you know it. Let's get ready to go downstairs and plan your birthday. And don't forget—your new horse will be wantin' to see you. Now let's get you dressed."

When the two came down the stairs, Laura's eyes scanned the dining room and hallway. She found Mrs. Delaney. "Where's Father?"

"He had to get an early start, dear." Noreen changed the subject quickly. "Now, you must get a good meal, so you'll have lots of energy to ride your new horse."

Laura's eyes filled with tears as she walked into the dining room where Liam was already seated. The cook was putting breakfast on the table.

"Mornin' Miss Laura! I made your favorite: muffins and hot cocoa."

Laura sat down slowly, staring blankly ahead.

Noreen made another attempt. "I'll bet your horse is eatin' her breakfast."

Still Laura did not speak, and the room was quiet enough to hear a pin drop.

Liam broke the silence. "Laura, let's eat our breakfast and get to the barn. Sky and Rose will be nervous in their new place, and they'll be looking for us."

Liam's words somehow pulled Laura out of her gloom. She realized he was doing his best to cheer her up. She smiled at him and wiped her tears, and then reached for her cocoa. "Yes, Liam, we must hurry."

Noreen turned to get the lunches she'd packed for the children, along with a bundle of carrots for the new horses.

"Good mornin', Miss Laura!" Philip said cheerfully. "Desert Rose is saddled and ready for you. Son, you may saddle your own horse." Liam nodded and headed for the tack room.

"Thank you, Mr. Delaney," Laura said politely. She eagerly went to the mare and led her out to the riding arena.

"I'll give you a leg up," Philip offered. "Keep in mind that she's still gettin' to know you, and you must move slowly and make sure she can see you."

Laura mounted smoothly. "Oh! She's quite a bit taller than Lilly."

"Indeed, she is."

Liam led Desert Sky into the arena and closed the gate. He mounted up with ease, and took a natural, balanced seat. The reins were positioned in his hands so he had gentle contact with the bit. His father had schooled him well, but as nicely as Sky was behaving, Liam knew he should use caution with a new horse.

Rose, the smaller of the two Arabians, had a quiet manner and was gentle for Laura. Sky was four inches taller—one hand, as horses were measured, a 'hand' being four inches—and more spirited, but well-trained, matching Liam's level of expertise.

Laura was thrilled. "Rose is so smooth compared to Lilly."

"You'll find her to be more responsive than your pony," Philip said. "You have a very good seat and soft hands. Now you must learn to use your legs to communicate to your horse what you want her to do. With Arabians, you don't need to kick them with your heels to move forward. Just give a gentle squeeze. Watch how Liam can make Sky move with just a little pressure from his legs." He turned to Liam. "Son, why don't you move the gelding out into a trot?"

Liam nodded, and in one smooth motion, he gently picked up his reins and applied the slightest leg pressure. The horse responded by elevating his head and moving into a nice, even trot.

"I didn't even see Liam move his legs," Laura remarked.

"That's the point, my dear. Now, why don't you try? I want you to barely squeeze with your legs, and at the same time, pick up the reins just a little. And remember, eyes forward—don't look at me."

Laura followed his instructions, and Rose responded instantly.

"Good girl! Now, you must always be able to stop your forward motion and halt your mare easily. Lower the reins, and rotate your hands very slightly so she can feel contact with her bit." Laura responded, with immediate results.

"I think you and your new friend will get along just fine," Philip remarked.

Liam pulled up alongside her and smiled. Laura's eyes were alive with excitement.

The Arabians were content and right where they belonged, with these children who loved them. They had a home where they would be the center of attention.

ᢓᢣ*Chapter Five* ᢓᢞᢣ

The week had gone by with Laura and Liam taking riding lessons in the arena every day. After each lesson, Philip allowed the children to ride around the estate.

Although Noreen didn't understand how two horses could entertain the children for so many hours, she was pleased to see them enjoying each other's company. But she wondered if the void in Laura's heart created by her father's absence could really be filled.

Just then, the phone rang. With a start, she answered. "Good mornin', Montrose Manor."

"Noreen, is that you?"

"Yes, Lord Meegan! I'm so happy to hear from you. I'll get Laura, she's in her room and she's been waitin' for your call all week."

"No! I can't talk to her right now."

"Please, Sir, she misses you so much."

"Noreen! I need to talk to *you.*"

"I'm sorry, Sir. Please go ahead."

"I'll be calling Laura this evening during her party, about seven o'clock. I'm calling now to make sure my packages arrived."

"Yes, Sir. I have them all wrapped with bows."

"Good. Now, is my daughter happy with her new horse?"

"Yes, Sir, but she misses you. I know she cries herself to sleep. I see her swollen eyes in the mornin'. But she's a brave child and tries to put on a happy face for us."

"Noreen, please…just tell me how she's doing with the Arabian."

"Philip said she has a wonderful seat. She spends hours at the barn with Liam."

"That's good news. Soon the tutor will start, and Laura will have other things to think about. If you feel more music lessons will help, please do whatever it takes."

"Excuse me for sayin', Sir, but what the child needs most is her father."

After a long moment of silence Aidan replied in a subdued, broken voice.

"I'll call tonight." There was a click and the line went dead.

Noreen dabbed her eyes as Laura came running into the kitchen.

"Mrs. Delaney, was that my father?"

"He'll call tonight, dear."

Laura threw her arms around her nanny. "Are you crying?"

"No, child, I must have got some onion from the stew in my eyes. Now, let's talk about your birthday. Cook and I are makin' your favorite dinner: lamb stew and soda bread. What kind of cake would you like?"

"Chocolate!" Liam shouted from the doorway before Laura could answer.

Laura giggled. "Of course—chocolate!"

"Now, you two, eat your breakfast. You don't want to be late for your ridin' lessons."

"Yes, Laura, today Father will give us his special lesson on balance."

"You two be careful," Noreen cautioned. "We have a party tonight."

After the children left for the barn there was a knock at the kitchen door. Mr. Callahan, the gardener, was standing with his cap in hand, holding a box.

"Good mornin', Mrs. Delaney. I waited for the children to be off. I have two kittens here from our cat's litter. I thought maybe, bein' that it's Miss Laura's birthday and all, she could have them. Sometimes the lass looks so sad. I'm hopin' the kittens will cheer her up, but my wife said I should ask you first."

"Oh, that's so thoughtful! They're adorable."

Evan Callahan had worked for Lord Meegan for over twenty years as the head gardener of Montrose Manor. He was short, with rounded features, and always had a smile on his face and a twinkle in his eyes. Evan and his wife, Anna, who worked as laundress of the Manor, had no children of their own. They had become surrogate grandparents to Laura.

"Why don't you and the missus bring the kittens when you come to the party tonight?" Noreen asked. "I'm sure it would mean a lot to Laura. Lord Meegan will not be able to make it, you know."

"I'm sorry he won't be here—but we'll be here with the kittens." Mr. Callahan nodded his head, and with a grin replaced his cap and hurried off.

Philip was confident the children and the new horses were well suited for each other, and that Laura would have no trouble learning to ride bareback, or without a bridle. He'd already taught Liam this method and his son was quite accomplished. For Laura's benefit, they were being instructed together. Philip began the day's lesson with an even tone.

"I believe ridin' without a saddle brings you as close to the horse as possible, feelin' the movement of each muscle in his body. Ridin' without a bridle gives the horse a chance to set his head in a natural position. With only a rope around the horse's neck, you'll be right in time with his natural rhythm. The rope is actually more for the balance of you, the rider, than it is for control."

Laura was eager to try, but a little unsure about having no reins.

"Miss Laura, you must not tighten up your legs," Philip cautioned. "Rose will not go forward when you're so tense. She can feel your every move, just as you can feel hers." Laura relaxed and Rose stepped into a nice easy trot. "Very good! Rose can tell you're ready to move on."

Laura beamed as she caught up to Liam. "I think I like riding without a saddle and bridle. Rose is very smart, and she knows what I want."

Liam smiled at her warmly. "You are very smart."

Laura turned her horse, looking back over her shoulder at Liam with a radiant smile that completely captivated him. It made his heart flutter. He blushed.

"Okay! Well done, you two," Philip said. "I think you need to go to the Manor and get all the horse hair off of you. I hear there's a party for someone special this evenin'…" Philip winked.

"Oh, I hope you'll be there!"

"I wouldn't miss it for the world, Miss Laura. Now off with the both of you!"

Beside the river, the children couldn't resist climbing a big tree. They managed to get sap all over themselves, and Laura tore her shirt as she jumped down.

"I'd better go up the back stairs and get cleaned up before anyone sees me."

Liam looked at his own soiled clothes. "I'd better go home and wash up, too. See you later, Laura Lye!"

She laughed and waved as she ran off. *I wonder why he called me Laura Lye. I like it!*

After Laura's bubble bath, Chloe brushed the girl's hair. "Let's put this pretty bow in your beautiful curls. It'll match your dress."

"Dress!" Laura cried out. "Do I have to wear a dress?"

"Now, Laura, it's your party. When will you ever wear all these lovely dresses if not to a party?"

"I wear a dress to church every Sunday," Laura protested.

Chloe just gave her a long look.

Laura sighed. "All right...I guess for my party. I wish Father would come. He likes me to wear dresses." *But what will Liam think of me all...girly?* Every Sunday after church Laura changed into jeans before Liam saw her.

"Laura, dear," Chloe said, "I know you like to use the back stairs, but for your party, I think you should be usin' the grand staircase."

Laura shrugged as she caught sight of herself in the mirror. "All right. That's fine."

Chloe stepped back to admire her. "You look like a little princess. You go on, now, and I'll be right down." Laura nodded cheerfully and headed for the door.

Gracefully descending the marble steps, Laura stopped in surprise to see the entire staff of Montrose—nearly twenty—standing below in the grand entryway. Everyone had a smile for her, and Liam's was the biggest of all. They began singing *Happy Birthday.*

A sad smile came to Laura's face. *They're all here...except Father.*

After dinner, Noreen turned down the lights, and Cook brought in the chocolate cake with nine candles aglow.

"Make a wish!" Liam cried. Tears filled Laura's eyes and her unspoken wish was obvious to everyone.

Liam wiped the tears from her cheek with his fingertips. "Laura, you look great tonight...that is, for a girl." They broke into laughter, and Laura looked at him affectionately. *Liam always knows just the right thing to say.*

Philip walked into the room carrying two giftwrapped boxes. "Now, Miss Laura, it's time to open some presents! These are from your father." Without hesitation, Laura tore into the packages.

"A new saddle! And riding boots! Liam, do you think Rose will like the saddle?"

"I think she'll love it. It's very fine leather. I'll show you how to clean it and keep it soft. It'll look wonderful on Rose. Now open the rest of your presents."

Mr. Callahan waited until Laura was done before he brought in the box with the two kittens inside. Her eyes opened wide with delight.

"They're darling—one grey and one white! Thank you!" Laura turned and gave him a big hug, and then hugged Mrs. Callahan. She then turned to her nanny.

"Can I keep them in my bedroom?"

"Yes, child. They're very young. They need you to take care of them."

"Oh Liam! Feel them! They're so soft and sweet." A sparkle came to Liam's eyes as he picked up the grey kitten.

Laura noticed how gently he held it to his face. "That one can be yours, but they'll have to live together in my room. You know family should always be together."

"Thank you for the kitten, Laura. I agree—they need to stay together so they won't be lonely. And I'll help you take care of them." He reached into his pocket and pulled out a small card. "This is my birthday present to you. I wrote it myself."

Laura opened the card and began to read the poem out loud.

Where're you off to, Laura Lye?
And what's that gleam there, in your eye?
Is that the river calls your name?
Is that the wind in Rose's mane?
Fly, you will, into the woods,
Just like a sparrow if you could.
But don't forget your happy home,
For here you'll never go alone.

Everyone clapped, and Liam blushed. *I didn't think she would read it out loud!* Laura threw her arms around him and gave him a kiss on the cheek. "Liam, it's wonderful! It's my best birthday present! I will always keep it."

Liam wanted to pull away and hide, but a strange feeling came over him as Laura's long hair brushed across his face. *Her hair feels like silk, and she smells so good, like...flowers.*

The spell was broken by the sound of a ringing telephone. Noreen answered and turned to Laura. "It's your father." It took no prompting for the girl to run to the phone.

"Oh, Father, I miss you! When are you coming home? Yes, thank you for the saddle and boots. Father, I got two wonderful kittens! I'm giving one to Liam—and he wrote me a poem ...Yes, but Father, when will you be home? Yes...Goodbye."

Laura's face was overcome with sadness, and once again, tears filled her eyes. Everyone felt her pain, but no one knew what to do—except Liam. He brought the little white kitten to Laura, gently placing it in her arms. She buried her face into its long hair.

"I can hear your kitten purring," Liam said. "She's happy to be yours."

Laura managed a smile. "Thank you."

Noreen swallowed her tears. "Liam, help Laura bring the kittens to her room. You two can play with them until bedtime."

Liam, never having been upstairs in the Manor before, followed Laura cautiously to her suite as he carried the box. He stopped dead in his tracks as he stared at the large, canopied four-poster bed with its gold satin comforter.

27

"Wow! Is this room all yours?"

"Haven't you seen my room before?"

Liam shook his head. "I've only been in the kitchen."

"Would you like to explore the Manor tomorrow?"

"I suppose, if it's all right with my mother."

"Liam, let's name our kittens. Look at yours—he's trying to get out of the box!"

"Well, I think I'll call him…Pooka. My mother taught me some old Irish words—it means mischievous. What are going to you name your kitten?"

"I'll name her…Creena! My mother told me it means heart."

The kittens playfully entertained the children, who were laughing when Noreen came to the door.

"I know you're havin' fun, but it's time for Liam to go home. Chloe is on her way up to put you to bed, Laura. Now, goodnight my dear, and have sweet dreams."

Laura ran to throw her arms around the nanny. "Thank you so much for my party, Mrs. Delaney. I love you."

Noreen gave Laura's hand a squeeze, but turned away before the children could see her tears. She motioned for her son to come. They said goodnight and left.

Chloe entered the room, shaking her head. "Now I have cat hair and a litter box to clean." But her heart melted at the sight of the kittens playfully attacking Laura's long hair. "It'll be no trouble at all, child." *Maybe she won't miss her father quite so much.* Chloe moved the kittens' box to a spot near the window.

"Goodnight Creena, goodnight Pooka."

"Laura, dear, do you want to wear this same dress for mornin' mass?"

"Oh, I can't go to church and leave my kittens."

"Yes, you will. It's your father's wishes that you be raised a good Catholic girl."

Laura nodded agreeably—she really didn't mind going to church. She got to see people from the village, and sometimes Mr.

Callahan would buy her ice cream afterwards. Laura kissed the kittens goodnight.

"Now, Creena and Pooka, be brave and don't cry. You're not alone."

⌒*Chapter Six* ⌒

After church the next morning, Laura raced up the stairs and quickly changed into her jeans to go to the barn. Philip said Sunday was a day of rest, so there were to be no lessons. The horses had been turned out in the pasture. She found Liam at the barn.

"Laura, I've taught Sky and Rose to come when I whistle."

"Show me!"

They went to the pasture gate, where Liam put his finger and thumb together in his mouth and demonstrated. The two horses pricked their ears forward, lifted up their heads, and galloped to the fence. Of course, their reward for coming was carrots.

"Liam, you have the magic touch with animals." A coy smile came to his face and he bowed, much to Laura's amusement. "Liam, I have one more carrot—for Lilly. Let's go give it to her. And then why don't we go back to the Manor and explore?"

"Sounds like fun, but I should ask my mother first."

"Well...I suppose," Noreen replied when her son asked permission. "As long as you don't touch anythin'. Laura, you know where you can go and where you don't belong...and no shenanigans."

"Yes, I know the rules."

Irish nobility spared no expense on their country estates, indulging in an extraordinary array of luxuries. Montrose Manor was no exception. It was a large, rambling structure in the French chateau style, completed in the mid-1800s. Construction of the Manor had provided years of labor for the surrounding villagers during the potato famine which had devastated the country.

Any visitor would be impressed the moment they stepped into the grand entryway, its expanse graced with Waterford crystal chandeliers and marble floors. The ground level was adorned with ornate leaded glass windows and warm rosewood paneling. Moving to the ballroom, one would be awed by the centerpiece, a unique Steinway grand piano. The immense living room was decorated in a rich baroque style, with deep rose and gold accents. Twenty-six guests could easily be seated in the formal dining room, but the family generally sat in the smaller, yet still elegant, informal dining room.

Liam followed Laura down the spacious hall into the expansive library, which was filled floor-to-ceiling with leather-bound books. Passing through the room, Laura paused at a doorway. Liam bumped right into her. She giggled.

"Oops—sorry," Liam whispered, his wide eyes scanning the immense collection. "I've never seen so many books in my life."

"There's even more here in my father's study—and you don't have to whisper." She opened the door to a spacious room paneled in rich mahogany.

"This is where Father spends most of his time...when he's here."

"I would, too," Liam whispered. "It's...perfect."

They moved on to the immense commercial kitchen, where Liam eyed a sheet of freshly baked cookies—*sweet biscuits.* Laura giggled again.

"You want one? It's okay—take a few." She did as well, and as they munched, Laura pointed out the huge walk-in pantry, the laundry room, and the hallway leading to the servants' quarters. Laura continued on from room to room with Liam trailing behind, mostly silent, as if he was touring a grand museum where a show of respect was of great importance.

"This place is so magnificent," Liam remarked. "How can you live here?"

"Oh, it is beautiful, but, you know...it's just home to me."

At the glass-enclosed indoor swimming pool overlooking the river, Liam gasped. "I've never seen a pool inside. Do you...swim in it?"

"Of course we do," Laura laughed. "My father swims laps every morning...when he's here." Her face saddened for a moment, but brightened again. "He taught me to dive. Do you want to swim with me sometime?"

"I never swam in a pool—only lakes and rivers. I'd love to, if it's all right."

"Sure it's all right, but we'll ask your mother anyway."

Laura took him up to the second floor, using yet another stairway. At the landing was a large hallway which led to the many spacious bedroom suites, each with its own bath. The rooms facing the

31

river had French doors leading to balconies with stairways down to the grounds. Rooms at the Manor's front had leaded glass windows and window seats.

Further down the corridor was another set of stairs. "How many stairways are there?" Liam asked.

"Maybe ten? But this one is my favorite for when I come in from the barn. I can sneak in if I'm dirty and not get in trouble. It goes down past the servants' quarters."

Liam smiled. "Knowing you, that's a good route." Laura stuck her tongue out at Liam and he laughed. "What's on the third floor?"

"Father has some offices, and his master suite is up there."

"Wow!" Liam shook his head. "I thought our five-room cottage was big. What's up in the tower? Can we get there from here?"

"I've been up there with Mother a few times…" A mischievous look suddenly came to Laura's face. "Let's go!"

"Is this one of the places you don't belong?" Liam asked cautiously.

She didn't answer him, instead saying, "Hurry, little boy, or you'll get lost." Laura scampered up the servant's stairway past the third floor to the tower stairs, knowing Liam would follow. He hesitated, but curiosity got the best of him, and soon he was right on her heels.

The thick stone walls of the tower made it dark, cool, and very quiet. The two children froze for a moment. The sound of their own breathing was all they could hear. An eerie feeling came over Liam as he reached for the door handle.

"It's locked. Maybe we should go."

"You give up too easily." Laura went to an alcove where there was a small wooden box. "Mother showed me where the key is. We must remember to lock the door and put it back when we leave."

"Why is the door locked?" Liam asked, concerned. "What's…in there?"

"You ask too many questions, Monkey Boy." Laura looked at him over her shoulder with an alluring smile that went straight to his heart. With her head slightly tilted, Laura's brown eyes sparkled through long dark lashes, giving Liam a look that warmed him—but worried him at the same time.

Liam wasn't sure about *that smile*. He slowly shook his head. *She looks like an angel—or is it the devil I see in those eyes?*

Whatever *that smile* was, Liam somehow knew it always got her what she wanted.

Laura dramatically opened the door, gesturing for him to enter the dark room.

"Laura, don't you want to turn on the light?"

"Are you afraid of the dark?" She mysteriously disappeared from view.

"Laura, where are you? Laura? Please answer me!"

There was a chilling stillness in the air.

"Boo!"

Liam jumped back and almost fell while she laughed out loud.

"That's not funny! I was worried about you."

"I'm sorry, I'm just playing. Here's a flashlight Mother kept up here—the light switch doesn't work. Now help me open the drapes."

Bright sunlight revealed a room filled with boxes and an old trunk, everything covered in dust and cobwebs.

"Laura, I really think this is one of the places we're not supposed to be."

"It's all right. This is where Mother kept things Grandmother gave her."

"Why would she keep them up here?"

"Father did not approve of my grandmother and her gypsy ways."

"Gypsy?" Liam asked. "What are you talking about?"

"My great grandparents were Travelers—you know…Tinkers. Some call them gypsies. My grandmother left them when she was sixteen and joined a dance troupe. Later, she met her Prince Charming."

"Come on, Laura, you're making this up."

"Maybe the part about the prince—but my grandfather really was a rich man."

Liam nodded slowly. "Okay…tell me more."

"Grandmother Maura did teach Mother a few things, including how to sing and dance to gypsy music. Mother wanted to name me

33

Maura, but Father would not have it. You see, Grandmother Maura was never really happy as a rich lady on a big estate. She ran off again to be a dancer, leaving my mother when she was only eight. My grandfather raised my mother by himself—but mostly she was in private schools. So Laura it is…my name, I mean."

"I like the name Laura," Liam said warmly.

She smiled. "Father never wanted me to learn their gypsy ways, but Mother showed me these things in the tower anyway. We would dress up like gypsies and sing and dance." Laura opened the old trunk and started going through it.

"Look! Here's my grandmother's cape and her tambourine! Let's pretend to be gypsies! Here's a mandolin for you to play and a red velvet sash you can wear. I'll dance in the cape and play the tambourine."

Liam was intrigued and began to rummage through the trunk. He found an old, tattered book filled with handwritten music.

"See this? I think I could learn these songs…"

"Go ahead and take it. No one will ever look at it but us."

On the back of the old book, Liam found a short poem, which he read aloud.

"Gypsy gold does not clink and glitter.
It gleams in the sun and neighs in the dark."

(Old saying of the Claddagh Gypsies of Galway)

Laura smiled. "I like that. It must be why I love horses so much."

Liam carefully picked up the mandolin, gently placing it on his lap. He blew some of the dust off and plucked a couple of strings.

"Ooh, it's way out of tune." He turned the keys to raise the pitches, and then began to play one of the melodies while following the sheet music.

"Not bad, Monkey Boy! With some practice, you could be a gypsy."

Laura put on the long cape and danced around the room while shaking the tambourine. She tripped over the hem and Liam barely had time to set the mandolin aside before catching her. They both laughed.

"I think you'll have to wait a few years until you fit into that cape," Liam remarked.

"I will wear it with pride someday," Laura vowed.

34

The children sang, danced, and played music for several hours. The room was growing dark when they put everything back into the trunk and locked the door.

"Liam, this will be our secret." She gave him *that smile* again.

Liam nodded slowly—he had never shared a secret with anyone before. The thought of sharing one with Laura filled him with extraordinary excitement.

ᴄ✍ Chapter Seven ᴄ✍

The next morning in the tack room, Liam showed Laura how to condition her new saddle. He took a small amount of saddle soap on a soft cloth and gently rubbed it in a circular motion into the surface. Warm sunlight streamed through the window, illuminating the saddle and releasing the wonderful smell of fine leather into the air.

"The more you rub like this, the softer it will be," Liam explained.

"Liam, is there anything you don't know about horses?"

"Oh, I'll never live long enough to know everything about horses. A horse can teach you, if you're willing to watch, listen, and feel. You must watch with your eyes, listen with your ears, and feel with your heart."

"Very wise words, my son," Philip remarked as he walked into the room. "Now, you two must hurry! Your new tutor will be at the Manor in one hour. It sure wouldn't hurt to wash off some of the barn before meetin' her."

"Can we give Sky and Rose some carrots before we go up to the Manor?" Laura asked.

"I'm sure it'll be fine, but you'd best hurry."

The children quickly finished cleaning the tack and ran to the pasture. Liam whistled, and the two horses came running to the gate.

"Oh Liam, Rose has a knot in her mane. I'll run back and get a currycomb."

"Bring one for Sky, too."

Laura returned and began to gently untwist the knot. "I don't want to pull too hard and break off her mane—it's the most beautiful hair I've ever seen."

Liam did not reply; his attention was drawn to Laura as she worked. *Laura, you have the most beautiful hair I have ever seen...or touched.*

Laura looked up to see Liam's gaze. "Isn't she gorgeous, Liam?"

He blushed and smiled. "Yes, she is, Laura Lye."

Time passed unnoticed as they groomed Sky and Rose. All who love horses know their mystical beauty and grace gives them a seductive quality, alluring enough to distract even the youngest soul.

Katie O'Brien was a devoted teacher in her early forties. A plain woman who dressed conservatively, she was tall and thin with short brown hair and green eyes, which were magnified by thick glasses.

Mrs. O'Brien was quite impressed as she pulled up in front of Montrose Manor. *What a wonderful place this is. I'll only have two children for three days a week—and at such a generous salary. This should prove to be quite agreeable.* She rang the door chimes and waited. After several long minutes, a servant came to the door.

"Oh dear, you must be Katie O'Brien, the tutor! Please come in. I'm sorry I took so long. We were all lookin' for the children. They seem to have gotten off somewhere—but we'll find them." There was an awkward silence.

"I hope the children do not make a habit of being late for their lessons," Mrs. O'Brien replied. "I pride myself in being prompt."

"My apologies—it will not happen again. Please, do come in. May I get you a cup of tea?"

"That would be fine," Mrs. O'Brien replied tersely.

The woman offered to carry one of the tutor's heavy satchels before showing her to the library. "Why don't you get settled here and I'll bring the tea." Suddenly she turned back. "Oh, I'm sorry—my manners! I'm Noreen—Liam's mother and Laura's nanny."

Mrs. O'Brien nodded politely. Noreen hurried off, trying and failing to conceal her upset.

Walking around the library, Mrs. O'Brien admired the beautiful marble fireplace framed on either side by an extensive collection of rare volumes. Pausing to look through the leaded glass windows, she noticed an older pickup truck racing up the driveway. The door flew open, and two children scampered out and up the steps into the Manor.

Soon, the sound of Noreen scolding them echoed through the hall. "Look how dirty you are! You were supposed to be here over an hour ago! Hurry to the library—Mrs. O'Brien is waiting."

When Laura and Liam entered the room, they were met by the unmistakable look of disapproval on the tutor's face.

"Children!" she said sternly. "I will *not* tolerate tardiness! My time is very valuable. Furthermore, I will not teach unwashed students. I expect you to be seated at the table, washed, and groomed *before* I arrive. Is that quite clear?"

"Yes, Mrs. O'Brien," they answered with lowered heads.

"Well, then. We shall start over tomorrow. I will be here at nine o'clock, and you will be here at eight-fifty sharp. You are dismissed!"

Noreen sent Laura to her room and Liam to the cottage for the rest of the day. She turned to apologize to Mrs. O'Brien again, but the indignant tutor was already out the door. Noreen went to find Philip, who was in the kitchen drinking a cup of coffee. Before she opened her mouth, he threw up a hand.

"Don't be blamin' me, now. I told them they had to be back for their lessons. They left the barn, and I thought they'd gone to the Manor. Later, I went to the pasture, and there were the two of them, covered in dirt, playin' with the horses."

Noreen folded her arms. "From here on out, Laura will not go to the barn before her tutorin'. Liam will do his chores, and then go to the cottage and clean up before the lessons. I think by keepin' them apart in the mornin', there will be less chance they'll drift off and forget the time."

Laura sat in her room for hours, until finally Mrs. Delaney brought her a tray from the kitchen.

"Now, here's somethin' for you to eat."

Laura looked up at her nanny with sadness in her big brown eyes. "I'm sorry for being late to meet the new tutor. It was completely my fault. Please, don't punish Liam."

Noreen had to smile—Liam had claimed earlier that it was completely *his* fault. "Laura, my dear, it will not happen again because you will not go to the barn until after your tutorin'."

"Please, Mrs. Delaney, I need to help Liam with the morning chores."

"He can manage on his own. Besides, I'm sure your father would not like to see his little girl muckin' boxes."

"Oh, but I like to do it! Mr. Delaney said mucking boxes is good for the soul."

Noreen started to smile again but quickly caught herself. "Laura, I said *no!*"

Laura jumped and threw her arms around the nanny. "Please don't be mad at me."

Noreen could not resist hugging the troubled girl. "I'm not mad at you or Liam, but I want you to take your tutorin' seriously." With that, she gave Laura a kiss on the cheek and left her to think about the importance of her lessons.

The next morning, the young students were at the desk in the library by quarter to nine, washed and groomed. Mrs. O'Brien arrived a few minutes later.

"Good morning, Laura and Liam. Now we can begin."

To determine their skill levels in reading and writing, the tutor had the children read aloud and then write a short story about their favorite activities. Their stories proved to be amusing. Each wrote about their time spent together with Sky and Rose.

"Now, I will give you some arithmetic problems to solve," Mrs. O'Brien instructed. Liam sat up eagerly, while Laura frowned and slumped in her chair.

"Laura, you must sit up straight like a lady," the tutor directed.

The testing continued in different subject areas, and Liam showed unwavering enthusiasm. Laura, on the other hand, was far from thrilled. Mrs. O'Brien's trained eye caught the differences between the two. *Miss Laura Meegan will certainly need some work on her motivation.*

"That will be all for today," Mrs. O'Brien said curtly.

After their lessons, the children politely thanked Mrs. O'Brien before they headed straight for barn.

"Liam, what do you think of Mrs. O'Brien?"

"I guess she's all right. The lessons are easy."

"I think they're hard. But at least she's not as mean as she was the first day!"

"She wasn't really mean. Have you ever gone to a real school?"

"No, my mother taught me at home."

"Trust me—for a teacher, Mrs. O'Brien's not bad. If you need help with your studies, I'll help you."

Laura smiled. "Thank you Liam. You're so smart!"

"I'm not any smarter than you are—I just pay attention in class."

Laura frowned and kicked some dirt at Liam. He laughed.

Mrs. O'Brien's normal schedule was to be Monday, Wednesday and Friday, with homework assigned for the days in between. Liam kept his promise, helping Laura every morning after breakfast.

Towards the end of the Friday lesson, the tutor was interrupted by a knock at the door. It was Noreen.

"So sorry to disturb you, Mrs. O'Brien. You have a phone call."

"Finish today's reading, students, and then you are dismissed. Remember your homework." The tutor grabbed her satchel and left the room.

Down the hall, Noreen spoke quietly to her. "It's Lord Meegan. He didn't want the children to know he was callin'."

"Thank you, Noreen." The tutor followed her to phone. "Yes, Lord Meegan, this is Katie O'Brien."

"Hello. I've called to see how the children are doing with their lessons."

"Of course, Lord Meegan. Your daughter is a bright child, but I'm afraid she has a tendency to daydream. Consequently, she is a little behind. Liam is an excellent student with a desire to learn. His reading and math skills are two grades ahead for his age. On their home-study days, he has been tutoring Laura."

"He has? Well, maybe he'll be a good influence on her."

"It has already made a difference, Sir."

"Keep up the good work, Mrs. O'Brien. I'll check with you in a few weeks."

Noreen was pleased at what she had overheard. "Is that right about my son?"

"Yes. You should be very proud of him," Mrs. O'Brien answered.

"Indeed we are. We hope he'll go on to college. He'd be the first one in our family to have a good education, thanks to Lord Meegan."

"Well, I must be on my way."

Noreen showed the tutor to the door. Then she brought a tray of biscuits and milk to the library, pausing at the door as she overheard her son.

"You must try harder to concentrate, Laura. A good education is very important."

Laura sighed. "Liam, what do you want be when you grow up?"

"I want to be somebody worthy of owning a castle like this one. What do you want when to be when you grow up?"

"I want to be a dancer and travel all over the world with my Prince Charming."

"Laura Lye, you and your gypsy heart!" They broke into laughter. Noreen smiled and entered the room, all the while wondering what Liam meant.

The next day was Saturday, Liam's birthday, and he was up earlier than usual. "Mother, I'm ten now. I'm too old for a party." Unlike Laura, who always looked forward to celebration, Liam never liked being the center of attention. Given a choice, he preferred to go unnoticed.

"Well then, what about a special dinner?"

"Okay—but just family."

"What about Laura?'

"Of course, Laura. She is family."

"Good—and that's very sweet of you. Cook will make your favorite dishes. Now, your first gift today is from Patrick, your father's new man in the barn. He's doin' your chores."

"I only just met him. Why is he doing that, Mother?"

"Well, there's certainly no rule that says you have to be old friends to be nice to someone. I'm sure it will make Patrick feel good. Just don't forget to thank him."

41

Patrick O'Brogan was a tall, good-looking man in his early thirties, with curly blond hair and smiling blue eyes. With a strong build and a gentle manner, he loved horses and enjoyed working in the barn.

Philip had hired Patrick on Chloe's recommendation. She had met him at the village dance, and it was love at first sight. Chloe convinced Philip to hire her boyfriend on a trial basis for the assistant trainer's job, and Philip took an instant liking to him, impressed with the man's knowledge of horses.

Patrick came from a poor family, and his work ethic was strong. He truly appreciated the job at Montrose, and showed it.

Liam enjoyed his birthday dinner that evening—roast lamb and mashed potatoes. In spite of his enjoyment of the feast, his attention was drawn to Laura, who'd surprised him by wearing a pretty yellow dress with a ribbon to match in her hair. Even Liam's obsession with chocolate cake was nothing compared to the pleasurable sensation of Laura's hair brushing against his face when she leaned in close to him.

"Make a good wish before you blow out the candles," she whispered.

Liam was quite distracted by the scent of gardenias coming from her hair.

"Liam—the candles are melting!" Laura cried. "Don't you have a wish?"

He grinned at her. Laura blushed. He thought silently, *I wish I could stay here at Montrose Manor and always be with Laura.*

After the cake, Liam opened his gifts, including a new pair of riding boots from his father.

"Son," Philip laughed, "the way you're growin', I hope they'll last you more than a few months." Noreen joined her husband in laughter, and then watched with delight as Liam began to tear into the large gift from her.

"Oh Mother—my own guitar! It's brilliant! Thank you—thank you so much!"

The six-string acoustic was not new, but had been well-cared-for and had a beautiful fret board. It had taken Noreen a long time to save enough to buy it.

"Do you remember the song about the children and the horses I taught you to play when you were seven?"

"Yes—let's see…" Liam began playing the melody, and the rich resonance filled the room. When he finished the song, everyone clapped. Liam smiled and bowed. He felt no embarrassment at being the center of attention in his family.

"I didn't know you could play the guitar," Laura said, surprised.

"My mother taught me when I was pretty young. She also taught me to read and write music."

"But I didn't teach him the poetry," Noreen remarked. "Now you can put your words to music."

Liam felt warm and safe, embraced in the love of his family. The special attention Laura gave him filled Liam with a feeling that was pleasurable yet mysterious. *This is the best birthday ever.*

43

ᴄ✺ Chapter Eight ✺ᴅ

Summer 1975

Now that tutoring was over for the summer, Liam worked with the horses every day alongside his father. One morning Philip gazed with pride at his young son.

"Liam, Patrick and I are goin' tomorrow to pick up two mares at Lord Meegan's stud farm in Kildare. Would you like to go with us?"

"You mean…Lord Meegan has another big farm?"

"Indeed—and a large home in Dublin to boot. He's a man to be respected."

"Oh, I do respect him! And I'd love to go. Can Laura come, too?"

"I guess—if it's all right with your mother. I'll ask her a bit later. Now don't you be tellin' Laura until I get permission."

"No, Sir."

Philip looked at his watch. "C'mon, Son—let's go up to the Manor for lunch. I'll talk to your mother while you're washin' up."

Noreen was reluctant. "I don't know, Philip. Lord Meegan's told me Laura's rarely been off the estate—only to go to church—and now you're talkin' about her goin' to a breedin' farm?"

"She'll be upset if Liam gets to go and she doesn't. I'll keep Laura out of harm's way—and you know Liam will, too. The two of them are inseparable anymore."

"I'll watch out for her, Mother," Liam announced, walking into the kitchen.

"Watch out for who, Liam?" Laura had suddenly appeared at the other door. Philip and Liam both looked to Noreen, who sighed and threw up her hands.

"All right, then—but just be careful."

"Careful about what?" Laura asked.

"I wonder," Philip said, rubbing his chin, "if a certain boy and girl who have a fondness for horses could behave themselves if they were invited to go to Lord Meegan's stud farm in Kildare tomorrow?"

44

"Oh! Mr. Delaney!" Laura cried, throwing her arms around him. "I promise! Thank you!" Suddenly she stepped back. "I mean—we promise!"

Liam nodded eagerly.

Noreen cautioned Laura at breakfast. "Now, I know you love the horses and all, but you must remember to stand clear at all times today. Laura? Are you listenin' to me?"

"Yes, Mrs. Delaney," Laura said between mouthfuls. Noreen smiled as she handed a basket of sandwiches and fruit to her son.

"Liam, you know what to look out for on a breedin' farm."

"Don't worry, Mother, I promise to look out for Laura," he replied resolutely. "We'd better get going—the lorry is waiting."

Laura watched excitedly from her elevated position on the bench seat of the horse van as they rolled out through the gates of Montrose. She tingled in anticipation of the journey before them, and soon the lush green countryside became the setting for her imagination. Philip began to point out the breeding and training farms along the way.

"Miss Laura, this is racehorse country, home of the Irish horse industry. The farm we're goin' to is where your father keeps his stallions and mares for breedin' and foalin'. When the foals are weaned, they come to Montrose, where I work with them until they are ready to go back and start their race trainin'."

As the lorry pulled into the grand stone entryway, Laura noticed the brass sign that read *Feyland Stud*.

"I know what that means," she announced.

"What?" Liam asked.

"Fairyland!" she answered proudly. "Father named the farm after Mother."

Philip drove the lorry slowly down the lengthy, tree-lined driveway. On either side were endless green pastures, each with grazing mares and foals in abundance. Some of the foals were contentedly nursing beside their mothers, while others ran playfully about.

"Ooh, look at the babies," Laura sighed. "I just want to take them all home."

Patrick smiled at the delighted girl. "Well, Miss Laura, I think their mothers might object if we took their babies away." He winked at her.

"Yes, you're right," Laura said thoughtfully. "They need their mothers to watch over them." Patrick was surprised and saddened by her sensitive insight.

Philip patted her affectionately on top of the head. "We'll have two mares foalin' at Montrose later this summer—the ones we're bringin' home today." The lorry rolled to a stop at the main barns.

"Welcome to Feyland Stud!" a short, slender man said cheerfully as he approached. "I'm Ian, the stud manager."

"I'm Laura," she announced, thrusting out her hand.

"Well, now, as I live and breathe—the image of ..." Ian hesitated.

"My mother?" Laura finished his sentence, standing up tall.

"Yes, child, your lovely mother Fey. We all miss her, but I'm certain you're going to light things up around here every bit as much as she did."

"Thank you, Mr. Ian," Laura replied proudly. The others smiled, relieved that the mention of Fey did not upset her.

"Well," Ian said, "if it's all right with Mr. Delaney, I'll take you on a little tour. We'll begin at the breedin' shed. They're just about to start." Philip nodded his agreement, and then turned to his son.

"Liam, make sure to hold Laura's hand and stay out of the way."

"Yes, Sir."

The breeding shed was actually a large room with high ceilings and padding on the walls. Ian motioned to an area on the side where the visitors could go to observe in safety.

They heard the approaching stallion before he came into view. His piercing calls to the waiting mare startled Laura, and her eyes widened as the large, angry-looking red stallion danced into the barn.

"It's okay, Laura," Liam assured her. "They have him under control."

"The rearin' and snortin' are just part of the matin' ritual," Ian added.

Just then the mare squealed loudly, and Laura jumped. Liam gave her hand a gentle squeeze.

"It's all right—the mare and stallion are just talking to each other."

"Are you sure he's not hurting her?" Laura asked.

Liam put his arm around her. "No, it's how she gets pregnant. Next spring she'll have a foal."

At a large foaling barn they saw a mare waiting to have her baby.

"Wow! She's really big," Laura cried.

"Yes," Ian said. "She's overdue—and we're expectin' a big baby. She's in foal to our largest stallion, Real Time—he's the one you just saw breedin'. We're keepin' a close eye on this mare."

"Why are we bringing home two mares to foal at Montrose?" Liam asked.

"That's a good question, my boy," Ian replied. "We have a very busy farm here, and we don't have time to watch late-foalin' mares when we've already moved on to the summer trainin'. When a mare gets into a late-foalin' schedule, we usually skip breedin' her until the next year. But we didn't do that with the two mares you're takin'. They're getting' old, and Lord Meegan wants one more foal out of each of them. So off they go to Montrose to have their babies and then retire."

"We'll keep a good eye on them," Laura promised. The men smiled, and Ian patted her on top of the head. "I really love all the babies," she added.

"Your mother loved to come here and see the foals," Ian remarked. "She picked out most of their names."

"Maybe I'll get to name a foal someday…"

"I'll bet you will," Ian said cheerfully. "You're goin' to like these two mares. They're very sweet, and I'm sure you'll enjoy their babies."

Philip looked at his watch. "Well, maybe we should go ahead and load up the mares so we can get on our way." Laura and Liam thanked Ian for the tour.

The handlers brought out Lady, a large bay mare with a star on her forehead, and Grace, a darker bay with no markings. The two horses loaded easily into the lorry.

As they rolled down the driveway of Feyland Stud, many of the mares in pasture picked up their heads and whinnied. Lady and Grace called back to them loudly.

"Oh," Laura said sadly, "they're saying goodbye to their friends. Are they going to miss them terribly?"

"Maybe at first," Philip replied, "but they'll have each other. Accordin' to Ian, these two have been friends for over twenty years, so we'll stable them right next to each other—for the rest of their lives."

"They love each other, like Sky and Rose," Liam added, which brought a smile to Laura's face.

That summer, Liam spent the early mornings helping his father in the barn and the rest of the day with Laura exploring the estate on horseback. Each day was a new adventure, with a different grove of trees or outcropping of rocks to discover. One day, they wandered quite a bit farther while riding the northeast corner of the estate. Unusual rock formations at the base of the hills got the best of Liam's curiosity.

"These rocks are different from the others," he observed. "See how some of them are kind of red? That means iron deposits. I learned that from a geology book." Liam prided himself in his reading.

Noticing an archway across the rocky surface, they dismounted and walked the horses carefully around for a closer look. Soon the two young adventurers found themselves facing a small crevice.

"Laura, I think there's a cave here. Do you feel the cool air coming out?"

"Let's find out where it goes!"

"You're too bold for your own good."

"Come on, Liam! Where's your sense of adventure?"

Liam wouldn't budge. "It's really dark in there. We could trip— or get stuck."

Laura rolled her eyes. "All right, we can go back to the barn and get flashlights."

"I suppose…But we'll need a few more things—like head collars and lead ropes for Sky and Rose. We'll have to tie them somewhere."

The two explorers rode their horses back to the barn, the excitement over their new discovery growing with each moment.

Upon their return to the rocks, Liam paused. "Now, promise you'll follow me closely and do as I say. No playing games. We could fall and get hurt."

"Okay," Laura agreed.

Liam cautiously climbed through the narrow passage, shining his flashlight ahead to reveal a sizable cavern with a high ceiling.

"Wow!" Laura exclaimed as she bumped into him. "This is even bigger than my bedroom!" The clay floor was level, and the two stepped several paces forward.

"It's so big!" Liam said excitedly. His voice reverberated loudly.

"Listen to the echo!" she yelled. "Monkey Boy!"

"Laura Lye!" They laughed until their sides ached, and it took a minute for Liam to catch his breath. "I wonder how our guitars would sound in here."

"Probably good! It makes your voice so deep."

"We could bring our guitars next time," Liam said. "I'll make straps for the cases, and we can carry them on our backs while we ride." Laura eagerly agreed.

Liam's attention was drawn to outcroppings on the far side of the cave wall.

"I'll bet the river used to run through here, millions of years ago," he said. "There was probably some change underground, and the water got cut off and sent the other way. I learned about it in the same geology book." Liam smiled proudly, but Laura was only half listening, distracted by something she'd heard. She put her finger to her lips.

"Shhh…listen," she whispered. There was a faint sound of trickling water. "Let's see where it's coming from." They made their way through a short tunnel and came upon a pile of rocks where daylight was streaming through. "I think that's where I hear the water."

"Let's move the rocks," Liam suggested. Laura's eyes widened at the size of pile.

"Do you think we can?"

"We won't know until we try."

They spent over an hour clearing the end of the tunnel. When they were finally able to walk through, they could see a meadow that gently sloped down to a stone wall which defined the edge of the vast Montrose estate.

"This could be an escape exit," Laura said.

"Escape from what?"

"You never know," she replied with a mischievous look.

"Laura Lye, you have a big imagination."

"I thought you said you need imagination to be a good song writer!"

"Yes, that's true, but with *your* imagination, my songs would be too wild." She stuck her tongue out at him. Liam pretended to ignore her and walked further out from the escape exit. They found a large overhang in the rock formation.

"Liam, this could be a shelter for Sky and Rose when it rains. I bet we could bring them around the other side and go into the cave this way." As they walked beneath the outcropping, Liam pointed to a darkened area a few feet away, where they discovered a spring filling a hollow in the rocks.

"This is going to be a perfect water trough for the horses," Liam said. He turned around. "I could close this in with a couple of tree poles across the front for a gate. It would be a safe shelter for Sky and Rose. I think I can get everything we need from behind the barn. I'll ask my father, of course. And I'll ask him if we can use Ol' Tommy, the draft horse. He's big enough to push his way through the brush and make us a path. We could harness the poles to him and stretch a tarp between them, like the American Indians used to do. I think they call it a…travois."

"We can't tell your father," Laura said with conviction. "We can't tell anyone about our cave."

"Why not?"

"They won't let us play so far from the barn."

Liam hesitated. "I guess I could tell my father we're building a fort in the woods—it would sound like it's a lot closer. But wouldn't that be…lying?"

"Not really. We are building a fort—for the horses. We just won't tell them how far away it is." She eagerly awaited his response.

Liam turned away. *How can one little girl make me so confused?* After a few minutes, he said thoughtfully, "Well, I guess it'll be all right. My father let me drive Ol' Tommy before. He'll just warn me to be careful, and I will."

"Great!" Laura cried. "We can haul everything we need: some straw to sit on, a couple of blankets…some hay for the horses, and—"

"Hold on. Do you plan on living here?"

"You never know…" She flashed him *that smile.*

Liam shook his head slowly. S*ometimes she scares me…and sometimes…*

Philip was busy with colts when they returned to the barn. As Liam had predicted, his father's response to the request was simply that they be careful. Laura and Liam wasted no time and busied themselves the rest of the afternoon building the travois.

The next morning Philip noticed Laura was distracted during the riding lesson.

"Miss Laura, Rose can't tell which direction you want to go unless you guide her. Your mind seems to be somewhere else." Liam shot Laura a glance.

"Sorry, Mr. Delaney," she said, straightening up in the saddle.

Philip studied the children. "Now, I recall—you two are off on a little adventure this mornin' with Ol' Tommy. Do you need some help with him?"

"Oh, no, Sir," Liam replied. "I know how to hook him up."

"All right, then. I have to go into Limerick for some tractor parts anyway."

It took the young adventurers quite a while to load up the travois with supplies before hooking it up to Ol' Tommy. Although the experienced draft horse had never seen a contraption quite like this, his gentle nature allowed him to trust Liam. Soon they began the long, slow trek to the cave, with Laura riding Ol' Tommy and Liam on foot, chopping small branches along the way with a hatchet. Instead of using the main path, they made a more direct route through the trees to the back of the cave.

When they finally got there, Liam was pleased. "I think we've cut off almost half a mile."

By the time they got everything unloaded and into the cave, it was almost dark. They decided to ride double on Ol' Tommy back to the barn as fast as they could, in spite of the bouncing caused by his lumbering gait, which was typical for draft horses. Laura had to hang on tightly to Liam with her arms wrapped around his waist. He became acutely aware of the warmth of her embrace and began to enjoy the sensation—until the darkened barn came into view and Liam realized how late it must be.

"Oh no!" Liam cried. "It looks like they fed the horses a long time ago." They brought Ol' Tommy into the barn where his hay was waiting. He was patient while they brushed him down. When they finally put him away and hung up the harness, Liam had a worried look on his face.

"Laura, let me do the talking when my mother scolds us for being late again."

"I'm not going to let you take the blame. It was mostly my fault for wanting to haul so much to the cave."

"Well, let's hurry back and face the music."

Sneaking in the back door, they were surprised to find no one but Cook.

"Where's my mother?" Liam asked.

"She left a couple of hours ago for church. Your father's already had his supper, Liam. Then he said he was goin' back to work on the tractor." She set their plates in front of them and watched as they hungrily dove in. "What've you two been up to? It's awfully late."

"At the barn with the horses," Liam replied with a mouthful of food. He noticed Laura was smirking, and shot her a glance. They hurried through supper, hoping to avoid more questions. After a hasty goodnight, Liam rushed off to the cottage to clean up and get into bed. Still in the tractor barn, Philip was unaware of his son's tardiness.

"Children, I'm sorry I missed you at dinner last night," Noreen said at breakfast. "I joined a new church in the village, and we've bible study on Tuesday nights."

Liam was confused. *Why is she going to church?* His mother was Protestant and his father was Catholic, but neither attended services. Although Philip had insisted Liam be baptized Catholic, he had never been conventional in his own worship, and never made Liam go to mass.

"You don't have to go to church to pray," Philip had observed. "After all, Jesus was born in a barn."

Noreen gave the children permission to go to their new "fort" for the day, since Philip told her there would be no time for riding lessons that morning. Cook packed the children a lunch, and they were on their way. At the barn, Liam found some leg wraps in the bottom of an old tack box. He decided the soft cotton rolls would make perfect straps for the guitar cases.

They arrived at the cave and dismounted, introducing their horses to the new pen. Sky snorted, unable to see the source of the running water.

"Easy, boy," Liam said, carefully leading his gelding. "See?"

Laura slowly closed the gate poles and got some hay. "Here you go, Rose…Sky, don't miss out. You like this place just fine, don't you?"

Once they were satisfied the horses were relaxed, Laura and Liam could hardly wait to start playing their guitars in their secret hideaway. They had already arranged bales of straw to sit on, and soon Liam eagerly began strumming. The remarkable fullness of the sound brought a smile to his face.

"Wow! This must be what chamber music sounds like."

"Well, I don't know what that is," Laura replied, "but it sounds brilliant!" She joined in, following his chords, and the two played for hours, stopping only to eat lunch.

They would have played longer, but Liam put his guitar down in the late afternoon.

"I think the sun is getting low. See how the light has moved to the big red rock over there? We should pack up and leave for the barn. If we're home on time, there won't be any questions. Time is the one thing that always seems to slip away from us."

The next morning on the way to the barn Liam heard something above them in a tree by the river. "Look! Honey bees!"

Laura looked up to see the lively buzzing in and out of a large hole in the trunk about halfway up. Liam began to climb.

"Monkey Boy, what are you doing? You're going to get stung!"

Liam did not even look back—he was on a mission. He paused, motionless, focusing on the hive. To Laura's surprise, the busy bees seemed to actually slow their flight—somehow calmed. Liam carefully reached into the hive, gently pulling out a piece of dripping honeycomb. He carefully climbed back down, unscathed.

"Liam, how did you do that without getting stung?"

"I hum to them. It's soothing, and they don't mind that I only took a little piece. They'll make more." He dribbled some golden honey into Laura's hand. She had never tasted it right from the hive.

"This is delicious," she laughed, as the sweet nectar dripped down her chin.

"Let's get our horses and go to the cave. We can wrap up the honeycomb and take it with us."

The children spent countless hours that summer in the cave. Liam continued to work on the skills of songwriting, and before long, he developed it to a level far beyond his youth. His inspiration came from the countryside, the horses, and, of course, Laura. Always eager to learn his songs, she sang harmony in the higher ranges. The cave was a haven for them, the perfect place to sing at the top of their lungs with no inhibitions.

On the island of Ireland, the rain comes and goes as quickly as the breezes blow. Laura and Liam's secret hideaway was the perfect shelter from the intermittent showers. As Laura had predicted, the natural rock overhang kept the horses dry.

"I love this place," Laura said during a downpour. "I feel so safe and dry here."

Liam did not answer right away, his thoughts drawn to the rhythm of the raindrops. "The rain is like a whispered voice, heard only by the soul."

54

Riding in the rain was always certain exhilaration, especially on the return trip, when the horses would fly through the woods to the dry barn and their waiting dinners. On those days, the children had to spend extra time cleaning the mud off the horses, bridles, and themselves. One such day, Patrick offered them a solution.

"Liam, I've made you and Miss Laura rope collars to go 'round your horses' necks. I'll get them and show you." He returned from the tack room with two loops made of soft braided cotton.

"I see you two ridin' bareback without a bridle in the arena. Sky and Rose are so responsive you'll be able to neck rein them with just the rope collars. But Liam, you need to ask your father for his approval, and then the both of you need to try them before you ride out on the estate."

"Thanks," Laura and Liam said at the same time.

"Now when you ride in the rain you won't have to clean tack— just yourselves." With that, he wiped some mud from Laura's face. She giggled and thanked him again.

The next day, Laura and Liam successfully demonstrated the use of the rope collars to Philip. He was pleased and added some words of advice.

"Right now you're in the safety of the arena. If you're goin' to ride without a bridle or saddle out in the open, you must be aware more than ever of what your horse is thinkin'." They nodded and brought the horses to a halt.

"I think you've got it! Now off with you—go and have fun!"

They eagerly rode off, the horses responding to the lightest touch of the collars. Galloping across the meadow like free spirits bound as one, Sky and Liam led the way with Rose and Laura close behind.

Philip felt a deep pride as he watched them. The horses were now responding better than they ever had for Michael O'Leary's son and daughter. Laura and Liam had learned their lessons well.

Patrick walked up and saw the smile on Philip's face. "What's so amusin'?"

"The children and their horses. They're off like the wild wind, without a care in the world. Ahhhh...to be young again!"

When the children returned to the barn they saw Patrick bedding two large boxes.

"Are we getting ready for the foals?" Laura asked excitedly.

"Yes, Lady is showin' signs of her milk comin' in, and Grace is due anytime."

"Oh, how exciting! I want to sleep in the barn and watch!"

"You'll have to get permission from Mr. and Mrs. Delaney first."

Philip walked up. "There'll be rules to follow if you attend a foalin'."

"I promise I will do everything you ask! *Please* let me watch!"

Philip studied the young girl and sighed. "I hope I'm not goin' to regret this. Rule number one: You have to be very quiet. The mare needs her privacy. Rule number two: You watch from the hayloft, where she won't be bothered. Rule number three: If at any time I ask you and Liam to leave, you go without question!"

"Yes, I promise!"

"I'll have to get permission from your nanny first. Now, off you go."

When they walked out, Laura remarked, "Liam, your father seems so serious."

"Yes, Laura, foaling is very special."

"Have you seen a mare foal before?"

"Yes. When things go well, it's so…beautiful."

"And when it doesn't go well?"

"I've only seen one bad foaling—and I wish I never had." After hearing the sober tone of Liam's voice, Laura decided not to ask any more questions.

Noreen cleared the table after supper, and Philip followed his wife into the kitchen.

"Lady looks like she's ready. The children want to sleep in the loft and watch."

"I don't know, Philip—Laura may be a little young yet."

Laura couldn't stand the suspense—she'd followed him. "Please! I have never seen any animal have a baby! I'm old enough."

"Philip, if there are any...complications, you send them both back to the Manor."

"Oh, thank you!" Laura gave her a hug.

Philip smiled. "Now, let's get some sleepin' bags and a snack for you. It may be a long night." He patted Laura on the head.

When Laura and Liam got up to the hay loft, they carefully placed their bedrolls at a good vantage point to look down at the mare. It did turn out to be a long night, and sleep soon overtook them. The first light of dawn was breaking when they awoke to a big thud as Lady dropped against the box wall.

"Laura, it's time," Liam whispered.

The bay mare was sweating as she pushed with every contraction. Soon, what looked like a large bubble appeared under the mare's tail. Laura gasped.

"Is that the foal?"

"Shhh—it's coming soon—the foal is inside that sack."

Within moments, the bubble broke, and a large amount of fluid gushed out. Laura started to say something again, and Liam put his finger to his lips. Suddenly, a pair of tiny hooves appeared, and Laura's eyes widened. Then, with a strong push, the mare delivered the foal. It just lay there, showing no signs of life. Philip broke the silence.

"Children, go to the Manor now." Patrick and Philip began to vigorously rub the foal with towels to stimulate breathing. Laura looked fearfully at Liam. She started to speak, but he shook his head and motioned towards the stairs. They descended from the loft and were headed out of the barn when Philip called them back.

"He's breathin' now—it's all right, you can stay." Laura and Liam smiled and turned around immediately.

"We have a good-sized bay colt," Patrick announced. Laura peered over the door as the mare got up and nuzzled her foal.

"He's so beautiful," Laura whispered.

It wasn't long before the colt began struggling awkwardly to get up, his long legs going every which way. Laura stifled a giggle with her hand.

Philip smiled. "It's time for us to leave for a while so the mare can bond with her baby. You can go back to watchin' from the loft, if you promise to be quiet."

The children dutifully agreed and went back up the stairs slowly. The colt bounced around for almost an hour before he finally managed to stand still and nurse. A few minutes later, Philip waved at the children to come down.

"What do you think we should call this little one? Of course, Lord Meegan will have the last word on it."

"I've already been thinking of a name," Liam proudly announced. "His sire is First Call and the colt was born at daybreak. So how about...First Light?"

"That's perfect!" Laura exclaimed.

"Very good, Son. I think Lord Meegan will like it just fine."

On the drive back to the Manor, Patrick and Liam chatted about the colt. Laura sat quietly, still absorbing the whole event. Later at breakfast, she was still silent, but not in a brooding way—she was wistful. Liam noticed her faraway look.

"Laura, are you all right?"

"Oh, I'm fine," she sighed. "I've just never seen anything so wonderful."

Later, the children hurried back to the barn to find the colt running and bucking around the mare.

"He's a good strong one," Philip said. "He's anxious to stretch those long legs."

"Why didn't he breathe at first?" Laura asked.

"Well, the whole time inside of his mum, it was like a very long nap. He just wanted to nap a little longer when he got outside."

Laura nodded. "I guess that makes sense. When can he go out and play?"

"I would let him go out now but it's a little damp from the rain...and Grace looks like she could foal today. I hate to upset her by movin' Lady out."

"Can I stay here and wait for Grace to foal?"

"Oh, it'll be a long day to wait. Why don't you and Liam go ridin' for a while?"

They returned a few hours later to find Patrick at Grace's box door. "Grace is drippin' milk. It looks like this will be an early one—probably this evenin'."

It wasn't long before the pregnant mare began pacing. She would make a circle, and then stop and look at her sides. Grace repeated this process for about twenty minutes, and then pawed at the ground and began to sweat.

"What's she doing, Liam?" Laura whispered.

"She's hunting for the right place to lie down and have her foal."

Just then, the mare dropped to the ground and began to push. The front feet and head were out in moments. One more push and the foal was born.

"This one is much smaller," Philip remarked as he began to dry off the foal with a towel. "We have a chestnut filly."

The foal was up on her feet much faster than the colt had been, and soon she was nursing.

"Mr. Delaney, why is the filly a different color than her mother?"

Philip tilted his head, pleased with Laura's keen eye. "Do you remember at your father's stud farm we saw a chestnut stallion called Wild Night? He's the sire of this little one."

Laura looked thoughtful. "I think her name should be Wild Honey."

"Very good, Miss Laura. I'm sure your father will like that name."

The next day the sun was shining brightly. Philip and Patrick put the two mares and their babies out into a large grass paddock. Laura and Liam watched the foals run and play until the newborns dropped to the ground to nap.

"They look like two lumps in the grass," Laura giggled. The mares continued to graze nearby, each with an eye on their babies.

Every day, Laura would spend hours watching the new foals play in the pasture. Sometimes their amazing energy would overcome their youthful agility, leaving them sprawled out on the ground in embarrassment as their feet went out from under them.

Although Liam spent his mornings helping his father work the long yearlings—colts not yet two years old—he always managed to find time during the afternoons to ride to the cave with Laura, the guitars slung on their backs. Along with the continued work on Liam's songs, they learned to play most of material in the old gypsy songbook. Their combined natural talents were impressive, and the music sparkled as it came to life.

ᴄᷓᴼ *Chapter Nine* ᴄᷚ

Although Laura's father did not return to the Manor for the holidays that year, he did call often and sent several lavish gifts for Christmas. Laura was able to endure the time without her father with a surprising degree of bravery, primarily due to her bond with Liam. Spring of 1976 marked a kind of new beginning for Laura. Her mother had been gone over a year now, but Laura had a newfound comfort in her life at Montrose. The entire Delaney family had extended itself wholeheartedly to include her, and she felt their love.

Lord Meegan promised Noreen he would come for Laura's tenth birthday, but the nanny decided not to mention it to Laura, knowing the girl would be crushed with disappointment if he did not arrive.

"Today, I want you to come home at noon," Noreen said after breakfast.

"You mean, for lunch?" Laura asked.

"Well, yes—but also to get cleaned up for your party tonight."

"Can't we get cleaned up later?"

Noreen folded her arms and looked sternly at the girl.

"Yes, Mrs. Delaney."

An hour later the children were riding along the river when Sky suddenly snorted and tensed up. He was focused on something in a tree.

"Look, Laura, it's a kite. I don't know where it came from, but I want to try to get it."

"It's pretty high up. Please be careful."

"Don't worry. Remember, I'm a Monkey Boy." Liam dismounted and began his ascent up the tree while Laura watched. She suddenly became distracted by a strange sound.

"Liam, do you hear that? It sounds like...crying."

Liam stopped to listen. "I can hear something from over there." He pointed towards the river. "I'll climb out a little to get a better look." Liam moved slowly out on the limb, which began to sag. "It's a dog—in the river! He's caught in a pile of tree limbs. He sees me now!" Just then, there was a large cracking sound. Laura gasped as both boy and tree limb dropped into the water below, which was running deep and fast. Liam was swept downstream into the pile of debris surrounding the dog.

"Liam! Are you all right?"

"I'm okay—I'm going to get him!" It wasn't long before Liam took hold of the frightened animal, who instantly gave his trust to the boy. Liam tried unsuccessfully to swim against the strong current. With one arm around the dog and the other around a limb, he called out again to Laura.

"Go back to the barn—to the tack room! There's a long rope with a loop in it!"

"Hang on!" Laura cried. "I'll be right back!"

She and Rose galloped as fast as they could, with Sky in close pursuit. Laura rode into the barn and dismounted at the tack room, wasting no time finding what she needed. She remounted and swiftly rode off.

Patrick was busy at the far end of the barn and looked up at the very moment Laura galloped away—without Liam. *There's somethin' wrong.* He called out to Philip.

"There's trouble with the children!"

Philip instantly ran to catch up to Patrick, who already had the truck running.

"I saw Laura tearin' out of here on Rose!" Patrick yelled. "Sky was with them—but no sign of Liam." Before Philip even had the door shut, Patrick hit the accelerator, heading down the trail along the River Maigue.

"Lord—that girl can ride! Where did she disappear to?"

Laura arrived at the river's edge, rope in hand. She quickly dismounted from Rose, who, along with Sky, was breathing hard.

"Liam!" Laura yelled. "Catch this!" She threw the lasso, and he grabbed it.

"Now what are you going to do?" he yelled.

"Slip the loop around you! I'll pull you out!"

"Laura! You can't pull me out! I'm a lot bigger than you!"

"I'll tie this end to the tree first!"

Laura wrapped the rope around, making a knot at the end, and turned to pull with all her might, to no avail. Suddenly, the hastily tied knot slipped—and so did Laura, sliding down the embankment into the river. She went under.

"Laura! Laura! Where are you?" Liam was just about to release the dog to dive under when Laura's head broke through the surface. She caught her breath for only a moment to choke out a desperate cry.

"Help! My foot...it's caught!"

"Laura! Grab on to a branch—I'm coming!"

"Look!" Patrick cried. "Over there! The horses!" He turned the truck sharply towards the bank, skidding to stop. Sky and Rose were looking intently at something down the bank. Jumping out of the truck, Philip was struck with terror at the sight of the children in the fast-moving water. He knew he had to act fast and kicked off his boots.

"Liam! Throw your rope to Patrick! I'll get Laura!" He dove in and swam swiftly to her.

Laura, barely able to keep her head above water, cried out something about her boot. Philip braced his body against the current and tried unsuccessfully to reach her foot below.

Meanwhile, Liam set the dog on top of the pile of debris, freeing a hand to grab the loose end of the rope, which he tossed to Patrick. Liam's effort caused him to sink underwater. He came up coughing, but managed to take hold of the dog again. Patrick pulled the boy and dog up to the safety of the bank, and then threw the rope to Philip.

Philip quickly secured the loop around Laura. "I'll have to go under to free your foot."

Laura only had the strength to nod once. Taking a deep breath, Philip dove into the dark disorientation of the swift, murky waters. He groped for Laura's boot, caught in the tangle of debris. Unable to free it, Philip's only option was to yank her foot out. He returned to the surface, gasping for air, but pushed on, realizing she was nearly unconscious. While supporting her limp body, Philip swam with one arm, as Patrick and Liam carefully pulled them out of danger and onto the bank.

Philip gently laid Laura on the grass, and the reality of her grave condition nearly overwhelmed him. She was hardly breathing and her lips were turning blue.

"Roll her on her side!" Patrick cried. Laura began coughing up water.

"Laura!" Liam cried fearfully. "Please be all right!"

Philip stroked the girl's face gently until her coughing subsided, and then lifted her into his arms again. "Patrick, get the horses back to the barn—I'll take the children. Son, get in the truck."

Philip raced up to the Manor, honking the horn repeatedly. Mr. Callahan came from around the side yard, and Noreen ran out the front door. She gasped when she saw the pale, drenched girl in the front seat. "My Lord! What's happened?"

"Laura needs a doctor!" The urgency in Philip's voice cut through Noreen's shock. She turned to her son, who was climbing out of the truck soaking wet.

"Liam, are you all right?"

"I'm fine! Please help Laura!" His voice was shaky—not from the cold, but from the terror. He still clutched the half-drowned dog in his arms.

Mr. Callahan took off his jacket and draped it around Liam. Philip was holding Laura close to keep her warm, in spite of his being soaked himself.

Iris had seen everything from the window and now appeared with an armful of blankets, bringing them to Noreen. Grabbing them, the nanny climbed into the truck and quickly covered Laura.

"We'll take care of the lad!" Mr. Callahan said. "You get goin'!"

Liam felt helpless as he watched the truck speed down the driveway. The kindly gardener put his arm around the boy.

"Don't you worry—Laura will be fine," he said gently. "Now, let's get you and your wet friend inside where it's warm and dry." Liam eyes lowered to the little dog still trembling in his arms.

"But it's all my fault," Liam said sadly. "Laura was trying to pull me—and the dog—from the river."

"Now don't you go blamin' yourself. It's goin' to be all right." The man concealed his own worry, silently saying a prayer as he walked Liam toward the Manor.

Philip drove swiftly into the village, arriving just in time to catch the doctor as he was leaving for lunch.

"Doctor McKay! It's Miss Meegan! She fell into the river!"

The doctor wasted no time getting Laura into the office, where he gave her a thorough examination. He then spoke gently to the young patient.

"You are a very lucky girl—you could have drowned. You've swallowed some water, and a little went down the wrong pipe, but you'll be all right. You've got a sprained ankle, though. I'll put a wrap on it, and you need to stay off it for several days."

The doctor turned to Noreen. "Give her this antibiotic as a preventative. We don't know what was in the water she swallowed. Keep her resting for a few days, and call me if there's any more swelling in her ankle."

Noreen held Laura close on the way home. "Child, you've scared the livin' daylights out of me." The nanny's eyes welled up with tears.

"Mrs. Delaney, please don't cry. I'm so sorry."

"I know you're sorry, dear—but you and Liam have got to be more careful."

❧

Liam was waiting restlessly at the front window of the Manor. He ran to open the door for his father, who was carrying Laura up the front steps. "Is she all right?"

Laura smiled, seeing that Liam had wrapped the little dog in a blanket.

"Yes, Son, she'll be fine in a few days, but you and I need to have a talk."

"Please!" Laura protested. "I heard the dog crying—he needed help."

"You should have come to us. You both could have drowned. Liam, you're older, and you know better." At that moment, the little dog lifted his head and licked Philip's hand.

"He's thanking you for rescuing him," Laura said. Philip, somewhat relieved, managed a smile while the children laughed.

65

"Now Miss Laura," he cautioned, "you can forget about playin' with the dog. I'll be carryin' you up to your room, and Mrs. Delaney will get you washed and put to bed."

"But what about my birthday party?"

"You need to rest," Philip insisted. "The party can wait."

They didn't even make it to the stairway before Lord Meegan entered the front door.

"Father!" Laura shouted. "You've come!"

"Yes, I have—and what has happened to my little girl?" He cast a disapproving look in Philip's direction, but changed it to a smile when he looked at his daughter.

"I'll explain it to you, Sir. I was just bringin' her up to her room to rest." Aidan nodded and followed them up the stairs.

While Noreen took over the duties of caring for Laura, the two men left the room and Philip proceeded to give an accounting of what had happened. Aidan listened intently without interrupting. Finally he spoke.

"After Noreen is finished with Laura—and you get into some dry clothes—I'd like you to bring your wife and son into the study where we can talk further about this."

"Yes, Sir."

Philip went to the cottage to change, and returned to the Manor to get Noreen and Liam. They walked solemnly down the hall to the study, each feeling guilty about Laura. The reality of the potential consequences hit them all as they entered the door, seeing the frown on Lord Meegan's face.

He studied the Delaney family for a moment before he spoke.

"The danger that has come to my little girl is of great concern to me. Perhaps a boarding school with supervised activities would the best place for her." All three began to protest at the same time, but Lord Meegan put up his hand. "One at a time, please. Noreen, you are the child's nanny."

"This is the first time anythin' like this has happened," she pleaded. "The children have been very good, and we all love Laura so much." Aidan did not respond and Philip spoke next.

"Sir, I have seen the children use very good sense when they're workin' on their ridin' skills. This behavior from them today was

66

completely unexpected—but not without reason. I think they just got a little careless, seein' the dog drownin' in the river."

"Sir," Liam said meekly, "I will never let harm come to Laura again. I promise."

The Lord of the Manor sat back in his chair, carefully considering their pleas.

"Well, I can see you all care for Laura a great deal. I know how happy she has been with your family, and it has brought peace to my heart. Thank God she's going to be all right. I will let this go for now. However, she is ten years old, and I think it is time she calms down and becomes more ladylike."

"Oh thank you, Sir," Noreen said, drying her tears. "We do love Laura so much."

After a few hours of rest, Laura wanted to get up to visit with her father. Chloe came to get him instead. Aidan had hardly entered the room when Laura started to get off the bed. "Father, can I still have my party tonight?"

"Careful now." Her father had a smile on his face in spite of himself. "Young lady, don't you think you've had enough excitement for one day?"

"Oh, Father, I can open my presents right after dinner, and Mrs. Delaney has already made the cake! Please!" Laura convinced him with *that smile.*

"You're just like your mother," he sighed. "I could never say no to her, either." He carried his daughter down the stairs and gently seated her at the dining room table. Liam came out from the kitchen.

"How's the dog?" Laura asked.

"He's just lying by the stove," Liam replied with concern. "And he looks so sad."

"Father, you can fix him!" Laura cried. "Please make him well."

"I'll take a look at him—but you stay right here." Aidan went into the kitchen, followed by Liam, where they found Philip trying to coax the dog into eating.

"I don't think he's doin' too well," Philip said quietly. Aidan looked at the emaciated animal. *He looks like he's living on borrowed time.*

"Philip, I think it would be best if you take the dog to the veterinarian right now. I'm sorry you'll miss dinner, but Cook will save you a plate."

"It's not a problem, Sir—I'll go right away."

"Thank you, Sir." Liam picked up the dog, wrapping him in the blanket. His eyes were fixed on the weak animal. "Hang in there, boy."

After dinner and cake, Laura opened gifts from her father, but to her, the best gift was having him there.

"Father, are you going to stay?"

"I will stay a few days to make sure you're all right, but then I must go."

Noreen watched Laura, expecting her to protest, but the girl didn't say a word.

The next morning, Laura was feeling better. Chloe put a wrap around her ankle for support and helped her get dressed. Aidan carried his daughter down to breakfast.

"Father, can we call the veterinarian and see how the dog is?"

"I have already called—Mr. Delaney went to pick him up. He's going to be fine, and, like you, young lady, he needs to take his antibiotics, stay warm, and rest." Just then, Philip came into the dining room, carrying the dog.

Liam rushed to meet him, taking the animal into his arms. "He looks a lot better!"

Laura smiled, and Aidan was relieved. "Liam, perhaps you should give your new dog a name."

"He's mine to keep?" Liam asked, looking to his father. Philip nodded. Liam thanked them both and hugged the dog.

"The veterinarian said he must have been abandoned," Aidan remarked. "It looks like he's been on the road for a long time now—looking for a home, I guess."

"How could anyone abandon a cute little pup like this?" Liam said, gently scratching the dog. Philip smiled and shook his head as he looked at Aidan, who quietly chuckled, noticing there was a large piece missing from one of the dog's ears. The white and brown mongrel terrier couldn't have weighed more than a wet rabbit.

Noreen raised her eyebrows as she looked at the skinny hound with the scruffy coat. *I guess beauty really is in the eye of the beholder.*

"I will call him Kite," Liam announced. "I was trying to get a kite when we found him."

"Kite is a grand name," Laura replied with a giggle.

Since Laura was confined to the house for a few days, Liam decided to keep her company as often as he could. After morning chores, he brought his guitar into the ballroom where she was playing the piano.

"I thought we could work on some songs together," he said.

"I'd like that, but my music teacher is coming soon for my lesson."

"What are you playing?" Liam asked. "It sounds classical."

"It's Mozart. That's what he teaches me."

"My mother taught me some classical—but it's been a while."

Aidan was at the entrance to the ballroom and heard Liam's comment. He was pleased with the boy's efforts to keep his daughter company.

"Perhaps we could arrange for you to take music lessons as well, Liam." The boy was startled by Lord Meegan's sudden appearance and shrank with humility.

"Oh, Sir, I don't know—you don't have to do that for me."

"No, I don't—but I want to. I think it works well for you both to learn together. Your mother says you've been a big help to Laura with her studies."

"Oh Liam!" Laura exclaimed. "I would love it if we took lessons together!" Liam's eyes shifted back to Lord Meegan.

"I would like it very much, Sir—uh, yes—thank you."

"Good! Then I will speak to the music teacher when he gets here."

Laura got up from the piano and limped towards her father.

"Careful, dear." He walked briskly to meet her with a hug.

"I'm being careful—and thank you, Father—for Liam. You're so wonderful! If you stay around for a few more days, you can listen to us practice." She flashed him that *smile*. Although Aidan was wise to his young daughter's persuasive ways, he was not immune to them.

"We'll see. I do have business to attend to."

Noreen appeared at the door. "Excuse me, Sir, but Laura's music teacher is here." A few steps behind her was a thin, balding man in his early fifties, wearing thick glasses and carrying a briefcase.

"Good morning, Lord Meegan. My name is Martin O'Sullivan." He bowed his head slightly, but intentionally did not extend his hand, protecting it from what he considered unnecessary contact. His hands were, after all, his livelihood.

"Good morning," Aidan replied. "I would like to inquire about the addition of another student to your roster." Laura smiled and looked over at Liam, who was nervously watching his mother. "Mr. O'Sullivan," Aidan continued, "I would like you to also instruct this young man, Liam."

Noreen's jaw dropped. "Lord Meegan...Sir...this is so kind of you...Sir."

"My pleasure, Noreen. Consider it an important part of his education. Besides," he added, glancing at his daughter, "perhaps more indoor activities will keep the children out of trees and rivers." Laura smiled, but Liam lowered his head in embarrassment.

Mr. O'Sullivan happily agreed to take on the new student. "Of course, I'll need to determine his skill level and begin from there."

Aidan and Noreen left the room while Laura went back to the piano. Liam found a chair and waited for instructions. Naturally, the teacher began with Laura, pulling some sheet music out of his briefcase.

"This is the next piece we will be learning. What key is it in?"

"Ummm...A minor."

"Very good, Laura. To begin, please practice your A minor scales, while I speak to Liam." She began slowly with the right hand, and Mr. O'Sullivan turned to the boy.

"Which instrument would you like to focus on, young man?"

"The guitar, Sir."

"You have some experience already?"

"Yes, Sir. My mother began teaching me chords when I was six, and she has taught me how to read music as well."

70

"Good! We will test your proficiency thoroughly later. For now, I will ask you to look at this sheet." He dug into his briefcase, pulling out a piece for guitar, which he handed to Liam.

"It's in three-four time in the key of A major," Liam said without being asked.

"Good! Later, I will determine how much the two of you will learn together and how much separately." Laura stopped playing for a moment when she heard this, and Mr. O'Sullivan noticed.

"Perhaps we should take Liam into another room for a few minutes, so each of you can concentrate on your respective lessons." Liam dutifully picked up his guitar and followed the teacher into the library.

"Now, why don't you put the new piece aside for a moment and play something for me that you know."

Liam thought for a moment, and began to play a slow but uplifting melody which went on for about three minutes and ended with a sustained major chord.

"That was very nice—but I don't think I recognize it."

"Well, it's a song I wrote about springtime. It's called *It Must Be Spring.*"

"I see...Well, this means you may have some future tendency towards composing. But, every composer must know the fundamentals of music, and then move on to theory. So, let us begin."

After a few days Laura was almost fully recovered, and Aidan left to rejoin the race circuit. Although she was saddened by his leaving, Laura was looking forward to wearing jeans and going outside again.

Kite was a constant shadow for Liam, who was thrilled to see the life coming back to the dog. A strong bond had already grown between them. The poor animal had never been cared for, and now he had a boy to love him. Kite may have been a funny looking mutt, but in Liam's mind, he was the best dog in the world. Soon, Liam had Kite doing a variety of tricks, much to everyone's amusement. Everywhere the children went, Kite was not far behind—even when they rode their horses to the cave.

One day, as the children were walking along the river path, Liam had an especially lively spring in his step.

"Laura, I never thought I would be so happy. I'm eleven years old, I live on a wonderful estate, and I'm getting a good education. I have my own horse, a cat, and now a dog. And I write and play music with my best friend in our own secret cave."

Pleased for Liam, a smile came to Laura's face. "I feel the same way—most of the time. I only wish Father would come home more, but I seem to make him sad. He really wants me to be a lady all the time, and I just can't do it. I like the way things are, and I never want them to change. Promise me, Liam, that things won't change."

"I can only promise I will always be here for you, and you will always be my best friend. As far as change...we never know which way the wind will blow."

"Wow! That sounds like something you would write in a song."

"You never know, Laura Lye." Liam had a distinct gleam in his eye.

"Liam, why do you call me Laura Lye?"

He laughed. "You remind me of something I read in a book about Germany."

"Oh, please tell me!"

"According to German legend, there was once a young maiden named Lorelei. She was..." He paused for a moment, suddenly feeling embarrassed. "She was beautiful, with long golden hair. She could be heard singing on a rock high above the Rhine River. Her beauty and hypnotic voice caused many a sailor to wreak his boat."

"Are you saying that I'm beautiful and I sing well...or that I'm a troublemaker?"

He smiled. "There's a song about Lorelei I'll sing to you someday. She was different things to each sailor. But you are my special Laura Lye."

Chapter Ten

Winter 1976

"**L**aura, your father called," Noreen said. "He'll be comin' home for Christmas this year." Laura, who had been gazing out the frosty window, turned excitedly to her nanny.

"That's wonderful! When will he be here?"

"Tomorrow. And I have another surprise—he'll be bringin' a friend with him."

"A friend? Is he bringing his horse trainer?"

"No, a lady friend. And she'll take you shoppin' in Dublin for new clothes."

"I don't need any new clothes—you buy me everything I need."

"Laura, dear, I think he wants you to spend time with her to get to know her."

"Why do I have to get to know her?"

"Now Laura, you must be fair to your father. He wants you to like his new friend, just like you wanted your father to like Liam."

"Can Liam go shopping with us in Dublin?"

"No. Liam would not want to go shoppin' for dresses."

"Dresses! Oh, no—I can't do that."

Noreen placed her hands around Laura's face, pleading with her. "Laura, for me and your father, will you please try to be the warm, sweet girl we know and love?"

Laura threw her arms around her nanny. "I'll try."

Laura was restless that night, wondering why it was so important to her father that she go shopping with his friend. She had a strong feeling things in her life were about to change somehow—and not for the better.

After breakfast she started out the door with Liam. .

73

"Hold it!" Noreen commanded. "Laura, today is the day your father will be arrivin'. I do *not* want you to go to the barn and come back covered in dirt."

"Please, Mrs. Delaney! I'll be back early and put on a dress."

"He'll be here around two o'clock. I want you back at noon—for a bath."

"Thank you," Laura replied sweetly, and headed out the back door. When they were a few steps away from the Manor, she confided in Liam. "I don't want to meet my father's friend and go shopping with her."

"I know, Laura, but sometimes we have to do things we don't want to. Maybe she'll be nice, and you'll like her."

"Liam, you're only trying to make me feel better."

"Well, is it working, Laura Lye?"

In response, she giggled, and broke into a run.

They always enjoyed the path down to the barn. The route followed the river, and around the bend were the cottages for the Callahans, the Delaneys, and Patrick. Just beyond, the beautiful stone horse barn came into full view, and that's where Sky and Rose lived.

"Today we should just ride around the estate," Liam suggested. "That way we won't lose track of time."

"You're such a worrier," Laura remarked.

"Somebody has to be one. Remember what happened the last time your father came."

Laura grimaced, recalling the disaster in the river.

They had been riding for several hours when Liam noticed the sun getting high in the sky. "We need to head back to the barn." As they were putting the horses away, he glanced at the clock in the tack room. "It's half past eleven, Laura."

Philip came down the barn aisle. "Liam, I'd like you to stay—the farrier will be here soon. You know you're his favorite when it comes to holdin' the horses." Liam smiled, always anxious to take on jobs of responsibility for his father.

Liam turned to Laura. "You'd better hurry—my mother will be looking for you."

Laura was on the path to the Manor when she saw Mr. Callahan helping his wife out of the car. The elderly woman was moving slowly. Laura ran to them.

"Can I help?" she asked. Mrs. Callahan's pained expression turned to a smile the moment she saw the girl. Her husband noticed.

"Well," he said, "you could come in and sit with Mrs. Callahan for a spell. She's been to the doctor and has to stay in bed for a while. I need to go back to the village for her prescription."

Laura cheerfully agreed and helped as Mr. Callahan eased his wife up the walkway and into the living room. He went to the kitchen to fix tea and sandwiches before leaving for the village.

After lunch Laura entertained Mrs. Callahan, singing some of her favorite songs.

"Laura, you have such a sweet voice. You know, I love to see you dance, too." Laura needed no more prompting than that.

The lady beamed with delight as she watched the girl flutter around effortlessly. *What a beautiful child—even with her face smudged and hay in her hair.*

Mr. Callahan returned to find Laura gently placing a quilt over his dozing wife.

"Laura," he whispered, "Mrs. Delaney is callin' for you."

"Oh no," Laura said, putting her hand to her mouth. "What time is it?"

"It's a little after two, my dear."

"I've got to go." She raced out the door and up the river path to the Manor, hoping she might go unnoticed if she sneaked in the servants' entrance.

Her father, however, was at the dining room window, impatiently waiting for her arrival. He now saw Laura running up the path and went to meet her at the back door. She entered to find him standing with his arms folded, a stern look on his face.

"Laura Meegan, where have you been? My Lord! Look at you!"

"Aidan, is this your daughter?" A tall woman with dark hair and disapproving eyes stood next to Laura's father.

"Yes, I'm afraid so," Aidan sighed. "Noreen, take her to her room to be scrubbed."

Laura hung her head in shame, as tears rolled down her dirty checks. "I'm so sorry."

"Child, I told you to be home at noon," her nanny scolded.

"But I was helping Mrs. Callahan!"

"Aidan," the tall woman said sharply, "I think there is a serious lack of control over this child."

"You may be right, Hannah."

Laura began to sob. Noreen took the girl's hand, trying to hold back her own tears. "Let's go to your room, now."

Laura cried all the way up the stairs. "I'm so sorry. I was helping Mrs. Callahan and I forgot the time."

"I know you're sorry, Laura, but it makes me look very bad to your father. He's talkin' about sendin' you to a boardin' school."

Laura threw her arms around her nanny. "Please don't let him send me away!"

"It will be up to you, my dear. You need to show them how you can be a lady."

Noreen helped Laura with a bath and shampoo. They picked out a nice dress and shoes, and she put a matching ribbon in Laura's hair.

"Now you look like a little lady! Hurry downstairs to meet the new lady."

Laura descended the grand stairway gracefully, and her father was pleased.

"That's more like my little girl." He gave her a hug. "Laura, I would like you to meet a very special lady. This is Mrs. Morann."

Laura gave the woman a little curtsey. "Pleased to meet you, Mrs. Morann."

"Well, there might be hope after all," the woman said sarcastically. "Laura, you may call me Hannah."

Hannah Morann had been married to a wealthy stockbroker who had passed away several years before. She had managed to spend most of the fortune he left her. With an appreciation for old world grace and a taste for the finer things in life, Hannah could see a great opportunity as Lady Meegan. Motivated and aggressive, Hannah wanted it all and she wanted it now. She was not about to let an undisciplined child spoil it for her.

Although Laura was doing her best, she shuddered at the thought of becoming familiar with this cold woman. Hannah's narrowed dark eyes gave her a severe appearance, enhanced by black hair pulled firmly back into a twist. Laura could feel the woman's heart of stone.

By the end of the day the staff was very aware of Hannah's presence. The pretense of charm she used around Aidan fooled no one. The older staff members remarked that she was nothing like Fey. Although Noreen and Philip had never known Aidan's late wife, they wondered what he saw in this woman.

"I suppose he's attracted to the fact that she's so proper and worldly," Philip remarked. "Maybe he's hopin' she'll influence Laura to be more of a lady."

"Oh, I don't think she's goin' to influence Laura," Noreen said decisively. "I can see the distrust in the girl's eyes already."

"Noreen, we must encourage Laura to try—for Lord Meegan's sake."

The next two days were agony for Laura, who was confined to the Manor. Aidan was taking no chance of her slipping into tomboy activities. She was to be on her best behavior and wear dresses at all times. Laura saw Liam only at breakfast in the kitchen.

"Liam, I miss spending time with you and Rose."

"I know. We miss you, too. When I ride Sky, I let Rose come with us."

"Thank you. She would be as lonely as I am, if you left her behind."

"Try to cheer up. Christmas will be here soon, and then they'll be gone, and we can go back to the cave and sing and play music." Liam hummed a little tune he had been working on, and Laura gave him a smile.

"I'll keep thinking about my horse, our music…and you."

"I promise it'll get better, Laura Lye. You must be strong for a while longer."

Liam got up from the table to go back to the barn and Laura watched as he made his way down the path. *What would I ever do without him?*

Laura strolled into the living room to find the large Christmas tree, which had just been delivered. She was looking forward to decorating it with her nanny and Liam, as they had done the year before. With a smile on her face, Laura recalled explaining to them the special meaning of each ornament.

"This one is a fairy. It was given to my mother by her mother. My mother's name, Fey, means fairy." She picked up a horse ornament. "This one is for my pony, Lilly, and the piano and guitar ornaments are for my music. Everywhere Mother traveled, she would bring me back one or two ornaments for the next Christmas. After the tree was decorated, we would have hot cocoa with marshmallows. Then we would sing and dance around the tree."

Laura was pulled out of the daydream when her father and Hannah walked in.

"Father, are you going help us decorate the tree?"

"The tree will be done when you get back from Dublin."

"Done? But Father, I always help decorate the tree."

Hannah smiled smugly. "I arranged to have it decorated by a professional designer."

Laura looked to her father with pleading eyes, but he looked down, and Laura instantly knew Hannah would have her way.

The next morning Laura was dressed in her best outfit and ready to go to Dublin.

Her father came to her room. "Laura, it's very important to me that you be on your best behavior for Hannah. Whatever she picks out for you, I want you to be gracious. She knows what all proper little girls should be wearing."

"Yes, Father, I'll do my best."

"Now that's my little lady." He gave her a hug.

It was Laura's first train trip and she was excited, bouncing from one seat to another to get a better look at the countryside—until Hannah put a stop to it.

"Laura, come sit like a proper lady of grace and gentility."

She obediently sat next to the woman for the rest of the trip, with her hands folded on her lap. At times, Laura thought she would burst inside. *How can anyone sit still for so long and not say a word?*

When they finally arrived in Dublin, Hannah took her hand. "Stay close to me, child, and do as I say."

Laura was intimidated by the big city. For the first time in her life, she was in silent awe, as she watched the bustle of people and cars, with the tall buildings looming overhead.

Hannah went from shop to shop, buying Laura fancy dresses with ruffles and bows. Laura never uttered a complaint, even though the patent leather shoes hurt her feet and the lace on her dress was scratching her neck. She was about as miserable as one little girl could get.

"Now Laura, I have a surprise for you," Hannah announced. "We are going to have lunch with my two daughters."

Daughters? Well, it might be fun to meet some girls my age.

When they arrived at the restaurant, there were two young ladies waiting for them at a table in the elegant tea room.

"Laura, these are my daughters, Peggy and Emily."

Laura felt a chill as the girls coldly examined her. Emily was sixteen years old, petite, with sharp features which she embellished with an excess of makeup. Her long auburn hair accented her piercing green eyes.

Peggy, fourteen, was clearly tall and thin, even when seated. The girl's skin was quite pale, and she used very little makeup. Her dark hair was pulled back like her mother's. In spite of the differences in their features, both girls were impeccably groomed and had the same brand of arrogance.

Laura wished she was at home with Liam. She was tired and uncomfortable. *How can I ever remember all my manners?*

Hannah ordered salads and tea for everyone. Laura could barely choke down her food, in spite of being very hungry. What she really wanted was one of Mrs. Delaney's sandwiches with cold milk—and to eat it in the hay loft with Liam.

Every time Laura moved, the older girls would laugh and mutter about her manners. Tears began to roll down Laura's cheeks.

"Laura!" Hannah sharply whispered. "The fashionable people of Dublin do not display their emotions in public."

It took all of Laura's energy to control herself, and when the awful day finally came to an end, she fell sound asleep on the train. Just before they reached their stop, Hannah shook her.

"Child! Wake up!" Laura rubbed her sleepy eyes and thought she was in the middle of a nightmare. Hannah's daughters were sitting directly across, giggling at her. She shook her head to clear her vision, but the girls were still there.

"My girls will be spending Christmas at the Manor with us," Hannah announced.

The stark reality of it all was almost too much for Laura. *Who are these people?*

Aidan was there to meet them at the train station, and as he picked up Laura, she hugged him tightly. He carried her to the car.

"This was a big day for my little girl."

Once Laura was put to bed she fell into a deep sleep, floating through a maze of images of her mother, interrupted by these cold strangers in her life. She woke up with a start. *Why are they here? And why does Father even like Hannah?*

In an effort to please her father, Laura picked out a dress and matching ribbon for her hair. Her first curiosity was the Christmas tree, so she went straight to the living room—where her jaw dropped. The tree was all done in gold balls and ribbons, and not a single one of her precious ornaments had been used. *This is the ugliest Christmas tree I have ever seen!* Laura ran back up to her room, threw on a pair of jeans, and slipped down the back stairs and out the door. *I can't take it any longer—I need to go to the barn!*

Liam was surprised to see her there. "Laura, what are you doing here?"

She threw her arms around him and started to cry. "Liam, please—let's ride to our cave." He could see her pain, so he asked no more questions. Throwing the rope collars around their horses' necks, they rode off like the wind.

Once inside the cave, Laura spilled her heart to Liam about the ordeal in Dublin and the horror of waking up to the ugly Christmas tree.

Liam gave her a hug. "I finished the song I wrote for you."

As he strummed, Laura calmed down and wondered how he could make her feel so good inside while Hannah and her daughters could make her feel so bad.

Christmas did turn out to be a lonely and horrible time for Laura. Hannah insisted it be a formal occasion with only Aidan, Laura, Hannah, and the girls, all dressed in their holiday best. First sitting down to a formal breakfast, the family then moved to the living room. In an almost regimented manner, each person was allowed to open one present at a time, giving proper thanks for the gift.

When it was Laura's turn, she obediently unwrapped one of the boxes with her name on it, with little expectation of the joy she usually associated with Christmas. As she opened the tissue paper to find yet another fancy dress she didn't want, Laura drifted off into the memory of a gift from her mother. The brown velvet riding cape—like her mother's—had made Laura feel grown up from the first day she wore it. Sweet memories of her mother now came flooding back. Laura could almost taste the fresh-baked scones and hot cocoa they enjoyed while opening gifts...

Laura's daydream was abruptly ended by Hannah's stern voice.

"Child, you have another gift to open."

After an embarrassing pause, Laura dutifully complied, removing the gift wrapping to reveal a box with an interesting logo on top—of a horse. A spark of hope struck the little girl as she lifted the lid—but then her heart sank.

"Now this is a proper riding habit for a young lady of distinction," Hannah proclaimed. Artfully displayed within were a tweed jacket and a pair of jodhpurs, much to Laura's dismay. *I'll never wear these things. I like wearing my jeans and cape.*

"Laura, you should thank Hannah for the lovely gifts," her father prompted.

81

"Yes, Father. Thank you, Hannah." Laura forced a smile, but inside her disappointment was overwhelming. *When will this ever end?*

The next day, she got her wish. Aidan, Hannah, and her girls were leaving, and Laura was glad to see them go. She loved her father, but did not care to ever see Hannah and her snobbish daughters again.

ᘓᕤ *Chapter Eleven* ᕬᘒ

Spring 1977

Springtime in Ireland was Laura's favorite season, always arriving with an abundance of colorful wildflowers. The smell of clover perfumed the air, and the buzzing of honey bees made sweet harmony with the chirping of the birds.

Although she missed her father, Laura was relieved that the ordeal of Christmas was now a fading memory. Life was good again. There was plenty of time to spend with Liam, enjoying music and their horses.

She was weaving flowers into Rose's mane when Liam came into the barn.

"Laura, today I'm going to train horses with my father," Liam said proudly.

"Can I stay and watch? I promise I'll be quiet, and I won't get in the way."

Philip walked in. "Laura, you're never in the way! You bring sunshine to us all every day." Laura flashed him a big smile.

Liam smiled, too, but he didn't allow himself to be distracted for long. He was honored that his father was asking him to help with the training. Learning about horses was exciting for him.

"I've got a colt in the arena we'll start with," Philip said. Liam nodded and eagerly followed his father while Laura looked on. "Son, if you pay attention, you can read a horse like a book. Watch this colt's ears. If you talk to him in a soft, reassuring voice, he'll listen and respond. When his ears and eyes are no longer on you, he's not listenin'. That is when an accident can happen. Just like a good school teacher, it's your job to keep him interested in you and learnin'."

Liam watched intently as his father demonstrated various training techniques.

Over the course of the next few days, Philip became confident enough in his son to let him start a colt on his own—a colt named The Real Thing.

The colt was nearly two years of age and showed promise for racing, but he was high-strung and had a short attention span. Liam was slow and patient with him. When the young horse showed signs of nervousness, Liam would stroke his neck and softly hum a melody. After only a week, the colt was doing everything Liam asked, and the boy wanted his father to see the progress. Philip watched, feeling the kind of fulfillment only a father could know.

"Son, I'm so proud of you. For only bein' twelve, you have the patience of a grown man—and a natural ability few have at all."

"I'm proud, too!" Laura added. The bond between Liam and his father was one Laura wished she had. Sadly, she had learned to feel comfortable without her own father. The Delaneys were her family now.

Philip patted his son on the shoulder and Laura on top of her head. "Now you two go have some fun! Get your horses and off you go."

Patrick and Philip looked on as they rode off.

"There they go," Philip said wistfully. "Flyin' on the wings of angels."

"You are very lucky to have a boy like Liam," Patrick remarked.

"Indeed, I feel very blessed. Noreen and I could only have one child and I could not ask for more than my Liam."

"He does have the gift. Soon he'll be training horses like his ol' man..."

"Oh, not my Liam—I want more for him. Yes, he has the gift, but he has many other talents as well. He's a very smart lad. I want him to go to college and make his mark in the world. Lord Meegan has promised to give him the best education, and for that, I will be forever in his debt."

"It sure is a big help to have Liam workin' with us," Patrick remarked.

"Workin' with us part time is fine—he can learn a lot from horses. It's somethin' that's good for any soul. But I know my Liam will go on to be someone special."

Later that week, Patrick walked up to Laura and Liam in the barn.

"There's somethin' Chloe wants to ask you up at the Manor."

"What does she want?" Laura asked.

"Oh—I think it's a surprise," Patrick replied mysteriously. That's all it took for Laura and Liam to race up to the Manor.

Noreen met them at the door. "I can't believe it—you're back early."

"Patrick said Chloe has a surprise for us," Laura said.

"Ah, yes…but you'd best wash up first," the nanny said with a twinkle in her eye. It didn't take long before they were at the table seated across from Chloe.

"I have some excitin' news," Chloe announced. "Patrick and I are goin' to be married in a few weeks! We plan to have a weddin' here at the Manor. I have a job for the two of you—we want Laura to be our flower girl and Liam to be the ring bearer."

Laura was thrilled—she had never been to a wedding. "Will I have flowers in my hair and a basket with flower petals, like I've seen in the magazines?"

Chloe nodded. They turned to Liam, who shrank in his chair, wishing he could be invisible. Chloe tried to make eye contact with him.

"Liam, won't you be part of our special day?" Liam just shook his head as he looked at the floor.

His mother intervened. "Your father and I are going to stand up for Chloe and Patrick. It would mean a lot to them for you to participate."

"I just can't!" Liam jumped up and ran out the door.

"I'm so sorry, Chloe," Noreen said. "He's such a shy boy."

Laura jumped up. "I'll talk to him." She knew exactly where to look—Liam's favorite tree along the river. Laura climbed up to sit next to him on the limb.

"Why won't you be part of their wedding with me?"

"I can't do it," Liam said firmly, looking away. "You know I don't like to be in a crowd—especially up in front of the world."

85

"Oh, Liam, it's not going to be a crowd—mostly just family."
Liam's frown did not change. Without a word he climbed a little higher
up the tree. Laura could not believe his stubbornness.

"Liam, pretend you and I are the only ones there. You can walk
with me."

"I'll think about it. Now, leave me alone."

"We could play and sing one of our songs for them as a present,
too."

"Now you're pushing. You know our music is just for us."

"That's silly!" she scolded. "Music is meant to be shared with
others. Your voice should be heard—you have a special gift from God."

With that she left him up in the tree. Laura walked briskly back
to the Manor, feeling more determined. *He's so talented, but no one will
ever know it as long as he's so shy.*

Several days passed without a word from Liam about the
wedding. Laura had decided to give him time to think about it. They
were in the cave, singing a song Liam had written months before—it was
actually a love ballad.

"I think this one would be good for Chloe and Patrick's
wedding."

Laura was surprised—yet pleased. "Oh, Liam, I knew you would
do it. Thank you."

"Only for you, Laura Lye, only for you."

The wedding plans were the talk of the Manor. Liam always
thought it was a waste of time and would go off to the barn. Laura, on the
other hand, was thrilled to hear every detail and involved herself as much
as she could. Her excitement doubled when Noreen showed Laura the
beautiful long dress she had made for her.

"And we'll put flowers and ribbons in your hair. Now off with
you!"

Noreen and Chloe smiled as they watched the girl run joyfully
down the path.

"Little Laura's so excited about your weddin' plans," Noreen
sighed. "I only hope she's not goin' to be too miserable when she hears

the news that Lord Meegan just got married to Hannah. Maybe if he'd made his only daughter a part of his weddin'…"

Chloe shook her head. "I still don't understand how he could have married that woman. I know it's really goin' to be hard for Laura. And he's not goin' to tell the girl himself—he's lettin' the beastly woman tell her."

"It's just not right," Noreen agreed. "I can't believe he's that wrapped up in his race horses—I think he's just takin' the easy way out."

"Then, after she's dropped the bomb on poor Laura, Hannah is goin' to help with my weddin' plans. Don't get me wrong—we appreciate Lord Meegan's generosity. He is payin' for the weddin' and all, but now everythin' will have to be her way."

"And we'll have Hannah for ten days to boot!" Noreen added. "At least she likes to travel and stay in Dublin with her fancy friends. She could be cursin' us here as the Lady of the Manor from dawn 'til dusk every day!"

"Oh heavens!" Chloe said, throwing her hands up. They both laughed.

Noreen knew the staff at the Manor would soon be in an uproar preparing for Hannah's arrival. She decided it was time to tell Laura about Hannah's visit.

"She's coming without my father? Why?"

"Your father has sent her ahead to help with Chloe's weddin'. We must be nice and show her respect."

"But she doesn't like us—anybody at the Manor—and she hardly knows Chloe. She just calls her the upstairs maid."

"Now, Laura, your father would be very unhappy if he heard you talkin' like this. He asked that you be here to greet Hannah when she arrives—and in a dress, with your hair properly combed."

◁◈ Chapter Twelve ◈▷

O n the morning of Hannah's arrival, Chloe helped Laura pick out a special dress and a matching ribbon for her hair.

"You look very nice," Noreen said when Laura came down the stairs. Forcing a smile, the girl seated herself in the living room. It wasn't really a long wait, but to Laura it seemed forever before the limousine finally pulled up. She greeted Hannah at the door, but the austere woman's first words were not exactly what the child expected.

"Ladies do not answer the door. That is a job for the servants." Laura was shocked by the woman's abruptness and had no idea how to respond. Hannah then turned to Iris. "I have packages in the car to be brought in. Then you can bring my bags up to my suite."

"Right away, Ma'am." Iris hurried out the door, anxious to get away from the domineering woman. Noreen came from the kitchen to greet Hannah.

"Welcome to Montrose Manor," she said cheerfully.

"Yes," Hannah replied with a wave of the hand as she marched through the entryway.

"Now, get Chloe, and have her meet me in the dining room. Make sure Laura is there as well. And have the cook make me a pot of tea." Laura's head was spinning as she walked cautiously behind the woman. A moment later Chloe and Noreen arrived to see Hannah instructing Iris to place the packages on the table.

Hannah dismissed the maid before turning to the others. "Please be seated." Chloe and Noreen exchanged worried glances and each took a chair. Laura followed suit without hesitation.

"I have brought gifts from Dublin," Hannah began. "Chloe, this one is for you—please open it." Chloe removed the lid carefully, and gasped in astonishment.

Hannah explained, "They are a pair of Waterford crystal toasting glasses for you and Patrick."

"Oh!" Chloe cried. "They're so elegant! Thank you—thank you so much." Hannah nodded, and then turned to Laura.

"Child, you may open your package." Laura opened the box to find an elaborate lace gown. "It's for you to wear at Chloe's wedding," Hannah said with satisfaction.

"I have a dress for the wedding," Laura protested. "Mrs. Delaney made for me."

Hannah frowned. "Laura, this is a designer dress from the best shop in Dublin. You will wear this one." Laura sadly looked to her nanny, who winked and shook her head once. Hannah continued.

"Now, I have wonderful news for everyone. Aidan and I were married last month. Laura, I am your new mother, and you now have two new sisters."

All eyes were on Laura as she stood frozen in time. Tears began to roll down her cheeks.

"Well, say something, child," Hannah demanded.

Unable to speak, her heart caught in her throat, Laura ran through the kitchen and bolted out the back door.

Noreen and Chloe were both utterly shocked at how the woman blurted out the news.

Hannah frowned. "It is certainly time for that child to grow up and realize the world does not revolve around her." She glared at Noreen. "Have the tea sent to my suite." With that, Hannah marched off.

"Oh, my heart's breakin' for the poor girl," Chloe said sadly.

"I'm sure she's run off to Liam," Noreen said, drying her own tears. "The poor child wasn't expectin' anythin' like this."

Liam was at the far end of the barn. He abruptly stopped what he was doing when he heard Sky calling. Knowing there must be something wrong, Liam ran to find his horse pacing at the door, and Rose missing altogether. He grabbed Sky's rope collar and mounted his horse.

"Where have they gone, boy? Show me." Giving the gelding his head, Liam clung to Sky's back as the horse shot off like lightning.

Disregarding her fancy dress, Laura jumped on Rose and galloped through the trees as fast as the mare would take her, branches tearing the delicate fabric to ribbons. By the time she reached the cave, Laura was crying so hard she couldn't see. She slid off Rose's back and dropped to the ground.

"Father would never do that! He loves me!" she cried. Rose patiently stood at Laura's side, and it wasn't long before Liam arrived.

"What's happened? Are you hurt?"

"He loves me," she sobbed. "He wouldn't do that."

Liam took her into his embrace, gently stroking her hair, and then began to sing to her. Laura fell limp in his arms, and Liam carried her into the cave to lay her down on the straw. He softly hummed to her while covering her with a blanket. She did not awaken for several hours.

"How did I get here with you?" she asked, rubbing her eyes.

"Are you all right?" Liam asked. "I've been so worried about you." Laura's eyes began to well up again as the pain of Hannah's words returned. Liam put his arm around her. "It's all right—you don't have to talk. I'll sing to you."

More time passed, and light grew dim in the cave.

"Laura, it'll be dark, soon, and everyone will be worried. Let's go home."

"It's not my home any more—I can't go back." She finally told Liam the whole story, and as he listened his heart began to break. Soon his sorrow turned to anger. *How could anyone hurt her like this? She's so trusting and loving—it just isn't fair.*

Laura's hair was soaking wet with tears. Liam wiped her face with gentle fingers, and then pulled her hair back and made a braid, tying it with the ribbon.

"Let's go back to the Manor together. I'll be there with you, so don't be frightened." Laura was too exhausted to protest. Liam helped her up on Rose.

As dusk approached, Noreen and Chloe made attempts to find Laura and Liam. Knowing they were most likely together was only a mild consolation to Noreen, who was frustrated that nobody had actually seen the two children. They went to Patrick's cottage to ask him.

"I know their horses were out earlier," Patrick said. "That's all I can tell you."

After Liam put the horses away, he took Laura's hand and they walked cautiously up the path.

"Liam, promise you will always be here for me."

"You know I will."

As they approached the steps, Laura began to tremble. Liam put his arm around her. "Laura, you'll be fine. You're the bravest person I know."

Hannah had been furious ever since Laura had taken off. *Wait 'til I get my hands on her. She will learn respect and how to act like a lady!* As Hannah paced near the window, she saw them coming up the path and went to meet them at the back door.

"Laura Meegan, where have you been? And look at you! Your dress is ruined!"

Liam held Laura's hand tightly, clearly trying to contain his anger. Laura, enraged beyond belief, did not hold back.

"You are not my mother and never will be! I hate you and your daughters! You will never be my family!" With that, Laura ran up to her room in tears. Liam started up the stairs after her, which only fueled Hannah's wrath.

"Stable boys do not belong in the house! Go back to your barn!" Liam froze in his steps while the angry woman marched up the stairs and into Laura's room. Without a word she grabbed Laura by the hair, jerking her off the bed and dragging the frightened girl in front of the mirror.

"Look at yourself. You are a disgrace! You do not have the makings of a young lady!"

"Good!" Laura cried. "I don't want to be one anyway!" Hannah's blood boiled at the girl's insolence. She spotted a large pair of scissors and impulsively grabbed them.

"If you want to be a boy, you won't need long hair!" Without hesitation, Hannah cut Laura's braid off to the scalp.

Laura's shock was immense. "You're wicked!" she screamed. "As wicked as the devil himself!"

Hannah responded by slapping Laura's face several times. Laura screamed out in terror and crumpled to the floor in defeat.

Laura's cries ignited a fury in Liam. He bounded up the stairs and into her room. To his horror, he saw Laura curled up in a ball on the floor with her long braid lying next to her.

Hannah started to push by Liam on her way to the door. Boldly blocking her exit, he gripped the woman's arm and jerked her to face him. The rage in his eyes rendered her powerless.

"Don't you ever lay a hand on Laura again!" His angry voice was deep and harsh. It was only Laura's whimpering that caused Liam to release his grip. Hannah, shaken by the boy's outburst, retreated from the room.

Liam knelt beside Laura. He carefully slipped the braid into his pocket, knowing the sight of it would only upset her more. He gently lifted her chin.

"Laura, are you all right?" She only nodded, unable to speak.

"Come with me. You can't stay here." Putting his arm around her waist, Liam helped Laura to her feet and they walked quickly out of the room and down the back stairs. They heard someone at the kitchen door, and Laura clutched him tightly. Liam sheltered the trembling girl as he looked to see who it was. He instantly relaxed at the sound of his father's voice speaking to his mother.

"Liam! Laura!" Noreen cried. "What's happened? We heard screams." Laura slowly pulled her head out of Liam's embrace to look up at her nanny.

"You poor dear! Your face—and your hair! Who's done this to you?"

"Hannah," Laura whimpered. Noreen pulled Laura into her arms.

Philip was livid. "Where is that cowardly woman?"

"Father, I took care of her. Can we please take Laura to the cottage?" Philip met his son's eyes in mutual understanding. He nodded once and picked Laura up, carrying her out to his truck.

"I'll be callin' Lord Meegan right away," Noreen declared. "I don't care if she threatens our jobs. She can't get away with this!"

Once in the safety of the cottage, Noreen tended to Laura's swollen face and put her to bed. She then made the phone call.

Aidan's voice was devoid of emotion. "Yes, Noreen, I was just informed by my wife of what happened earlier."

"Oh! I'm sure she gave you *her* side of the story. Did she tell you she slapped Laura so hard she has bruises on her face and a swollen eye? And did she tell you she chopped her hair off to the scalp? Did she tell you how it all started? How she just blurted it out that you were married and now she was Laura's new mother? Now, did she?"

There was dead silence on the phone.

"Lord Meegan, are you there?"

His voice softened. "I will be home tomorrow morning. Just keep Laura with you until I get there."

"Bless you, Sir. She needs you."

Laura's exhaustion left her unaware she was in Liam's bed. Noreen did not wake her until late the next morning.

"Laura, darlin', your father is on his way. I've drawn you a bath, and I've made pancakes."

"I don't want Father to see me. I don't want anyone to see me. Look at my hair." She began to cry again.

"You'll feel better after a hot bath. Liam stayed in this mornin' to have breakfast with you." At that news, Laura managed a smile and agreed.

As the children finished their breakfast, Chloe came into the cottage, accompanied by a young woman.

"Laura, this is Molly, my sister. She's a hairdresser in the village. She'll cut your hair into a cute style."

"I have no hair to cut."

"Oh, sure ya do, sweetie," Molly assured. "I can make you look like a little pixie." Molly ran her fingers through what remained of Laura's hair. "You have the perfect face for it."

Laura was doubtful, but Molly wasted no time. Wrapping a towel around the girl's shoulders, she snipped away until the blonde hair was about two inches long everywhere.

"Now you're a little pixie!"

Laura looked in the mirror. "Chloe, I can't be in your wedding," she said despondently. "I have no hair to put flowers in."

93

Liam was quiet while the women were talking, but now he spoke up. "I can make you a crown with wire and we can weave flowers and ribbons into it."

Laura gave him a brave smile. "You saved me last night. Thank you."

When Aidan arrived he drove straight to the Delaney cottage. One look at his precious little daughter and he welled up with tears.

"Oh Laura, I'm so sorry I didn't come and tell you everything myself. This all could have been avoided. Can you ever forgive me?"

"Just tell me it's not true."

"Dear, it is true—Hannah and I are married. I thought it would be good for you to have a mother again. Hannah is a good woman, and she means well. You should not have yelled those hateful things at her. You have love in your heart for everyone."

"I'm sorry, Father. I don't feel love in my heart for her or her daughters."

"Give it time. You'll come around."

"But look what she did to me! My hair is gone—and she hit me."

"I promise you nothing like it will ever happen again," he said firmly. "Now, we should go to the Manor."

"No, Father. I want to stay here with the Delaneys."

"Laura, I insist you come with me."

"Can Liam come, too? Please, Father—he saved me last night."

Aidan looked at Liam, who boldly met Lord Meegan's eyes. "All right, dear." He put his arm around his daughter reassuringly.

At the Manor, Liam took Laura's hand, and they slowly followed Aidan. Hannah was waiting for them in the living room, and as she started towards them, Laura began to tremble. Liam squeezed her hand.

"Be brave, Laura Lye," he whispered.

Hannah said, "Laura, darling, I would like to apologize to you for last night. I lost my temper. It will never happen again."

Laura could see right through Hannah's feigned sincerity to her cold, hard eyes. She was not swayed by the woman's empty words.

Laura bolted from the room, running up the stairs, with Liam right behind her.

Aidan put his hand on Hannah's shoulder. "Give her time—she's still in shock over everything."

"Aidan, I just do not know if I can take her intolerable manners. And why is that stable boy going up to her room?"

Aidan frowned, narrowing his eyes. "Hannah, Liam is like a brother to Laura and he will always be welcome in our home."

"Well, maybe if she kept better company, she would not be a tomboy."

Aidan's patience was growing thin. "That boy has been a blessing for Laura. He's helped her through some very difficult times."

Hannah could clearly see Aidan was adamant. "I will respect your feelings on the matter, Aidan."

"Now, regarding Laura—you will *never* lay a hand on her again. Is that understood?" Aidan's directness was unnerving to his new wife.

"Yes, I do apologize. I was trying so hard and...she was so rebellious. I just lost my temper. It will never happen again. I promise."

✍ *Chapter Thirteen* ✍

Summer 1977

Chloe and Patrick's wedding day arrived with a gentle breeze and a clear blue sky. The ceremony was to be on the expansive lawn bounded by Mr. Callahan's prized rose garden—said by many to be the most colorful in the south of Ireland. With the river running alongside and the Manor as a backdrop, the setting was spectacular. Everything was in place, with flowers, tables, and chairs all set up. In keeping with tradition, the Irish flag proudly flew behind the altar.

Laura, the flower girl, was in her room putting on the white and blue dress her nanny had made. Aidan had approved it as the right choice for his daughter, since the dress clearly matched Chloe's wedding gown. He quietly asked Hannah to return the one she bought in Dublin, and she agreed.

Noreen came in and sighed as she saw the beautiful child before her. "Laura, you look like a princess! I have somethin' else for you," she added with a twinkle in her eye. From a white box she set down, the nanny lifted a wreath of flowers and gently placed it on Laura's head. A dozen long blue and white ribbons trailed halfway down the girl's back. A glowing smile came to Laura's face as she ran to the mirror.

"Now I look like I have long hair! These pretty ribbons are perfect!"

"It was Liam's idea," Noreen said proudly. "And he made it himself."

It warmed Laura's heart to think of Liam's kindness. She grabbed the basket of rose petals. "I'm ready now!"

Chloe's sister Molly was putting the finishing touches on Chloe's hair. She carefully placed the veil on the bride's head. "My dear sister…If I do say so myself, you look like an angel from Heaven above."

Chloe was truly a divine sight in her traditional white Irish lace gown, with Celtic blue braiding on the bodice, and the handmade veil that had been worn by her mother and grandmother.

The bride then reached for the symbol of time-honored tradition: The Magic Hankie. It had been passed down to Chloe from her mother, who carried it at her own wedding. The custom was to then stitch it into a bonnet for the bride's firstborn to wear at the christening. Chloe, the eldest of five children, had worn the bonnet for that ceremony, and now it had been changed back into a hankie for her wedding. She would save it for her own firstborn, continuing the practice.

The entire Bailey family would be part of Chloe's special day. Sean Bailey looked forward to the honor of walking his daughter down the aisle, and his two boys, Bobby and Danny, were in the wedding party. Bridesmaids Molly and Kelly were wearing blue to match Noreen's matron-of-honor dress.

All the men, including Liam, were wearing tuxedos. Danny, just fourteen, had the unusual distinction of being the only groomsman who could knot a bow tie.

"Now, hold still," he said to Patrick, who nervously stood in front of the mirror.

Although restless, Patrick was thrilled at the prospect of finally being part of a family again—especially the Bailey family. He had lost his parents tragically when he was a teenager, and he had no siblings or any other living relatives.

Philip walked around the ornate white and gold wedding carriage, satisfied that it was draped perfectly with flowers. He patted Ol' Tommy affectionately on the neck.

"Old boy, you look more like a show horse than a draft horse." Ol' Tommy was gloriously decked out in blue ribbons braided into his mane and tail. Philip carefully took his place in the coachman's seat, with the rescued dog, Kite, sitting obediently beside him.

Leaving his cottage with the bride and her father aboard, Philip sat a little taller as he headed towards the arched bridge, which was framed by graceful willows as old and stately as the Manor itself. Ol' Tommy pranced over the bridge, proudly bringing his passengers into view. An Irish Uilleann piper played while the guests looked on in anticipation. The sweet sound of the instrument, softer than Scottish bagpipes, was perfect for the festive occasion.

As the ceremony began, Laura met Liam's eyes.

"Thank you for my crown," she whispered. Laura flashed him *that smile,* and while it made him feel good, he still blushed.

"You look beautiful, Laura."

"Well, you look quite handsome, Monkey Boy." With confident smiles they walked down the aisle hand-in-hand to wait for the bride and groom.

Chloe and Patrick made a perfect couple. All could see their deep love for each other, and tears of joy were shared by many.

When they were pronounced Mr. and Mrs. O'Brogan by Father O'Malley, Patrick joyfully kissed his bride. Everyone applauded and cheered as the couple eagerly made their way to the carriage. Philip and Ol' Tommy whisked them off for a ride around the estate. Laura watched wistfully, dreaming of the day she would be a bride.

"I want to have Ol' Tommy pull my wedding carriage," she sighed.

"Well, it's a nice thought," Liam said gently, "but I doubt he will be around 'til then." Laura's face saddened at the thought of losing a friend like Ol' Tommy.

The reception in the Manor was in grand style, with a lavish buffet. The top layer of the wedding cake was soaked in Irish whiskey, to be saved in a tin for the christening of the first born. The cream cake layers had lucky charms contained within, each attached to a ribbon. The silver trinkets were in the shapes of hearts, clover leafs, horseshoes and crosses. Only one was a gold key—to open the doors of success and happiness. The wedding party was to pull one charm from the cake before the cutting. Laura pulled a heart from the cake and Liam pulled the golden key.

Everyone raised their glasses to the bride and groom with the traditional Bunratty Mead. The sweet golden nectar was very popular and one small glassful could bring anyone to a mood of celebration. Philip gave a heartfelt toast to the newlyweds, followed by Lord Meegan thanking everyone for coming. He gave the blessing:

Be the eye of God dwelling with you,
The foot of Christ in guidance with you,
The shower of the spirit pouring on you,
Richly and generously.

After the feast of rich food and drink, Laura boldly asked the bandleader if she could make an announcement. He smiled and handed her the microphone.

"Excuse me." She jumped a little as the sound of her own voice surprised her, and then giggled. "Sorry! Anyway, Liam and I have a wedding present for Chloe and Patrick." She turned to the newlyweds. "We wrote a song we want to sing for you."

Hannah gave Aidan a questioning look and he simply shrugged his shoulders. No one had ever heard the children sing together.

Liam walked on the stage carrying the guitars, and handed one to Laura. He looked nervously at Laura as he began playing the melody. She joined in, strumming the chords. When the two began singing, their harmony so perfect and their tone so pure, a hush came over the crowd. Aidan's face lit up with pride, as did Noreen's and Philip's. Liam's voice was surprisingly strong, and Laura's was clear and sweet. Their hours of practice in the cave had brought them to this moment.

Noreen was in disbelief that her shy Liam could stand up in front of everyone and sing his heart out. Even Laura was surprised at how well he did. The children left the stage with everyone applauding, including the band members.

Chloe and Patrick tearfully hugged them. "You two were brilliant! Thank you so much! What a special weddin' gift!"

Philip beamed. "Son, I had no idea how well you can sing and play! And Laura—you're so good together!"

"Thank you, Mr. Delaney," Laura replied modestly. She knew it was Liam who really stole the show.

Compliments came from many others throughout the afternoon. Father O'Malley was one of the admirers.

"Son, I haven't seen you in church. Are you Catholic?"

"Yes, Sir. I…"

The priest put his hand on the boy's shoulder. "It's all right, Son. I was wondering if you'd be interested in singing in our choir on Sundays." Liam looked to Laura, who nodded her approval.

"I'd like that, Sir. I will ask my parents." Liam went right away to find his father.

"Son, if you want to start goin' to church it's up to you. You know what I believe. Now you need to find out what you believe."

Liam looked concerned. "What about Mother? You know how she is about the Catholic Church."

"I will have a talk with her, but she and I—well, we don't see religion the same way. With her bein' Protestant and all, if we hadn't fallen so hard for each other when we met we might not have ever married." He paused. "Just remember, Son, you were baptized Catholic—just like me—but you have the freedom to choose your own belief. I've never felt you had to report to a church to talk to God, but you decide for yourself. And don't worry about your mother."

Mr. O'Sullivan, the music teacher, was the next one to compliment Laura and Liam. "You both put on a fine performance for Patrick and Chloe. Liam, you've never demonstrated your vocal ability to me before. Have you had voice lessons?"

"No, Sir."

The teacher studied the boy for a moment. "I have never heard an untrained voice sound like that. You've quite a vocal range for a young man. It is a rare gift you have."

"Thank you, Sir," Liam replied modestly.

"I look forward to seeing you both at tomorrow's lesson. Perhaps we'll try something new."

Laura and Liam were complimented by many more people that day, and the celebration went on well into the evening.

The following day Mr. O'Sullivan's scheduled lesson included a vocal exercise for Liam. Again, the instructor was quite impressed.

"I do believe that with the proper guidance, you have great promise as a vocalist."

Liam smiled, but still seemed somewhat self-conscious. Laura could hardly contain her excitement until the teacher left.

"Liam, did you hear that? You can be a star!" Liam shook his head.

"It makes me feel good to sing, but I'll never be a star."

100

"Liam Delaney! You can be anything you want! Everyone needs someone to believe in them, and I'm *the someone* who believes in you."

She had seen a profound transformation come over Liam during their performance at the wedding. Somehow he was a different person when he had a microphone. He could stand up tall and sing in a powerful voice with all the confidence in the world, but when Liam stepped off the stage he reverted to the shy boy who wanted to go unnoticed. Laura somehow knew that singing gave him the power to be free.

⊙⁄ᵒ Chapter Fourteen ᵒ⁄⊙

Winter 1977

The newlyweds didn't have to be concerned about finding a home. Chloe simply moved into to Patrick's cottage. She still had her housekeeping duties in the Manor, but her younger sister, Molly, moved into the room next to Laura's, taking on Chloe's duties as night nanny. Molly, young and full of life, was small, with beautiful brown eyes and red hair—at least *this* month. After all, she was a hairdresser.

During the day, Molly's talents were appreciated by the patrons of the village hair salon, but in the evening her favorite subject was Laura. Reassuring the girl her beautiful blonde tresses would soon be long again, Molly played with Laura's hair, showing her how much fun it was to be feminine. Laura, now age twelve, was beginning to see herself as the pretty young lady she was becoming.

Christmas had come and gone without any trauma, although Laura did not experience much enjoyment. Hannah and her daughters were tolerable at best. They stayed at the Manor for four long days. In spite of Laura's efforts to be quiet and polite, Emily still managed to point out every little thing she did wrong. Peggy, plagued by allergies, almost succeeded in getting the cats evicted.

One of Laura's least favorite moments was when Kite followed Liam into the Manor, much to Hannah's horror.

"Get that mangy critter out of the kitchen!"

Relief came to Laura—and the staff—the day her father announced he was taking Hannah and her daughters back to Dublin. Aidan and Hannah stayed at Dublin House, Lord Meegan's large mansion in Merrion Square, not far from his office. Although his busy life in Dublin resulted in Laura not seeing her father very often, it was a price she would willingly pay for peace at the Manor.

The instant they were gone, Laura was off to the barn to meet Liam and go riding. The moment she saw him, her outlook on things brightened considerably.

Liam was quite tall for a thirteen-year-old, and his good looks made him appear even older. His voice was changing, and became even deeper and stronger when he sang. Every time he picked up his guitar, Laura became excited with anticipation. She was, naturally, his biggest fan.

Philip was proud of his son and gave him regular encouragement whenever he heard Liam playing the guitar. In contrast, Noreen would leave the room. Philip saw this as a demonstration of her disapproval of Liam's singing in the Catholic Church choir. After realizing she had lost that argument, Noreen became withdrawn and distant to everyone except the members of her own church.

One day in the cave Laura noticed Liam was unusually quiet.

"Liam, is something bothering you?"

"I'm worried about my mother and her church group," Liam sighed. "She's spending more and more time with them and she never sings anymore."

"I know," Laura said. "She leaves the room now when I play the piano. She used to enjoy listening. Maybe you should talk to your father about it."

"You're right. I'll talk to him tomorrow morning."

"I'll spend some time with Lilly first so you can talk in private."

He smiled at Laura. *She always knows how I'm feeling and just what to say.*

The next morning, Liam spoke to his father after they turned the horses out.

"Father, have you noticed a change in Mother?" Philip did not answer right away, so Liam continued. "I'm worried about this new church group. She spends so much time with them, and we hardly ever see her. She never sings anymore."

Philip looked grim. "I know, Son, I don't like it either. I don't even know if this new group has a house of worship. It's not the Protestant church she used to go to. The word around town is that they're into some kind of faith healin'. I've tried to ask her about it, but she just clams up." Philip's jaw tightened and his eyes narrowed. "Then out of the blue, last Sunday, she brings the Deacon MacDara to the barn to meet me."

"What did you think of him, Father?"

103

"Don't tell your mother, but I took an instant dislikin' to him. There's somethin' about him not to be trusted."

"Mother wants me to stop singing and playing guitar."

Philip looked squarely at his son. "Liam, never give up your music." He softened, smiling. "I used to sing in a few pubs in my day, but I never had the talent you do. You truly have the gift of song."

"Why did you give it up?"

Philip rubbed his chin. "Well...I enjoyed playin' music with the boys, but we were mostly paid in pints. You can't support a family on the Guinness, or even work the next day. It's very tough to make a livin' in the entertainment business. You need a good education, too."

"Yes, I intend to go to college."

A few days later Laura stopped playing the piano to run after her nanny.

"Mrs. Delaney, why do you leave the room when I play the piano or sing?"

"The Deacon says music is entertainment and entertainment is evil." With that, she abruptly turned and walked away, leaving Laura stunned.

Why is it evil? What kind of church doesn't believe in music?

The next day, Philip and Patrick were loading some horses to go to Feyland Stud. "Can Laura and I go with you?" Liam asked. "I would like to see how First Light is doing with his training."

"Sure, Son. You did all the ground work with him. I'll tell your mother later you'll be goin' with us." He wondered if Noreen would even notice the children were gone.

Ian welcomed them warmly at the main barn of Feyland Stud.

"Ian, how is First Light doing?" Liam asked.

"He has the conformation, the size, and the desire. If we can get him to settle and run, he could be a real stakes winner. But he's a handful and he's very strong-willed."

When they walked into the stud barn, Liam could see the tall colt looking over the top of the door, his ears pinned back and a glare in his eyes.

"Can I go to him by myself?" Liam asked. "I think he might remember me."

"It's up to your father." Everyone looked at Philip.

"Be careful, Son. You know these young studs can be dangerous."

Liam nodded and approached the colt while softly humming a melody. The colt flicked one ear forward. "Remember me, boy? I used to scratch your withers."

Liam slowly opened the door and put his hand out, which the cautious colt sniffed without objection. First Light then turned his head to the side, inviting the young horseman to greet him. Liam moved closer, stroking the colt's neck, working his hand down to the withers. The look in the colt's eye softened the moment Liam's fingers began to massage the sweet spot. His ears moved forward, a sign that he was calm.

"Goood boooy," Liam said, satisfied.

As the others approached slowly, all eyes were on Liam.

"Amazin'," Ian said quietly. "Is that the same temperamental stud?"

"He has a way with all animals," Patrick said.

Ian looked at Philip. "Any chance of us keepin' Liam to help us start this guy?"

Philip shook his head. "I'm afraid not, with his school work and all. He'll be goin' to college, you know." Ian raised his eyebrows and nodded his head in approval.

Liam now had the colt in a kind of trance. "If you give him a chance to come to you and work with him on his terms, he'll be fine. As a foal, he was the only one we couldn't catch out in the pasture. But I took my time. I sat down in the grass and hummed like I had no interest in him. He couldn't stand it and would come right up to me. Let it be his idea."

Ian was impressed with Liam's technique. "Our jockey, Shane, might be just right for this colt. Would you explain to him how it works, like you told us?"

105

The boy beamed. "Sure, I will!"

After Liam met the jockey, they spent an hour together working with First Light.

"I think he likes you, Shane. But please call me anytime if you have a problem with him." Shane thanked him with a firm handshake.

"Liam, if I had my way," Ian said, "you'd be here workin' with him every day."

Liam smiled proudly. "I think he'll run for you. Just remember, he likes to have his withers scratched before you do anything. It's like warming up his engine."

Shane laughed. "I think I know just what you're talkin' about."

Ian wished them a safe journey back to Montrose and soon they were headed down the road. Liam's sense of accomplishment deepened when he caught Laura smiling at him.

She summed up the day cheerfully. "You really do have the magic touch!"

ᠭᡔᡃ *Chapter Fifteen* ᡔᠬ᠗

Summer 1978

The warm summer night was heavy with humidity, with the feeling of an approaching storm in the air. Liam opened his bedroom window, but the breeze carried an electric charge with it into the room and made it hard to fall asleep. The boom of thunder off in the distance only added to his restlessness, and as the storm moved closer, Liam buried his head beneath the pillow to muffle the sound. He finally drifted off to sleep.

Liam was jolted awake by a terrible crackling noise, followed by the screams of horses. He stumbled to the bedroom window and stood in disbelief. "My God!" The hay storage barn had been struck by lightning, and flames were already shooting through the roof.

Liam ran into the hallway. "Father! The barn!" he shouted.

"I see it, Son! Get dressed!" Liam threw on his clothes and followed his father out of the cottage. As they raced out the door, Noreen called the fire brigade.

Patrick was already at the barn, using a hose to direct water at the flames—to no avail.

"Ol' Tommy's in there!" Patrick cried. "He's the only one!"

"I'll get him!" Philip shouted. "Liam! Get the other hose and water down the horse barn so the fire doesn't spread from here!" Liam wasted no time in following his father's instructions.

"Philip! Be careful!" Patrick was spraying as far as possible with the hose, but still the flames grew.

Philip grabbed several lap blankets from a carriage and plunged them into a water trough, dousing himself thoroughly as well. He raced into the burning barn, where the intensity of the heat nearly knocked him over. Throwing the wet blankets over his head, he pushed forward. Smoke was now so thick he could only make his way by following the sound of Ol' Tommy's panicked cries.

When he finally got to the horse's box, Philip grabbed the head collar and lead rope. The latch burned his fingers as he fumbled to open the door. Ol' Tommy thrust his muzzle into the head collar and nickered to his friend. Philip threw one of the wet blankets over the frightened horse's head, and they made their way blindly back through the barn, following Patrick's frantic calls to them from the other end.

Halfway through, Philip and the horse froze at the terrifying sound of a loud crack from above. Ol' Tommy snorted loudly and planted all four feet in place. In an instant, the flaming timbers collapsed on man and horse. Philip's last act was to pull Ol' Tommy's head into the shelter of his arms.

Outside, Patrick's heart sank as he saw the roof cave in. He stood helplessly in shock, crying Philip's name in vain.

"Father!" Liam cried. He rushed towards the inferno, but he was grabbed by two of the firemen who had just arrived.

"Lad! You can't go in there!"

Liam fought to break free. "My father is in there! I have to get him!"

Patrick ran over and fiercely embraced the struggling boy. "Liam! Listen to me! You can't help him—he's in God's hands now."

Liam fell to his knees and sobbed uncontrollably. Patrick, stricken with shock, stood motionless, his hand on Liam's shoulder.

"Your mother..." Patrick murmured.

Liam slowly raised his head, and through his tears saw her standing halfway between the cottage and the pyre that had once been a barn. Noreen's expressionless face revealed nothing.

Laura ran from the Manor as fast as she could, panicked by the sight of embers shooting through the night sky—and the fear of what she might find. Before her, against a backdrop of flames and flashing emergency lights, was the silhouette of Liam on his knees.

"No, Father, no! You can't leave me!" His heart-wrenching cries stabbed Laura to her very soul. It was more terrifying than she had imagined. She sank down next to Liam, wrapping her arms around his waist. He buried his face in her hair.

The fire had been confined to the hay barn and was extinguished within an hour. When it was all over, there was nothing left but smoking rubble.

While Chloe drove Noreen and the anguished children back to the Manor, Patrick stayed behind until the last of the fire crew and Garda left. The still of the night was broken by the slam of the coroner's rear door. In a gesture of final farewell, Patrick placed his hand on the van and lowered his head in silent prayer.

At the Manor, the staff was awake, gathered in the kitchen. Mrs. Callahan, overcome with emotion, swept Laura into her arms. Noreen pushed past her son as if he did not exist, seating herself across the room in silence. She stared blankly into the distance, blind to the hurt in her son's eyes. Shocked, Molly pulled the heartbroken boy into her warm embrace.

When Patrick finally arrived at the Manor, he was exhausted, defeated, and covered in soot. Chloe ran to her husband and hugged him tightly. Together, they wept.

The night dragged on, everyone silenced by grief. Patrick finally stood up.

"I'd better check on the horses. It's nearly daybreak and time for their breakfast."

Liam jumped up. "I'm going with you."

"Me too," Laura announced, grabbing Liam's arm.

Chloe looked at Noreen, who had been lost in her own world all night. Deciding to take matters into her own hands, Chloe said, "Children, you should stay here."

"Sky and Rose need us," Liam protested. "And Kite's still in the cottage."

Patrick was outraged by Noreen's withdrawal. He looked scornfully at the woman, wanting to shake her back to reality. Seeing no point in keeping Laura and Liam in the house, he gave a nod of approval. They needed no more than that to head for the door.

Outside, the pungent smell of smoke hung in the air. Laura and Liam went right to work helping Patrick, with Kite tagging along. When they were finished, Liam looked solemnly at Laura, and then at Patrick.

"Can Laura and I stay here with our horses for a while?"

Patrick knew Liam needed time, and Laura would be more comfort to the boy than anyone. He put his hand on Liam's shoulder. "I'll leave you, then, but promise me you two'll stay away from that smokin' rubble." *I'll take care of Ol' Tommy later,* he thought.

Liam agreed, and Patrick gave him a hug before he walked to the truck.

Laura went to Rose again, making sure she had calmed down. She put her arm up over the mare's withers and leaned against her warm body. The gentle rhythm of Rose's breathing and chewing was soothing to the exhausted girl. The sweet smell of hay replaced the acrid odor of the night's terror. Laura slipped easily into the refuge of sleep, sinking into the straw below the mare. The gentle caress of Rose's soft nose and the warmth of her breath was a much-needed comfort. A beam of morning sunlight blanketed Laura's weary body, and she drifted into a dreamless slumber.

As if from some great distance, Laura heard Sky's nicker, and she was brought out of the veil of sleep by Rose's insistent nudge. She opened her eyes to discover the belly of the gentle mare above her head. Although Rose had long since finished her breakfast, she had remained immobile while Laura slept.

Laura sleepily rubbed her eyes. "Rose, how long did you let me sleep? We have to check on Liam and Sky."

Giving her mare a hug, Laura quietly slipped out. She peeked through Sky's partially open door to see Liam crumpled in the corner on a pile of straw, sobbing. Sky gently nuzzled him while Kite lay in the crook of his arm. Slowly slipping in through the door, Laura went to the gelding's side. Sky picked up his head and greeted her with his warm breath against her face. She gently stroked his neck.

"Sky, we're going to make it better." She lay down beside Liam in the straw, wrapping her arms around the boy and his faithful dog.

In spite of the tragedy that had befallen Montrose, all was now calm.

When the morning barn crew arrived, they began to deluge Patrick with questions about the fire. Laura knew it would be too painful for Liam to even hear questions about the disaster. She went to Patrick.

"I need to take Liam on a ride."

"I don't blame you, girl. I've got a basket of food Chloe sent down. Take it with you." Laura thanked him and threw the contents into a knapsack. She got the rope collars and handed one to Liam.

"Let's get out of here," she said gently.

After several minutes, they broke into a gallop, as always, but Liam showed none of the usual signs of enjoyment. To Laura, he looked like he was a million miles away.

When they got to the cave, Liam put Sky into the corral, going through the motions as if in a trance. Laura took his hand. She had never imagined Liam as being vulnerable—he had always been the strong one for her.

In the cave, Liam sat in silence for hours while Laura held him, gently stroking his hair. She was reluctant to say anything for fear of making him relive the tragedy. Finally, she was overcome with exhaustion, and fell asleep against his shoulder. Hours passed before Liam gently nudged Laura awake.

"Laura, it's getting late. I want to stay here by myself tonight. Would you go back to the Manor and let everyone know I'm all right?"

Laura shook her head. "I can't leave you all alone."

"Please…I'm asking you to do this for me. I need you to do this for me."

She looked at him with deep sadness in her eyes. "Yes, Liam, I'll tell them—but I'm coming back."

Laura took off, and as she expected, Sky followed her and Rose all the way to the barn. After putting them away, she ran to the Manor.

Chloe met her at the door. "Laura! We've been worried about you."

"Sorry we didn't come back earlier. We fell asleep."

"Where's Liam?"

"He needs some time alone. He asked about his mother. How is Mrs. Delaney?"

Chloe shook her head and turned away. "She's gone off to her…church. The Deacon came and picked her up. I've called your father—he'll be here in the mornin'."

"Can I stay with Liam tonight?" Laura asked. "He needs me."

111

Chloe turned to meet Laura's pleading eyes. "Well, I guess…you two have stayed in the loft before watchin' the mares foal."

Laura bit her lip to stop from confessing the truth about where they were staying. Chloe went to the kitchen to pack them a dinner. "Now, you're sure you'll be warm enough?"

Laura nodded. "We've got our sleeping bags."

"All right, then. But please, check in with us first thing in the mornin'."

"I promise. Thank you."

As Laura left the kitchen with the basket of food, a wave of guilt came over her for having lied. At the barn, she gathered a few more things, including a flashlight and another sleeping bag. She pulled Sky and Rose out and then looked at the full knapsack and bulky bedroll. "Rose, this won't be easy. You're going to have to help me."

She led her mare alongside a tack trunk in the barn aisle, using it to climb up with the heavy load. Rose remained motionless. Laura patted her on the neck.

"Thank you. You're the greatest. You, too, Sky! Now, let's go see Liam."

By then it was almost dark, and Laura knew riding Rose at anything faster than a walk would not be safe, especially with her cumbersome load. Once inside the forest, the only illumination came from moonlight darting out from behind the clouds. The trees cast an eerie maze of shadows. Laura began to tense up, and the sudden hoot of an owl caused Rose to balk. Sky snorted loudly, and leaves rustled above as the giant owl took off. Laura nearly fell off as it passed over their heads. She forced herself to go on, knowing Liam needed her. The clouds finally parted as she arrived at the cave.

Laura was able to safely dismount in the moonlight. After she settled the horses, she found her way into the main room of the cave, but there was no sign of Liam.

"Liam! Where are you?" She frantically dug for the flashlight, but its illumination did not reveal his whereabouts. Laura ran through the far tunnel, making her way out to the open field below.

There in the moonlight stood a broken boy, staring up at the sky, his shoulders shaking. As Laura got closer, she could see Liam's tears. The moment he saw her, Liam opened his arms and she ran to him. No words were spoken, and none were needed. Time stood still as love passed through their hearts.

Rain began to fall softly. Laura held Liam tightly and could feel that he was still trembling. Gently taking his hand, she led him back into the cave.

Liam collapsed on the bed of straw, and Laura pulled the sleeping bag over them. Holding him close and shielding him from the world outside, she provided the warmth he so desperately needed. They drifted off to sleep.

Sunlight was streaming through the cave when they awoke.

"Liam! We need to go back to the Manor! I promised Chloe."

Liam shook his head. "I'm not ready to face the world alone."

"You'll never be alone. I'll always be right by your side."

"Sweet Laura, you have no idea what could happen now that my father is gone. Mother and I will probably have to move again, and I won't have money for college." He lowered his head. "The only thing I'm really afraid of is never seeing you again." He started to cry, and Laura put a comforting arm around him.

"Liam, my father will not make you leave. He'll be home this morning—he'll make things better. He promised to pay for your college, and Father's a man of his word. Now let's go to the Manor."

With no strength to oppose her, Liam climbed on his horse and they rode to the barn.

Chloe stood at the window of the Manor, anxiously watching for the children. Patrick had told her earlier they must have slept in their fort in the woods.

"They'll be runnin' up the path any moment," Molly reassured.

"Laura should have told me where they were goin'."

"Remember, they're just children," Molly said. "And she's only tryin' to comfort the poor boy."

"Oh, I know you're right. And it's a mountain more than his mother's doin'. If I could get my hands on that woman! Oh, I'm sorry, Lord! That's not a good Christian thought."

When Laura and Liam arrived, Chloe greeted them with a hug. One look into Liam's eyes was enough—she couldn't bear to scold them. She and Molly helped them get cleaned up as Cook made breakfast. Not knowing what to say to poor Liam, the three ladies sat in silence at the kitchen table as the children ate. Their hearts shared his pain, but all they could offer was the small comfort of their presence. The deafening silence was broken when someone came in the front door. Laura jumped up and ran to the entryway.

"Oh, Father, please help! Liam needs us."

"My darling, I'm here now, and I'll take care of everything." She led him by the hand into the kitchen and right to the table. Liam instinctively stood up, trying to put on his best face for the Lord of the Manor. Grief suddenly consumed Aidan, and he embraced the devastated boy. No emotions were spared at that moment. Finally Aidan spoke in a weak voice.

"Son, I'm so sorry about your father." Aidan stepped back and looked deeply into Liam's eyes. "Now, I want you to trust me. You and your mother will always have a home here. And I promised your father you would have the best education. I'm keeping that promise."

"Thank you, Sir," Liam replied as he began to weep again.

Aidan cleared his throat. "I'll never forget all your father has done for me. He was a great man, and everyone will miss him." Laura hugged her father, and then Liam.

"Chloe, I would like to speak to Noreen about the arrangements."

"Where *is* my mother?" Liam asked.

"I think she's still with her church group," Chloe said cautiously.

Liam stood up straight, facing Aidan. "Sir, it would be best to check with me on the arrangements." His tone was surprisingly decisive and Aidan raised his eyebrows.

"Of course, Son. If it's all right with you, I would like to have your father buried here on the estate, in our family plot."

"Thank you, Sir, it would be an honor. Could we get Father O'Malley to do the service? My father and I are Catholic. My mother is…well, I really don't know…"

"I'll call Father O'Malley," Aidan reassured. "I'll make the arrangements and take care of everything."

Liam spent most of the next few days at the cave, playing his guitar and writing a new song. Laura would join him whenever he asked her to, but she gave him the space he needed to begin healing.

In the early morning on the day of the funeral, the mortuary delivered the coffin and set everything up in the grand entrance of the Manor. The casket was covered with and surrounded by an array of beautiful flowers. Guests would be able to come into the Manor before the services for a private moment, to leave a flower, say a prayer, or otherwise mourn as they wished.

There was a nicely framed photograph of Philip on display that Chloe had selected from her wedding album. Strikingly handsome in a tuxedo, the coachman was proudly driving the carriage as it was pulled by Ol' Tommy in all his glory.

Patrick had made arrangements for Michael O'Leary to come early, his lorry loaded with a black Shire horse and funeral coach for transporting the coffin to the plot.

Philip Delaney was a man well-regarded by many, and soon people began arriving from several counties to pay their respects. Everyone assembled outside the Manor, and a Uilleann piper began to play softy while the pallbearers carried the coffin to the coach. Lord Meegan stood at the top of the stairs and looked out over the mourners.

"Philip Delaney loved this estate, and put his heart and soul into making it a fine home for us all. Let us now give him one last tour of the grounds before he goes to his final resting place."

Patrick climbed up front with O'Leary, and Liam rode in the back with Kite at his side. The piper continued to play as the coach slowly rolled off towards the bridge.

Laura took her father's hand, and everyone followed the piper in procession to the family cemetery while the funeral coach encircled the estate.

When it returned, Father O'Malley began the service with prayer, and then asked Patrick to say the eulogy.

"Philip Delaney was more than just a good trainer of horses and a good friend. He was a guidin' light for so many—includin' me. He knew I didn't have a lot of experience but he gave me the opportunity to work by his side at this wonderful place. For that I will forever be in his debt. Philip was a man with a big heart and he had a passion for everythin' in his life...his family...his horses...his love of country..." He paused to wipe his eyes.

"The finest mark he left on this land is standin' before me—his young son, Liam. Philip had a grand vision for his son's future which I hope to be a part of. I know he's lookin' down on Liam now with great pride in his heart."

Liam picked up his guitar and looked towards the Heavens.

"I wrote this song for you, Father. I call it *Now I Set You Free.*"

Father, you gave your life to save an old friend.

And now your time here has reached an end.

On that tragic night, no one was to blame.

I only ask, please fire me your eternal flame.

So someday, you, I hope to be,

With all my love, I now set you free.

There were no tears spared anywhere. Even Noreen, who had remained in her state of withdrawal, was finally weeping.

Aidan dried his eyes. "Thank you Liam. Patrick was right—at this moment, your father has the greatest pride in you. We all do.

"There are no words to describe how much I will miss this fine man, Philip Delaney. The care and guidance he has given my daughter while I've been away is immeasurable. I intend to repay this debt of kindness by seeing his plans through for his son's future." Aidan looked at Liam.

"Liam, your future may not yet be written, but on this day of remembrance, you have shown yourself to be the kind of man your father had in his vision."

Father O'Malley delivered a closing prayer, and the Uilleann piper began to play again. Everyone returned to the Manor for an old-fashioned Irish wake—a celebration of life. Hannah saw to it there was plenty of food and drink, including ale and whiskey. The piper was joined by a drummer and a fiddler, and the music came alive. Most everyone began to dance, but Liam sat in a corner trying not to be noticed. Laura brought him a plate.

"You need to eat something."

116

"I need for this day to be over," he sighed. "I don't want people to pity me."

"Liam, they're not here to pity you. Everyone here loved your father. They're here to pay their respects and to support you and your mother."

"I'm sorry, Laura. I just want to be alone somewhere—with you."

"I know. It'll be over soon."

Laura spotted the picture of Philip and Ol' Tommy and asked Chloe if she could have a copy. She didn't know how or when, but someday Liam would want it.

Several hours later the long day finally came to an end. Everyone was physically and emotionally spent, and the day of remembrance was complete.

The next morning, before leaving for Dublin, Aidan called Noreen into his study.

"Noreen, first I want you to know that you and Liam will always have a home at the Manor. But Liam has expressed worry over some things. Can you shed some light on this?" Noreen fidgeted in her chair before speaking.

"Lord Meegan, it has been very difficult for me since my husband passed on. Every time I look at Liam, he reminds me of Philip. I'm sure you can understand how I have to put some distance between us until the pain is easier to take." Noreen's words rang true in Aidan's heart, and he felt genuine compassion for her.

"Yes, Noreen, I do understand completely. Time will make things easier for both of you." Aidan opened his desk and handed Noreen a check. "I want to give you this as assurance that you have nothing to worry about and Liam's future is secure. It should be more than enough to send him to Trinity College with board for four years. Also, I will continue to pay Philip's wages—to you." Noreen's eyes widened as she looked at the check, and she jumped to her feet.

"Bless you, Lord Meegan! You are a good man." She left the room abruptly. Aidan had an unsettling feeling he couldn't quite put his finger on.

There was, in fact, more to Noreen's withdrawal than the world knew. She carried a dark secret. Months earlier, she had been diagnosed with a tumor. The recommended treatment would have broken the family financially. In desperation, Noreen turned to Deacon MacDara, a faith healer from the village who promised a complete cure. She put her life in his hands, concealing the illness from her own family.

Her Protestant minister warned her, "The pretense of healing and salvation is but a cloak of deception enshrouding this Deacon. He preys on the sick and the weak for his following." Noreen chose to ignore the minister's advice, placing her trust entirely in MacDara.

It didn't take long for the rumors to reach the faith healer that Noreen had come into money. He began working on a plan, knowing she would be an easy mark in her weakened physical and emotional condition. In his mind, the only obstacle would be Noreen's son, Liam. The Deacon would have to either convert him as well, or see to it that he was out of the picture entirely.

There was a big change in Liam's life after his father's death. The feeling of emptiness was a hole in his heart. Every day, he missed his father's words of wisdom and encouragement—and, of course, his love.

Liam soon learned he could not depend on his mother, who further distanced herself from him. Her devotion to the new church—and its powerful Deacon—hurt Liam deeply.

The truth was, it was easier on Liam with his mother gone. When she was around she would preach to him about his evil music and sinful ways. She never spoke of his father anymore, and was always quick to praise the Deacon.

One evening, Liam noticed the photograph of his father was no longer on the mantle. He asked his mother about it.

"He's gone," she replied blankly, turning away.

Liam saw this as a clear sign she no longer wanted anything more to do with him or his father's memory.

Chloe and Patrick saw the changes in Noreen and took it upon themselves to care for the boy and make him feel like he still had a family. And, of course, Laura was a constant beacon of love and support for Liam.

One morning, Liam stood mesmerized as he watched Laura, sunlight glistening magically through her hair. *Laura is the truest part of me.*

⊖ Chapter Sixteen ᏆᎦ

Spring 1978

"**W**ill you be coming to the Manor for Christmas?" Laura asked her father anxiously on the phone.

"No, my dear, but I have an even better idea. I would like you to come here to Dublin."

"Oh, no! I couldn't leave Liam. This is his first Christmas without his father. And Mrs. Delaney...I don't think she wants to celebrate."

"Well, let's invite Liam to join us in Dublin. The two of you could ride the train together, and I'll show you all around the city. I'll bet Liam would like to see Trinity College."

"Thank you, Father. I'll ask him today." Laura knew her father was sincere about helping Liam, but also guessed the offer was a bribe to get her involved with Hannah and the girls. Laura thought it would be worth it if Liam could come, so she promised to work on the idea. She hung up the phone and ran to find Liam in the barn.

"That sounds like a fine idea to me," Liam said. "My mother is so against any kind of celebration now that we're probably not going to have Christmas."

When his mother returned that afternoon from another church meeting, Liam told her of Lord Meegan's invitation.

"If this is what Lord Meegan wants, then so be it," she replied flatly. Liam was sure she wouldn't even miss him. He shrugged his shoulders and returned to the barn.

Patrick's response was enthusiastic. "That sounds like it'll be a grand trip! And don't you worry about Kite or your horses. I'll take care of everythin'."

Liam's excitement about the upcoming trip grew over the next few days. This would be an entirely different kind of journey for him. Until now, Liam had always associated traveling with the upheaval of moving. The experience was always the same: rolling down a long road with all the family's worldly possessions in the old pickup truck. The trips had always provided plenty of time for Liam to dwell on the fear of being the new kid in school again.

The day finally arrived. Chloe waved goodbye from the platform at the village train station as Laura and Liam took their seats by a window. Not only was this Liam's first train trip, but they were traveling first class. He felt privileged, and did his best to act mature, especially as more passengers boarded at the Limerick station. But his childlike thrill was revealed by the look of wonder on his face as he gazed up at the tall buildings.

"This is a big city!"

Laura giggled. "Wait 'til you see Dublin."

The train wandered through the countryside, traveling up through the small towns and villages of Thurles, Bally Brophy, and Monasterevin. Aidan met them at the Pearse train station in Dublin, greeting them both with open arms.

"I'm so happy to see you. We're going to have a wonderful time." He looked into his daughter's eyes. "Will you please try to accept Hannah and the girls for me, so we can be a family?"

Laura sighed. "I will try, Father."

"Thank you, dear."

Earlier that week, Aidan had spoken to Hannah about the children's upcoming visit. "Hannah, I know you will put an extra effort into making Laura and Liam feel at home with us for Christmas. You know the boy lost his father recently, and Laura's been trying to help him. Now, I know my daughter can be stubborn, but remember—she is just a child. She needs time to get to know what a warm person you can be." Aidan searched his wife's eyes for a sign of compassion.

"Aidan, my dear, women of true class always do their best to make guests feel comfortable in their homes—regardless of their upbringing." She punctuated her statement with a glowing smile. The truth was, Hannah was not happy Aidan had invited a stable boy to stay with them.

As it turned out, Hannah was pleasantly surprised at Liam's courteous behavior and eloquent vocabulary. His English was exceptional, and he made it a point to speak without his parents' Irish brogue. Hannah, who had never really paid attention to Liam, became aware of his love of books and poetry. To her, this was a new dimension for a working-class boy, having always seen stable hands as uneducated and crude at best.

Emily and Peggy attended a prestigious boarding school in London and were only home for the holidays. They instantly took notice of Liam's good looks. Now almost fourteen, he had grown very tall and seemed older than his years. Emily, the eldest of the two girls, flirted with him at every opportunity. Annoyed by Liam's obvious bond with Aidan's daughter, Emily was quick to point out everything Laura did wrong, openly laughing and sneering at her, with her sister Peggy egging her on.

Their abusive behavior did not have the intended effect on Liam. In fact, he was irritated with their rudeness. Knowing Laura was on her best behavior, he gave her constant encouragement, helping her to avoid conflicts.

Once Laura and Liam started touring Dublin with Aidan, they soon forgot about the family tensions. Trinity College impressed Liam so much as they toured that at times he was speechless. After viewing *The Book of Kells* in the Trinity Library and Museum, Liam found his voice again.

"This must be the largest library in the world! I could spend weeks here."

Aidan seemed pleased. Liam's appreciation for the culture and history of Ireland was endless. Laura, too, responded to the boy's enthusiasm.

On Christmas morning, Hannah surprised Laura with a beautiful, silk-covered photo album. The first photos were of Laura as a young girl with her father and mother. Inside the front cover, Hannah had written: *To my beautiful Stepdaughter.*

Moved by Hannah's thoughtfulness, Laura looked up at her father's new wife, now seeing her in a different light. "Thank you."

In another surprising gesture, Hannah presented Liam with a gift-wrapped package. The boy was momentarily struck speechless, almost forgetting his manners.

"Thank you, Mrs. Meegan," he remembered to say.

"You may call me Hannah," she said, smiling. "Now, please—open it."

Carefully unwrapping the gift, Liam was thrilled to discover a rare, first-edition, leather-bound book of poems by Robert Louis Stevenson.

"Oh, my God!" Liam exclaimed. "I mean—thank you. This is wonderful. Laura, look! It's called *Songs of Travel.*" He turned back to Hannah. "Thank you so much—he's my favorite poet and author! I've read *Treasure Island,* and also *Child's Garden of Verses.* But I've never had a leather-bound book of my own. Thank you very much."

"He's one of my favorite English authors," Hannah said.

"Actually," Liam said as politely as possible, "he's a Scotsman."

Hannah nodded. "I stand corrected. Thank you for your literary knowledge."

Laura beamed with pride. *He's so smart!*

Aidan was amused, but more than that, he was overwhelmed with Hannah's thoughtfulness. He gave her a warm hug and a kiss. Hannah was surprised by her own reaction, a feeling of joy that was rooted in family—something she rarely experienced with her daughters.

Emily sat back and observed Liam with great interest.

The last two presents were large matching boxes for Laura and Liam from Aidan. He urged them to open the packages together. Upon discovering the contents, Liam was again without words, but Laura shouted loudly enough for the both of them. "Electric guitars and amplifiers! Just like real musicians have!"

They were Gibson hollow body guitars, known for their warm resonance. The Fender amps each had one input for a guitar and one for a microphone. The expensive equipment was made in America and sought after by musicians worldwide.

"My only request," Aidan said with a smile, "is that you wait until you are at the Manor to play your guitars. For you talented musicians, I'm having the large room in the tower sound-proofed and made into a studio. I'm having a stage built, complete with lights, so you can put on shows for us."

"Thank you so much, Sir," Liam said in soft, broken voice. Strangely, he abruptly left the room. Aidan looked concerned and turned to Laura.

"I hope I got the right things. I was told this is what all the musicians want."

"You have no idea how perfect your gifts are," Laura said quietly, hugging her father. "Liam's just...overwhelmed. He didn't want anyone to see him get emotional. Thank you, Father. You're wonderful."

On the train trip home, Liam expressed his gratitude to Laura. "I can't believe how kind and generous your father has been to me. And Hannah, too."

"My father is very special," Laura beamed, "and he thinks you are, too!"

Liam blushed. "I feel very lucky to be treated this way, Laura Lye."

Liam had already decided he would not mention Christmas—or the gifts—to his mother. When he walked into the cottage, she was getting ready to leave and showed no interest in even hearing about Trinity College. Liam stood there feeling empty, knowing she would never share his dream of attending college. He would have to study hard on his own if he was to be accepted to the prestigious university.

Aidan made Laura promise that she and Liam would wait until he came home before seeing the new studio. The moment finally arrived.

Laura and Liam stood in the hallway in anticipation. Aidan dramatically threw open the double doors, stepped aside, and waved them in with a bow. Laura ran in, throwing her arms up in the air as she twirled around in pure joy.

"Father! It's fantastic!" As if in the most wonderful dream, Liam entered slowly, not believing his eyes. What had once been a dark, dusty room was now transformed into a brightly lit, wood-paneled studio with a raised stage and plenty of space for seating. The musty old drapes had been replaced by bright blue theater curtains. The custom track lighting included a bank of motorized colored spotlights for the stage

"Lord Meegan—I mean, Sir—it's…amazing!" Liam stammered.

With an uncharacteristic grin on his face, Aidan flipped the master switch, illuminating the stage in a multitude of colors. Laura shrieked and danced in delight, while Aidan laughed easily. Excited as he was, Liam remembered that he was still considered a guest in the Manor. He offered his hand in thanks, but Aidan was caught up in the moment, dismissing the formality to give the boy a warm hug.

"Me, too!" Laura cried as she ran over and squeezed into the embrace.

Aidan wished he could stay to prolong the excitement, but business called back in Dublin.

Noreen Delaney was going through the motions of her duties, completely uninterested in the studio project. Even when the musical instruments arrived from Dublin she made no comment. Iris was the one to inform Laura of the delivery.

Liam wasted no time setting up their equipment. While he was working, Laura wandered around the room and noticed her grandmother's trunk in the corner. She raised the lid and found a note from her father: *This was your grandmother's. I thought you might like it.*

"Liam—look! I can't believe it!" She showed him the note. "I thought he didn't want me to have anything of grandmother's." Liam smiled as he read it.

"Your father is full of surprises." He finished hooking up the equipment and turned on the amps, strumming the first chord in the new studio.

"Wow!" Liam exclaimed. "What a great sound! These guitars are the best!"

"Father is the best!" Laura gushed. Liam agreed.

The young musicians played for hours. Finally satisfied that it was a great first session, Liam sat back, looking thoughtful. "I think the way I write songs in here is going to be different than in the cave."

Laura looked worried. "What does that mean?"

"It's all right, Laura—we still need the cave. But we can do rock songs here and ballads there."

ᕙᕗ *Chapter Seventeen* ᕙᕗ
Spring 1979

S ix months had passed since Philip Delaney's death, and in that time Noreen only spoke to her son when absolutely necessary, and then only a few words at a time. Liam was understandably surprised one evening when she approached him.

"Liam, I want to talk to you."

"Yes, Mother?" Liam was guarded, but hopeful.

"I am going to marry the Deacon," she blurted out. Liam gasped.

"Mother, please! I can't believe you would do this!"

"Liam! I will not have you passin' down your Irish judgment on me! I have a chance for a new life, and I'm not goin' to let it slip away."

"Mother! What about—"

"Not another word! I've made up my mind. We'll be marryin' this Saturday—I don't expect you to come." With that she headed out the door, leaving her son devoid of anything but devastation. Kite licked Liam's hand, and he picked up his small friend.

"I think we're on our own now, Kite."

Working in the barn early the next morning was Liam's only solace. He was doing his best to fill his father's boots, knowing Lord Meegan continued to pay full wages to his mother. The work occupied his hands, but his mind was troubled, wondering what the future would hold for him with the Deacon in the picture.

Liam was several minutes late for tutoring, and twice that morning Mrs. O'Brien had to call for his attention. Both she and Laura were puzzled—Liam was always the good student. One look into Liam's eyes told Laura he needed her.

She waited until class was over to speak to him. "Let's go for a ride. I think we need to get away."

Once they were in the privacy of the cave, Liam told Laura of his mother's plans and how the distance between them was growing. She looked up at him thoughtfully.

"Liam, your mother has been gone for a long time now. Let her go." At first he couldn't believe what Laura had just said, but then he realized her words were true. Laura reached for his hand, while Liam looked into her sympathetic eyes.

"You amaze me, Laura Lye. You see right into my soul. What would I ever do without you?"

"It's not going to happen—you're stuck with me, Monkey Boy." Liam smiled and she gently wiped his tears away. They dropped the subject of his mother and moved on to playing their guitars.

Chloe was stunned by the news that Noreen was to marry the Deacon. She told Patrick about it that evening.

"I've already taken over most of her duties as mother and nanny. I feel like I should call Lord Meegan, but it could make things worse for poor Liam. Noreen might just pack up and leave."

"At least with him here, we can keep an eye out for him," Patrick replied. "I just don't know how much longer he can go on like this. He works his tail off in the barn, all the while keepin' up with his studies and his music. Now his mother rewards him like this."

Chloe shook her head in dismay. "He's only a boy! The woman must be daft!"

Patrick rubbed his chin. "I think she's fallen into evil hands…"

The Deacon had never made an effort to meet anyone at Montrose, so it was not surprising that none of them were invited to the wedding. The most profound change came suddenly: Noreen's new husband moved into the Delaney cottage.

Deacon Larkin MacDara was tall, with black hair and eyes that could pierce to the very soul. He had a look that would intimidate, and the toughness to validate it. Everything he said was law, and no one dared question him.

Liam wallowed in a mire of inadequacy, unable to measure up to the Deacon's expectations. There was no pleasing the high-and-mighty preacher, with his harsh judgment of Liam's music, work with racehorses, and reading of anything but the Bible.

127

The boy did his best to be invisible to the Deacon, leaving for the barn each morning before dawn. Chloe and Cook made Liam's meals and kept him in clean clothes. He would return to the cottage when he knew the Deacon and his mother were at church, and he made sure to shower and go to bed before they came home. Liam did not even have the comfort of Kite, who had been banned from the house from the first day the Deacon moved in. Patrick and Chloe took the little dog in, reassuring Liam that Kite was still his.

One night while showering Liam began to feel uneasy, as if he wasn't alone. While drying off, he heard a crash in the living room. Liam tied the towel around his waist and ran into the room to find the Deacon smashing his acoustic guitar into pieces.

"What are you doing?" Liam cried.

"I'm destroyin' the Devil's work! It's evil, and I will not condone it in my house."

"This is Lord Meegan's house!" Liam shouted. "And he lets my family live here! You're not my family, and you have no right to destroy my property!"

Without a blink of his eye the Deacon whipped off his leather belt and began striking Liam repeatedly on his wet, bare body and face. The preacher became more enraged with each lash of the belt.

"There will be more of that comin' if you tell another soul! And, things could happen to your mother if you don't watch your step..."

With that, the Deacon turned and stormed up the stairs. Nearly broken from the beating, Liam picked himself up from the floor and stumbled to gather his clothes. With no other thought but escape, he left for the barn.

The numbness now turning to throbbing pain, Liam slowly ascended the steps to the loft. Only when he was in the safety of the bed of straw did he allow himself to cry, thrust into the paralyzing grip of isolation and fear.

When Patrick came into the barn the next morning, something seemed odd to him. He stopped to listen, but heard only the sound of the horses chewing their hay. He rounded the corner and stopped in his tracks, surprised to find Liam there doing his chores—in silence. Normally, the boy would be singing or talking to the horses.

"Good mornin'," Patrick said. "Everythin' all right?"

"Everything's fine," Liam replied almost inaudibly, turning away. Patrick was not convinced and moved forward, catching a glimpse of Liam's bruised face.

"My God! What's happened to you?"

"One of the colts threw his head last night. The strap on the head collar caught me across the face." Patrick stepped forward again, but Liam lowered his head, trying to hide his shame. "It's nothing."

Patrick could see Liam was uncomfortable and decided to let him be. "Okay, well, just be careful."

Liam nodded and continued to work.

Later when Laura asked about his face, he shrugged and gave the same excuse. She could tell from the look in his eyes there was more to the story, but she also knew he didn't want to talk about it.

The next day, when they left the barn for the cave, Laura was curious about why Liam didn't bring his guitar.

"I'm not really in the mood to write anything new today, but I'll sing along with you if you want." His response seemed strange to her, but again, Laura had the feeling it was best to just be there for him.

Liam kept the shameful secret of the beating for weeks. He became more withdrawn as the stress began to take its toll on him.

One evening, after his mother and the Deacon left for church, Liam was reading by the fire, taking advantage of a rare moment of refuge from the turmoil. Within the pages of poetry in the leather-bound Stevenson, Liam found a world of tranquility no one could touch.

Suddenly, a chill went down Liam's spine. Before he could even look up, the book was snatched from his hands—by the Deacon.

"This is the word of Satan! Let it burn in Hellfire!" With that he thrust the book into the flames. Liam lunged toward the hearth in an effort to save the cherished first-edition. The Deacon responded by lashing Liam across the face with his belt, sending the boy to the floor. The enraged man continued strapping him relentlessly.

Liam crawled to the rocking chair, using it to get to his feet. With a rush of adrenaline, he picked up the chair and swung it, knocking the Deacon to the floor. Liam escaped, making his way to the safety of the hayloft, where he hid for the night.

The next morning, when Liam missed breakfast at the Manor, Laura knew something must be wrong and hurried to the barn. Noticing fresh bruises and a deep cut on Liam's face, she decided it was time to speak up.

"Liam, I can see the pain in your eyes—and look at your face. Are you going to keep pretending you're all right?" He turned away but Laura grabbed his arm. "Liam—you can't hide from me anymore."

"I…I can't…tell you," Liam said through tears.

"You know you can tell me anything."

"It's got to be kept a secret."

"I would die before I would ever reveal your secrets to another soul. You know you can trust me."

Liam shook his head. "It's not a matter of trust. I don't want to involve you."

"I'm already involved—the same as you are with me."

"Laura, this is something evil and I don't have the right to bring you into it."

"Now you're scaring me, Liam. We've never kept secrets from each other before. No matter how bad this is, I won't let you keep it to yourself. You've always been here for me—and I'm here for you." She took his hand, leading him up to the loft.

Finally, trembling, Liam told Laura the frightening story of how the Deacon had smashed his guitar and beat him at every opportunity.

Liam looked intensely into Laura's eyes. "I believe he is the Devil himself. He threatened to kill my mother—and even Kite. I'm afraid of him and his power."

Laura wept, but gathered her strength for him.

"No one is more powerful than my father. He will take care of that evil man."

"Laura! You promised not to tell a soul!"

"All right—I'll keep my word. But you must promise not to keep anything from me."

Liam agreed and reluctantly removed his shirt to show her his wounds. Laura concealed her shock and anger over the many deep cuts on his back, and went to get disinfectant and bandages from the tack room.

After carefully dressing his wounds, she gave Liam a tender kiss on the cheek.

Liam moved into the barn, sleeping in the hayloft every night. He made a point of getting up early each morning to wash up in the tack room before Patrick arrived. Later, when Molly left for work in the village, Liam would take a proper shower at the pool house in the Manor. It continued to be his secret, shared only by Laura.

"Liam, how long do you think you'll be able to keep this up?"

"Until I can figure something else out."

"Doesn't your mother even wonder where you are?"

"She's not aware of me anymore. In her mind I'm gone—just like my father."

Weeks went by that summer with Liam completely avoiding the Deacon. As careful as Liam was, Patrick guessed something was going on. His suspicions were confirmed one night when he let Kite out of the cottage. He watched as the dog went straight to the barn. A few minutes later, Patrick saw a flashlight beam in the loft, and realized it must be Liam.

Patrick knew it had been nearly impossible for the boy to accept the Deacon, and figured sleeping in the barn was the only way Liam could have any solitude. He decided to say nothing and let it be, never dreaming that Liam was in fear for his very life.

Laura kept a close watch on Liam every day. There were no new cuts or bruises she was aware of, but she could see the emotional scars that formed instead. *He never smiles anymore.* Her heart was breaking for him, and she felt helpless.

"Liam," Patrick asked one morning, "would you be in charge of the farm today while Chloe and I transport a couple of colts to the stud farm in Kildare? I'll take Kite with us so he's not underfoot."

Liam actually smiled, pleased that Patrick trusted him with the responsibility. He couldn't wait to tell Laura.

As soon as he found her, he said, "I'm in charge of everything today while Patrick is gone."

"I'll help you."

Liam assigned her several duties, and then went on with his own. At noon, Laura went to the Manor to pack a lunch basket for them. A steady rain had been falling all morning, so Liam had brought the horses in. He was cleaning tack in the barn aisle and humming a melody when he heard someone approach.

"Laura, I'm over here," he called out. There was no answer, and suddenly Liam's blood ran cold. He looked up to see the Deacon's face, twisting with fury.

"Get out MacDara! Leave me alone!"

"I've warned you about workin' with these racehorses. Gamblin' is evil, and you are a sinner! Now it's time for you to learn I mean what I say!"

With a buggy whip already in hand, the Deacon lunged. The first crack caught Liam across the face and sent him to the floor. With the whip rising and falling relentlessly, MacDara beat Liam with blind rage, pinning him to the ground in defeat.

"You are a sinner, Son of Satan!" Liam tried to cover his face, but the sting was unbearable. His cries turned to piercing screams.

As Laura neared the barn, she could hear the chilling shrieks. Dropping the basket, she ran, her heart pounding against her chest, fearful of what she would find. The unreal scene in the aisle before her shocked Laura to her very core.

"Stop! Stop! You're going to kill him!"

The Deacon cracked the whip at Laura, just missing her face. She recoiled in terror and ran out, but realized there was no one to help Liam but her. Laura instinctively grabbed a shovel leaning against the wall. With a powerful grip on the handle, she raced back into the barn and ran full-speed at the Deacon. With all of her rage focused into one swing, Laura hit the demonic man squarely in the back of the head. He crumpled to the ground, the whip flying from his hand. Blood began to pool under his expressionless face.

"Liam! Are you all right?" He groaned as she kneeled at his side. "Liam! I think I killed the Deacon! We have to get out of here!"

Liam's excruciating pain would barely let him stand, let alone walk. He staggered outside, leaning on Laura, who then eased him down on a trunk. She ran to get Rose and Sky, but she was forced to pass by the Deacon's limp body on the way. The sight of his blood overcame her, and Laura vomited against the wall.

When she recovered, shaky and lightheaded, she grabbed the rope collars and threw them on the horses. Sky and Rose snorted and sidestepped as Laura led them past the Deacon's body.

"Come on, you two. We've got to go." Laura managed to get the horses outside.

"Liam, I'm going to help you, but we have to hurry. Climb onto Sky's back, and we'll ride to the cave, where we'll be safe."

Fighting to stay conscious, Liam struggled onto Sky's back and slumped over the withers, unable sit up. As they rode, Laura kept the pace slow so he wouldn't fall off.

"Liam, stay awake," she called. "We'll be there soon."

Liam's agony was so intense he could barely move when they arrived. Laura tried to help him dismount, but did not have the strength to support his limp body. He buckled to his knees.

"Liam, please try to help me get you inside the cave." He struggled to his feet, and she guided him to safety. When they reached the straw bed, he collapsed. He was pale, cold to the touch, and soaked in perspiration—and blood.

"Oh Liam! I don't know what to do—you need a doctor!" Laura trembled as tears flooded down her cheeks. It was all up her now—Liam had passed out yet he was shivering intensely. Laura quickly covered him with a blanket, realizing there was no time to waste.

"I don't care if I have to ride through that barn again—I will be back with help." *They can put me in jail for killing the Deacon—as long as they save Liam!*

Laura jumped on Rose and took off at a gallop, with Sky following. As she approached the barn, she could see Patrick parking the lorry. *Thank God he's home!*

"Patrick! We need you!" He turned to see the hysterical girl on her mare, and the gelding with no rider.

"My God! Where's Liam?"

"He needs us!" Laura sobbed. "The Deacon was beating him—I killed him! There was blood all over! Please help us!"

"Of course—but you have to calm down. What are you talkin' about?"

"In there." She pointed to the barn. Patrick ran to look. There was blood everywhere, but no sign of the Deacon—or Liam.

"Laura, where's Liam? There's no one here."

"The Deacon—I killed him in there!"

"Laura, tell me where Liam is!"

"At our secret cave—I'll show you."

"Cave? What cave?"

"Follow me!" Laura spun Rose around and took off toward the forest at a full gallop. Patrick jumped into the truck, grinding the gears in his pursuit. He followed to the end of the road, where Laura was impatiently waiting. There, Patrick leaped on Sky's back and rode after her the rest of the way. At the cave, she led him to where Liam lay unconscious.

"Dear God! Laura, do you have any water here?"

She returned with a canteen, and Patrick carefully raised Liam's head.

"Drink, Liam. We're goin' to get you to a doctor. But first we need to get you to the truck." Liam slowly took a few sips of water.

After a few moments, he was able to struggle to his feet. Patrick carefully helped Liam onto Sky's back, and then jumped up behind him. As he held Liam close, Patrick could feel the blood soak through to his own shirt. He knew there was not a moment to spare.

"Laura, ride like the wind! Tell Chloe to call an ambulance!

Feeling the weight of both Patrick and Liam on his back, Sky walked carefully with his precious cargo.

Laura cried Chloe's name as she and Rose got to the cottage. Chloe burst out the door.

"What's happened, child?"

"We need help! It's Liam! He needs an ambulance—the Deacon beat him!"

"Glory be to God! Where's Patrick?"

134

"He's bringing Liam in the truck!"

Chloe turned on her heels and ran to make the phone call. She returned to Laura, who was now crying so hard she could no longer speak.

"They're on the way. Come down off your horse. Everythin' will be all right. I'll help you with Rose."

As they were putting the mare away, Sky came galloping into the barn, riderless.

"I'll put him in his box," Chloe said. When she reached for his rope collar, her heart sank to see it was covered in blood, as was Sky's back. Before she could say a thing, she heard the approaching siren. *I only hope they're not too late.*

The ambulance attendants were ready and waiting when Patrick pulled up. The unconscious boy was slumped against him. They carefully placed Liam on the stretcher and into the ambulance as Patrick quickly filled them in on what little he knew. "He's in shock, and I'm afraid he's lost a lot of blood."

Chloe bit her lip and pulled Laura close. "Dear, you go with Patrick. I'll go in the ambulance with Liam."

As Patrick drove Laura to the hospital, he noticed she was staring at his blood-soaked shirt. She seemed unaware of the blood on her own clothes. He reached over for her hand.

"Laura, it's time to tell me the whole story."

In a quivering voice, she began describing how the beatings had been going on since Mrs. Delaney married the Deacon. The fear on Laura's face turned to anger.

"The Deacon beat Liam all the time for no reason! He called him a sinner because he played music. He even smashed his guitar!" Patrick put a hand on her shoulder as she continued. "He said Liam was lazy and no good when he was reading or studying. He burned all his books."

Patrick's jaw tightened as he fought to control his own anger. "Don't you worry child. I will see to it that Liam is safe. This will never happen again. The Garda will find that evil man and lock him up where he belongs."

"No! He'll get out of jail and beat Liam harder next time."

"There'll be no next time! I'll take care of the coward myself." At that point, killing the Deacon with his bare hands was Patrick's clearest thought.

Chloe was pacing nervously in the waiting room when they arrived.

"How could Noreen let this happen to her son?" she sobbed.

Patrick shook his head. "She hasn't been right since Philip died. Dear God, I feel like we've let the lad down. I knew somethin' was wrong. I just thought Liam was upset, with his mother marryin' the Deacon and all."

Chloe embraced her husband, and then pulled Laura into the hug. "We've let Liam down, but we're here for him now, and we'll never let anythin' like this happen again." They turned anxiously as a man dressed in scrubs came into the waiting room.

"I'm Doctor Hewson. Are you Liam Delaney's family?" Patrick, Chloe, and Laura looked at each other and nodded their heads.

Chloe spoke up. "I take care of the boy."

The doctor raised his eyebrows as he noticed the blood on the man and the girl. "Is there anybody else hurt?"

"No," Patrick replied solemnly. "I'm afraid this is all the boy's blood."

The doctor hesitated, and then looked to Chloe. "Ma'am, may I have a word with you?" Chloe glanced at Patrick and shrugged before following the doctor to an alcove. "The boy has lost a lot of blood," the doctor began. "He has a concussion. He'll be staying here for a while. I'm afraid there will be some scars." Dr. Hewson studied the shaken woman before he continued. "I need to tell you that some of Liam's wounds are old and were never treated. I would say this young man has been abused for some time now." He glanced at Patrick.

"Oh no!" Chloe cried. "Patrick would never lay a hand on Liam!"

"Well, somebody's been beating him—and almost killed him."

"Please," she begged. "It wasn't my husband—it was the boy's stepfather, the Deacon MacDara. Patrick can explain."

Wanting to know more, the doctor brought Chloe back out to the waiting room and made clear exactly what had been happening to Liam. Patrick's face turned red with anger. Chloe and Laura cried as they hugged each other.

Just then, an officer arrived, and the doctor went with him to fill out the report that would be filed with the Garda.

The officer returned to address Patrick. "I'm Officer Devlin. I understand you're not the boy's parents."

"For the love of God, no!" Chloe blurted out. "We would never let this happen to him!" They explained the situation to the officer as best they could, but halfway through, Laura interrupted.

"The Deacon is an evil man! You can't let him ever do this again!"

"Now Miss, did you see this Deacon do any of these things?"

"Yes! I saw him beating Liam with the whip, and he wouldn't stop, and I hit him."

Patrick put his arm around Laura. "Now Laura, just tell the officer what the Deacon did to Liam."

"Liam was afraid to tell anyone—but he told me."

"Told you what, darlin'?" the officer prompted.

"That the Deacon's been beating him for a long time."

Just then another officer came in and Devlin waved him over. "I'd like you escort this poor family home, now. I'm goin' to finish my report so we can get a warrant to arrest one Deacon MacDara."

"Can't we see Liam first?" Laura pleaded.

"I'm sorry, darlin'. The doctor said he'll be sleepin' all night. We can't even take a statement from him 'til mornin'."

"We should go home now," Patrick said after the officers left. "We need to get cleaned up, and we can't do anythin' more here." Laura was too tired to object.

On the way back to the Manor, Laura fell asleep in Chloe's arms. Patrick carried her up the stairs, and Chloe tucked her into bed. Then Patrick left for Noreen's cottage—to look for the Deacon.

The cottage was dark when Patrick got there. He flipped on the light and found Noreen rocking in her chair, a blank look on her ashen face. *Dear God, she looks so frail.*

"Noreen, Liam's in the hospital." She did not react. "Noreen!" Patrick shook her but she still did not respond. "Noreen! Where's the Deacon?"

She slowly turned her head to look up at him.

"He's gone," she answered in a faint voice. "He took the money...from the bank...Our money...Liam's college money...All of it."

Patrick could see Noreen was not well at all.

"Your son is in the hospital. Noreen, do you hear me?"

"He's gone," she murmured, wringing her hands while still rocking. "Gone..."

Just then, the Garda arrived.

"The Deacon's taken off," Patrick told them. "He managed to take all Mrs. Delaney's money—and she needs a doctor."

After a brief attempt to question her, it became obvious to the officers that Patrick was right—the woman needed medical attention.

"We'll take her to the hospital right now," the officer said.

Chloe and Patrick stayed the night with Laura at the Manor. Patrick felt that as long as the Deacon was at large, Laura was not safe.

Lord Meegan arrived at the Manor before Laura awoke the next morning. Chloe and Patrick filled him in on all the details.

"You should have come to me right away when you first noticed the change in Noreen," Aidan said. "That poor boy. I must go to the hospital and see him now."

"What about Laura?" Chloe asked. "She needs to know you're here."

"I'll be back soon. When she wakes tell her I've gone to see Liam."

Aidan drove quickly to the hospital. He quietly entered Liam's room, without waking him. The cuts and bruises on the young boy were shocking. *It's unthinkable that he's been so afraid to tell someone he needed help.*

Liam tried to open his swollen eyes. Disoriented, he could not make out the figure before him. "Father, is that you?"

"No, Son, it's Aidan. I've come to help you." Aidan tried to mask his anguish.

"Where am I?" Liam was barely able to speak through swollen lips.

"You're in the hospital and you're safe now."

"Laura?"

"She's fine—she's at the Manor sleeping. I know she'll want to see you later today. Right now you should rest. I promise you everything will be all right."

Liam drifted off to sleep again, and Aidan left the room. As he walked down the hall, he could feel a great anger welling up inside. *How could a mother let this happen to her child?* He was almost to Noreen's room when Dr. Hewson came out.

"Aidan," the doctor said, extending his hand. "It's good to see you again. Sorry it's under these circumstances. I've given Mrs. Delaney a sedative. She won't be awake for hours." The doctor paused. "Can you come with me?"

Aidan nodded and followed the doctor to his office, where they sat down. Dr. Hewson looked solemn before he began.

"Were you aware of Mrs. Delaney's illness?"

"Illness? What illness?"

"Mrs. Delaney was my patient over a year ago. She has a malignant tumor which could have been treated when I first diagnosed the cancer. But she never came back. Now it has spread throughout her body. She may only have a few days at best."

"Dear God, we didn't know. Ryan, please keep her comfortable and spare no expense—I'll be responsible for both Noreen and Liam. When the boy is ready to come home, I'll bring him to the Manor and care for him there."

Dr. Hewson shook his head. "I'm sorry, but Child Protection Services has been contacted. He'll be sent to a foster home or a state facility when he's discharged."

"No. They're not taking him away from the only real home he has ever known. I'll call my attorney—we'll find a way."

Dr. Hewson looked thoughtfully at Aidan. "Very well. I'll keep him in the hospital as long as I can so you can make the necessary legal arrangements."

"Thank you, Ryan."

Solicitor John MacDonald, attorney at law, was just finishing a conference call when Lord Meegan came into the front office asking to see him.

"I'm sorry, but he has a full schedule today," the new secretary protested.

Aidan brushed past her into MacDonald's private office. "John, I need your help and I need it now."

The secretary came running into the office, but MacDonald waved her away. "Cancel my calls until further notice."

After an hour, they came out and shook hands. "Aidan, I'll call you as soon as I can get the judge to sign these papers."

"Thank you John, I owe you. This is very important to me."

Laura was picking at her breakfast when Aidan walked in.

"Father, we need you!" She threw her arms around him. "Please help Liam."

"Laura, darling, I am taking care of everything. Now wipe your tears. Let's go to the hospital together and visit Liam."

On the way Laura poured her story out to her father. At times, it took all his strength to conceal his emotions from her. The thought of his little girl driven to the desperation of trying to kill a man was almost more than he could take. Aidan had spent his life trying to protect Laura from the outside world by keeping her at Montrose—and when she needed him the most, he had been gone. *Things will have to change.*

ᢙᡌ Chapter Eighteen ᢙᡌ
Fall 1979

L iam spent a week in the hospital recovering, while Aidan's attorney set the wheels in motion for a custody hearing. The judge would require Mrs. Delaney's signature, since she had actually demonstrated she was of sound mind. However, she was drifting in and out of consciousness. It was several days before Dr. Hewson called Aidan to say Noreen was coherent enough to discuss Liam's future.

"Oh, Sir, I'm so sorry!" Noreen cried, wringing her hands. "I truly believed the Deacon when he said he could heal me. I had no clue he was so...evil. The things he did to Liam...And he got all the money you gave me for Liam's college. I'm so sorry." She began to weep, and Aidan gently took her hand.

"Don't worry about anything—it was not your fault. I'll take care of Liam now—as if he were my own son." Noreen nodded and squeezed his hand.

"You are a good man, Lord Meegan. I will gladly sign the papers for you. I know Liam will be cared for. He's a good boy, and he deserves a chance in life."

It took all Noreen's strength to put the pen to paper, but a smile came to her face as she signed. A moment later, she drifted off into unconsciousness.

Aidan brought the signed documents to John MacDonald's office. The attorney assured him there should be no problem in getting legal custody, as long as a blood relative did not come forward to contest it.

"On that other matter, John...I checked with the Bank of Ireland. It's confirmed—MacDara wiped out the account. Please tell me we can prosecute him."

"Only if the law can catch up to him, but I have a feeling he's slipped through the cracks. I've already checked with the Garda. They told me a man fitting his description was last spotted in the south of France. According to the captain, if they do nab him, you'll be only one of many who seek retribution."

"Well, it would give me great pleasure to see that devil locked up, but I obviously have more important things to worry about. Thank you and keep me posted."

"Of course, Aidan. Shall I ring you in Dublin when I hear some news?"

"No, John. From this point on I will be where I belong: with my daughter and my entire extended family at Montrose Manor."

The next day Aidan brought Laura to see Liam in the hospital, as he had done each day, but this visit was going to be different.

"Liam, your doctor says you're healing well. We're all happy to hear that."

"Thank you, Sir. I am feeling stronger."

"Good. Now, are you up to talking about your future?"

Liam hung his head, trying to forget about the depressing visit from a social worker two days before.

Laura took his hand. "Don't worry, Liam—we'll help you. Won't we, Father?"

"Of course we will—and I have a possible solution. But it is up to Liam."

A hopeful look came to the boy's eyes.

"Tell us, Father!" Laura cried.

Aidan began cautiously. "Well, Son, I know you are aware of your mother's condition." Liam nodded slowly. "I've been told you haven't been able to visit her yet, but I've spoken to her. She's very sorry for everything that's happened to you. She loves you very much." Liam turned away to wipe his tears, and Aidan continued, "Your mother agreed it would be best for you to come and live with us in the Manor. You wouldn't just be a guest—I'd be your legal guardian, and you'd be a member of the family."

"Thank you, Father!" Laura cried, embracing him.

"Hold on, dear. We haven't heard from Liam yet."

The boy could no longer hold back his tears. "It's the answer to all my prayers. I would be...honored, Sir."

"It's settled then," Aidan replied, beginning to choke up. He bowed slightly. "And the honor shall be mine." Laura was literally jumping for joy.

"Wait," Aidan added. "There's more. I would like to announce that I will no longer be making my regular residence in Dublin."

"Father, does this mean you're coming home to live with us?"

"Yes, my dear." Laura dove into her father's arms. "And Hannah and her daughters as well." Laura pulled away, and her smile faded to a frown. "Don't worry, my dear—the girls will only be there on school vacation and holidays." Laura sighed with relief.

Liam sat up as straight as he could. "Sir, as soon as I'm strong again I'll continue to earn my keep, helping Patrick."

"Son, you don't have to work. I will take care of all your financial needs."

"But Sir, I want to help. I love horses and I learned so much from my father."

"You need to rest. We'll talk about it later. And please, I would like you to call me Aidan. We're family now."

"Family is a grand thing!" Laura said cheerfully.

Liam sat back in his bed, warmed by a sense of belonging—something he hadn't felt since his father was alive.

Dr. Hewson met Aidan and Laura in the hallway the next morning. He had a serious look on his face.

"Good morning, you two," he said politely. "Laura, why don't you go visit Liam? I'd like to speak to your father for moment." She agreed and left them.

"Aidan, Noreen's condition is worsening. It would be best if Liam sees her now."

"I understand, Ryan." The two men joined Laura at Liam's bedside.

"Your mother's been asking for you," Dr. Hewson said. "I think now would be a good time for you to go see her." Liam nodded, understanding the doctor's meaning.

Aidan helped Liam out of bed, while Laura got his robe. They helped Liam slowly down the hall, and the doctor stopped them just outside her door.

"We'll wait out here. Remember, your mother is very weak."

Liam nodded, and Laura squeezed his hand. He walked cautiously into the dimly lit room. When his eyes found the frail, gaunt woman lying flat on the bed, he couldn't believe it was his own mother.

"Liam?" she said faintly. "Is that you?" She squinted, trying to focus.

"Yes, Mother—I'm here." He came to her side.

"My precious son...I'm so sorry. Can you find it in your heart to forgive me?" Tears rolled down her face, and Liam gently wiped them away, kissing her on the cheek.

"Of course, I forgive you," he said, taking her hand. "I love you." She smiled while Liam looked into her eyes. "Mother, why didn't you tell Father and me that you were ill? We could have helped you."

"I was taken in by the Devil himself, Son. I'm so sorry. I believed the Deacon would heal me—but he poisoned my heart instead."

"I understand. Just rest now."

"Liam, will you sing *Danny Boy?*"

Liam took her hand. He felt a strange sense of completeness, as if God had blessed her in that moment. He began to sing his mother's favorite song, and a peaceful smile came over her face. Noreen's eyes gently closed.

When the doctor entered the room, Liam was still softly singing. Dr. Hewson listened for a pulse and shook his head.

"Son, she's gone now."

"I know—I just wanted her to hear the whole song."

The funeral was a small gathering of staff and family, including Noreen's brother, Peter Malone, from Galway. Noreen Delaney was buried at Montrose next to her husband, and Liam sang *Danny Boy* for his mother one more time.

Patrick stood with Chloe, one arm around her and the other holding an umbrella to shield them from the steady afternoon showers.

"It certainly is a gloomy day to end all," she quietly remarked. "My heart's breakin' for poor Liam—fourteen years old and no father or mother."

"He has Laura. She'll get him through," Patrick replied. "Lord Meegan will care for him—and we'll be here, too." He looked to the skies. "I owe it to my friend Philip to watch over his son."

144

There was no wake planned, but Iris and Cook put out refreshments in the dining room of the Manor for the guests.

When Peter Malone saw his opportunity, he approached The Lord of the Manor.

"Lord Meegan, I'd like to have a word with you—in private if you please."

Noreen's brother was a short, rounded man with dark features. Wearing a faded, ill-fitted suit, he looked as though he had probably scraped together everything he had for train fare. He stood in Aidan's study, nervously twitching.

"It's about the boy, my nephew, Leo."

"His name is Liam," Aidan corrected.

"Oh yeah—Liam. Well, I guess I'll be takin' him home with me now."

"Is that so?" Aidan replied with raised eyebrows. "Maybe we should have Liam in on this conversation. I'll be right back." He left the room.

Before Aidan returned with Liam, he only told the boy he was needed in a meeting with Peter Malone. Naturally, Liam was curious.

"So, Mr. Malone, you want to take your nephew to live with you?" Aidan asked.

Liam was shocked and began to protest, but Aidan waved a hand at him. "Let your uncle speak. Tell us, Malone, what are you going to do with him?"

The man cleared his throat. "Well, I have a small farm up north—I could use a strong lad to help out. Of course, just until he's ready to go to college."

"You plan to send him to college, do you?" Aidan mused.

"Oh, yes. Noreen had money for his education. I'll be takin' that with us, too."

"Then you haven't heard..." Aidan raised an eyebrow. "The money was swindled from her by Larkin MacDara."

Malone suddenly looked troubled. "How much is left for us?"

"Us?" Aidan asked, feigning surprise.

"Uh—I mean...for him—the boy."

"Well, that would be...nothing." Malone's face began to redden. Aidan had clearly made his point and sat back comfortably in his chair.

"I'll tell you what I'll do for you, Malone. I will keep Liam here and become his legal guardian. I'll assume full responsibility for him—financial and otherwise—and send him to a fine university. And you will sign away any legal rights to him." Aidan's decisive tone left the man stunned.

"Why on earth would I do that? He's me own flesh and blood!"

Aidan didn't bother to reply. He was already writing out a check. He held it up for Malone to see. "I think a check for ten thousand pounds will convince you. Now sign these papers." He shoved the documents in Malone's direction, making a point of holding back the check.

Malone quickly scribbled his signature and snatched the check from Aidan's hand. He left without even a goodbye.

Liam stood dumbfounded. "I—I don't know what to say. No one has ever done anything like this for me."

"Son, you're part of my family now. You've brought life back to my little girl, and I owe you a great debt of gratitude. And I will always honor the memory of your father and mother."

"Thank you, Sir. I will never forget your kindness."

The next morning John MacDonald filed the documents and Liam became the legal ward of Lord Aidan Meegan.

Liam and Kite moved into the large suite on the second floor, across from Laura's room. Through the French doors was a private balcony with a stairway leading down to the river—perfect for Kite to come and go as he pleased. Standing at the railing, Liam felt the cool breeze coming off the river Maigue. The view was spectacular. He felt privileged, yet overwhelmed. The changes in his life had been so abrupt Liam was unsure of how to react. *Everyone is so...generous.*

Other changes had taken place at the Manor. Hannah hired a prestigious decorator from Dublin to remodel the large master suite on the third floor for her and Aidan. Two suites on the second floor were being redone for Emily and Peggy. Fortunately for Laura and Liam, they wouldn't be coming to the Manor until Christmas.

To Laura's surprise, Hannah showed genuine compassion for Liam, often checking on the healing of his wounds. Her generosity included buying him new clothes and—most importantly to Liam—several leather-bound books to replace what the Deacon had destroyed.

In yet another sign of her new approach to family unity, Hannah no longer objected to Laura's wearing jeans. The Lady of the Manor could now clearly see the difference between the scruffy tomboy of yesteryear and the well-groomed young lady Laura had become. At thirteen years old, Laura was increasingly conscious of her own appearance, with Molly happily guiding her along.

It had been over a month since Liam joined the Meegan family. He seemed to be adjusting well. One night at dinner, Aidan made an announcement.

"I would like to introduce my friends and business associates to the new members of my family. A Christmas ball would be the perfect opportunity—formal, with dancing and music. Speaking of music—Laura and Liam, I would like you to perform several of your songs." Laura nodded enthusiastically.

Hannah was pleased. "I am planning a shopping trip to Dublin. Laura, you and I and the girls will wear ball gowns. Liam, you and Aidan will wear tuxedos.

"Hmmm—a ball gown," Laura replied thoughtfully. "That sounds so elegant! Thank you." Liam just nodded and Laura wondered how he really felt about all of this. She waited until dinner was over to speak to him in private.

"I'll do anything for your father," Liam said, "but I'm afraid I'll look like a fool."

"That's silly! You'll look very handsome in a tuxedo."

"It's not what I will look like—it's what I'll act like. I've never danced or been in a social situation with…the privileged class. I don't want to embarrass your father."

"I know just the person who can teach us ballroom dancing," Laura announced. "Molly. She goes to lots of dances. I'll ask her later."

Molly agreed to give them lessons in the privacy of their music studio. The next night, she came up the stairs with some record albums of ballroom music. With her guidance, it didn't take long before Laura and Liam were right in step.

"You two are amazin'!" she remarked. "You both have a natural rhythm."

Liam discovered he actually liked dancing. Laura thought it was heavenly.

The next day Iris found Laura in the living room.

"Miss Laura, your father would like to see you in his upstairs office." Laura thanked Iris and headed up to the third floor, curious about the unusual summons.

"Laura, darling," Aidan began with sincerity, "you are almost fourteen now, and old enough to appreciate and care for possessions that are only worthy of a fine lady. I've wanted to give you these since your...since your mother..." His voice broke and tears came to his eyes. "It's all of her jewelry. She would want you to have it."

Aidan opened an elegant box filled with strings of exotic pearls and rare, precious stones set in gold and silver. Laura was speechless as she picked up a necklace.

"I remember mother wearing these pearls." She held them close to her heart.

"I have fond memories attached to every piece," Aidan said, wiping his eyes. "Now I'll cherish the occasions when you wear them." Laura hugged her father.

Aidan stepped back. "My dear, I think these should stay in my vault up here until you need them. You'll have the combination—so whenever you want them..."

"Father, thank you. I will be honored to wear Mother's jewelry."

The party invitations were sent out and Hannah was in a flurry with all the arrangements.

"Children, I would like to go to Dublin tomorrow for our new clothes. We will take the early train, so be dressed in your best and ready to go."

Once they were in Dublin, Liam and Aidan were fitted for tuxedos. Liam had never been to a fine clothing store, let alone one for custom tailoring. When the haberdasher brought the measuring tape up the inside of Liam's thigh, the boy blushed.

"Lad, you must stand still to be fitted properly."

"It will all be over soon, Son," Aidan reassured him, to no avail. Liam turned a brighter red, knowing Hannah and Laura were still there.

"I think," Aidan said, "Liam and I will visit the Trinity College library while you ladies go shopping." He glanced at Liam, who nodded gratefully.

"Whatever you like, dear," Hannah replied.

"Liam, what's your favorite color?" Laura asked sweetly.

"I guess...blue. Sky blue. Why do you ask?"

"Oh—you'll find out," Laura teased. A moment later Hannah stated she was ready to go to Cleary's.

"Have fun at the library," Laura said, and off they went.

It didn't take long for Hannah to find what she wanted for herself and her daughters. Laura took longer. She had something special in mind. At the fourth shop, she spotted a beautiful sky blue ball gown. It was off-the-shoulders with a low back.

"This is the one I want," she announced.

"Oh, dear," Hannah said. "It might be a little mature for you."

"Please? It's for a special occasion. May I try it on?"

"Well, I suppose...It is the only gown that has caught your eye."

A few minutes later Laura glided out of the dressing room gracefully, feeling like a princess. An uncharacteristic smile came to Hannah's face.

"Laura Meegan, you are stunning!" she gasped. "It fits you like a glove. Now, we must hurry—Liam and Aidan will be waiting for us at the restaurant."

❦

Hannah turned to Liam after they took their seats. "Well, how was the library?"

"It's the most amazing place—I could spend days there."

"Son," Aidan said, "I want you to know that all the books in the library at the Manor are yours to read, any time you wish."

Liam smiled broadly. "Oh, thank you, Sir. I will take very good care of them."

"Well, ladies, how did the shopping go? Did you find your gowns?" Laura and Hannah glanced at each other, sharing a smile.

"Yes, we did!" Laura replied.

Hannah no longer felt threatened by Aidan's daughter, and now took pride in the positive changes she was seeing in her. The love and understanding of a good man helped Hannah accept her—and even a stable boy—into her life.

ᴄ✑ *Chapter Nineteen* ❧
Winter 1980

Hannah hired the best holiday designer to transform the Manor into a winter wonderland. Her vision was to create an enchanting setting that would capture the Christmas spirit for the family's guests from the moment they stepped into the grand entry.

Snow-covered boughs with silver ribbons draped the windows and grand staircase. An archway of frosted mirrors, reflecting dangling illuminated crystals, created the experience of entering an ice tunnel which led into the ballroom. The vaulted ceiling was covered by dark blue velvet with thousands of twinkling lights, providing the illusion of an evening of dancing beneath the stars. Each table was graced with wintry white boughs and silver julep cups filled with flickering candles.

Aidan finished getting dressed and went downstairs to find Hannah.

"My dear," Aidan whispered, "not only do you look fantastic, but you have set the stage for a spectacular event. The Manor has never been in such grand glory." Hannah beamed with pride.

The first guests were to arrive shortly, and Aidan and Liam were waiting for them in the entry. They were quite the pair, dressed in their tuxedos. Liam, now six-foot-three, was taller than Aidan, who looked up at him in admiration.

"Liam, you are a handsome gentleman," Aidan remarked. "I'm proud of you."

"I agree," Hannah added. "You look very distinguished in your tuxedo."

Liam smiled. "Thank you—that means a lot to me."

Emily and Peggy had arrived earlier. They were plotting incessantly about which eligible men would be coming from Dublin, and who among them they would select for dance partners. When the two girls came into the grand entry, they both fell silent the moment they laid eyes on Liam.

"Liam, make sure you save me a dance," Emily said as she gave him a wink. Liam blushed and did not say a word, anxiously looking around for Laura.

∽

Earlier, Molly had carefully studied Laura's golden locks, running her fingers through her tresses as she spoke. "Yes! Your hair is long enough now to put up. I can make cascadin' ringlets. And I brought some little sparkle clips from my salon. They'll go well with your mother's diamond necklace."

Molly went right to work on the transformation, her hands never stopping until she was satisfied. She finished with a light spray of gardenia perfume to Laura's neck and shoulders. A pink gloss applied to Laura lips was the perfect final touch.

The artist now stood back and admired her work, a perfect blend of elegance and sophistication in the striking form of the young lady before her.

"Laura, you are breathtakin'! Now go downstairs and *wow* them!"

∽

Hannah and her daughters had joined most of the guests in the ballroom by the time Laura gracefully descended the grand staircase. But her stunning radiance did not go unnoticed. Liam was awestruck the moment he caught sight of her. *My God! She's so beautiful.* His heart skipped a beat, and for a moment he could not catch his breath.

Aidan, who had just finished introducing Liam to a guest, turned to see the subject of the Liam's sudden preoccupation. The Lord of the Manor was taken aback at the vision of loveliness before his eyes. *She looks so much like my beautiful Fey.* Then Aidan was in motion, and in a grand gesture of chivalry kissed his daughter on the cheek and offered her his arm. Laura, in her glory, flashed her father *that smile,* and then turned her brilliance to Liam. Liam, overwhelmed, could do nothing but follow as Aidan escorted his daughter through the ice tunnel and into the ballroom.

All eyes were on Lord Meegan and daughter. The crowd parted to let them pass.

"My dear, you are dazzling," Aidan whispered to Laura. "Your mother would be so proud to see the beautiful young lady you've become."

Touched by his words, Laura looked up at her father affectionately with soft brown eyes so much like her mother's that a tear came to Aidan's eye.

A hush came over the room as Aidan approached the microphone.

"Good evening, all of my cherished guests! Welcome to Montrose Manor for an evening of celebration among family and friends. It gives me great pride at this time to introduce the members of my own fine family." He turned and put his arm around Laura, who was smiling proudly as she glanced at Liam. Aidan continued, "This is my daughter, Laura, who some of you have met before, but none have seen looking quite so grown up." There were several cheers followed by applause.

To Laura, the entire event was a kind of fairy tale, with a roomful of unfamiliar faces who were suddenly her friends. Her gaze once again fixed on Liam, whose glowing smile, directed at her, made him incredibly handsome.

Aidan then introduced Hannah, Peggy, and Emily, who indulged themselves in the glory of being in the spotlight.

"And now," Aidan said with anticipation, "I would like to introduce the newest member of my family, Liam Delaney. He's the sophisticated young man right here."

Liam was uncomfortable walking up onto the stage, until Laura took his hand. A warm feeling came over him, inspiring him to wave at the crowd.

Among the guests were many business associates, horse breeders and trainers, as well as longtime friends of the Meegan family. Most knew about the death of Liam's parents and responded with cheers and applause to welcome him. Naturally, Patrick and Chloe were the loudest. Aidan smiled and waved in a gesture of thanks to the crowd. He put his arm around Liam, and the applause grew. After a moment, Aidan put his hand up, and the crowd quieted.

"In just a few minutes, I will begin the first dance with my lovely wife, Hannah, who is responsible for the creation of this fine event." More applause followed, and Aidan concluded, "Please indulge yourselves in the hospitality of the evening."

Aidan's only sibling—his older brother, Aengus—was among the guests. Their parents had passed away years before, and although the two brothers were co-owners of Feyland Stud Farm, Aidan and Aengus maintained very little contact. Their good looks and strong family resemblance were all they really had in common.

Aengus and his wife, Rachel, lived in the large Manor at Feyland, yet no longer had any involvement in the breeding, training, or racing. Their two sons had never shown any interest in horses or their Ireland home. After graduating from college, they both left the country. Rachel was an extremely attractive lady, well-bred and well-known in the highest circles of society.

Aidan saw his brother and Rachel approaching, and he made a point of beckoning them to come over and meet Liam. They were polite, but Rachel had a clear look of disdain—as if she were meeting the new stable hand.

When Aidan had visited months before to tell Aengus and Rachel the good news of his guardianship, the two were cordial, but were actually displeased. After Aidan left, Rachel openly expressed her objections.

"After all, the boy has no pedigree. His parents were poor people—barn help. Does this mean a stable boy is going to inherit the Meegan estate someday? It should be designated for our sons—and, of course, Laura."

Aengus rubbed his chin. "Aidan may think he is finally getting the son he could never have, but you can rest assured, I'll intervene in good time."

Liam had already greeted a seemingly endless string of guests, and Laura noticed his discomfort at meeting Aengus and Rachel.

"My, you are handsome, Monkey Boy," she remarked with a smile.

"Laura, you are..." Liam stuttered, spellbound by Laura's radiance. The sky blue gown glowed in the firelight.

"Well, what do you think?" She twirled around and flashed him *that smile.*

"I can't...describe...how you look..." *She looks so grown up!* Liam's infatuated thoughts were interrupted by the beginning of a drumroll.

"And now," the maestro announced, "the first dance is about to begin with our gracious host and hostess, Lord and Lady Meegan." The drummer did a cymbal crash, and the violinists began dramatically accenting the entrance of the host and hostess.

Hannah beamed with pride as Aidan escorted her on his arm to the center of the dance floor. The orchestra began playing *The Vienna Waltz*, and the Lady of the Manor, elegant in her silver gown, glided across the floor with her handsome Lord. The sparkle of Hannah's elaborate tiara beautifully complimented her diamond necklace, and the couple looked every bit the part of royalty. Their dance ended with thunderous applause, and the guests were invited to join in.

"Liam, shall we dance?" Laura asked with anticipation.

"I don't know, Laura—I really feel out of place."

"Come on Liam." But he hesitated too long. A young man stepped up.

"My name is Timothy O'Donnell—of the Dublin O'Donnells. May I have the pleasure of this dance, Miss Meegan?"

Laura looked from the young man to Liam, her eyes pleading for him to act. Embarrassed, Liam looked away, but he did not expect Laura's next reaction.

"Why, yes, Mr. O'Donnell," she said coyly, offering him her hand. As they walked off to the dance floor, Laura glanced over her shoulder at Liam, who stood paralyzed, furious with himself.

As the two began to waltz, it was apparent that this newcomer was experienced, and Liam suddenly found Laura's gracefulness anything but enjoyable to watch. A strong feeling of jealousy came over him. *Who is this 'Mr. Dublin', anyway?*

Liam hated the stirrings of resentment he felt and decided to step out onto the terrace and cool off.

But just a few moments later, Liam turned his head and caught a glimpse of Laura, her gown shimmering in the moonlight as she approached him. To Liam, the sparkles in her hair were a halo. His gaze was fixed upon her, revealing the longing and hurt in his eyes.

"Liam," she asked sweetly, "are you unhappy with me?" He slowly shook his head but did not speak, still ashamed of his own jealousy. "Please come inside, Liam. It's cold out here."

Laura was trembling in her off-the-shoulders gown, and she ignored Liam's hesitation, throwing her arms around him. He instinctively embraced Laura to shield her from the cold. Her skin felt like silk, and the warmth of her body melted into his. Liam impulsively lowered his head, drawn to the fragrance of gardenias from her neck. It was intoxicating to him. A wisp of Laura's hair swept slowly across Liam's cheek, and he tingled inside. Liam's role as Laura's protector had been transformed. His heart was pounding with desire.

Laura looked up with innocent eyes. "Please say something…"

Laura's gaze was all it took. With his inhibitions finally disarmed, Liam lifted her chin and kissed her soft, inviting lips. The kiss was tender and enchanting, and they both allowed it to linger. Liam started to feel weak in the knees. He leaned into her more, and now he could feel Laura's heart pounding.

Then, as if suddenly slapped in the face, Liam came to his senses and pulled back. "Laura, I'm so sorry! I don't know what came over me."

"Liam, don't be sorry—it was wonderful—"

"We'd better go inside now," he said, ignoring her.

When they got near the dance floor, Laura stopped to face him. "Will you dance with me now?"

The thought of Mr. Dublin dancing with Laura again was more than Liam could stand. Without hesitation, he took her hand.

The moment they went into step together, Liam felt like he was being whisked away on a magic carpet. Laura's sweeping motions made it appear as if she were floating. Her gown flowed behind each of her graceful steps as if it had a life of its own. To Liam, they were the only two people in the room.

Laura felt like the belle of the ball, as if she were with her Prince Charming. Liam's natural feel for the rhythm of the music made him smooth and decisive as he led her in the dance. She wished the moment would last forever.

Emily spotted them from across the room. *Liam is far too gorgeous to be wasted on that little girl.* She walked right up behind him and ran her fingers through his hair.

"Hello, handsome," she said charmingly. "Remember, you owe me a dance."

Liam paused only to give her a distracted look. Then, ignoring Emily, he twirled Laura in the other direction.

Emily was shocked. *Nobody refuses me...*

After the lavish buffet, Aidan took the microphone. "Is everyone having a good time?" There was a loud applause and several hoots and hollers. "I have a special surprise: the children will perform for you."

Laura and Liam sang two love ballads Liam had written. Liam wished he had picked some other songs to perform instead. The lyrics now took on a new meaning for him, and every time he looked at Laura, he blushed. Liam was sure he would forget a line or miss a chord on the guitar, but he made it through both songs, somehow. The guests did not notice his nervousness, and everyone responded with roaring applause.

Laura and Liam stepped off the stage, and Aidan embraced his daughter.

It was after midnight, and the ball was almost at an end. Aidan had the family join him on stage as he took the microphone.

"Ladies and gentleman," he said cheerfully, "I hope you are all as fulfilled as I am tonight." Aidan patted his stomach, and the crowd laughed. "On behalf of the entire Meegan clan, I wish you a Merry Christmas and a prosperous New Year. *Sláinte!*"

The guests applauded, and one of them—a long-time friend of Aidan's—called out, "Would the lad be kind enough to sing *Danny Boy?*"

"Would you mind, Son?" Aidan asked, turning away from the mic. "I know everyone would enjoy it."

Liam was unable to refuse Aidan, the man who had saved him in his time of need. Liam took the microphone. "This is for my mother," he said solemnly.

After the heartfelt rendition of *Danny Boy* there were very few dry eyes in the house. The applause was warm and sincere, but Liam was left feeling emotionally drained and he had no desire to stay and socialize.

"Thank you and good night!" Liam slipped off the stage, grabbing Laura's hand to lead her out of the ballroom.

"Liam, where are we going?" she asked. "We have to say goodbye to the guests."

"I said goodbye, and now I'm leaving. Are you coming with me?"

She nodded, and they disappeared upstairs to the music studio. He turned to her with concern in his eyes.

"Oh, Laura, I don't fit in with these people. I don't know what to do or say. I'm sorry I kissed you like that—I don't know what came over me."

Laura pouted. "I was hoping you kissed me because you think I look beautiful and you want to make me happy."

"I did—I mean I do—but it's not right. I stepped over the line."

"Liam!" she protested. "It was our first kiss, and I will *not* let you spoil it for me. It was wonderful..."

"I was...overwhelmed with the moment. It was a wonderful kiss and...I'll never forget it." Laura gave him a hug and looked longingly into his eyes. Liam was drawn closer to her, but caught himself and pulled back.

"It's late—we'd better go to sleep."

Liam closed his bedroom door without even a parting glance. The truth was, Liam could not get Laura out of his mind. *She's come into my heart, and I know I don't have the right. Just when my life seems to be going well, I have to go and complicate it.*

Laura felt a mixture of warmth and frustration as she went into her room. She looked at herself in the mirror, turning her head from side to side. *There was nothing timid about the way Liam kissed me—it was pure magic! Someday, I intend to marry him...*

The next morning, Liam went down to breakfast early. His guilt about kissing Laura made him dread the thought of facing Aidan. He quickly ate his breakfast and hurried off to the barn.

When Cook was pulling fresh-baked scones out of the oven, Laura came downstairs. The others were all sleeping in. Laura asked if Cook had seen Liam.

"Oh yes, Miss Laura. He was up bright and early and he barely touched a bite. I think he's gone off to the barn." She set the hot pan on the counter. "What would you like for breakfast?"

She turned to see that Laura had disappeared. Cook smiled and shook her head.

When Laura approached the barn, she saw Liam helping Patrick turn horses out. As soon as Liam saw Laura, he blushed, lowering his head to avoid eye contact.

"Good morning, Liam," she said in a sweet voice. "I missed you at breakfast."

"Uh…I wasn't very hungry." He walked past her like he was too busy to talk.

Laura had to run to catch up. "Liam, will you go riding with me?"

"No, not today. I'm helping Patrick with the colts."

"No, that's all right," Patrick replied, overhearing. "I'm feelin' last night's party a bit." He rubbed his head. "It's goin' to be a light day. Go ahead and go for a ride."

"Come on, Liam, we could ride to the cave. We haven't been there since…"

At that moment, Laura realized they had not been back since the horrific day when the Deacon almost beat Liam to death. Judging by the look on his face, Liam remembered the trauma at the same moment and did not respond.

Patrick broke the silence. "You know, I haven't mentioned your cave to anyone, but I'm not sure your father would approve of you two bein' so far away from the Manor."

"Oh, please, Patrick," Laura protested. "We've been going there since I was nine years old. It's safe. You know—you were there. We promise, we'll always be careful."

Patrick hesitated and looked from Liam to Laura. "I'll want to go with you and check the place out for myself. I was a bit busy with Liam when I was there before. I'll drive the truck as far as I can go, and then ride double with—well, Liam's getting' so big, now. Maybe I should ride double with Laura."

Once they arrived at the cave, Patrick was awestruck. "This place is amazin'! The main room is darn near as big as my cottage. I see the horses have their own shelter. You two are very resourceful. How did you get everythin' here?"

"Ol' Tommy," Liam replied. They were silent for a moment as everyone felt sadness for the loss of their old friend.

Patrick thoroughly inspected the inside walls with a flashlight until he was convinced it was safe. "This must be a great place for your singin' and playin'."

Laura responded to his comment by singing one line of a song.

"Good Lord, you sound like an opera singer!" Patrick said, making them laugh. Then he gave them a wink. "Go ahead and enjoy—I don't see any harm in your comin' here."

"Thank you, Patrick. If you like, you could ride Sky to the truck," Liam suggested. "Just turn him loose—he'll come back to Rose."

Patrick agreed and left.

Liam picked up Laura's guitar and started to play softly, without singing. Laura felt like he was holding back from her.

"Liam, please talk to me."

"What's bothering you, Laura?"

"It's not what's bothering me—it's what's bothering you."

"Laura, I just don't understand how things can change so fast. Our lives can be turned upside-down with just a twist of fate. Not long ago, I was the son of a horse trainer, and I worked in the barn. Now both my parents are gone, and I'm living in a castle with all sorts of luxuries—and a new family. I feel like a kite in the breeze, never knowing where the wind will blow." Laura moved closer and Liam continued.

"I couldn't go on if I lost you," he said sadly. "I'm frightened that things will change between us."

"Liam, I will always be here. You are my friend and my life. Nothing will change between us. I promise, I will always love you." Laura's heart was pounding, and she longed for him to kiss her.

Liam looked deeply into her eyes. "You are the one true thing I have to hold on to. I will always love you."

Liam stood up, walked over to the wall, and bent over to pick up a white stone. Laura watched closely as Liam carved something onto the cave wall. He finished and stepped back to reveal the inscription:

My Friend, My Life, My Love—Liam & Laura

"I will always remember this moment," Laura said softly.

The holiday break came to an end and tutoring resumed for Laura and Liam After the first session, Aidan summoned Mrs. O'Brien into his study.

"I wanted to know how Liam is doing," he began. "With all that he's been through, I've been worried he may have fallen behind."

The tutor shook her head. "Liam is an amazing student. He seems to try even harder now, and he told me of his plans to go to Trinity College."

"We do want the best for him."

Mrs. O'Brien hesitated. "Actually, I've taught him all I can. He's at least two grades ahead of his age group and ready for advanced courses. I think he should go on to a preparatory school—for perhaps two years—and then right into college."

Aidan raised his eyebrows. "This news is impressive. I knew the boy was smart, but—college so soon? Perhaps you're right. However, I think we should wait until this school year is over before we send him to a prep school. He's had to make so many adjustments. I think he needs time before another big change comes into his young life."

Mrs. O'Brien nodded. "I'm sure that is the best decision."

৫⁄৯ Chapter Twenty ৩⁄৯

Spring 1980

Laura and Liam both had birthdays coming up, and Hannah planned a combined party. Liam was not thrilled about the idea of having a celebration, but he didn't want to risk hurting anyone's feelings by objecting. Laura picked up on his mood and decided to tease him.

"You know, Monkey Boy, you think you're more mature than me, but we'll be fourteen years old at the same time for two weeks."

Liam smiled. "Yes, Laura Lye, but in two weeks I will be fifteen."

Emily and Peggy arrived home during spring break from school in London. It didn't take them long to settle in. They were helping Hannah with the decorations for that evening's party when Laura came into the room.

"All this decorating for me?"

"Don't be such a selfish, spoiled brat!" Emily replied. "It's Liam's party, too."

Laura felt awful. "I didn't mean it that way—I meant to say—it looks wonderful."

"She's too young to know about proper manners," Peggy remarked.

Hannah responded with her usual ineffectual scolding. "Now girls, it's Laura's birthday—try to be nice."

Ignoring their mother, the sisters laughed and gave Laura their sneers.

Cook prepared a birthday dinner including all of Laura and Liam's favorites: soda bread and salad, lamb with mashed potatoes and gravy, and, best of all, Liam's favorite: chocolate cake. There were

162

fourteen candles on one side and fifteen on the other, divided by icing that spelled out *HAPPY BIRTHDAY LAURA and LIAM.*

Afterwards they opened presents, including a special one from Hannah: a leather-bound book for Liam's collection.

Emily was feasting her eyes on Liam, admiring his muscles, which had filled out since she last saw him at Christmas.

"Now for your big presents," Aidan announced. "Go ahead and open them, my talented children." Laura did not hesitate.

"An electric piano!" she exclaimed, thrilled. She examined the chrome logo on the front. "Fender Rhodes—it's so wonderful! It's perfect for our studio. I love it—and I love you, Father." She threw her arms around him.

"Liam, open your present," Laura prompted.

He carefully opened the big box to find a beautiful new Martin six-string acoustic guitar. He gasped, "Thank you, Sir! I don't know what to say…except…you're the greatest." He stood up and gave Aidan a hug. "Thank you so much for everything."

"You're very welcome, Son. They tell me a songwriter needs a good acoustic guitar for those spontaneous moments of creativity."

Laura and Liam couldn't wait to take the electric piano and guitar to the studio. Emily, on the other hand, wanted to keep Liam around as long as she could.

"Liam," she said flirtatiously, "why don't you play for us?"

Liam squirmed and did not reply.

Aidan intervened, saying, "I think we should take the instruments up to your studio now. It will take a while to set everything up. Liam, we'll need to use the freight elevator for the piano. Your back might be able to take the strain of the stairs, but mine will not."

The next couple of days had everyone filled with anticipation over the upcoming events. The first would be a trip to Dublin, where Lord Meegan was to be the guest of honor at opening ceremonies for the Grand Hotel. He was the founder of a large property development company that built the enormous structure. Following the ceremony, there was to be a formal ball. Aidan also planned to take the family to

Kildare to the Curragh Racecourse. His colt, The Real Thing, would be running.

Hannah, Emily, and Peggy were, of course, very excited about the ball. To them, everything else paled by comparison. Laura and Liam, on the other hand, couldn't wait to be around the horses and experience the thrill of the races.

❦

"I hope The Real Thing wins for us," Liam said to Laura that day in the studio. "As a young colt he showed promise as a runner. I really liked working with him."

"This is his first race, and we get to see it! Father is so proud that the whole family will be there."

Liam's smile quickly turned to a frown. "I'm never comfortable when Emily is around. She makes me nervous."

Laura agreed. "She's always mean to me. But why does she make you nervous?"

"I don't like the way she looks at me...and I don't like her touching me."

"Oh, she doesn't mean anything bad by it. Besides, sometimes it's hard to resist you." Laura gently ran her fingers through Liam's dark wavy hair.

Liam found it difficult to hide how much he enjoyed Laura's caress.

❦

That night dinner at the Manor was informal, and Emily made a point of sitting next to Liam, much to his dismay. Hannah and the girls were engrossed in talking about the ball—what gowns they would be wearing and who from Dublin society would be there. Aidan politely listened, nodding every so often.

Liam, on the other hand, had an annoying challenge: trying to simply eat his dinner in peace while ignoring Emily's foot as she repeatedly rubbed it against his leg. Every time he shifted away, she moved in closer. Just as Liam was swallowing a large piece of soda bread, Emily placed her hand on the inside of his thigh and squeezed. He jumped up, banging his knee on the table and choking on the bread.

The conversations stopped and all eyes turned to him. His face was beet-red. Emily offered him a glass of water, but Liam backed away from her so fast he stumbled. He was finally able to catch his breath.

"I'll be fine...but may I please be excused? I'm not feeling well."

"Oh, dear," Hannah remarked. "Maybe I should call the doctor."

"No, thank you. I just need to go to my room."

"Are you sure? Maybe you could just rest in the living room for a minute. We have chocolate cake for desert."

"We can save him some cake," Aidan remarked. "Son, you do look a bit flushed. Go ahead up to your room. We'll check on you in a while."

It took over an hour for Liam to calm down. He was lying on his bed, writing a song, when his concentration was broken by the sound of his door being opened.

"Emily! What are you doing in my room?"

"I've come to check on you," she replied in a sickeningly sweet voice. Boldly, she walked over and sat on the bed, putting her hand to Liam's forehead. He brushed it aside.

"Now what's this?" she purred. "Are you writing a love letter to me?"

"No! Now get out and leave me alone!" Liam crumpled the paper in his fist.

Emily gave him an innocent, hurt look. "Well, you don't need to be hostile with me! I'm just trying to be friendly."

"Please leave."

Emily got off the bed and sauntered around the room with a mischievous look on her face. Suddenly, her attention fixed on the top of the dresser.

"Hmm...what's in this wooden box?" She picked it up and turned to face him.

Liam's irritation turned to anger and he sprang to his feet. "They're private things that belong to me!" He grabbed at the box, but she held it close and spun away from him, turning towards the bed.

"Kiss me, and I'll give it back," Emily teased.

When he stepped forward she dropped the box and grabbed hold of Liam's hair, pulling him in. To his horror, Emily kissed him firmly on the lips. He drew back, but she wouldn't release him.

"You know you want me."

Liam was boiling mad. "Get out and don't come back!"

Unaffected, Emily taunted him further. "C'mon—I know you're as turned on as I am. You're just a little shy. I'll come back later, when everyone's gone to bed."

As she turned to leave, she noticed the contents of the box on the floor. "What's this, lover boy?" Emily mused, picking up the long blonde braid. "Is this a trophy from your last conquest?"

Infuriated, Liam lunged at her. "Give it to me!"

Liam's demand only spurred Emily on in her mischief, and she clutched the braid tightly.

"I'll give you what you want tonight when I come back," she said beguilingly. With that, Emily ran out the door and down the hall.

Liam stood motionless, stunned by her behavior. He heard her door slam and the lock click. Emily had gotten the best of him and it was clear she was planning to cause more trouble. He wiped his mouth, trying to rid himself of the bitter taste of the unwanted kiss. *She's disgusting, with her heavy makeup and that stench she soaks herself in.* Liam locked his door, took a shower, brushed his teeth, and got into bed.

But he didn't fall asleep. Wide awake, staring at the ceiling, Liam's thoughts drifted back to the Christmas Ball and the kiss with Laura. She smelled like gardenias, and her kiss tasted like honey. Her skin felt like silk, and her hair felt like...*The braid...She never knew I kept it...*

A knock came at the door. "Go away!" Liam cried, thinking it was Emily.

"Liam, are you all right?" It was Laura's sweet voice—he jumped up to let her in.

"Sorry, Laura. Come in."

"I just wanted to make sure you were all right before I went to bed. Can I get you anything?" She could see Liam looked pale and shaky. "Are you cold?"

"No, I just need to sleep. I'll be fine in the morning." He knew Laura wasn't convinced. She gently touched his arm.

166

"I hope you're better soon. Goodnight." After she left the room, Liam locked the door.

Liam had a restless night, plagued by nightmares of trying to escape from Emily. Sometime after midnight he heard someone trying his door—it had to be her.

The next morning, Liam was dressed and down in the kitchen before anyone else was awake—including Cook. He helped himself to a large piece of chocolate cake and a tall glass of milk before he hurried off to the barn.

Later that morning, Hannah spoke up in concern when she saw Liam was absent from the breakfast table. "Is Liam still feeling ill?"

Emily spoke up before Laura could respond. "I'm sure he's fine. I checked his room, and he's left already. He must be off playing with those horses again."

"How sisterly of you to check on him, dear," Hannah replied.

Laura was confused. *Emily's acting strange—and so was Liam.* She excused herself and went out the back door.

Liam was busy helping Patrick put the horses out when Laura arrived.

"Good morning!" she yelled at them from the end of the aisle. Patrick waved, but Liam simply nodded. As Laura got closer to Liam, he looked away.

"I'm going riding," she said. "Do you want to come with me, or should I just let Sky follow along?" Liam finally met her eyes.

"Can you wait until I'm finished here? I can come with you then."

Laura nodded, looking at him curiously before she went to groom Rose and Sky. *He looks troubled.*

As soon as Liam finished, they rode off to the cave at a gallop.

Emily entered the barn just as Liam and Laura rode off. She glared in their direction as they disappeared from view. It was the first time Emily had ventured down to the barn. *Why would anyone want to be around these smelly animals?* She looked around and spotted a horse curling its lip at her.

Patrick saw this and smiled. "Mornin', Miss!"

Emily didn't bother to greet him. Instead she asked, "Why is that creature making that funny face?"

Patrick shrugged. "I guess he thinks you smell funny."

"Well! I'm never coming down here again!" Emily hurried off.

Patrick chuckled as he watched the city girl retreat. "Now there's a fish out o' water for you." He patted the colt on the neck. "You're right—she sure does smell funny."

Once inside the cave, Laura started to rub Liam's neck. "Wow! You're really tense!"

He stepped away. "Laura, please don't touch me right now. I've got to tell you what's been going on, and I need to be able to think straight." Laura nodded, and Liam described everything that had happened the night before with Emily—except the part about the braid. "She made me feel ill, starting right there at the dinner table."

Laura's initial shock turned to compassion. She touched Liam's cheek with her fingertips. "It's all right. I understand."

"Laura, she's been after me since the Christmas Ball."

"Oh, I agree—this is more than just flirting. I think we need to tell Father."

"No, Laura, please don't tell him. I'll handle Emily myself. Your father is so proud to have his entire family together—I don't want to spoil things for him."

"All right, but you have to promise you'll tell me everything that happens."

"Laura Lye, you know me too well. I could never keep anything from you."

On the way to dinner that evening Laura had an idea. "Liam, why don't you sit next to Father so you can talk to him about The Real Thing. You don't want to listen to the girls talk about the ball at the Grand Hotel anyway." A smile came to Liam's face. *She's a real angel.*

Emily walked into the dining room to find Liam already seated, Aidan on his right and Laura on his left. She pouted and plopped herself in the closest available chair, which was nowhere near Liam. Hannah made her usual night-before-a-trip-to-Dublin announcement: "Now make sure you have everything you will need for the journey."

Liam went to his room after dinner to pack a few things. Again, he locked the door to keep Emily out. He did, however, leave the balcony door ajar for Kite. The dog had eaten a mouse in the barn earlier—Liam knew Kite would probably have an upset stomach and would have to go out.

A little after midnight Liam woke up with a jolt. Emily was under the covers, rubbing her body against his. He bolted out of bed and backed against the wall.

"Emily! How did you get in here?"

She ignored his question. "When you get cold and lonely, come back to bed and I'll warm you up, gorgeous."

"Emily, let me make it clear to you once and for all. I do *not* want you, and I have *no* intention of getting involved with you."

"Oh lover boy, you're just shy. Let me help you get over it."

"Get out now."

"Liam, are you a virgin?" He blushed, bright red. "You are! I'll fix that for you." She untied her negligee.

That was all it took for Liam. He grabbed Emily by the arm, dragging her out of his bed to the balcony. "Out you go!"

Liam pushed Emily through the door and tried to close it, but she grabbed his arm, trying to kiss him again. He pulled her off—by the hair.

"Ooh, Liam! I like a man who's strong and takes control."

"You're out of control! Now don't bother me again."

He gave Emily a shove. Just before losing her balance, she thrust her hands at Liam's face, scratching him aggressively with her long fingernails. She fell out onto the balcony, tearing her silk nightgown on the door.

"Jerk!" she screamed. "I'll go to Aidan and tell him you tried to rape me!"

"I can't believe you would upset your mother and Aidan with a lie like that. Now leave me alone!"

Liam slammed the French doors and locked them. Furiously, Emily began pounding on the glass while she continued to scream. Now Liam could hear knocking from the hallway door. He went to open it, and Peggy pushed her way in.

"What is going on here, Liam? Where's my sister?" Her attention was drawn to Emily's cries from across the room. She raced to the French doors and unlocked them.

"Good Lord, what's happened to you?"

Emily threw her arms around her sister and sobbed dramatically.

Laura, now at Liam's door, glared at the scene with arms folded. "Yes, Emily, tell us what's going on."

Continuing the melodrama, Emily put her hand to her forehead, looking like she was about to faint. "Liam asked me to come to his room," she whimpered. "He said he wanted to talk to me. I...I shouldn't have come." She glanced at Liam and cringed, as if in fear. "Then he kissed me, but I pulled away from him. He grabbed me and tried to...rape me! I barely escaped to the balcony. Thank God you came along, Peggy."

Laura watched Liam as he shook with anger, his face reddening. He was too upset to respond, so Laura spoke for him. "Liam would never do anything like that. Tell the truth, Emily! You've been chasing him since Christmas. You ought to be ashamed of yourself."

Peggy took another look at her sister, who was still crying, half-naked in her torn nightgown. She then looked at Liam, whose face was red with anger and deeply scratched.

"It's obvious who the victim is here!" Peggy snapped. "I guess this is what you'd expect from trash like a stable boy." With that, she helped Emily into the hallway. "I'll take you to your room—then get Mother."

"Please!" Emily said, loud enough for Laura and Liam to hear, as she allowed Peggy to help her out. "Don't upset her and Aidan with this! They're so happy we're a family now. I'll just keep away from the monster, and we'll be back to school soon."

Laura shut the door and got a damp cloth from Liam's bathroom. She began treating his scratches.

"We need to go to Father with the truth *before* the drama queen tells her tale."

"No! Laura, please—let me handle it."

She nodded and gently brushed Liam's hair away from his face. Comforted by Laura's tender touch, Liam began to relax. Laura finished by applying a little salve to his face, and then kissed him sweetly on the cheek. Impulsively, Liam turned and kissed Laura on the lips. He came to his senses and pulled back gently.

"Laura, thank you. I needed you to believe in me."

"You're welcome." She smiled. *That felt like more than just a thank you kiss.*

Liam began to worry. "I sure hope Emily didn't wake up the rest of the Manor."

Laura shook her head. "Molly is spending the night out of town, and there's no way Father and Hannah could have heard anything from their suite on the third floor. Liam, why did you ever let her in your room?"

"I didn't. I left the French doors open just enough for Kite to go in and out. Emily must have come in that way." Kite had slipped back into the room unnoticed. He now heard his name and came over, tail wagging.

Liam looked down at the dog and said, "Yes, Kite, you caused us a lot of trouble tonight. If you're going to eat mice, you'll have to live in the barn." Kite licked his hand as if to say *I'm sorry.* Laura and Liam both smiled.

"Liam, would you like me to stay with you for a while?"

He looked longingly into Laura's eyes. "I think I'll be fine, Laura. You should go back to your room. We both have to get up early, remember?"

Laura gave a little pout and Liam responded by giving her a hug.

The next morning, Liam hurried off to the barn with Kite so Patrick could take care of the little dog while the family went to Dublin.

Patrick looked quizzically at Liam. "Are you all right? You look a bit pale, and...how'd you get those scratches on your face?"

Liam looked down for a moment. When he looked up again, there were tears of anger in his eyes. "It's that Emily. She won't leave me alone."

Patrick nodded. "I wondered why she came to the barn yesterday. First time I've ever seen any of them down here."

"What was she doing here?"

"Well, I guess chasin' after you. She got here just as you and Laura rode off."

Liam decided to tell Patrick the whole story. He listened intently while studying the boy.

"That's a tough one, lad. You know most rich people get what they want, and some don't care who they hurt in the process."

Liam shuddered. "I'm not sure what to do—except I've got to watch my back and never put myself alone with her."

"That's probably good thinkin'." Patrick put his hand on Liam's shoulder. "I'm glad you talked to me, Son. I'll always have an ear for you."

"Patrick, that means a lot to me. Thank you. Now, I'd better hurry, or they'll leave for Dublin without me."

⌒ Chapter Twenty-One ⌒

I t was not until everyone was seated aboard the train to Dublin that Aidan noticed the scratches on Liam's face.

"What happened to you?" All eyes were on Liam as he lowered his head.

"I was playing with Kite on my bed last night," Liam quietly replied. "He got a little too excited and scratched me." Liam had just lied directly to Aidan—and he hated himself for it. It went against everything he had been taught as a boy.

"Oh dear, let me see," Hannah said, looking closely at Liam's face. She reached forward, but Liam pulled away and turned his head. Judging by the look on Emily's face, she was apparently enjoying Liam's discomfort.

"It's nothing, really—I'll be fine."

"Father," Laura suddenly interjected, "do you think The Real Thing is going to win at the race?" She succeeded in diverting Aidan's attention.

"Of course he's going to win, my dear—that's why he's entered."

In spite of Laura's efforts, the trip to Dublin continued to be uncomfortable for Liam. Emily glared at him, sneering when no one else was looking. Liam gazed out the window, pretending not to notice.

Once they arrived at the hotel, each of the Meegan party got their own rooms. Liam was relieved he would finally have a place to escape from Emily.

Before they left the lobby, Peggy brushed past him, muttering a warning: "If you even come near my sister I will call the Garda."

Liam took a deep breath and turned away.

The Grand Hotel Ball was scheduled for that night. In spite of Hannah's plans to take the three girls shopping for gowns, Emily and Peggy took off on their own. Somewhat unnerved, Hannah asked Laura to shop with her. Laura cheerfully agreed, relieved she didn't have to spend time with the girls. Also, she wouldn't have to worry about Liam, who had gone to Trinity College.

It didn't take long for Laura to find a lovely yellow chiffon gown. Hannah made her own perfect choice for the event—an elegant black formal. Satisfied, they moved on to selecting their race-day outfits.

"Laura, what do you think the owner of the winning racehorse should wear?"

"Hannah, you're asking me? You're the one who's up on all the latest fashions."

Hannah smiled. "Well, I have never been to the races, but I have seen the photographs in the newspaper. I want to make sure I am properly dressed. We will be sitting in an owner's box.

"I think this black and white suit with the matching picture-hat would be nice. Laura, how about this lovely spring dress for you?"

Laura had been thinking more about the horses than the event, and naturally assumed she'd wear jeans.

"Look—here is a hat to go with it," Hannah suggested, gently placing it on Laura's head and turning her towards the mirror.

"It frames your lovely face just right. It gives you the look of sophistication."

Laura tilted her head slightly. A mischievous smile came to her face as she thought of Liam. "This will do nicely."

Returning to the hotel, the two took seats at a table for four in the tearoom, where Hannah discussed the evening's agenda.

"Tonight, we will be joined by the O'Donnell family at the banquet table. You remember, Laura—you danced with Timothy at our Christmas ball. You made a lovely couple."

Laura winced, knowing how Liam would react.

Late as usual, Emily and Peggy burst into the tearoom, laughing and talking excitedly about their new clothes. Laura stayed only long enough to have a cup of tea and part of a scone, and then politely excused herself. She thought it would be best if Liam knew about Timothy before the ball. She rang his room.

"Thanks for calling, Laura. Can I come to your room?"

"Sure," she replied, wondering what was on his mind.

174

Liam looked worried as he walked in. "I've been trying to avoid Emily since I got back from Trinity. She was waiting in the lobby for me. I had to race in and lock the door, but she followed me and knocked for a long time before finally giving up."

"No wonder she and Peggy showed up late for tea," Laura remarked. "I thought I saw a devilish look in Emily's eyes." Laura studied Liam for moment. "Why don't you stay in my room tonight? Emily won't be able to find you, and there are two beds here. We'll have to be careful—Father and Hannah are in the room across the hall."

"It is risky," Liam sighed. "But I just might have to."

Laura told him the O'Donnell family would be seated at their table. "Mr. O'Donnell is the architect for my father's firm—they've been friends for years."

Liam groaned. "Does that mean you have to dance with Mr. Dublin?"

"Liam, he has a name—it's Timothy—and he's not a bad person."

"He's too old for you, Laura."

"C'mon—I'm not dating him."

"You can say that again!" Liam blushed, embarrassed at how possessive he sounded, but Laura was actually pleased. She gently touched his face.

"Liam, I can put a little makeup on your scratches so they don't show. Do you want me to?"

"I don't know. Will it look funny?"

"Just sit still, and I can make it look a lot better."

Laura carefully applied flesh-toned cream to Liam's face, blending it in. When she was finished, she kissed him quickly on the cheek.

"You're as good as new, Monkey Boy!"

Liam felt uncomfortable with the strange substance on his skin, but one look in the mirror convinced him he looked far better.

"Thanks, Laura. I guess I'd better go get dressed."

As planned, the ball was attended by all the fashionable people of Dublin. Liam was greeted at the entry and ushered to his place at the Meegan table. As he was seated, he looked around for Laura. He turned to see her entering the ballroom, and his heart skipped a beat. *She's gorgeous...she illuminates the entire room.* Laura caught his gaze and smiled sweetly, a sparkle in her eyes.

Just then Timothy O'Donnell jumped up from his place at the end of the table.

"Laura! Laura Meegan!" He waved at her and caught her attention. "You're seated down here next to me."

Liam's heart sank. He slumped into his chair in disappointment. Looking at the empty place next to him, he noticed the card was turned away. Just as he reached for it, he heard a familiar voice.

"Hello, handsome. What a coincidence—we're going to be dinner mates."

It was Emily. Liam's impulse to escape was undeniable, but his fear of creating a scene was stronger—and Emily knew it. She sat down next to him, waving at her mother and Aidan on the other side of the table. They smiled and waved back. Emily turned to focus her attention on her powerless victim.

"What's wrong, Liam? Cat got your tongue? Looks like she got your face, too."

Emily smiled triumphantly.

Across the table, Laura turned away from the egocentric Mr. Dublin to see the sadness and defeat in Liam's eyes. She mouthed the words, *I'm sorry.* Liam's view of Laura was suddenly blocked by Emily's arm.

"Care for some buns?" she asked playfully, passing him the bread basket. Liam just shook his head and passed it along.

A welcome diversion came when the master of ceremonies tapped on the microphone and asked for everyone's attention. He welcomed the guests and then introduced Lord Meegan, presenting him with a special plaque. Aidan gave a speech thanking everyone from the investors to the laborers for the completion of the Grand Hotel. For a while, Liam felt safe. Emily wouldn't dare interrupt the ceremony.

Timothy O'Donnell was always on the hunt for beautiful girls. A tall, thin eighteen-year-old Trinity student, he had his light green eyes focused on Laura Meegan.

Timothy fancied the way Laura filled out the low-cut chiffon gown. Her body had matured since he'd last seen her at the Christmas Ball. *She's a little young, but I like them that way.*

After the speeches ended, dinner was served, and the waiter set a large, rare piece of prime rib in front of Liam.

"Be sure to eat every bite," Emily taunted. "You're going to need your strength later." She placed her hand on his knee, sliding it up his thigh. Liam grabbed her hand firmly, throwing it off. Emily winced in pain but continued, determined. "Now, now—let's play nice."

Liam lost his appetite. He looked in Laura's direction again, but could see there was no hope—she was busy with her own problems. Dinner finally came to an end and Liam made his escape swiftly, cutting a path through the shuffling guests.

Unfortunately for Laura, Liam was moving in the opposite direction. Timothy used the bustle of the crowd to his advantage. He suddenly took Laura's arm and decisively escorted her out to the terrace.

"Let go of me," Laura said firmly, pulling away.

"Is that kid Liam your boyfriend or your brother?" Timothy asked sarcastically.

"Liam is my best friend, and my father is his legal guardian."

"What? Did his parents kick him out?"

"No, his parents are deceased."

"Well, since he's not your boyfriend, I think you need one. Me!"

Laura looked at him in shock. "I'm fourteen and too young to date."

Timothy stepped forward, pulling her in. "Oh, that's not a problem. I'm every father's dream beau for his daughter." He suddenly kissed her—forcefully.

Laura pulled back in disgust and tried to slap him, but missed as he ducked.

"Ahhhh, a little wildcat! I like my women to put up a fight." When he tried to kiss her again Laura kicked him squarely in the shin and quickly escaped back to the ballroom.

Someone touched Laura on the shoulder and she instinctively sidestepped.

"Laura, it's me," Liam said, calming her down. "Are you all right?"

"Let's get out of here—to my room."

Laura was able to control her emotions until the elevator doors closed. She threw her arms around Liam and began to cry. He kissed her on the forehead.

"Everything's going to be fine."

As soon as they got safely inside her room, Liam locked the door. Laura told him everything that had happened with Timothy, and Liam's face reddened.

"I ought to go punch Mr. Dublin right now."

"No—please stay here with me. We don't need any more trouble tonight."

"You're right. With Timothy chasing you and Emily after me, this should be a safe enough place to hide."

"Liam, let's have our own party here with just the two of us."

Liam smiled. "Life is always best when it's just you and me." He took Laura's hand and led her to the balcony, where they could hear the band playing.

"Miss Meegan, may I have this dance?"

"Mr. Delaney, I would like that very much."

He gently took her into his arms. They swayed to the music, and they both started to relax as their troubles faded away.

"Miss Meegan, you look lovely tonight." Secure in Liam's arms, Laura laid her head on his chest.

The radiating warmth of Laura's body was more to Liam than just a comfort—it was a bond unlike any other, a bond that felt everlasting.

When Laura lifted her head and looked at Liam soulfully, he knew she felt it too, and the last of his inhibitions melted away. He did only what came natural. Lifting Laura's chin, Liam kissed her tenderly, allowing it to linger before he broke the silence.

"I'm going to say goodnight now and go to my own room. I'll see you at breakfast."

ᢏᢒ *Chapter Twenty-Two* ᢒᢘᢓ

Not every owner had the kind of hands-on involvement with the horses that Aidan Meegan had. His pride in his Irish-bred racehorses ran deep, and Aidan always made a point of checking on the horse and the jockey the day before a race.

The train ride from Dublin to Kildare was long enough to add to the anticipation about going to the center of horse racing culture in Ireland. Laura and Liam were asking as many questions as Aidan could field, but he was more than happy to answer them, sharing the bond of excitement with these two young teens.

Ever since his brother Aengus lost interest in going to the races, Aidan had felt a void. His emptiness deepened dramatically with the loss of Fey, who had accompanied Aidan to every race. The delight in Laura's eyes mirrored her mother's.

"Father, is this the biggest racecourse in Ireland?"

"Some say it's the most important. Curragh Racecourse is the headquarters for flat racing, hosting all five classic races."

"Where did the name Curragh come from?" Liam asked.

"The Gaelic word is *Cureach*—it means racecourse. There is an Irish legend about it." A gleam came to Aidan's eye as he began to spin the tale. "Long ago, Kildare and the Curragh were owned by a Norman landlord. Our St. Brigid went to him and begged for a little plot of land to give to the poor. But he refused. She then asked, 'Would you give me the amount of land my cloak would cover?'

"The landlord laughed heartily and of course agreed. St. Brigid laid her cloak on the ground, and it began to spread out. To the man's amazement, the cloak continued to spread until it covered what is now Curragh. Since that day, it has belonged to the people of Kildare."

"What a wonderful story," Laura cried. "It all sounds so magical."

As the train rolled to a squeaky stop, Aidan looked out over the familiar sights. White buildings trimmed in green overlooked the endless grassy fields dotted with grazing sheep. In the foreground was the green turf racecourse, with the trainers, jockeys, and groundsmen moving busily about. Aidan found it especially rewarding that today he would be seeing the Curragh anew through Laura's and Liam's eyes.

The day before a big race was always a whirlwind of activity around the track. Laura and Liam followed Aidan as he wove his way through horses and their handlers to the stable area. They met Toppy Corcoran, who was to ride The Real Thing. Toppy was the leading jockey in the country. He was short, lean, muscular, and good-looking. He cheerfully shook Liam's hand.

"I understand you worked with The Real Thing as colt."

"Yes, my father and I both worked with him," Liam proudly replied.

"This colt has the heart of his grandsire, the great Nijinsky," Toppy remarked. "He has racin' in his blood."

"My father mentioned Nijinsky. I guess he was pretty famous in Ireland."

"He was famous the world over," Aidan said, "but his roots are here. All my horses are descendants of the great Nijinsky. He won the Triple Crown in 1970 and is the last horse to do so. He's also the leading sire of stakes winners."

"The Triple Crown—does that mean three different races?" Laura asked.

"Yes," Aidan said, "but not just any races. They're the Epsom Derby, 2000 Guineas Stakes, and St. Leger Stakes."

"You can feel the excitement in the air around here!" Laura remarked.

Aidan smiled. "Nothing makes an Irish heart beat faster than the thunder of hooves in the finishing stages of a great race."

"With that sentiment, I must bid you all farewell for the day," Toppy said with a tip of his hat. "I'll have to excuse myself to tend to my duties. It was real nice to meet you two. Aidan, I've got a real good feelin' goin'."

"*Slán leat—go mbeannaí Dia duit*," Aidan said warmly.

"I know what that means," Laura said. "Goodbye—and may God bless you."

At dinner that night Laura and Liam were talking excitedly about the day with Aidan as Hannah politely listened. Peggy and Emily, on the other hand, were completely disinterested in anything that had happened at the track.

The dawning of Race Day marked a flurry of activity at the Grand Hotel, and in the Meegan clan everyone was to be dressed and ready at ten o'clock.

Peggy came to the lobby a few minutes late. "Emily has cramps today and wants to stay in her hotel room, and I think I should stay with her."

"Are you sure you don't mind staying, dear?" Hannah asked.

"Not at all—someone needs to be with her."

Laura and Liam were thrilled with the news, and Laura knew the real reason Emily didn't want to join them. She wanted to be with her new boyfriend, Lawrence O'Donnell. In Laura's mind he wasn't any better than his younger brother Timothy, but hopefully he could be new entertainment for Emily.

The day was perfect for horse racing. The sun was out, but there was a cool breeze in the air—just enough to make the horses feel frisky and fresh.

Aidan looked at his watch. "It's time for the parade ring. Let's go to the paddock area."

They found a crowd forming around the oval paddock, watching as the first of the jockeys came out to parade their mounts before the betting audience. Toppy and The Real Thing appeared, with Toppy wearing the royal blue and gold silks of Feyland Stud.

"Father, do we have money on The Real Thing?"

"Of course we do! The going looks good, as they say in the Irish racing circuit. The track is not too firm and not too heavy. The racecourse at Curragh is widely recognized as a fair galloping track, and The Real Thing will do well here. He has a good draw—his position in the starting stall is number two."

Laura was reading her race card. "Father, what's a maiden race?"

"It's a race for horses that have not yet won. There are only six horses in this race, and they'll run five furlongs. Our horse is running against Silver Wings, Celtic Heat, Royal Heir, Irish Mist, and Dare Me."

As the jockeys rode out to the starting gates at the far end of the track it was clear the young colts were full of energy. Some were trotting, but some bounced and sidestepped along the way. Each member of the Meegan family watched through binoculars.

It was time for the colts to enter their starting stalls. It took several tries for The Real Thing to settle in. Liam held his breath while Laura gripped his hand.

"And they're off!" the announcer began. "Silver Wings takes the lead, with Celtic Heat and Royal Heir in second and third spot, followed by Irish Mist, The Real Thing, and bringing up the pack with Dare Me! Irish Mist takes the lead! Dare Me and The Real Thing move up into second and third spot..."

"Go! Go! Go!" Aidan shouted, jumping to his feet. Laura and Liam were screaming incoherently. Hannah, still seated, looked at her husband in disbelief at his raucous behavior, but no one else noticed; the entire crowd was in an uproar.

The announcer could barely be heard. "It's neck and neck with Irish Mist and The Real Thing! With less than a furlong to go, The Real Thing moves up the outside to pass Irish Mist! It's the Real Thing! The Real Thing! The Real Thing wins by a nose!"

"We won!" Laura screamed, hugging her father.

"We did indeed!" he shouted. Laura grabbed Liam's hand, and they jumped for joy. Aidan's racing spirit was rejuvenated. Sharing the excitement with his daughter, the familiar thrill of victory was his once again. Hannah's entire demeanor changed when she realized the Meegan box was now the center of attention. Quite aware of the eyes upon her, she majestically rose to her feet and placed her hand on Aidan's arm.

"I believe," she announced, adjusting her hat, "it is time for us to go to the winner's circle and have our picture taken."

Followed by the children, Aidan and Hannah strode proudly through the crowd as people congratulated the Lord and his Lady.

Liam began to feel the sense of pride that was his due. He stepped right up to Toppy and enthusiastically shook the jockey's hand. He then stroked the colt's neck.

"Goood boy," Liam said soothingly. The horse immediately calmed at the familiar, soft-spoken tone, and turned to sniff Liam's hand. "You were the first horse my father let me work with. He'd be so proud

183

of you now." Laura squeezed his hand, and a bittersweet smile came to Liam's face.

The photographer assembled the group, and naturally Hannah made sure Aidan was between her and the horse. She was in her glory posing for the win photo that would be in all the newspapers—including the society pages of the Dublin Times.

The excitement of the victory by The Real Thing carried through to the trip home from Dublin. Emily and Peggy had flown directly back to London, adding to Laura and Liam's pleasure.

They were happy to be home and stopped at the Manor only long enough to change into jeans before running off to the barn. Patrick was thrilled to hear all the details. He had listened to the race on the radio with Chloe.

"Me and Chloe have some good news of our own."

"C'mon," Laura said. "Don't keep us in suspense."

"We're expectin' a baby in the fall."

Laura threw her arms around him. "That's wonderful news!"

Liam patted him on the back. "Congratulations!"

"How about we go up to the cottage," Patrick suggested. "You can congratulate the mother-to-be." They agreed and off they went.

"We're hopin' it'll be a boy," Chloe said excitedly. "And we have a special name picked out." She glanced to Patrick, who smiled. "After your father—Philip Liam."

"That would be an honor," Liam said, clearly moved. "Best wishes to you both."

Chloe and Patrick hugged. The two young visitors waved goodbye and returned to the barn, where they got their horses ready and rode off to the cave.

When they arrived and dismounted, Liam heaved a sigh of relief. "I feel like I'm home again—here in our private place."

A dreamy look came to Laura's face. "Liam, do you ever think about having children of your own?"

"No, I can't say I've given it any thought."

"Well, I have," Laura said matter-of-factly. "I want two children—a boy like you and a girl like me. They can grow up here at Montrose Manor and ride horses like us."

"Laura Lye, you are a dreamer."

"And you don't have dreams?"

Liam gently lifted Laura's face and looked into her eyes. "You know I do. Sometimes that's all you've got to hold on to. But we've got to concentrate on our education and our music. We're a long ways off from worrying about children."

"I guess you're right," Laura sighed.

One afternoon in late spring, Mrs. O'Brien was ending another class session with Laura and Liam when Aidan came in to the study.

"Liam, we would like to talk to you about your education," he said.

"Can I stay, Father? Or is it...private?" Laura asked.

"Yes, dear. You can stay." Aidan turned to Liam again. "Mrs. O'Brien has informed me that your progress has been exemplary."

"Thank you, Mrs. O'Brien," Liam said humbly.

"The problem," Aidan continued, "is that you are ready to advance in your studies to a level she cannot provide." Both Laura and Liam looked puzzled.

"Allow me," Mrs. O'Brien interjected. "Liam, you are at least two grades ahead of your age group. What you really need is to attend a preparatory school—and when that is complete you can go right on to Trinity."

Liam felt overwhelmed. "This is...incredible news. I don't know what to say."

"Where will he be going?" Laura asked apprehensively.

"Mrs. O'Brien recommends the Glenstal Abbey for gifted boys," Aidan said. "It's in Murroe, County Limerick. He can come home on the weekends and holidays."

Laura shrunk in her chair. "When will he be leaving?"

"He should start in the fall," the tutor answered.

Liam began to ask a multitude of questions, which Mrs. O'Brien and Aidan both answered, caught up in his enthusiasm. Nobody noticed that Laura had left the room.

Later Liam went up and knocked on Laura's door.

"Who's there?" she asked in a weak voice.

"It's me—Liam—can I come in?"

"No. I want to be by myself."

"Laura, please—I want to talk to you about school."

"There's nothing to talk about! Now leave me alone!"

Liam didn't know what to do, and walked away feeling helpless. Laura did not come down for dinner that evening, and Liam asked about her.

"I'm afraid she's not feeling well," Hannah said. "I sent a tray to her room." She leaned closer to Liam and quietly added, "I think it's her time of the month."

Liam was surprised. He had never thought about Laura that way.

After dinner he went back upstairs to find the tray of food, hardly touched, in the hall just outside Laura's room. He knocked several times, but there was no answer, so he slowly opened the door, only to find that her room was empty. It gave him an uneasy feeling. *It's almost dark out...where would she go?*

Liam decided to go for a walk. As he approached the bridge, he saw Laura's silhouette in the moonlight. Relieved he had found her, but still worried, Liam went to her.

"Laura! I've been looking all over for you."

"Well, you found me. What do you want?"

"I'm sorry if I've done something wrong."

"What you do is your business and not my concern." With that, she ran from Liam and headed straight for the Manor.

"Please wait, Laura! I want to talk to you!"

The next morning at breakfast Liam asked Laura if she would like to go riding. "No, thank you," she snapped. Laura quickly turned and left.

Hannah gently touched Liam's arm. "When young girls are having cramps, they get a little...moody. They prefer to be left alone."

"Thank you for the advice," he replied. "I think I'll go to the barn now." He was fairly certain Laura's behavior had nothing to do with female problems.

Liam was scratching Sky's withers when Patrick came around the corner and bid him good morning. In need of a sympathetic ear, Liam asked Patrick if he had a couple of minutes for a talk.

"Sure, Son, what's on your mind?"

Liam described his predicament as best he could. "I don't understand why Laura's mad at me."

"I can tell you this: women are a great mystery. Sometimes when they say 'I don't want to talk to you,' it means they do. And when they say to leave, it means they want you to stay. It's then that you have to listen with your heart, not your ears."

Liam shook his head. "But Laura is different. She's always honest with me."

Patrick laughed. "She's not bein' dishonest—she's just bein' temperamental. Remember, she's not a little girl anymore."

Liam thanked Patrick for his advice and went about working with the horses, but he couldn't get Laura off his mind.

Later that day Hannah announced that she and Aidan would be going out for the evening. "Cook will have your dinner for you."

"What about Laura?" he asked.

"She's still under the weather and asked for a tray to be brought to her room."

After eating his meal alone, Liam went upstairs. "Laura, can I come in? Please—I want to talk to you."

She finally opened her door and looked up at him with sad eyes. "I don't want you to leave me. Everyone I love leaves me."

"I'm not going away—I'm just going to school. I'll be home every weekend."

"What if I need you in the middle of the week?"

"Just call. We can talk any time you need me."

"It won't be the same."

"Laura, you knew I would be going off to college, and we would have to be apart."

"But I thought it would be years from now," Laura whimpered. "I need you to stay and always be here."

Liam put his hand to his heart. "I will always be here for you. You must try to see this as good news. I'll get through college sooner than expected, and then we can be together." Liam wanted only to make

Laura feel secure again. He lifted her face and gently wiped her tears. "Don't you understand—this is all for us and our future." Liam gave her a tender kiss, and then stepped back and gazed into her eyes. "Laura Lye, you are the love of my life. I'll miss you every day, and when we're apart, just reach into your heart and you'll feel me with you."

ᗡᕲ *Chapter Twenty-Three* ᕲᗡ

Summer 1980

"I've been thinking about a grand idea," Aidan announced one night at dinner. He had everyone's full attention. "How about a family holiday aboard the Queen Elizabeth II to America?"

"A cruise?" Laura exclaimed. "That would be grand!"

"America? I would love to, Sir," Liam said.

"You can count the girls out," Hannah remarked. "They both get seasick and would be miserable." Aidan did not appear to be disappointed. Hannah continued, "When do you plan this adventure?"

"I thought we could all go to Emily's graduation in London and sail from there."

"That should work out well," Hannah said. "Emily plans to visit her new boyfriend's family estate in York for the summer, and Peggy will be traveling to Spain with friends."

"Then it's settled!" Aidan declared. "I will book passage for the four of us on the transatlantic crossing from Southampton to New York City." Laura jumped up and hugged her father in delight.

"Thank you, Sir," Liam said humbly. "I've only dreamed of seeing America."

Later, while walking with Kite, Liam turned to Laura. "I guess Emily has a steady boyfriend now. That's good news. It will keep her busy. Maybe going to her graduation won't be so bad."

"The best part is that the day after, we'll be on the cruise!" Laura added.

ᗡᕲ

A few days later they were stepping off the train in Dublin for another shopping excursion arranged by Hannah. The plan was to split up, with Aidan and Liam going to the tailor, unaccompanied by the ladies.

"After we're fitted," Aidan said, "I will take Liam to Meegan Enterprises and show him around. You ladies always take so long to shop."

Hannah smiled. "Well, we have to look good for our men. Right, Laura?"

The shopping day was a great success for everyone, but at dinner in the Grand Hotel Laura noticed Liam was quiet. Hannah did most of the talking, primarily about preparations for the cruise.

"We need to get passports for Laura and Liam as soon as possible."

"We'll take care of everything tomorrow," Aidan reassured her. He looked at his watch. "Seamus and Kate O'Donnell are joining us in a few minutes for drinks. I'm sure you two can find something to do."

"Don't worry about us," Laura said. "Liam, let's go for a walk."

They strolled through the gardens of the hotel, stopping by the fountain.

"Liam, what's bothering you tonight?"

"Can you read me that well, Laura Lye?"

"Yes I can, Monkey Boy." She smiled sweetly.

"It was the tour today at Meegan Enterprises. Don't get me wrong—it was really a grand place—very modern." He paused.

"Well then, what's wrong?"

"Your father wants me to come into the company after I graduate from college."

"You don't have to decide what you want to do now."

Liam shook his head. "He was so proud. I could tell it would mean a lot to him."

"The important thing is what you want, not what Father wants."

"But he's done so much for me. I owe him everything."

"Liam, we've talked about you graduating from Trinity and then making a career with your music."

"I know, but without your father I would have no future. I would probably be in a home for unwanted children."

"You can't give up on your dream because of a tour of Meegan Enterprises."

"Laura Lye, I don't know what I would ever do without you," Liam said. "You'll never have to worry, I'll always be here." She looked deep into his eyes.

"You promise?"

Laura nodded. "Liam, am I your…girl?"

"Of course, you are. Why do you ask?"

"You never call me your girlfriend or show any public display of your affection."

He looked at her thoughtfully. "Let's go to your room and talk."

Once in the privacy of Laura's suite, Liam carefully chose his words.

"Laura, I have thought about this more than you will ever know—it haunts me night and day." Laura became concerned and took Liam's hand before he continued, "I will never forget where I have come from, nor will I ever forget where you come from. I have the utmost respect for your father and all he has done for me. I know he thinks a lot of me, and so far he's proud of what I have accomplished." Laura started to speak, but Liam put a finger to her lips. "Please let me finish while I have the courage."

"Liam, you're scaring me."

"Don't be scared—just be understanding. Laura, I love you with all my heart and soul, but I don't think this is the time in our lives when we should share it with anyone. First of all, we are very young, and most people would not take it seriously."

"I don't care what people think," Laura replied boldly.

"Yes, you do. You are a Meegan, and that carries with it a certain responsibility. Your father expects you to go to college, and he wants the very best for you. I have no pedigree and no means to support you. I'm still in his legal custody—the poor stable boy with no parents and no money."

"Liam, Father loves you like a son."

"That's my point: a *son*—your *brother*. I'm included in his family because he trusts me to be honorable. And being his daughter's boyfriend would change everything."

"But Father is the most understanding person in the world."

"He may very well be, but *you* are the most important person in *his* world."

Laura started to cry. "Liam, will you ever be my boyfriend?"

"I promise you that someday I will be worthy of you, and in your father's eyes it will be right. Until then we must be patient and only have our special moments when we're alone."

Laura wiped her tears and looked at him thoughtfully. "Is this why you study so hard and practice your music so much?"

"Yes, Laura. I am determined to be someone of importance for you, and someone your father will be proud to call his son-in-law."

"Does this mean we're secretly engaged?"

"No, that will happen when the time is right. Our commitment to each other is in our hearts and shared by us alone." He kissed her tenderly, but pulled back before it could turn to passion. "I'd better say goodnight."

"Are you sure?" Laura asked with pleading eyes.

"Yes, I'm quite sure." Liam's heart was full, but his good sense prevailed.

After he left, Laura thought over everything he had said and agreed with most of it. Keeping their powerful love a secret would be difficult, but her resolve was strong.

Liam slept better knowing Laura understood how he really felt.

Finally the day to leave for London arrived. Hannah was running around like a mother hen making sure they all had everything ready to go. Aidan shook his head. "Hannah, relax. We have what we need, and we'll buy what we've forgotten."

"Aidan, I just know we left something important."

"We have our passage tickets, air tickets, passports, and each other. Now let's go, or we won't make the flight to London."

Having never flown before, Laura and Liam were both a little nervous as they boarded. When the plane took off she grabbed his hand and squeezed it tightly, but he smiled, finding the acceleration to be a thrill.

"I think I'm going to like flying. I hope the boat trip is fun, too."

"Liam, it's an ocean liner—not a boat," Laura laughed. "It's one of the biggest, most luxurious ships ever built."

"Excuse me, Miss Meegan. Sounds like you've been reading the brochure."

"It's not very often I know more about something than you, so I need to point it out." She gave him a satisfied smile and he shook his head.

"You underestimate yourself, Laura Lye."

The graduation ceremony at the university was long, with hours of boring speeches. Laura reminded Liam to cheer up, because the celebration dinner would be at a nice hotel and there would be plenty of great food.

They all met Emily's new boyfriend, Elliott Fox. He had sandy-brown hair, hazel eyes, and a muscular build. His appearance was Emily's main focus, but her secondary attraction to him was that he came from a rich family. Quite sure of himself, Elliott talked mostly of his own accomplishments all through dinner. As far as Laura and Liam were concerned, he was just fine—anything to keep Emily occupied.

After dessert, Hannah announced they were going to turn in.

Liam walked Laura to her room and said goodnight. When he turned down the hall, he could see Emily at his door. *What now?*

"Hello there, stepbrother," she said in her most seductive voice.

"Emily, where's your boyfriend?"

"Oh, he's having a drink with some friends at the bar."

"I'm really tired, and I don't have the energy to fight with you, so just leave."

Liam unlocked his door and tried to step in, but Emily pushed her way past him and flopped down on the bed.

"Emily, I mean it! I will pick you up and throw you out into the hall."

She opened her coat to reveal her naked body. Liam was shocked.

"What are you doing? You're crazy!"

"Come on Liam, just one kiss goodnight."

Liam turned and headed for the door.

"Wait! Where are you going?" she called after him.

"To the bar. I'm getting your boyfriend to deal with you. I wonder what Mr. Blueblood will think of his girlfriend naked in my hotel room?"

Emily pulled her coat closed. "Okay—I'm leaving!" Brushing past him she muttered, "What a waste of your beautiful, hard body. You...in a hotel room, all by yourself. Someday, you'll figure out what to do with all those muscles."

After that Liam was wide awake and very restless. Even though he had no desire for Emily, the sight of a young woman's naked body had stirred things in him. He wanted to call Laura, but thought better of it. His thoughts drifted into a fantasy about Laura.

The phone rang three times before he answered it.

"Liam, are you all right?"

"Uh...yes," he replied, embarrassed. "I'm just happy it's you."

"Who else would you expect to call this late?"

He told her the entire story about Emily's visit.

"Liam," Laura asked in a soft, inviting tone, "would you like to stay with me?"

He blushed at his own thoughts. Using every bit of restraint he could muster, Liam replied, "No, Laura. I'm sure she's given up, and I'm really wiped out. Thanks for the call." He hung up, got up—and took a cold shower.

◡◡ *Chapter Twenty-Four* ◠◠

Laura and Liam were in awe at the magnificent ship before them. "Wow! Have you ever seen anything like it?" Laura asked.

Liam shook his head as he gazed at the *Grande Dame* of the seas.

The group was ushered across the ornately decorated gangway and into the Grand Promenade of the ship. After being checked into the log, they were met by the concierge and shown to their suites.

"Lord and Lady Meegan, I present the Queen Mary Grande Suite."

"This is splendid!" Hannah remarked. The concierge smiled and promised to be at their beck and call for anything, and then brought Laura and Liam to their private suites.

It wasn't long before all passengers had boarded and the announcement was made that the ship would be underway in ten minutes.

"Oh, Liam! Let's go to the rail and wave to everyone."

"But we don't know anybody to wave to."

"It doesn't matter—it's what they do!"

As they pulled out of the harbor Aidan looked at his watch. "At seventeen hundred hours we will assemble in the Premier Lounge for a Bon Voyage toast."

"That's nautical time for five o'clock," Liam said.

"Very good, Son," Aidan replied. Laura smiled at Liam.

After they were seated in the lounge a distinguished gentleman in uniform appeared at the entryway and proceeded to their table. Aidan stood up to greet him with a vigorous handshake.

"Aidan, my friend, I'm so happy you finally made it on my ship before I retire."

"Hannah, Laura, Liam, I would like you to meet an old friend of mine, Daniel Riley. It just so happens he is the honored captain of this fine vessel."

Laura and Liam stood to greet him and began asking questions about the ship. He answered as many as time allowed.

"Please excuse me now; I must prepare for my reception party. I will see you this evening. It was a pleasure meeting you all."

Captain Riley turned to Hannah and bowed slightly, touching the brim of his hat. "Lady Meegan."

"Please—call me Hannah," she gushed, instantly taken with the tall, distinguished gentleman. "We are most honored to be your guests." As the captain left, she glanced around the lounge to see who had taken notice of the personal greeting.

"Father, can Liam and I explore the ship until it's time to dress for the reception?"

"Of course! I want you to enjoy yourselves on this trip. You may be on your own as long as you return for meals and the events we've planned."

"Thank you, Father." Laura grabbed Liam's hand. "Let's go!"

Moving from deck to deck, they took in all they could, finding everything from swimming pools and hot tubs to a casino and a library. The Princess Grill Dining Room, decked out in red and burgundy, was formal. The Lido had a casual atmosphere younger passengers preferred.

Liam noticed the clock. "I think we'd better change for the Captain's reception party." Laura cheerfully agreed.

It didn't take long before Laura was standing in front of her mirror in a pale peach chiffon gown, adorned by her mother's pearls. When she was finished applying her lipstick, Laura was startled by a whistle of approval—from Liam, standing at the balcony door. He was sharply dressed in a black tuxedo.

"How did you get into my suite?" she asked, surprised.

"Ah, don't you know? We have adjoining balconies." He smiled and presented her with a small gardenia. "I thought you might like to wear this in your hair."

"Ooh, this is perfect!"

Liam gave Laura a quick kiss on the cheek. "The fragrance of the gardenia is very intoxicating."

196

"Well, then, I shall wear one every day," she replied sweetly.

Liam offered Laura his arm, and they proceeded to the reception. They were greeted by Captain Riley and had their photo taken with him.

Hannah and Aidan, already seated at the table, caught sight of Laura and Liam.

"Hannah, is that my little girl?"

"Yes, Aidan, she has grown into a beautiful young woman. And Liam is quite the dapper gentleman, as well."

"My dear, I have to give you the credit for Laura's desire to finally give up blue jeans for gowns." Hannah beamed, pleased with the compliment.

Also seated at the table was the Bianchi family from New York. Robert Bianchi was a friend and business associate of Aidan's. He was traveling with his wife and their two teenagers.

Robert had known Aidan since they were young men and was a major investor in Meegan Enterprises. Robert, in his early fifties, was a short, good-looking man with graying hair and a cheerful smile. His wife Catherine was refined and petite, with blonde hair and radiant blue eyes.

Sixteen-year-old Jon, with his long, wild blond hair and sparkling blue eyes, had the kind of adorable presence that appealed to all women. Always the entertainer, Jon was gifted with a natural wit which would bring a smile to anyone's face.

Although her smile was also engaging, Jennifer was more reserved than her brother. A small strawberry-blonde with green eyes, the fifteen-year-old was glad to meet some teenagers.

"On the trip over to England there was no one our age," Jon remarked. "I think the trip back will be real cool. Do you like rock music?"

"Yes, we do," Laura answered. "And we play and sing."

"So do we!" Jennifer said. "Maybe they would let us use the piano in the lounge. Jon can bring his guitar."

Laura was surprised. "You brought your guitar?"

"I don't go anywhere without it," Jon answered. "I'm going to be a rock star."

In a demonstration of his talents, Jon began presenting the menu as if he were the maître d'. "Tonight's gourmet offerings include grilled

197

Scottish bay scallops, wrapped tenderloin with black truffle Madeira sauce, white asparagus, and chateau potatoes." Robert and Aidan chuckled, and people at the next table applauded. Jon took a bow.

"As you can see," Robert said, "my son is shy and withdrawn."

Laura giggled, and Jon flashed her a broad smile accented by big dimples.

Liam was instantly irritated and leaned over to Laura. "I don't think he's all that amusing. I can read the menu myself."

Laura ignored Liam and continued to watch the charming American boy.

Once the dinner was served, Liam relaxed and enjoyed the culinary delights, right down to the chocolate mousse.

The orchestra was assembled on stage, and the cruise director gave the official welcome to the guests aboard the QE2 and invited them to dance.

Liam saw his opportunity to get Laura alone, and offered her his arm. But the dance floor was crowded, and after the first number he was ready for a change.

"Can we go for a walk and get some fresh air?"

Laura agreed and headed for the table to grab her wrap.

"We're really enjoying the cruise, Father. Thank you. We're going for a walk on deck—we'll say goodnight, now." She turned to the Bianchis. "It's been a pleasure meeting you." They smiled and nodded, but Jon jumped up.

"Jen and I will go with you," he announced. "Maybe we can go to the lounge and see about that piano."

"Sure!" Laura replied cheerfully. "It sounds like fun."

Liam shot her a disapproving glance. While Jon and Jennifer turned to bid the others goodnight, Liam took Laura's hand and walked her away from the table. "Laura, what have you gotten us into?"

"Don't be so shy! They seem really nice. We could have fun with them."

"I don't like to play music with anyone but you."

"Liam Delaney, tell me: how you are ever going to play in a band if you won't play music with anyone but me?"

"You know that will be a long ways off, and not until after I graduate college."

"It won't hurt you to start making some friends now."

"I don't think I like him. With his long shaggy hair, he looks like trouble."

"Your hair is long, too."

"My hair is to my collar—and combed. That guy has it way past his shoulders and it looks…wild."

"I think it's sexy—and his name is Jon."

Liam set his jaw and narrowed his eyes. He was interrupted before he could object.

"Let's rock 'n roll!" Jon exclaimed as he grabbed Laura's hand and started away. Liam was shocked, but he wasn't about to let Laura go off alone with him.

Two steps ahead of Jennifer, Liam followed them down the staircase to the lounge, which was empty except for a steward cleaning up.

"Good evening!" Jon said boldly. "Jon Bianchi, guitarist. You don't mind if we rehearse here, do you?"

"It's okay by me," the steward replied. "Nobody is going to come down here tonight, with the Captain's party going on upstairs. I'm just finishing up now."

Jon thanked him and ran to get his guitar. Liam was not impressed with Jon's brashness, but before he knew it Jon returned, already strumming a few chords.

"So, what kind of music do you guys play?" Jon asked.

"Mostly Irish songs," Laura replied from her seat at the piano. "And ballads Liam has written. But we're fast learners."

Liam scowled, but she ignored him and started to play one of their songs. When she began singing the verse, Liam did not join in. Laura looked hurt.

"C'mon Liam! Sing with me." Intimidated, he joined in half-heartedly.

"Not bad," Jon said politely. "Jen and I will do a song now."

They were quite good, making the teenagers from Ireland seem average. Liam was not about to be upstaged, though, and when Jon started playing a Beatles song, Liam not only joined in, but overpowered him. When they finished, someone in the back of the room began clapping—and it was not the steward.

"Hello there! You kids sound good. How long have you been playing together?"

Jon looked at his watch. "About an hour. Hi, my name is Jon and this is my sister Jen—we just met Laura and Liam tonight at dinner."

"I'm Greg, the drummer for Foolish Pleasure." He was in his late twenties, with wild blond hair and green eyes, and a medium build but well-muscled arms. Jon and Jen jumped up to shake his hand. Laura gave him a big smile and waved. Liam just nodded and looked away.

"We're playing every night in the Rock 'N Roll club," Greg said. "Come by tomorrow around two, when we're rehearsing. Maybe you kids could play a set."

Everyone but Liam was excited and thanked him. Greg wished them a good evening and left. Liam looked at the clock above the bar.

"One o'clock—that's late for me. I'm going to turn in. Laura, get your wrap."

"Where are you going?" Jon protested. "The night is young."

"Liam's right," Jen interjected. "It's been a long day. We'd better call it a night. We'll probably sleep in. See you tomorrow after lunch?"

"Sure," Laura replied. "Where shall we meet you?"

"At the Rock 'N Roll club," Jon answered, flashing a big smile at Laura.

Liam took Laura's hand and quickly rushed her towards the door with a final, "Goodnight!"

A moment later, Laura pulled away. "Why did you order me to leave?"

"Why did you tell them we'd meet them?"

"Why not? They're fun to be with, and they're good singers."

Liam lowered his head and sighed. "I'm sorry. I just feel uncomfortable around them—especially Jon. I don't like the way he looks at you."

"He doesn't mean anything by it. Just give them a chance."

Reluctantly, Liam nodded agreement.

Once they were back at Laura's suite and had the door shut, Liam took her into his arms. "You look so wonderful tonight. I don't want to share you with anyone!"

Laura was flattered, but didn't want to encourage his jealousy. "Liam, you're going to have to trust me. I'm not interested in anyone but you. But we have to meet other people and interact with them some time in our lives."

"I don't want things to change. You're my life, and I don't want to share you."

"I feel the same way, but we can't live in the shelter of Montrose Manor forever."

"I'll try to be friends with Jon and Jen. It's not easy for me, you know. I'm shy."

"Oh, I do know, Monkey Boy!"

∽ Chapter Twenty-Five ∾

L aura was disappointed that none of the Bianchis showed up at breakfast. Still, she talked excitedly about their experience playing music in the lounge.

"Today we're going to meet them in the Rock 'N Roll club!"

Hannah frowned. "I certainly hope you are not going to start playing that loud music. And that boy Jon looks like a wild hooligan."

Aidan shook his head. "Now Hannah, I think it's wonderful the children have found friends with the same interest. Jon's simply following the current styles in America—he's a nice boy from a good family." Laura smiled, pleased with her father.

"I'm sure you'll all have fun," Aidan remarked. Liam, more interested in eating than talking about Jon, hadn't said a word.

That afternoon Laura and Liam arrived at the club to find Foolish Pleasure rehearsing. Liam liked the band and their style. Laura picked up a tambourine and started shaking it while she danced around.

Greg smiled as he watched her. "Hey, the girl has real rhythm!"

"And she's a real looker," Jon said from behind the mixing board where he was eyeing the vast array of VU meters.

"We ought to have her in the band," Greg quipped. "The guys in the audience would rather look at this pretty little thing then my mug!"

Liam was irritated by the remarks and ready to speak out when one of the band members handed him a guitar.

"Let's hear your stuff."

Laura sat at the piano and began playing the opening to one of Liam's love ballads. Liam took the lead, and Laura joined at the chorus.

The harmony worked well, and Greg was impressed. "Very nice!"

"Good job," the guitarist chimed in.

"Guys, why don't we take a break and let these kids entertain us." He stood up from the drum set and handed Jen his sticks. "Your brother says you drum, too."

"My sister has many hidden talents—if you give her a chance." Jon winked at Liam, who wasn't sure what he meant—and wasn't sure he wanted to know.

Jon thanked Greg for the use of the instruments, and then turned to Liam. "I think Jen and I could learn your song."

Liam started again, and after the chorus, he allowed space for a solo. Jon's guitar work added a colorful dimension, and when the song ended the members of Foolish Pleasure applauded. Even Liam was pleased.

The veteran band decided to take an extra-long break to listen to this new talent. The teenagers spent most of the afternoon playing. They worked through four of Liam's songs. At one point, a young cocktail waitress, quite taken with Jon, flashed him a big smile and brought him a beer on the house.

Greg found this amusing. "Jon, I see you've already got a fan club."

"What can I say?" Jon replied, throwing up his hands. "They love me."

"Listen," Greg said, putting his hand to his chin. "How would you guys like to play a set during our break tonight? We'll see how it goes, and take it from there."

"You bet!" Jon replied. "What time should we be here?"

"You'll start when we break around eleven." A big grin came to Jon's face as he shook hands vigorously with Greg. Jon turned to the others and shrugged.

"Well—we're committed now! It's sink or swim…when they throw us overboard."

Even Liam laughed, in spite of being bothered that Jon made the agreement.

Laura could tell something was bothering Liam when they returned to her suite. She gently touched his face.

"What are you worried about? The performance—or Jon?"

"I'm actually looking forward to the music," Liam said. "But Jon…"

"C'mon," Laura sighed. "I think you really like him. He makes you laugh."

"All right—he's funny—and he's a good guitarist, but sexy...I don't see it."

"I'm afraid you'd have to be a woman to see it." Laura flashed him a coy smile.

Liam shook his head. "You really know how to rattle me."

"Monkey Boy, you know you're the only one for me. Relax and have fun! Here we are on a grand cruise with kids our age—and playing music with a well-known rock band."

"I know you're right, Laura. I'll try."

The young musicians reported early to the Rock 'N Roll club and played four songs during Foolish Pleasure's break. They were well-received, and Greg told Jon they were welcome to play every night at the same time. Everybody agreed. Satisfied, Greg returned to the stage with his band to do their next set.

"We need to celebrate!" Jon exclaimed. "Let's go find a hot tub."

"I'm in!" Laura said excitedly. Jen agreed, and everyone turned to Liam.

"I guess so," he shrugged, knowing he was out-voted.

They met later at the pool deck, minus Jon. Jen removed her cover-up to reveal her skimpy bathing suit.

"I love your bikini!" Laura said. "I want to get one just like it."

"Thanks," she said, glancing at Liam to see if he noticed. "They have them at the gift shop."

The thought of Laura in a revealing bikini with Sexy Boy around worried Liam.

Jon walked up with a devilish look on his face. "Guess what I scored?" Out of a towel, he pulled a bottle of Dom Perignon champagne and four plastic cups.

"Where did you get that?" Liam asked.

Jon grinned. "Well, I sort of...borrowed it from my father's suite. Room service brought two bottles while I was there, and I thought Father should share the wealth! Besides, he'll never remember if he ordered one bottle or two."

"That's for sure," Jen agreed. "He's a great businessman, but when he's on vacation, he misses the little things."

Liam shook his head. "Laura, I don't think we should."

"C'mon!" Jon laughed. "We're celebrating the beginning of our music careers!"

"One glass won't hurt anything," Laura said. Once again Liam was out-voted.

Jen admired Liam's great body while sipping her first glass of champagne. *He must work out—he's got such broad shoulders.* Just then Liam turned to reach for his glass and Jen noticed the scars on his back.

"Liam, what happened to your back?" she asked with concern.

Liam turned red. "It's a long story, and we don't need to get into it."

Jon was enjoying himself and didn't notice Liam's awkwardness. "I've got an idea! How about we stow away on the ship for months and never go back to school." The girls laughed.

"We could earn our keep playing music in the club," Laura added.

"I don't think I'd like missing school," Liam said. "I have plans for the future."

"Music is my future," Jon said, grabbing the bottle. "Here, you need a refill." Before Liam could refuse, Jon filled the glass again. Liam drank the second glass of champagne and began to relax enough to laugh.

"We must do this every night after our gig," Jon suggested. They all cheered and agreed. The excitement of performing live with an established rock band was contagious, and drinking champagne in the hot tub was the perfect way to celebrate. The four were feeling very grown-up.

The second night's performance was even better, with more in attendance.

"Hey Greg," Jon asked after the show. "Do you think you could score us a bottle of champagne, as a kind of …tip?"

Greg smiled, remembering when he was that age. "Sure—why not? They comp us with drinks, so I'll order a bottle for you guys. Promise me that's all you'll drink."

"Sure, man! You're really cool—thanks."

The next day, the teenagers rehearsed in the early afternoon, and Jon felt hunger pangs when they were finished.

"Let's grab a burger and fries on the Lido," he said.

"Well," Liam replied, "I've never had a burger and fries—but it sounds like food."

"You're kidding...right?" Jon asked, disbelieving. Liam shook his head.

"I've never had them, either," Laura confessed.

Jon put his hand to his forehead. "You two must have just climbed out of the potato patch. Hamburgers and fries are a staple of the American teenage diet. Please don't tell me the champagne was your first drink."

Liam was embarrassed. "I'm afraid we're a little behind your American ways."

"Not a problem," Jon assured. "Hang with me, and I'll catch you up to speed."

"Laura, what are we in for now?" Liam asked.

Jon wiggled his eyebrows suggestively, and Jen rolled her eyes.

It wasn't long until Liam was on his third burger—with all the trimmings.

"By the way," he said, picking up a French fry, "in Ireland we call them chips."

"Whatever you call them," Jon said, "I think you've got the hang of it."

The week went by quickly, with the four enjoying their music together. Liam learned a lot from Jon on the guitar, and Jon really liked Liam's singing and song writing. "I hate for this cruise to come to an end tomorrow," Jon sighed. "We're getting so good together."

"How long will you be in New York?" Jen asked. "Do you think you guys could come and stay at our home for a while?"

"That's a great idea!" Jon exclaimed. "Let's talk to our folks about it."

As much as Liam wanted to play music with these new friends, he still wanted his time alone with Laura. He tried to signal her not to accept the invitation, but she ignored him, thrilled by the idea.

"I'll definitely ask my father," she said cheerfully. Liam rolled his eyes.

Jen began talking about the Captain's Gala dinner which was only a few hours away. She had just started describing her dress when Jon jumped up.

"I've got to go!"

"Me too—I'll go with you," Laura said. Before Liam could say a word, the two were gone.

Laura found her father having a drink with the Captain. "Father, may I talk with you?"

"If you'll excuse me, Daniel—I've hardly seen my daughter all week, and now she wants to talk to me."

"I've got things to attend to anyway." Captain Riley tipped his hat and left.

"Father, Liam and I have become best friends with Jon and Jen. They've invited us to go to their home in New York and stay for a few days. Can we, please?"

"Laura, you know we only planned to stay in New York for one week, and I want you to see all the sights."

"Please? It would mean so much to us..." Laura gave him a pleading look with her big brown eyes. Aidan shook his head in defeat.

"I'll talk to Robert and Catherine about this tonight and see what we can come up with. Now, Hannah was looking for you—something about a hair appointment."

"Oh, I forgot—I have to hurry! 'Bye, Father. I love you." Laura rushed directly off to the beauty salon. The stylist was just finishing with Hannah when Laura showed up.

"I'm sorry I'm late. Can I still get my hair done?" The beautician smiled.

"I can get started right now, but you might be a little late for the Gala."

"Thank you," Laura sighed.

Hannah stood up to leave. "We shall see you later, dear."

Laura took a seat and glanced at the person in the chair next to her. To her surprise, it was Jon. "What are you doing here?"

"I decided to get a haircut. It's always easier to persuade my father when I have shorter hair."

"Oh Jon, I like your hair. Don't cut it off."

"Don't worry—I'll just have it cut to my shoulders and styled so it looks neater."

It wasn't long before the other beautician finished with Jon and he was on his way. It took a while longer for Laura's style. She thanked the hairdresser and ran off.

Laura quickly put on her long, black, beaded gown. The torso was form-fitting, low-cut, with spaghetti straps. While applying her lipstick, Laura saw a card and a small gardenia on the dressing table. She read Liam's note.

Laura, I've looked everywhere for you. I hope to see you soon at the Captain's dinner. Love, Liam.

Laura pinned the gardenia in her hair and hurried off.

Meanwhile, Liam's frustration was building as he continued to look for her. He ran into Jen just outside the Princess Grille.

"Jen, have you seen Laura anywhere?"

"No I haven't—and Jon seems to be missing, too. We might as well join our parents at the table. Those two will show up eventually."

"Jennifer, you look very pretty tonight," Robert said when Liam and Jen arrived. "Where's that brother of yours?"

"Oh, he'll be along."

"Liam, is Laura on her way?" Aidan asked.

Liam shrugged. "It always takes her a long time."

Standing at the top of the Grand Stairway was Jon, looking quite dapper in his tuxedo, with his newly styled hair. He was taking in the lively scene below him. From behind, he heard the sound of hurried footsteps and the rustling of a ball gown. He turned to see the breathtaking image of Laura, with her blonde, cascading ringlets sweeping across her bare shoulders as she ran.

"Wow...Laura! You look so...hot!" He smoothed his tuxedo as he regained his composure. His tone softened. "May I escort you to your table, Miss Meegan?"

Laura smiled, and Jon bowed slightly as he offered her his arm. He returned her smile with a penetrating glow uniquely his own. No female was immune when Jon's deep blue eyes made contact with hers.

Arm-in-arm, they glided down the staircase, both of them caught up in the thrill of the moment, enjoying the attention—and feeling very grown-up.

Jon chuckled. "Here we are, looking so high-class, and I'm sure I'm going to trip on your gown and fall flat on my face." Laura giggled again, and Jon added, "I guess that would really be a grand entrance." That was all it took for Laura to laugh out loud.

In the dining room, several conversations faltered—including at the Meegan-Bianchi table. The onlookers were now silenced, looking in awe at the approaching pair.

"That handsome young couple is having a grand time," Hannah remarked.

Liam choked on his bread when he saw Laura on Jon's arm.

"Look at Jon," Jen remarked. "He looks like a model, right out of GQ."

Jon's charisma was undeniable as he escorted Laura to her chair, pulling it out for her. Glancing at his parents, he took a little bow.

"Well, what you think?"

Catherine touched her son's arm. "You look so handsome!" she gushed.

"Nice job with the hair," Robert added.

"My darling daughter," Aidan praised. "You look magnificent— a lady of the world, to be sure."

Laura beamed, and then looked to Liam, but he turned away. The waiters began serving the many courses of wonderful cuisine to satisfy every palate—except Liam's. While everyone else seemed to be having a wonderful time, Liam's face went red, and his hands were shaking.

Laura was the only one to notice Liam's upset. *I've really done it now.*

Before dessert, Jon got up from the table and excused himself. Liam jumped up and followed him, and Laura knew she would have to intervene. Just then her father touched her arm.

"Laura, now would be a good time to discuss your idea for a visit with the Bianchis." Robert and Catherine smiled at her, and now she was stuck.

"Jon, we need to talk," Liam said sharply when he caught up with the American.

Jon was startled by Liam's tone, but responded with his usual good nature. "Sure, Liam—what's on your mind?"

"I want to know what's going on with you and Laura."

"Not as much as I'd like!" Jon had no idea that was a very wrong answer.

Liam narrowed his eyes and set his jaw firmly. He clenched his fists and his breathing got heavier. Jon picked up on the body language and took a step backwards.

"Hey, man, it's a joke! Lighten up! I think she's cute but nothing's going on."

"What about that entrance together? And what were you doing alone with her earlier, when nobody could find you?" Liam took a step towards Jon.

"Nothing! We both got our hair styled! Hey, you're worrying about nothing. I value you guys as friends. I would never hurt your sister."

Liam unclenched his fists and lowered his head. "She's not my sister."

"She's not? But I thought—"

Taking a deep breath, Liam leaned against the rail, looking emotionally drained. "It's true—she isn't my sister. Aidan Meegan is my legal guardian. My parents are both dead. They worked for him, and I was just the poor stable boy. Now Lord Meegan, as they call him in Ireland, has taken me into his family, and he's sending me to the best schools. He even calls me his son."

Jon put his hand on Liam's shoulder. "None of that makes any difference."

"Well, this might: I'm in love with Laura, and have been since she was a little girl. She loves me, too."

Jon raised his eyebrows and leaned back. "Wow! I'm sorry...I didn't know."

"No one knows," Liam said. "And they can't. It would really complicate things."

"Man," Jon pondered while he rubbed his chin. "I guess it would. You're not sleeping with her, are you?"

"No! We're not stupid—just crazy in love. We both want to go to college, and I want to establish a career before we tell everyone. I have to prove I'm worthy of her."

Jon put his arm around Liam. "Thanks for telling me all of this. I'll keep it to myself. I won't even tell Jen—unless you want me to."

Liam was incredibly relieved to finally share his secret with someone. He gave Jon a hug. "It means a lot to me to have you for a friend."

Jon hugged him back. "I feel the same way, Big Guy."

Just then Laura and Jen appeared.

"Hey! What's going on?" Jen asked. "The two best-looking guys on this ship are out in the moonlight, hugging each other?"

Jon turned to the girls. "What? It's not okay for me to think Liam's a hunk?" They all laughed, and Liam blushed as he stepped back.

Laura took Liam's hand. "I need to talk to you," she said sweetly. Liam nodded and they walked off hand in hand to a secluded area. When she started to explain about the hair appointment and dramatic entrance, Liam put his arms around her.

"It's all right Laura—Jon already explained. And now, he knows everything."

"Liam, what do you mean *everything?*"

"I told him you're my girl."

Laura impulsively kissed him, with elated spirit. Liam indulged in the passion, responding with an emotional surrender that was the culmination of everything he'd been going through that evening. Suddenly, he came to his senses and pulled back.

"Laura, we need to be careful. Someone will see us."

"But I'm so happy! You told someone I'm your girl."

"I admit it felt good to say it. And I trust Jon—he's my friend."

"Can I tell Jen? She's my friend, and I trust her."

"Yes—tell her—but make sure she understands their parents can never find out."

Liam pulled Laura in for another kiss. "By the way, you look exceptionally wonderful tonight." She gave him *that smile*.

They got back to the table just in time. The Grand Finale had begun, with the lights dimmed and the waiters parading with trays of Baked Alaska Flambé. The orchestra was playing *When the Saints Come Marching In.*

Laura's eyes sparkled, as did Liam's—and only he and Laura knew why.

With his spirits lifted, Liam's appetite returned. He ate three servings of the Baked Alaska. When he finished, his gaze fixed hungrily on Laura's plate. She laughed easily and pushed her uneaten dessert in his direction.

Jon was explaining to his parents that Liam was a good influence on him.

"See? I cut my hair—and he's even got me thinking about college."

"Can we adopt Liam?" Robert asked. Catherine nodded and they laughed.

There was no more need for Jon to sell the idea of taking Laura and Liam in as guests. It was all settled—they were going to spend a week in the city, seeing all the sights, followed by a week at the Bianchi home. Aidan and Hannah would to return to Ireland as scheduled. Laura and Liam would fly home on the Concorde by themselves.

The QE2 docked early the next morning in New York harbor. They were all sad to see the cruise come to an end. Saying their goodbyes to the members of Foolish Pleasure, the teenagers thanked them for the opportunity to perform.

Greg turned to Liam. "Remember, I'm serious about your songs. I want you to send me a few, especially that one—*I Remember When.* You guys have a lot of talent. Keep up the good work."

The Bianchis and the Meegans hugged each other and parted. Just before the Bianchis got into their limousine, Jon turned to Liam.

"Hey, Big Guy! We'll see you and the pretty one in a week!"

⟨ᴼ *Chapter Twenty-Six* ᴼ⟩

New York City lived up to every expectation of what a major metropolis should be: a colorful palette of endless activity. The tourists from Ireland wasted no time taking in all the sights. Their eyes fixed on the Statue of Liberty as she stood proud and tall guarding the harbor, with Ellis Island just across the water.

"Over twenty million immigrants came through here hoping for a new life in America," Aidan said solemnly as he gazed out to the east. A deep feeling of respect came over Liam—a kinship with these wayward souls who came from nothing.

A carriage ride through Central Park was next on the agenda, and Laura lost herself in memories of Ol' Tommy pulling the carriage at Chloe and Patrick's wedding.

Liam was surprised at the vastness of the park. "It gives you a sense of being on a green island in the middle of an ocean of city."

The Meegan family had fabulous rooms at the Waldorf Astoria Hotel. They enjoyed a wonderful dinner, and then took a ferry tour of New York harbor. After nightfall, the flickering lights of the city skyscrapers formed indelible images in the minds of the two teenagers.

Aidan had been to New York City many times, and he wanted to make sure Laura and Liam saw as much as possible. He had planned a full week, and each morning at breakfast he would go over the day's itinerary. The second day they saw a show at Radio City Music Hall, and then went to Rockefeller Center and the St Patrick's Cathedral.

The next day, at the Empire State Building, Liam's anticipation heightened. He recalled what he had read before leaving Ireland. "Get ready for a long elevator ride—it's 102 floors to the observatory."

When they stepped out at the top, Liam was in disbelief. "The cars and people look like ants. This is spectacular—I'll never forget this."

"You can see forever!" Laura added.

The days and nights were filled with so many activities that Laura and Liam, in spite of their youth, began to show signs of fatigue.

Between the tours, the shopping, and shows on Broadway, the simple Irish country kids were no match for the Big Apple.

Liam could have spent days at the Metropolitan Museum. His knowledge of the historical periods was impressive. Aidan said he was pleased to see the young man's appreciation for both art and artifact.

Times Square at night is a spectacle known to millions, and the fourteen-year-old girl from Ireland was the latest to be mesmerized by the myriad of lights.

"Have you ever seen anything so bright?" she asked.

"The only thing brighter is the sparkle in your eyes," Liam whispered. Laura flashed him a smile. It was one of the few stolen moments they had together that week.

The day arrived for Aidan to return to his business concerns in Ireland. Before he and Hannah left for the airport, Aidan hired a car for Laura and Liam. He took Liam aside while they waited for the limousine to arrive.

"Son, your attention to detail is remarkable—whether you're critiquing a sculpture at the Met or studying the barrel-vaulted ceilings at Grand Central Station. I have every confidence that after your visit with the Bianchis, you'll get yourself and Laura safely home. You're very mature for your age, and I have a great deal of trust in you."

They embraced, and Liam felt a special pride in having earned Aidan's respect. The day would surely come when he would be able to ask Aidan for his daughter's hand.

After receiving a generous tip in advance from Aidan, the limousine driver made a point of going well beyond the normal courtesies for his young passengers.

"The North Shore of Long Island is where real estate is expensive and only the richest of the rich live. And if you don't believe it, just ask 'em—they're proud of it!"

Liam chuckled while he gazed out at the rugged North Shore terrain, dropping to the sea in a series of bluffs, coves, and wooded headlands. The private estates were magnificent, surrounded by acres of groomed land. Finally the limo pulled into a long, winding tree-lined drive, which led to a large, two-story stone manor with prominent front columns of imported white Italian marble.

A moment later, Jen came running out the door to greet them.

"Laura! Liam! You're here!"

"Hello!" Laura answered as she and Liam got out. The girls embraced while Liam stretched.

"Where's Jon?" he asked.

"He's washing his car. He'll catch up with us in a while." Liam raised his eyebrows, impressed that Jon had his own car.

After the travelers settled into their rooms, Jen took them downstairs where Jon was waiting. Without a word, he swooped Laura up and whirled her around.

"I've really missed you, girl! I can't believe it's only been a week." Jon's next stunt was to jump into Liam's arms. "I've missed you too, Big Guy!" Everyone laughed as Liam dropped Jon on a nearby couch.

"After lunch, Jon can take us for a drive to show you some of the island," Jen said.

"You have a driver's license already?" Liam asked. "In Ireland you have to be eighteen."

"Wow!" Jon exclaimed. "That's a long time to wait. Here it's sixteen. Now...you have to check out our studio." He led the way to the to the huge basement room, complete with separate glass booths for drums and vocals. Each headset had its own controls, and the entire layout was clearly designed for performing and recording.

"I can't believe this. It's amazing!" Liam exclaimed. He looked at the lighted mixing board and effects boxes. "It looks like some kind of starship with all the lights. Can you make your own recordings?"

"That's what it's all about," Jon replied smugly.

"I think I would live in this room," Liam sighed.

"He just about does!" Jen laughed. "He only comes out for food."

Jon smiled sarcastically. "We'll get back in here soon enough, and you two will find out how much of an appetite we can work up. But first, let me introduce you to my baby." They followed Jon to the six-car garage, where he presented his black Trans Am T-Top with gold trim that looked like it had just rolled off the showroom floor.

"Is this your car?" Liam asked.

Jon smiled proudly. "My father's going to let me drive it for the week you're here."

"How come you can only drive it this week?" Laura asked.

"I'll answer that," Jen quipped. "You see, Jon doesn't seem to understand the meaning of the words speed limit. One more ticket and he'll have his license revoked."

"My father's very uptight about bending the rules," Jon moaned.

"Father is concerned you will have an accident," Jen corrected. "You've only been driving for eight months."

"Yeah, I get the picture," Jon griped. "If I drive like a little old lady, and then I can have my keys back. Now let's go for a spin!" Liam helped Jon take the top off, and they all climbed in.

The Irish teenagers had never been cruising before. As Jon got out on the open road, they were thrilled by the sense of freedom, with another teenager driving—and having no particular place to go. With the top off and the latest rock music playing loudly, they felt very grown-up.

"That's great guitar on the radio," Liam remarked. "What band is it?"

"It's The Police," Jon replied. Liam looked blank, not recognizing the name. "They *are* from your side of the pond—England. Well, anyway, they're really hot."

They enjoyed the scenic drive through the small villages on the way to the harbor. People were out and about in every town, some shopping and some—particularly the younger ones—cruising around in their fancy cars, just like Jon and company.

At a stop light, a convertible pulled alongside. "Hey, Bianchi!" the driver yelled. "What's the matter—you got car trouble? You're driving slower than my grandma!" The young heckler and his car mates all laughed uproariously. Jon gave him a hand gesture, and they were left in the dust by the other car when the light changed.

Jon drove down to the marina. "Let's go check out our sailboat."

"You have your own sailboat, too?" Laura asked, surprised.

"She belongs to my father," Jon laughed, "but he never takes her out. Jen and I do, all the time. Tomorrow, if the wind is up, we'll take you sailing."

Jon brought the car to a stop. When they stepped out, Liam was awed by the rows of expensive yachts in their private berths.

"I've never seen so many beautiful boats in one place. Which one is yours?"

"The long white one right over there. Technically she is an offshore cruising yacht. The *Sienna Sun* is a Cape George thirty-six-foot cutter."

It was a short walk down the ramp, but Liam stood back for a moment to take in the sleek design of the vessel. Jon unlocked the main cabin door and they all boarded, Laura and Liam in wonderment. The yacht was true perfection, with all the latest equipment and appointments, including beautiful mahogany wood throughout.

"It's a real beauty!" Liam said. "Is this how all American teenagers live?"

"Not as many as you might think," Jen said. "Jon and I are blessed with successful parents who also happen to be generous." She looked at her brother. "We appreciate it—unlike some of our friends, who think it's their birthright to have the best."

Jon agreed. "I don't plan to live off my parents' money forever like some guys I know. I plan to make something of myself."

"Me, too," Jen agreed.

"I admire that," Liam said. "It would be too easy to just indulge and never earn your keep, but I wouldn't feel very good about myself."

"What do you guys do for entertainment?" Jon asked.

"Well," Liam said, looking at Laura, "I read a lot, we ride horses almost every day...and let's not forget—we play music."

Dinner at the Bianchi Estate was, in the old Italian tradition, always an event of sorts, with lively conversation and an array of interesting dishes.

Mr. Bianchi turned to Laura and Liam. "I trust you're enjoying yourselves on Long Island so far." They nodded enthusiastically. "Liam, you're a very good influence on Jon. He's planning to continue his education—maybe even abroad."

"Thank you, Mr. Bianchi," Liam replied. "I'm glad to hear that. Jon, you should consider going to Trinity College with me."

"I'd like to check it out...Hey! I could come visit you guys."

"What about me?" Jen cried. "Can I go, too?" she asked, looking at her parents.

"Maybe," Robert said thoughtfully, "we can arrange for the both of you to go for a visit later this summer. I'll talk to Aidan about it."

"Oh!" Laura exclaimed. "That would be wonderful!" The teenagers talked excitedly about the possibilities.

After dinner the young group went for a walk around the estate to the cliffs, where they enjoyed a dramatic view of the sea. A gentle breeze cooled the warm balmy night. Jen shivered, rubbing her arms.

"Let's go inside—to the music studio."

They all filed in, Jen to her drum set and Jon to the Marshall Stack amplifier his guitar was plugged into. There were two more guitars in stands next to another Marshall. Liam was again overwhelmed by the vast array of equipment.

"Go ahead," Jon said with a wave of the hand. "Choose your weapon."

"The red guitar looks good to me," Liam said, picking it up.

"It's a pretty nice axe," Jon said with a smile. Liam assumed the slang term referred to the guitar, and switched it on.

"I think you'll like the keyboards, Laura," Jen said. "We've got a Fender Rhodes and a Mini Moog." She walked over and turned everything on for Laura, showing her the functions of the knobs on the synthesizer.

Laura played a tone that sounded like a string section. "This is brilliant!"

They started off with a jam session. Laura had fun trying out different timbres.

"How come you have so many instruments for just the two of you?" Liam asked.

Jon grinned. "Well, my father's got the idea that if he keeps buying us the latest equipment it'll keep us home more often—and out of trouble."

"Like driving around in fast cars," Jen quipped. Jon sneered at her.

"Our musician friends hang out here because we've got the best gear. I guess my father's pretty smart." Jon hit a power chord, and the group was on to another song. They played until they ran out of steam.

"I don't know about you guys, but I'm beat," Jen said with a yawn.

"Me too," Laura agreed. They switched off the amps and headed for their rooms.

A few minutes later there was a knock on Liam's door.

"Come in, Laura."

"How did you know it was me?" she asked, closing the door behind her.

"Well, I didn't think it would be Mr. Bianchi coming to tuck me in," he smiled.

"I miss spending time alone with you," Laura said sadly. "Can I have a hug?" Liam took her into his arms and kissed her tenderly.

"I miss our time together, too, Laura Lye. This is all exciting and fun, but I'm looking forward to going home."

"Me too. I feel so immature—like a little girl who's never been anywhere."

Liam nodded. "I know Jon is only eighteen months older than me, but he's done so many things I feel like he's ten years older."

"But sometimes he can act like he's ten years younger," Laura laughed. That brought a smile to Liam's face, and he kissed her goodnight.

❧

Morning sun danced through the windows, bringing a clear day but no wind.

"After breakfast we'll take a drive to the beach," Jon announced. "Grab your swim suits and a towel."

The cook asked if they would like a picnic lunch, and Jon flashed a big smile at her. "No, thank you, Isabella—you need a break from all your hard work." The small Portuguese woman giggled and patted Jon on the cheek.

"I bet you haven't tried New York pizza yet." Jon said. Laura shook her head.

"We've never had pizza—of any kind."

Jon threw up his hands. "You've got to be kidding, right? You're serious? We'll have to fix that. Kids in America need pizza like kids in Ireland need...What do you guys eat, anyway?" They all laughed.

Jon drove along the winding coastline until they came to a beautiful beach with golden sand, where they stopped and spread out towels. When the girls came out of the changing room Laura was wearing a new bikini she bought on the cruise ship. Liam was quite taken with her, but he was torn between the impulse to cover her up and the urge to kiss her passionately. He blushed at his own thoughts.

Jon yelled, interrupting Liam's fantasy, "Last one in the water has to wash my car!" Jon was already at a dead run when Liam jumped to his feet. He sprinted easily past the not-too-tall American and jumped into the water first. Jon was the next one in, with Laura soon to follow. Jen stopped short of the water, putting her hands on her hips.

"I'll accept my defeat, but we're taking it to the drive-through car wash."

"Drive-through car wash?" Laura asked while looking at Liam.

Jon laughed. "You two are really going to have to catch up to the eighties!"

Liam splashed Jon in the face and they played like young children. He tried to wrestle Liam under the water unsuccessfully—but not without a great deal of effort from the bigger teenager. Liam was impressed at how strong Jon was for his size.

Jen and Laura, back on the beach, had retreated from the ruffians.

"Look at my brother. Why do guys always have to play around like that? Is it to prove who's the strongest?"

"Liam's never had anyone to wrestle with," Laura smiled. "He's really enjoying being with Jon. You know, Liam was an only child and his parents both died not long ago. I'm all he has." Jen gave her a hug.

"He's very lucky to have you, Laura."

"No, I'm the lucky one." She gazed affectionately at Liam.

"I feel blessed to have Jon for a brother," Jen sighed. "He's only eighteen months older than I am, but he's always taken care of me." Her contented look faded. "I've been worried about him the last couple of years, though. All of his wild parties, drinking, smoking pot—and sex with different girls..."

Laura's eyes widened. "Jon does all those things?"

"I'm afraid so, but not so much since school got out. And since he met Liam, he's almost turned into a saint."

"Jen, have you..."

"Go ahead and ask me, Laura."

"Well...do you do all those things?" Jen shook her head.

"I've tried smoking pot—I really don't like it. And drinking—maybe a little champagne, like on the ship, but not getting drunk like some of the kids. And sex? No way! Jon would kill me if he found out, and I really haven't met...that special guy. What about you?"

Laura's eyes widened again. "Oh, no! The first drink Liam and I ever had was the champagne on the ship. And, forget about the other two things." Laura blushed, feeling young and inexperienced again. The heart-to-heart was interrupted when Liam and Jon came up, shaking cold water all over the girls.

"You two are as welcome as a couple of wet dogs!" Jen yelled.

Jon just shrugged. "I'm starving!" he said. "Let's go to Pizza Mia's." The others agreed, so they changed into dry clothes and jumped into the car.

"I wish I had a hairbrush," Laura complained. "Then maybe I could do something with this wet mop of mine."

"That's why I cut my hair short," Jen replied. "I just run my fingers through it."

"I love your long hair, Laura," Liam said. "I have a comb. I'll help you braid it."

Jen looked from Liam to Laura in disbelief. "If I had a guy who was willing to braid my hair for me, I would have left it long."

"Not many guys can braid hair," Jon laughed.

"Liam braids ropes for the horses at home," Laura said.

"Oh, I'm not making fun of him," Jon said. "I'd love to be able to braid your hair...Wait—that didn't come out right!" They all laughed.

Pizza Mia's was packed with kids doing what American teenagers do best—eating and hanging out. Jon and Jen knew almost everyone, and they introduced their new friends. Jon's best buddy from school was sitting at the next table.

"Chad, we want to take the *Sienna Sun* out tomorrow if the wind is up. I could use another set of hands."

While eyeing Laura, Chad answered, "It would be my pleasure."

Jon's ex-girlfriend, Donna, was at the same table. "Can I come, too, Jon?" she asked sweetly.

"I guess," he said with a shrug.

Jon ordered the pizzas, and while they waited some other guys came to the table.

"Hey, Jon—long time no see. You've only missed about a dozen really great parties. What gives, man?"

"Have you nothing better to do?" Jon replied with a wave of the hand.

"Sooorry, man," the boy replied sarcastically. As he turned to rejoin his buddies he muttered snidely, "What's up with him? Does he think he's too good for us now that he has these Euro-friends?"

Laura and Liam were embarrassed by the comments.

"Don't pay any attention to those creeps," Jen said. "They need to grow up."

Just then the focus shifted to the hot pizzas being served. It didn't take long before the two large pans were empty. Liam ate most of the pepperoni pizza by himself.

"Well, how did you like it?" Jen asked when they were out by the car.

"The pizza was great." Laura answered. "But I think it was a little noisy there."

"That's a fact," Jon said. "They're like a pack of wild animals."

"You'd never know these kids come from families in the social register," Jen added. "None of them have any manners. Sorry about those rude boys earlier."

By mid-morning the next day there was a nice breeze.

"It's going to be a perfect day for sailing," Jon announced after breakfast.

"How long did it take you to learn to sail?" Liam asked.

"Not long. It's not all that complicated. I'll teach you if you want."

"I'd love to learn."

"You got it!" Jon said.

The cook appeared. "Excuse me, Jon. I make you a picnic lunch today?"

He smiled. "That would be great, Isabella."

"Four people?"

"No—there are two more—six. Thank you very much." She nodded and left. Jon sighed. "I almost forgot Donna. I can't believe she's still speaking to me."

"I don't know how you do it," Jen laughed. "You break a girl's heart, and she still wants to be with you."

Liam shook his head. "You broke her heart? And now you're seeing her again?"

"Well," Jen explained, "he's running out of girls on the island. He has to start recycling." Everyone laughed except Jon.

"Hey! I didn't ask them to fall in love with me. I can't help it if I'm charming."

Once aboard the *Sienna Sun*, Liam closely watched every move Jon made. With help from Chad and Jen, Jon maneuvered the yacht out of the harbor like he'd done it a thousand times. Soon the three had the sails up and they were underway.

"Now that we're out in the open, I'll show you how to handle her," Jon said. He began to show Liam the changes that came about in speed and direction as he worked the sails. Liam was a fast learner, and Jon didn't have to repeat any instruction twice.

Liam discovered the *Sienna Sun* was more than just beautiful— he could see what Jon meant about the yacht being seaworthy. He began to feel like his spirit was already in the right place for the world of sailing. To Liam, working the sails was somehow similar to the process of training a young colt on long lines. A sailboat and a colt were both wild forces he could tame—if he paid attention to all the elements.

With the wind in his hair and sea mist in his face, Liam took the helm with a feeling of exhilaration. The flapping of the sails was a unique counterpoint to the swells of the ocean. The rhythm of nature was calming, encouraging his mind to fall right in step with his soul.

Donna flipped her blonde hair back to fix her eyes on Liam. She found him to be worthy of her gaze, but then glanced at Laura, wondering if she would be Jon's next girlfriend. Donna's gaze returned to the muscular Irish teenager with the dark wavy hair.

"Hello? Earth to Donna," Jen said.

"Sorry, I was hypnotized by those incredible blue eyes."

Laura heard this and almost spoke out, but then she thought better of it.

"Forget it, Donna," Jen said. "He's got a beautiful Irish girlfriend." Jen glanced at Laura, who smiled.

About an hour later Jon helped Liam guide the *Sienna* to a sheltered cove. "Let's drop the sails and anchor here for lunch. Isabella made us a gourmet picnic."

In the galley Jen spread out the feast, which the six teenagers proceeded to devour. After they ate, Chad pulled out a bottle of Tequila and shot glasses.

"I brought a little something for dessert. Anyone want a shooter?"

"Sure, why not?" Donna said, smiling at Liam. Chad poured her a shot, and then took one for himself.

"Who's next?" he asked, raising the bottle.

"No, thank you," Liam answered decisively.

"Chad, we shouldn't," Jon said. "I may need your help getting her back in."

"Don't be so uptight," Chad replied as he poured another. "It's just a couple of shooters. Laura, how about you?"

"Oh, I'd better not," she answered. Chad shrugged and downed it himself. He poured another round.

"Take it easy," Jon scowled. "The wind's picking up—I'm going to need you."

"Don't worry," Chad said. "Get her under way—I'll be up." Jon shook his head, disgusted. Liam jumped up and offered to help him.

"I'll be up in a couple minutes," Jen said. "I'm going to tidy up the galley." Jon nodded, and he and Liam went topside to pull up anchor.

Chad refilled the shot glasses, and he and Donna gulped down the drinks. Chad, a tall, good looking blond with a dark suntan, considered himself quite the ladies' man. Some of the girls called him Chad the Cad. He eyed the cute Irish girl as she helped Jen finish with cleanup. Refilling the glasses, he pushed them towards Jen and Laura

"Come on! One shot won't hurt you ladies—or are you just little girls?"

"Okay—but this is it," Jen replied, taking the glass. She downed it quickly. Just then a gust of wind blew through the cabin. "I'd better get topside." Jen headed up and Chad turned to Laura, nodding towards the other glass on the table.

Laura noticed how easily Jen gulped down the tequila. *I am not going to be the only 'little girl'.* She took the shot and downed it in one gulp. Laura's face turned bright red and her eyes filled with tears. The burning sensation took her breath away. Chad started laughing, and Laura was humiliated as she gasped.

"Warms you right up," Chad declared. "That's why all the good sailors keep a bottle aboard. Here, have another, it'll go down easier." Laura was determined to be accepted as an equal, and took the drink. Donna followed suit, and Chad kept pouring, drinking right along with them. By the time Laura swallowed her third shot, she could barely taste it. At that point she was feeling very good—in fact, a little too good.

The skies had darkened and the wind velocity was gaining.

"Chad!" Jon yelled. "You'd better get up here—it's starting to get rough!"

Chad staggered up the stairs and stumbled out onto the deck. Jon shook his head. "Great! You're in no shape to help. Go below and keep Laura and Donna there. Jen, I need you to stay here—and Liam…"

"I'll be wherever you need me," Liam said.

"Thanks!" Jon yelled into the mounting wind. "Just follow my lead!"

Chad stumbled below and turned on the heater. It wasn't long before Donna passed out on the couch, and Chad the Cad took advantage of the situation, leading Laura to the berth in back. She lay down on the bed and started to go to sleep.

"Not so fast, my pretty one," Chad said, taking off his shirt. "I think you owe me a little thank-you." He climbed on top of her, planting a kiss firmly on Laura's mouth while his hands roamed her body. Even in her drunken state, Laura was well aware of his groping. She tried to wrestle free, but with little ability to coordinate, her efforts were useless. Chad ignored her struggling and forced his tongue into her mouth. Laura wanted desperately to cry out to Liam, but she could barely breathe.

On deck, the others literally had their hands full. Jon was shouting orders left and right, but he kept his cool. Jen, not so confident, clearly looked worried as the waves crashed against the hull and onto the deck. She was having a hard time holding her sail. When it whipped around and knocked her over, Liam pulled her up and grabbed the line with his other hand.

Suddenly, they all heard a scream from below deck.

Liam nearly rushed off. Jon looked intently at him, shouting, "I need you here, man!"

"I'll go!" Jen yelled. She rushed down into the cabin to find Chad all over Laura. "Chad! What the hell are you doing? Leave her alone!" Chad jumped up and Jen could plainly see Laura's half-naked body. Jen rushed at him with full force, knocking him against the wall. As Chad crumpled to the floor she began kicking him, her anger unleashed.

Laura staggered up the steps to the deck, dressed only in pants. She fell to her knees, vomiting over the side of the boat.

Liam was shocked but he held his post. He managed to get his windbreaker off to toss over Laura's shoulders. Jen came out with a beach towel and went to Laura's aid.

"Get her back inside before she falls overboard!" Jon yelled. "It's wild out here!"

Jen took Laura below and got her dressed, ignoring Chad, who was passed out on the floor. She figured he wouldn't be a threat to Laura anymore, so Jen rushed back up the stairs to take her place on deck.

The three struggled against the elements, and at last made it safely into the harbor.

Jon stormed into the cabin and found Chad still passed out on the floor.

"Get up!" Jon yelled.

Chad rolled over and groaned, blinking his eyes as he tried to focus. The five-foot-eight-inch tall Jon grabbed the much taller boy and pulled him to his feet. "You loser! How could you do this? She's only fourteen!"

A defiant smirk came to Chad's face. "Hey man, don't get so righteous. I wasn't doing anything you wouldn't have done."

That remark was all it took to send Jon over the edge. In one smooth motion he threw a right cross and sent Chad flying into the wall, where he slumped to the floor again.

"You're lucky it's me and not Liam!" Jon shouted. This time Chad knew enough to keep his mouth shut.

"Now give me your keys," Jon demanded. "You and Donna are taking a taxi home. You can pick up your car tomorrow."

Chad was about to protest, but saw the fury in Jon's eyes. He pulled the keys out of his pocket and tossed them in Jon's direction.

"I was counting on you to help me sail today," Jon scowled. "It got scary out there, and you let us all down. If it wasn't for Liam's help, we could have been in real trouble. Here you were, warm and dry, taking advantage of a young girl who happens to be my guest and my friend. I guess it's not hard to see who your real friends are. Now get off my boat before I throw you off."

Jen helped Laura to the car, while Jon and Liam worked together in silence cleaning up the boat. They had just shared a harrowing experience—and survived. The two friends had formed a bond which did not require any spoken words.

Catherine Bianchi was concerned with Laura's condition when they got home.

"It was real wild out there and Laura got seasick," Jon explained.

"I really don't feel well myself," Jen added. "I'll help Laura to her room—then I'm going to lie down."

"I'm so glad you're home safe," Catherine said. "It was a good idea to take Chad to help you bring the boat in." Jon just glanced at Liam and rolled his eyes.

The girls, emotionally and physically spent, did not join the family for dinner.

"Liam, how did you like the *Sienna Sun?*" Robert asked.

"She's wonderful—and I learned a lot from Jon about sailing."

Jon looked thoughtfully at Liam for a moment, and then spoke. "Father, I think I learned a few things of my own from Liam. I believe it's time I grow up and leave my wild friends behind. I really feel good when I'm with Liam. He makes me think about life—instead of just living for the moment. I trust him—I can depend on him in any situation. He's the kind of person I want to be."

Liam was embarrassed and didn't know what to say, but Robert smiled as he glanced at the young man from Ireland. "I can see Liam is a good person." Robert turned to face Jon again. "Son, it's very important to surround yourself with people you can count on. Some are what you call fair-weather friends. When a storm comes, they take shelter and hide, whereas a true friend will weather the storm right alongside you."

"You got that right!" Jon exclaimed. "Whoa! Now I'm scared—my father's advice is making sense." They all laughed, and Jon put his hand on Liam's shoulder. "Thanks for being there. You are my best friend."

Liam's discomfort faded. "Thank you—that means a lot. I feel the same way."

ᓚᓂ *Chapter Twenty-Seven* ᓂᓯ

The next morning Jen went to Laura's room to see how she was doing.

"Well, I've got a really bad headache," Laura said, rubbing her temples. "And I feel pretty embarrassed."

Jen sat on the bed and massaged Laura's neck. "Do you remember much after drinking the tequila?"

"Not really, but I think Chad had something to do with me having half my clothes off…and then I got sick."

"I had no idea Chad was capable of being such a monster," Jen said. "He's always been a girl-chaser, but you're younger, and you just met him. I'm so sorry."

"Thanks for stopping it when you did." Laura gave Jen a hug.

"It would have been Liam coming to your rescue, but he was needed on deck."

"I know." Laura put her head in her hands.

"Here—I brought you something to make you feel better." Jen handed her two aspirin and a glass of tomato juice.

It wasn't long before Laura did feel better, and the girls joined Jon and Liam in the studio. Laura apologized for her behavior and for having messed up the boat.

"I'll forgive you this time," Jon said, "but next time, you scrub the deck."

Laura was profoundly embarrassed. "There will never be a next time." She turned to Liam. "I promise."

Liam gave her a smile and a hug. "The important thing is that you're all right."

"And I was only kidding about scrubbing the deck," Jon added.

"I know I learned my lesson," Jen added. "Tequila is bad news—and so is Chad."

"He's history in my book," Jon agreed. "All right. Enough—let's play music!" He began strumming his guitar, but was interrupted by a knock on the studio glass. He looked up to see Donna.

"Jon, can I speak to you?"

Jon continued to tune his guitar. "I'm busy. What do you want?"

"Jon, please? Just a few words in private."

He sighed as he put his guitar in the stand. "Excuse me, guys—this won't take long." Jon stepped outside the studio, intentionally leaving the door open. "All right, Donna. What's on your mind?"

"I'm so sorry for getting wasted on your boat yesterday. I know I blew it with you. I really wanted us to get back together, and I was nervous. I thought a shot or two would help."

Jon looked at her with disgust. "That's your problem—you think the answer comes in a bottle. You need professional help. I'm moving on with my life, and I'm leaving the wild parties and people behind—and that includes you."

Donna turned and ran out crying. Everyone had heard, and Jen made a feeble joke. "Jon breaks another heart."

He gave her a dirty look. "I'm not trying to hurt anyone—I'm just being honest with her." Another knock came at the door. "Now what? Oh, Father—sorry. I thought it was Donna again."

"Son, I have tickets for the rock concert at Jones Beach Amphitheater tomorrow night—if anyone's interested."

"Are you kidding? It's the Journey concert! It's been sold out for months! How did you get these?"

"Oh, this old man still has connections. Remember, I have clients in high places."

"Father, you're the greatest!" Jon exclaimed, giving him a hug. The others thanked Robert, and he left with a smile on his face.

Jon turned to Liam. "Wait—let me guess. You guys have never heard any music from Journey, right? They're only the hottest thing going! They should have the best sound and lights and everything."

"I can't wait!" Laura exclaimed.

The next day Laura's enthusiasm was somewhat dampened as they entered the amphitheater. The sheer volume of foot traffic was overwhelming. Laura feared that if she let go of Liam's hand, she would be swallowed up by the crowd. The young Irish girl had never seen so many loud, pushy people in one place.

When Journey began to play, Laura's feeling of intimidation subsided as she shared everyone's enthusiasm for the music and multi-colored light show. Laura could see Liam was completely captivated throughout the performance.

"The lead singer has such a great voice," Laura said in the car on the way home.

"You mean Steve Perry," Jen sighed. "Don't you think he's sexy?"

"I suppose he's cute," Laura replied. Liam rolled his eyes.

"Hey, Big Guy," Jon said. "What did you think of the lead guitarist—Neal Schon?"

"All the musicians are great—their showmanship is brilliant. And Steve Perry—he can hit the highest notes and hold them. Do you guys go to all the concerts?"

"I wish!" Jon replied. "We see as many as we can get tickets for, but sometimes they sell out really fast. During the summer we have all the big name concerts here—sometimes twice a month."

"Wow!" Liam said. "This is all pretty exciting. What a difference from the quiet life Laura and I are used to."

Laura nodded.

The inspiration from the concert stayed with them right into the next day in the studio. Liam had just finished working out the music for a song he'd written about sailing on the *Sienna Sun*. The four of them played it through successfully after three tries.

"I think we're ready to record this song," Jon announced. "Let's give it a shot."

Liam looked at the recording console, which still reminded him of the control panel on a spaceship. "Are we going to be recorded on that big tape in the other room?"

"Well, yeah—that's what it's there for."

"It seems so professional—and expensive. What if we make a mistake?"

Jon chuckled. "Don't worry about it. I've got plenty of tape. Let's try a run-through." Jon pressed the record button. "Ready...one...two...three...four...." Jon hit the first chord and they fell right into step, but Liam was weak on the vocals in the first verse. They finished the song and Jon paused the recorder.

"All right, so you were thinking too much about the tape and not enough about the song. It happens to the best musicians. What we do now is just forget about the tape and just let it roll." He appeared to be in deep thought for a moment. "I've got an idea. Where do you feel the most comfortable working on your songs?"

"That's easy," Liam answered, looking at Laura. "Our cave back home."

"Cave?" Jon asked. "Whatever. Just close your eyes and that's where we are."

Liam agreed and began the process as Jon suggested. A few moments later, an easy smile came to Liam's face and he slowly nodded, his eyes still closed. Jon counted off again, and they did another take.

"Yes!" Jon proclaimed. "We've got it! Now let's listen to it."

After rewinding, Jon hit play. The recording was incredibly clear, and Jon looked pleased. He turned some knobs on the console, adding effects to the vocal track.

"That's just a touch of reverb—almost like a cave." The effect gave Liam's voice more depth and fullness. "Now I'm going to try some overdubs with the Moog." Jon dialed a few knobs on the synthesizer and produced one sound like crashing waves, followed by another like seagulls.

By the time Jon was finished with the mix, the song that started out as a simple story about sailing could have been the soundtrack for a Hollywood movie.

"It sounds like we're professional musicians!" Liam said, grinning at the others.

"Oh—but it could be," Jon replied. "My friends, this is a sign of things to come…"

"We do work well together," Jen said. "But there is this problem of the Atlantic Ocean separating us. How can we be a band?" Laura's smile turned to a frown and Jon shook his head as he looked at the girls.

"You give up too easily," he replied. "Where there's a will, there's a way."

Still smiling, Jon made a cassette copy for each of them. After dinner he played the tape for his parents, and they listened intently.

"It's really good!" Robert exclaimed. "I'm impressed with all of you—and I really like the title, *Sailing the Sienna Sun.*"

"It has a nice ballad feel," Catherine remarked. "It reminds me of some of our best times on the yacht." Jon was thrilled his parents finally approved of—and actually enjoyed—some of his music.

"Laura and Liam, I'm so pleased you have come into my children's lives," Robert said. He studied the four teenagers for a moment, and a sly smile came to his face. "So your departure tomorrow won't be such a sad event, I've been working on having you spend more time together." He had everyone's undivided attention. "I called Aidan yesterday. Jon and Jen can go to Ireland for the last two weeks of their summer vacation."

The teenagers jumped up and hugged each other. Jon was the most excited. He kissed his father on the cheek, and then danced around the room with his mother. It was obvious from Catherine's delight that Jon was the apple of her eye. Jen, hugging her father around the neck, was definitely Daddy's Girl. Her sparkling green eyes and beautiful smile were a reflection of her father's.

Liam's joy turned to melancholy as he thought of his own mother and father. *I wish they were here to be proud of me, like Jon's parents.* "I'm really tired," Liam said. "I think I'll go to bed."

Laura could see the sad expression on his face and knew something was wrong. "I think I'll go, too. Thank you all for everything." She turned and followed Liam upstairs and into his room.

"Liam, why are you sad?" She took him into her arms.

"I'm not sad now. You're here."

"Were you thinking of your parents?" Laura asked compassionately. Liam nodded and his eyes began to get watery.

She kissed him on the cheek. "I think we're both a little homesick."

"You're right. I'm ready to go home—with you—to Montrose Manor."

The next morning on the way to JFK, Jon decided to avoid the sadness of parting by talking about the Concorde.

"You guys are so lucky," he said. "I've heard you fly at 55,000 feet, and you go twice the speed of sound!"

"It will only take three and a half hours to London," Liam replied.

"Father," Jon said, "I think that's how we should fly when we go for our visit."

"Do you, now?" Robert replied, looking in the rear view mirror at his son. "I hear passage on a cargo ship is much more economical."

"Very funny," Jon said with a smirk.

The traffic was snarled on the way, and there wasn't much time for goodbyes.

"Keep writing those songs, Big Guy," Jon said. "We'll be crossing the pond before you know it." They all hugged before Laura and Liam rushed off to check in.

"I'm really going to miss them," Jon said, watching the two disappear ahead. Jen, already in tears, only nodded.

"Cheer up kids," Robert said. "You're going to see them in a month."

Liam admired the luxurious appointments of the Concorde as they were seated. "Relax," Laura said, taking his hand. "This is just another chapter in our adventure!" Liam smiled, and Laura looked at him thoughtfully. "Lately, it has been quite an adventure. I think I've grown up several years since we left Ireland."

"We've both grown up," he replied. "America is a grand country—but a little too fast for me." Just then, the supersonic jet accelerated for takeoff.

The flight was exhilarating, yet smooth, and Liam enjoyed it thoroughly. Before long they were touching down at London's Heathrow airport. After a seemingly endless check-in at customs, finding the gate for their flight to Shannon was an enormous challenge in the huge terminal. Liam held Laura's hand securely while they made their way through the bustling crowds.

"What would I do without you?" she asked as they boarded the Aer Lingus flight.

"You'd still be in New York," he laughed.

"I admit I've been a little intimidated—but that's what I have you for."

"Is that all I'm good for?"

"You know better than that," Laura said, giving him a squeeze.

"What I do know is that I'm homesick for Ireland."

"Me too, Monkey Boy!"

Hannah and Aidan were anxiously waiting for them at the airport.

"Our world travelers are home safe," Aidan said, giving them both hugs.

"The Manor has been so empty without you," Hannah added. "Welcome home."

The moment they arrived at the Manor, Laura and Liam changed into jeans and went to see their horses. Kite sped to Liam when they walked into the barn.

"Hey, little guy, I've missed you!" Liam picked up the excited dog.

"Look at you two travelers," Patrick said, coming around the corner. "It seems like you've been gone a lifetime. You've grown up!" He hugged them warmly.

"It's good to be home," Laura sighed. "But I'm still feeling the jet lag—I'm not sure what time it is. Are Sky and Rose in the pasture?"

"As a matter of fact, they are," Patrick replied.

One whistle from Liam and the two horses came running to greet them. A smile came to Liam's face as he hugged Sky.

"So, tell me about America," Patrick said. "Did you see the Statue of Liberty?"

"Yes we did," Liam replied. "And she is a grand lady—just like America."

"Grand—and fast-paced as well," Laura added. They took turns telling stories of their experiences—leaving out certain details.

"Tell us more about your visit with the Bianchis," Aidan said at dinner.

"Do all American teenagers have cars?" Hannah asked.

"It seems that way—they can drive at sixteen," Laura answered. "But I think some of them are a little...unruly—and maybe a little too young."

Aidan raised his eyebrows. "A very adult observation, my dear. What did you think about the land of opportunity, Son?"

Liam looked pensive for a moment as he gazed at Laura. "America was certainly a grand experience we'll never forget. We really had a fine time at the Bianchi's—Jon and Jen have become our best friends. But my heart belongs to Ireland. There's no place like home." He got up from the table and gave Aidan a hug. "Thank you for the wonderful experience, Sir. Thank you for everything you've done for me."

Tears came to Aidan's eyes. "I'm so happy you came into our life," he said in a choked voice. "You've been through so much for your young age. I'm very proud of the man you're becoming." Laura jumped up and hugged them both.

Hannah, never having seen a glimpse of appreciation from her daughters—let alone the love she was now experiencing—got caught up in the emotion. Tears came to her eyes as she reached for Laura's hand, giving it a squeeze. "We are happy to have you home."

With morning came a beautiful day for riding—and the horses were frisky. As they galloped through the meadows, Liam felt as though he and Sky were in flight. They seemed to barely touch the ground, and new lyrics began to form in his mind—a song about flying on the wings of his horse.

"Now we're home," Laura said, once they were in the cave. Liam opened his arms and she fell into them.

"Sometimes I'm afraid to grow up and live in the real world," Liam sighed. "I'm not sure if I can fit in."

Laura looked at him with kindness in her eyes. "Liam, you'll be brilliant. I know you'll always make good choices and do the honorable thing. You did much better than I did in America."

"You did fine."

"I don't know—I've got to learn about other boys. They're not like you. They all want the same thing: sex."

Liam laughed. "So...you think I don't want sex?"

She looked at him coyly. "Do you want to have sex with me?"

"Oh, Laura Lye, you sweet thing. Just because I don't try to force myself on you doesn't mean I don't want you. I could never disrespect you—or your father. I know someday we'll be together when we're older."

"How long do we have to wait?" Laura pouted. "Until I'm an old lady?"

"It'll be worth the wait—trust me."

She impulsively gave him a passionate kiss. "Are you sure you want to wait?"

"Don't tempt me!" Liam said, pulling away.

Laura coyly smiled. "It's good to know I can tempt you."

Soon they were back into their comfortable daily routines at Montrose. Liam had so many songs in his head he could hardly wait to write them down.

One afternoon Iris brought Liam a post from America. At first he thought it was from Jon, but then realized it was from Greg, the leader of the band Foolish Pleasure. He excitedly opened the letter.

"They're recording *I Remember When,*" he said excitedly. "Now I'll find out if anyone else likes my songs."

"They will love them as much as I do," Laura said sweetly.

Aidan entered the room. "Liam, the Glenstal Abbey has an interview appointment for you tomorrow. We can all go to Limerick together and see the school."

Liam was thrilled with the news, but then glanced at Laura. Her smile had faded. She couldn't believe it was happening so soon.

"Father, he doesn't start until September. Why do they want to see him now?"

"It's just an interview, Laura. Don't you want to go and see the school?"

"I guess," she replied sadly.

ᴄ✐ *Chapter Twenty-Eight* ᕤꙨ

Glenstal Abbey School for Boys, set on five hundred acres of some of the most beautiful countryside in Ireland, was once a castle built in the romantic Norman style. The name Glenstal means *Stallions of the Glen,* and the buildings were surrounded by streams, woodland paths, and a lake. Highly regarded, the school had small classes to allow individual attention.

Liam was nervous at the beginning of the interview, but the counselor took an instant liking to him and soon the young man felt comfortable. The suggested curriculum included math, physics, history, English, and classical music. Even though Liam had never played rugby, the counselor suggested he join the team.

"With your size and muscular build, you're a natural."

"Thank you for the offer—but I don't think I'll have time."

The interview continued with Aidan at Liam's side, while Laura and Hannah walked around the grounds.

"Hannah, I wish Liam didn't have to go away to school," Laura sighed.

"You know, dear, your father has been speaking of sending you to a girl's school, where you will learn the proper ways of a young lady of distinction."

"No, Hannah," Laura protested. "You can teach me what I need to know."

"Well, I am flattered child, but you need more education than I can give you."

"I don't see a problem with things staying the way they are," Laura argued. Hannah stopped walking and faced the fourteen-year-old.

"Part of growing up is learning how to adjust."

Laura pouted, but offered no more argument. *Father will listen to me.*

On the trip home, Liam talked excitedly about the classes he would be taking in the fall, while Laura sat quietly and looked out the window. When they arrived at the Manor, she excused herself.

"I don't feel well. I'm going to go to bed—and I don't want any dinner."

Hannah studied Laura as she left the room. "It must be that time of the month again—it has always made both my girls so moody."

Liam knew better, and later went to Laura's room.

"Laura, are you all right?" She looked up at him with her big brown eyes, but said nothing. "Please don't be sad. I know you're upset about my leaving for school in the fall, but we've been through this. You know it's for our future. The sooner I get through school the sooner we can be together."

"You don't have to be so happy about it." Liam took her into his arms.

"Laura Lye, you know I'll miss you very much, and I'll come home every weekend. So let's make the best of our time together. We have a whole month before school starts. Remember, Jon and Jen will be here soon."

"I don't want to share you with anybody—even them."

"I promise you we'll find time to be alone. It means a lot to me, too." He gave her a goodnight kiss, but she clung to him.

"Laura, we must be careful—especially at home." Reluctantly, she let him go, and managed a little smile before he left the room.

Laura was certain the idea was Hannah's—not her father's. *I'll talk to him alone…*

"I'm going to help Patrick with Wild Storm—the new colt," Liam said to Laura at breakfast. "Do you want to go riding afterwards?"

"I'll join you later—I have something to do first." Liam nodded and hurried off.

Laura found her father in his study. "May I talk with you about school?"

"Sure, dear, what's on your mind?"

"Hannah told me you were considering sending me to a private girls' school."

"We have discussed it, but I would talk to you before any decision was made."

"Good—then we can talk about it now. I don't want to go off to school by myself. Why can't I just be tutored here until I can go to college with Liam?"

Aidan sat back in his chair and raised his eyebrows. "Mrs. O'Brien feels she can only take you so far. Besides, you need to be around young girls your age. If you go to St. Andrews Catholic School, you would be coming home on weekends—you can ride the train home with Liam. I just want you to think about it before you say any more."

Laura nodded slowly, giving her father a sad look as she left the room.

When Laura got to the barn, there was a lot of commotion going on in one of the horse boxes. Patrick was yelling, "Whoa! Whoa...easy boy. Liam, are you all right?"

"I can't give up on him yet," Liam said, his voice straining. "Let me try again."

Laura hurried to where Patrick was standing. The young horse, Wild Storm—fully tacked, with saddle and bridle—was rearing into the air, striking out with his front hooves. Liam was firmly hanging on to the reins, keeping his body close to the colt's side, well aware of the danger of allowing the horse to break free.

"Liam, give up—he'll hurt you again," Patrick insisted. Liam ignored the warning, his focus completely on the colt. Liam and Wild Storm crashed into the wall several more times. Patrick could only look on in frustration, knowing if he intervened the colt would become more agitated.

Liam was finally able to put his arm over the colt's neck. Wild Storm had quit rearing and was now just circling, with Liam maintaining his firm grip on the bridle. As the colt's pace slowed, Liam began to rub his neck and withers.

The young horse still resisted, shaking his head and neck. Liam gently touched him and began to hum soothingly, persisting until the colt's eyes no longer showed fear. As the colt relaxed and listened, his ears tipped towards Liam. Then Liam saw the final sign he had been looking for: Wild Storm began to lick his lips.

Satisfied that he'd accomplished his goal, Liam released the girth of the saddle and eased it off, and then massaged the colt where the saddle had been. Wild Storm now stood quietly while Liam pulled the bridle off, easing the bit from his mouth.

Patrick shook his head as Liam left the box. "I don't know how you do it. I would have written him off as a renegade."

"This colt is just frightened and misunderstood," Liam said, his voice weak. "He's only acting out of fear—" Liam winced.

"Are you hurt?" Laura cried.

"Lad, I'm goin' to have a look at you." He lifted Liam's shirt. "This doesn't look good at all. I hope you don't have any broken ribs."

Liam tried to strengthen his voice. "I've been hurt worse."

"You don't have to be tough for me. I've been injured by horses enough times to know you're hurtin'. We'd better go to the Manor and have Lord Meegan take a look. He'll want to bring you to the doctor and have those ribs taped up."

"But—"

"Liam," Laura said through tears, "you're going to the Manor with us now!"

Liam was surprised at her directness. He started to walk off with the saddle, but stopped in mid-stride and groaned. "I guess I am a little sore."

Laura took the saddle from him while Patrick ran to get the pickup.

Hannah saw the truck racing up the drive and knew there must be something wrong. She rushed to get Aidan.

From the front porch Aidan could see Liam was hurt—he could hardly get out of the truck. Aidan ran to Liam's side.

"Patrick, tell me what happened—and I want the whole story."

Patrick explained as quickly as possible while Aidan examined Liam's bruises. "Son, I appreciate your trying to gentle this colt, but you are far too valuable to me. I can get another colt, but I cannot get another son! We are going to the hospital to have your ribs x-rayed and there will be no argument."

By this time, Liam was in so much pain he offered no protest.

The examination at the hospital revealed that Liam had three cracked ribs and a dislocated shoulder. A strong painkiller made the corrective procedure on the shoulder bearable, and the doctor cleared his patient to return home with strict orders for bed rest and no more horse activities until further notice.

Aidan carefully helped Liam to his bedroom when they got home.

"Son, I feel terrible about all this. If anything ever happened to you…" Aidan choked up and tears came to his eyes. "I would never be able to forgive myself. Promise me you will not take chances like that again."

"I'm really sorry I upset you," Liam said. "I promise to be more careful."

Laura walked into the room. Aidan looked at her and said, "I'm sure you're in good hands now, Son. I'll leave you to your nurse." Aidan kissed Laura on the forehead as he left. From the doorway, she watched him disappear down the steps.

"Liam, why did you keep working with the colt after you were already hurt?"

"I just wanted to give him a chance. He's not a bad colt—he was just scared."

"Well I was scared when I saw him run you into the wall. I know you have a special way with animals, but you can't risk your life for them."

"Laura, you risked your life for me. You went after the Deacon with a shovel."

"That was very different and you know it—he would have killed you. I had to do something. Liam, I love you, and I can't stand the thought of you getting hurt. Please promise me you won't put yourself in a position like that again."

"Only if you promise me you will be my nurse."

Laura brought Liam lunch and spent the next few hours reading to him. He slept peacefully for several hours in spite of the awkward near-sitting position recommended by the doctor.

Patrick and Chloe came by to check in on Liam. "How about we take care of Kite for a while—to keep him from jumpin' on you and such?" Liam agreed to the plan. They wished him well and left. Aidan heard the two from within his study.

"Patrick, can I see you for minute?"

"Yes, Sir," he replied, glancing at Chloe.

"I'll get the dog and see you out back," she said.

"Patrick, come in and have a seat," Aidan said. Patrick nervously took a chair. "Don't worry—I'm not blaming you for what happened to Liam. I know he's very enthusiastic about training horses and he does have a special way with them. But I can't take a chance on his getting hurt."

"I understand, Sir, but—if may I speak my mind—the lad was right about Wild Storm. I've been workin' with him real slow, and talkin' to him calmly—like Liam said. The colt has really come around. Liam just wanted to give him a chance."

"I can appreciate what you're saying, Patrick." Aidan sat back in his chair and sighed. "You know I care a great deal about the horses and their training, but Liam is like my own son. I want you to send the colt to Feyland tomorrow. Let the trainers there deal with him. Tell them how well the colt has responded to Liam's techniques—they can take it from there. As far as Laura and Liam...Sky and Rose are the only two horses I want them to handle."

"Yes, Sir, I do understand. I think the world of Liam, and I certainly owe it to Philip to watch out for him."

Just before dinner the phone rang. Jon was calling from Long Island to confirm his flight times. Laura told him about the accident.

"Should I come right now and help him?" Jon asked, concerned.

"No, Jon, that's all right. Come in two weeks like you planned— Liam will feel more like having visitors then."

"Can I talk to him?"

"He's still sleeping. Why don't you call back at about eight o'clock our time?"

At seven o'clock, Laura knocked softly on Liam's door.

"Come in, Nurse Laura."

"Now how did you know it was me?"

"Lucky guess." He smiled at her. "I know you've been looking in on me a lot."

"Can I help feed you?" she asked, setting his dinner tray down.

"No. I do have one good arm—but I would like your company."

"You've got it! The Callahans picked flowers from the garden—see, over there in the vase? Cook made your favorite dinner with chocolate cake for desert. And Jon will be calling you at eight o'clock. I'm going to bring the phone in for you."

Liam smiled. "Wow, I can't believe all this attention I'm getting."

"Well, don't get too used to it, Monkey Boy, because this is the last time you're hurting yourself." Liam's ribs hurt too much to protest. Liam began eating his dinner while Laura plugged in the phone.

A few minutes later it rang.

"Montrose Manor," Laura answered cheerfully. Her smile quickly turned to a frown. "Oh—it's you, Emily. What do you want?"

"I want to speak to my mother, if you don't mind."

"Your mother is out right now—and I'm expecting an important call from America at any moment."

"Oh, sure you are. Who would call you from America? Anyway, tell my mother I called. It's important that she call me back as soon as possible."

Without responding, Laura hung up the phone.

"I hope she's not coming for a visit," Liam frowned. The phone rang again. Laura sighed and picked it up. "All right! I'll give her the message."

"Huh? Is this Laura?" It was Jon.

"Jon! I'm so glad it's you. Here's Liam—now don't wear him out."

"Hey Big Guy, how are you feeling? I miss you—I wish I was already there."

"I'm a little sore," Liam answered. "But I have a grand nurse."

"Is that a nurse or a watch dog?" Jon laughed.

"She's just making sure I get well so we can do things when you guys are here."

"Liam, are you really going to be all right by then?"

"With Nurse Laura I can't do anything but heal."

"We can't wait to get there! I can't wait for the flight either—my father's letting us take the Concorde. Jen wants to say hi, so I'll say goodbye for now. Take care."

"Thanks for calling, Jon. See you soon."

"Hey good lookin'," Jen said cheerfully, taking the phone. "How are you doing?"

"I'm doing all right, Jen—can't wait to see you guys."

"Me too—but I'll let you rest. We love you! Get well soon. Bye to both of you!"

"Okay—enough chatting," Laura stated when he hung up. "It's time for your breathing exercises, and then I'll ice your ribs. After that, you need to get some sleep."

When she was done Laura kissed him on the cheek and turned out the light. With the medication he'd been taking, Liam quickly fell into a deep sleep.

At breakfast, Hannah asked Laura if she had taken a call from Emily last night.

"Oh, I forgot! I was waiting for a call from Jon."

"Laura, it was important, and you should have told me as soon as I came in."

"I'm sorry," Laura said. *What could be important in Emily's life?*

"Emily is engaged to Elliott," Hannah announced. "They are having an engagement party next week at the Fox estate in York. Aidan and I must attend to meet the family. I am sure Liam will not be able to travel yet. Do you wish to come, Laura?"

"Oh, I'd better stay here and make sure Liam takes care of himself."

ᑲᕷ *Chapter Twenty-Nine* ᕷᑲ

A cool breeze wafted through Liam's French doors early one morning, tempting him to violate his prescribed bed rest. For over a week he'd dutifully complied with Nurse Laura's orders, but the spirit of the outdoors was calling him. He carefully made his way out to the balcony and took a deep breath—but then winced, holding his side.

"Mr. Delaney!" Laura barked, appearing at the doorway. "I don't recall giving permission for you to wander about."

"I know," he confessed, "but I just can't stand it anymore. I can't sing, I can't play my guitar, I can't ride my horse…"

"Time heals all wounds," Laura said, leading him back to bed. "Especially with a little love." There was a knock at the door, and Laura jumped back.

"Come in," Liam answered. When Aidan and Hannah entered, they looked surprised to see Laura.

"It's a good thing I checked in on my patient early," she quickly explained. "He was out on the balcony."

"I don't blame him," Aidan chuckled. "Convalescence is a tough sentence for an active young man."

"Thank you!" Liam replied, glancing at Laura.

"Don't get me wrong, Son—Laura's only following the doctor's instructions." He put his arm around his daughter. "And she's doing a fine job at that."

"Thank you, Father," Laura replied smugly.

"Now children," Hannah said, "we will be leaving for the airport in a few minutes. Here are the phone numbers where we can be reached."

"Don't forget," Aidan added, "We'll be picking up Jon and Jennifer at Heathrow on our way back."

"We can hardly wait," Laura replied. "And I'll watch Liam like a hawk."

Liam nodded. "I can vouch for that."

Aidan and Hannah were still laughing as they left the room waving goodbye.

❧

The next morning when Liam opened his eyes, he found Laura standing beside him. "I've brought our breakfast. After we eat, I plan to take Rose out for a short ride."

"Can I watch from my balcony?"

"I'll help you out there, and you can read until you see me in the meadow."

After Liam was settled, Laura hurried to the barn to get Rose ready.

Liam's attention was drawn to Laura the moment she came into view, the scene before him like a painting unveiled. The sky was a cloudless blue, the meadow a brilliant green, laced with wildflowers abloom. But nothing could match the beauty of Laura on her horse, galloping across the meadow, her cape flowing in gentle rhythm with her long golden hair. Rose, in perfect harmony, moved with elegance, her mane and tail floating in the breeze. The poetry in motion was complete with Sky and Kite a few steps behind. Liam could not have loved Laura more than at that moment in time.

❧

"Laura, I will carry that image in my heart forever," Liam said later when she returned. She gave him a tender kiss, allowing it to linger. "Now that's the kind of medicine I need," Liam said dreamily. "I'm feeling a lot better. I think I'm ready to spend more time outside."

"We'll see about that. For now I'm going to get your lunch—we can eat on the balcony together."

Iris handed Laura a letter when she got to the kitchen. "There's a post for Liam."

"Thank you—I'll take it up with his tray."

Laura noticed that the return address was a recording studio in New York, and she could hardly wait until Liam awoke from his nap. Liam stirred when she came into the room, and awoke with a smile. Laura gently stroked his hair. "You have a letter from America."

"Is it from Jon?"

"No, it's from a recording studio. Hurry, open it!"

Liam's eyes widened as he read the letter. "It's a contract for *I Remember When*. They say my song has been recorded by Foolish Pleasure and is soon to be released. They're going to pay me a percentage of the sales."

"That's wonderful news!" Laura exclaimed, dancing around the room.

"I didn't think they would pay me for my music."

"You write the best songs in the world. You should get paid. You're going to be rich! How many songs did you send to Greg?"

"There were three—*I Remember When, It's Been a Long Time,* and *Echoes from My Heart.*"

"Liam, this is so exciting—we should call Jon and Jen right now."

"We'd better wait until this evening. It's the middle of the night in New York."

Laura's excitement stayed with her all afternoon. Liam made the phone call at five and told Jon about the contract.

"That's totally cool!" Jon cried. "I'll have to call you Big Time instead of Big Guy! Wow! I'll call Greg today and try to get a copy of the recording to bring with us."

"Do you think you can get it on such short notice?"

"Hey! Remember who you're talking to. If it can be done, Jon can do it."

Liam chuckled. "Jon, hurry and get here—maybe I'll be able to laugh by then."

Laura took the phone. "Jon, that's enough excitement for Liam today. We'll hang up now. See you in a couple of days."

The next morning while Liam was resting, Laura decided it would be a good time to visit the horses.

When she got to the barn, Patrick and Chloe were both examining Philip's old pickup truck.

"What are you doing?" Laura asked.

"It's a surprise for Liam," Patrick answered. "Soon he'll be wantin' to drive, even if it's only around the estate. This truck is all his father left for him, so we're thinkin' about fixin' it up with a new paint job and all."

"That's a wonderful idea!" Laura cried. "What can I do to help?"

Chloe answered. "Well, my little brother Danny works in the village body shop. He's comin' by to help Patrick get it down there today. You can help us decide what color Liam might want."

"Sky blue is his favorite color," Laura stated.

"And just in time," Patrick said, looking past her. "Here's Danny now. Laura, you remember Chloe's brother—from our weddin'?"

Danny Bailey was a good-looking seventeen-year-old with strawberry blonde hair that carelessly swept across his brow, sometimes hiding his dark brown eyes. This accented his shyness, but his smile was warm and engaging. He was tall, although shorter than Liam, and had a muscular build from playing rugby.

"Yes, I do," Laura replied cheerfully. Danny looked thoughtfully at her.

"I think I remember you—it was four years ago."

"Our flower girl, Laura Meegan," Chloe said.

"I'm fourteen now," Laura announced.

"I couldn't help but overhear about the color," Danny said. "Sky blue it is. The truck should be done in a few days, but first she needs a new battery."

Patrick gave him a jump start with his truck, and they drove it slowly to the tractor barn on the deflated tires. Laura went on to the barn to get the carrots.

"Sky, I know Liam really misses you," she said, stroking his neck. "But he'll be down here soon enough. In the meantime, we have a surprise for him."

ᥱᔊ *Chapter Thirty* ᥲᔌ

"**I**'m concerned that Jon and Jen will be bored in Ireland," Laura said to Liam as she fluffed up his pillow. "They always have so much to do in New York." Their friends were due to arrive that day with Hannah and Aidan.

"They'll be fine. They're here to visit with us—not tour Europe. Besides, who wouldn't love Ireland? It's the most beautiful place in the world."

"Liam, I know you're a traveler now, but you haven't seen the entire world yet."

"Well, it's my world—the most beautiful place with the most beautiful girl."

Laura gave Liam a lingering kiss, taking advantage of one of their last few moments of privacy before everyone arrived.

"I hate the thought of you leaving me in a few weeks for school," Laura sighed. "Oh! I forgot to tell you—Father wants to send me to a private girls' school. I'm sure it's Hannah's idea, and I don't want to go. I know you can help me talk him out of it."

"Well…what school is it?"

"St. Andrew's Catholic School for Girls, in Murroe."

"You can come home on the weekends, can't you?"

"Yes," Laura sighed. "Father said you and I could ride the train together. He also said I should meet other girls my age. I don't agree—I've got you."

"I like the idea that we can ride the train to and from school, which means spending more time together—Friday afternoon and Monday morning. Think about it…if you don't go away to school, you'll be alone here during the week."

Before Laura could argue any further, Liam silenced her with a tender kiss.

"My, what have we here?" Molly asked pointedly from the doorway. Laura and Liam pulled away from each other, blushing. Molly smiled as she shook her head. "Don't bother tryin' to hide it—I know young love when I see it, and I've been seein' it for awhile. You two have it bad for each other."

"Do you think anyone else knows?" Liam asked.

"I'm pretty sure Chloe suspects somethin', but don't worry—your secret is safe for now. Lord Meegan and Hannah are the ones you need to be careful around."

"I know," Laura sighed. "Thank you for understanding."

Molly raised her eyebrows and looked from Laura to Liam. "I hope you two are not doin' foolish things…" Liam turned bright red and lowered his eyes.

Laura shook her head decisively. "Oh no, we're not…sleeping together."

"I believe you, but we need to talk about protection—just in case." Molly, contemporary and always outspoken, was not about to let them brush it off because of their embarrassment. "I'm not judgin' you two—I just want you to be prepared in case your passion gets out of control." Liam was still in retreat from the conversation, so Molly focused on Laura. "Has Hannah talked to you at all about sex?"

Laura rolled her eyes. "She said all proper young ladies wait until marriage."

Liam chuckled. "I guess Emily missed that talk."

Molly smiled, and then continued. "Liam, perhaps it would be best if you talk to Patrick—and I wouldn't put it off. I'm sure he would be more than happy to give you some advice." Liam nodded, and Molly turned back to Laura. "You and I will talk later."

Molly left the room and the two looked at each other in disbelief.

"Laura, we need to be more careful! We're lucky it was just Molly."

"You can trust Patrick, can't you?"

"He's been a great friend to me. We've talked about a lot of things."

"Did you mention me?" Laura asked coyly.

"Well, I asked about women in general. He didn't know it was about you."

"Someday the world will know," Laura sighed.

Iris called up the stairs. "Your guests are pullin' up!"

252

"Go ahead and greet them," Liam said. "I'll be there soon."

"Are you sure I can't help you down the stairs?"

"No! I want to come down myself. Now get going." Laura raced down the stairs to meet everyone. Jon was coming through the door when she got to the grand entry.

"My little Colleen!" he exclaimed, picking her up. "We made it to Ireland at last!" He twirled her around and the others laughed.

"You'd better pull in the reins when you greet Liam," Laura cautioned. "Remember, he's still very sore."

Jen greeted Laura with a hug. "Is he still in bed?"

"I'm on my way," Liam called. They looked up to see him slowly descending the stairs.

"Son, you're doing so much better," Aidan remarked. "I guess Nurse Laura has done a grand job."

"She certainly has," he replied. "Hey, my friends—welcome to Ireland!" Liam gingerly extended his hand.

"I guess a handshake will have to do," Jon said. "But what I really want is to give you a bear hug."

"Not if you want me up and around for anything else."

Cook entered the room, and Jon gave her an engaging smile. Her face lit up. "Welcome to Montrose Manor! I've got an Irish lunch prepared for you."

"Thank you—I'm famished from the journey," Jen sighed.

They followed Liam into the dining room to find a vast assortment of fine cheeses on the table, along with Laura's homemade soda bread. Cook brought in a large tureen of Irish stew and began serving as everyone seated themselves. A chocolate cake with Irish cream filling, made especially for Liam, was elegantly displayed on the sideboard.

The conversation was lively during lunch, with talk of traveling, Emily's engagement party, and Liam's news from the recording studio.

"Son, I'm very proud you got your first song published," Aidan remarked. "I'll look over your contract this afternoon." Liam thanked him.

"I have a copy of *I Remember When*," Jon said. "Does anyone want to hear it? I brought my tape player. I wasn't sure if our tapes would play on your machines. I even brought an adapter for your weird outlets."

"I see you have skills in logistics, Jon," Aidan smiled.

After lunch Jon played the tape. Everyone was pleased—even Liam, who was always critical of his own work.

"Sounds like a hit to me!" Jon said. "It'll soon be at the top of the charts."

"Wow!" Laura said. "This is exciting! But...it's time for this patient's medication and rest." Aidan smiled, but Liam was slightly annoyed.

"C'mon, Laura, they just got here!"

"You can visit with everyone after your nap," she insisted. "Don't worry—I'll give them a tour but I won't show them the studio without you."

"She's tough," Jon laughed. "You'd better do what your nurse says, Big Guy."

Jen entered her large guest suite and spun around to take it all in. She ran to the window seat, which was framed in elegant draperies that matched the green and pink floral tapestries on the wall. The large cherry-wood bed was adorned with a matching comforter. Laura had placed pale pink roses on the marble bedside table, adding just the right finishing touch.

"This room is fantastic!" Jen cried. "And what a killer view. You really do live in a castle." Laura smiled, pleased with Jen's enthusiasm.

Jon's room had a more masculine feel, with blue and cream tones. His jaw dropped as his eyes fixed on the massive marble fireplace, framed by bookshelves filled with leather-bound classics. He reached for a copy of *A Tale of Two Cities*.

"I started reading this for my English lit class last year, but I never finished it." He walked towards the French doors leading out to the balcony which overlooked the River Maigue. "I think I just found a good place to finish this book."

Jen laughed. "You came all the way to Ireland to read?"

"Why not?"

Laura laughed. "Now, I'm sure you guys are still trying to get your bearings. This is the same side of the Manor as Liam's room. The stairs from the balcony lead to the path along the river."

"Are there any fish in there?" Jon asked.

"Plenty: brown trout...and salmon, I think. If you want to fish I'm sure Patrick, our horse trainer, and his brother in-law, Danny, would be happy to take you. Danny's the same age as you."

"That would be great." Jon smiled. "This whole place is fantastic. All of the stone arches and gargoyles...and the history. I can't wait to see the ruins."

"Liam gets excited over stuff like that," Laura remarked. "If you like history you'll have plenty to do with him."

"The Big Guy and I have more in common than I thought," Jon remarked.

Laura peeked in on her patient and was satisfied he was sleeping. "Let's go see the grounds," she whispered.

"I just love it here," Jen said as they strolled through the rose gardens. "I want to see your stables—and meet Sky and Rose. I've heard so much about them." Jen stopped to smell one of the blooms just as the head gardener, Mr. Callahan, stood up.

"Oh! So sorry I've startled you, Miss!" He brushed himself off and removed his cap. "I'm very pleased to meet you fine young people. The missus just made a batch of sweet biscuits, and I know she'll be wantin' to meet Miss Laura's friends from America."

"That would be wonderful! My name is Jen, and this is my brother, Jon."

"Evan Callahan at your service." He bowed. "I won't be goin' with you, though. I confess I've already had enough of the biscuits." He patted his stomach, and they all laughed. They proceeded to the cottage, taking in the sounds and sights along the way.

"The air is so fresh and the river is so clean!" Jon exclaimed, walking with an excited, bouncing stride. "I can't wait to go fishing."

Mrs. Callahan greeted them at the door, drying her hands on her apron.

"Please come in. My name is Anna. How do you like Ireland so far? I bet it's not so grand as America."

255

"I think Ireland is wonderful," Jon proclaimed. "Everything is green and beautiful. I just may have to move here." He winked at Anna, and she laughed heartily. Jon continued, "America is dazzling, yes, but the pace is very fast, and it can be dizzying." He spun around comically and pretended to lose his balance, to everyone's amusement. "I'm looking forward to just breathing the air and listening to the river."

Anna was quite taken with Jon. "You're welcome to stay here if you like," she said with a girlish giggle. Jon gave her a wink, which added to her delight.

"He's always charming the ladies," Jen remarked.

They thanked Mrs. Callahan for the biscuits, and then rushed off to the barn.

"Laura, I just love your stables!" Jen said. "If I were a horse, I'd be happy living here. The circular layout of the stalls is very cool. Every horse has a view of the arena and they can watch each other." Jen walked over to one of the boxes, and the mare inside nickered at her. "All your horses look happy. Are Sky and Rose here?"

"Only at night," Laura replied. "During the day they go out to play. Let's go meet them—and Lilly, my old pony." As they walked out, Laura turned to Jon. "Liam trained Sky and Rose to come when he whistles—but I can't do it. Can you?"

"Sure—watch this." He placed his thumb and forefinger in his mouth, and Jen covered her ears. Jon produced a loud, piercing sound that made Sky and Rose pick up their heads from where they were grazing. They galloped to the gate, to the delight of the American visitors. Laura gave the horses each a carrot.

"Hey!" Jon protested. "Let me do that part, too."

Laura handed out carrots, holding back a few. "These are for Lilly."

"Do you like to ride?" Laura asked.

"I do," Jen answered, "but I'm not too sure about Jon. He had a bad experience."

On the way back to the barn, Jon spotted a shiny, sky blue truck coming up the driveway. "Wow! Look at that—what a classic."

The truck rolled to a stop, and the driver and passenger stepped out.

"I want you two to meet Danny and Patrick," Laura said as they approached the truck. "Danny just finished painting the truck as a gift for Liam. Danny and Patrick, this is Jon and Jen from America." Danny politely shook Jon's hand, but his gaze was fixed on Jen.

"My wife, Chloe—that's Danny's sister—thought up the idea to surprise Liam with the truck," Patrick explained. "By all rights, it's his anyway. It belonged to his father. We just wanted to fix it up for him."

"What a great idea—and a really great job!" Jon said, admiring the vehicle from all sides.

Just then Chloe came from the cottage to greet them. "Oh! You must be the fine young Americans we've heard all about. Oh, my manners." She smiled warmly and extended her hand. "I'm Chloe."

"I heard a rumor there's a couple of good fishermen in this group," Jon said, looking at Danny. "I'd like to give it a try while I'm here." Chloe nudged her little brother, who was distracted by Jen's smile.

"Uh—yes! I'm going in the morning," Danny replied. "If you want to join me, meet me here at the barn at half six."

Laura smiled, seeing the puzzled look on Jon's face. "That means six thirty."

"You got it!" Jon said, smiling broadly as he shook Danny's hand.

"Speaking of time—we'd better get back to the Manor or Liam will be coming down here looking for us," Laura said.

"Laura, I've talked to your father about givin' Liam the truck," Patrick said. "He told me we could bring it by after dinner tonight. It'll be a surprise he won't forget." Patrick smiled in anticipation.

Jen caught Danny staring at her again, and he blushed. She responded with a warm smile. Laura couldn't help but notice the connection. *Oh, what do we have here?* "Let's go see if Liam's up yet," Laura said.

Jen's smile never faded as they walked along the path. "I've never met more friendly people," she sighed. "Have you, Jon?"

"Never," he replied, giving Laura a hug. "I just love the Irish!"

Laura giggled, and then nudged Jen. "So, you think Danny is a fine thing, do you?"

Now it was Jen's turn to blush. "Oh! Without a doubt." The girls laughed and Jon rolled his eyes. As they got further up the path Laura pointed out the trees she and Liam used to climb, and told them the story of Monkey Boy.

☙

Liam was in the study with Aidan going over the contract.

"It looks good to me, Son. It's on an itemized basis, so if a song is a big hit, you can renegotiate for more money."

"Oh, I just want my music to be recorded—I don't care about the money."

Aidan raised his eyebrows. "You should always care about the money. Foolish Pleasure and the record company will be making a profit. You should receive your fair share. Take what you've earned and spend it at a later time as you see fit."

Liam nodded. "That sounds sensible. Thank you, Sir."

"You're quite welcome." Aidan looked towards the door. "I believe our guests have returned. Go ahead and join them."

Liam heard voices as he walked out of the study.

"Shh! Jon, he might hear you," Laura cautioned.

"Hear what?" Liam asked pointedly, looking straight at Jon.

"I'm, uh, going fishing with Danny tomorrow morning, and you can't come because you're not healed yet," Jon said quickly.

"That's okay," Liam replied. "I like to eat them, not catch them."

Aidan had followed Liam out of the study. "We can have a big fish fry with your catch tomorrow night."

"Everyone might go hungry," Jon laughed. "You haven't seen me fish. I rarely catch anything—except a cold."

"Oh, you'll do fine fishing in the Maigue," Aidan smiled. "They jump right on your line."

As they headed towards the studio, Liam turned to Jon and Jen. "I hope you're not disappointed—we don't have recording equipment, but we do have nice gear."

They entered the studio, and a smile came to Jon's face. "This is outrageous! We could put on a real show here." Liam handed Jon his guitar.

"You play, I'll sing—if I can."

258

"Instead of playing drums," Jen said, "which I see you don't have, I could play the electric piano and do some backup vocals." Laura agreed and picked up her guitar. It wasn't long before the group was right back in the spirit of the music.

After an hour Laura insisted that Liam take a break and rest before dinner. She helped him to bed.

"Laura, I do appreciate everything you're doing for me, but I don't want to miss out on Jon and Jen's visit."

"Trust me—you'll see plenty of them. I just want you to pace yourself. Father wants to take Jon to Dublin to see Trinity College before he leaves, and I know you'll want to go. So rest up now, and get stronger."

"Yes, Nurse Laura." He gave her a big smile.

After finishing a wonderful lamb dinner, Aidan caught Laura's eye and nodded towards the patio. She took the hint.

"It's such a lovely evening. Let's all go out and enjoy it."

They agreed, and soon Chloe, Molly, and Patrick came up the path to join them. "Where's Danny?" Jon asked.

"I believe that's him comin' up the drive now."

They all turned to see Danny driving up in the shiny, sky blue pickup. He drove past the parking area and right up to the patio.

Liam's jaw dropped. "Is that my father's old truck?"

"No, lad," Patrick proudly announced. "It's your new truck!"

Liam walked slowly towards the pickup, tears in his eyes as he shook his head in disbelief. "It's better than new. Who took out the dents and painted her?"

"That would be me," Danny said with pride as he stepped out of the truck.

"Danny did all the work at O'Grady's," Chloe gushed. "That's the body shop in the village where he works."

"Chloe and I wanted to do somethin' special for you," Patrick said, "after everythin'…that's happened. Anyway, it's time you learn to drive."

Liam turned to give the two a careful hug, protecting his ribs. Then he turned and shook Danny's hand. "I don't know what to say, except...she's beautiful!"

"You're most welcome," Danny replied. "She's a classic—and it was an honor." Liam slowly pulled himself in behind the wheel and Molly snapped a picture.

"I'll give you drivin' lessons when the doctor says you're ready," Patrick said.

⌒ *Chapter Thirty-One* ⌒

Jon was up early, having charmed Cook into making a special breakfast for him. He thanked her and hurried off to meet Danny, who he found checking the tackle box.

"Good morning, Jon! Are you ready to catch some fish?"

"I hope so," Jon laughed.

They hiked down the trail to the river, talking about how well they had surprised Liam. Danny led the way to what he said was his favorite bend in the Maigue, and they stopped at the water's edge, where he set Jon up with a rod.

"Now just watch me." Danny cast his line, and in seconds he had a bite. Skillfully setting his hook, he slowly reeled in the fish as he guided it towards the bank. Jon was amazed at Danny's technique as he pulled out a beautiful brown trout.

Jon made an attempt but was rather clumsy with the cast, and then got the line hung up on rocks. Danny helped him cut his line and start over.

"Jon, you're trying too hard. The fish are there, and they will bite—just relax and ease your line out."

Jon tried several more times but he couldn't cast out to the pool.

"Okay, Jon, let's start over again. I hear you're a musician. Fishing's like playing your guitar—you have to find your rhythm, and then settle in."

Jon began to relax and get a feel for the rod. He was able to cast much farther out. In a few moments, he got a bite and a smile came to his face.

"Now you're fishing!" Danny proclaimed

In less than two hours, they had eighteen trout.

"How many can we catch? Is there a limit?" Jon asked.

Danny chuckled. "At Montrose you can fish all day, but I think one more each, and it will be plenty for a fry." Jon agreed, and in a few minutes they each had one more catch.

The two teens enjoyed the cool morning air on the walk back to the Manor. "Danny, you seem to know something about music. Do you play?"

"I fool around on the bass, but I'm not that good, and my bass guitar is old."

"We need a bass player in our group," Jon said. "Will you join us tonight?"

"Oh, I wouldn't be good enough to play with you guys," Danny said, embarrassed. "I heard Liam has a song recorded by a top American rock group."

Jon wouldn't take no for an answer. "We just need a steady bottom. I can tell from your casting that you've got good rhythm. You'd be a great help to us. Bring your bass when you come to the fish fry tonight."

Danny hesitated. "I wasn't invited." Jon looked at him as if he was crazy.

"Hey, man, you caught most of the fish—you're invited!"

Danny shook his head, clearly uncomfortable. "I'll have to ask my sister Chloe." He looked at Jon and realized the American didn't understand. "We're from the...working class. We don't usually socialize with the Royals."

Although he was surprised, Jon was not about to accept Danny's objection.

"I'll talk to Aidan and make sure everyone is invited—everyone who contributed to fixing up Liam's truck, everyone who caught these fish—and that's all there is to it!"

"We'll see," Danny said, unconvinced. "Anyway, you did great today."

"Thanks—I had a great teacher," Jon grinned.

They brought the fish in through the back door of the kitchen, and Danny said he had to get to work at O'Grady's.

"Don't make any other plans for tonight," Jon smiled. "I'm counting on you to be here." Danny nodded and left. A moment later Cook appeared.

"My, that's quite a catch!" she exclaimed.

"I'll clean them—and help you cook tonight, too," Jon said cheerfully.

"That won't be necessary," she replied, giving him a big smile.

In the dining room, everyone was just finishing breakfast. Jon came bouncing in with a big smile on his face. "We caught a truckload of the most beautiful trout!"

"Oh, there'll be no living with him now," Liam laughed.

Jon ignored him. "We have plenty for a big fish fry tonight. I would like to include Molly, Chloe, Patrick, and the real fisherman—Danny."

Hannah frowned, but Aidan spoke up. "It will be fun to have you all here."

"Great! Thank you. I invited Danny to play music with us after dinner, too."

"Wonderful!" Jen gushed.

"What instrument does he play?" Laura asked.

"He's our new bass player."

"We can sure use one," Liam remarked. "I had no idea Danny played. Did you also happen to stumble upon a set of drums for Jen?" Everyone laughed but Jon.

"No, but I'm working on that, too."

"He's always got big ideas," Jen laughed. "Sometimes they even work."

"Jon," Aidan asked, "would you like to go to Limerick with me today? Jen and Laura are going riding, and Hannah will be taking Liam to a doctor's appointment."

"I would love to go. Let me talk to the cook—I told her I would clean the fish."

"That is unnecessary," Hannah declared. "That is not our guests' job!"

"I caught them, and I told her I would clean them," Jon said, shrugging. He rushed off to the kitchen before Hannah could say another word.

When Jon walked in, he was surprised to find the cook already had a helper: Mr. Callahan. They were almost finished cleaning the trout.

"I do a might more than just prunin' roses," the gardener said. "You're on holiday, young Jon—go enjoy yourself."

Jon thanked the man, and then told the cook about the other planned guests.

She smiled. "It's very thoughtful of you to tell me how many will be comin'. I usually don't know until the eleventh hour."

"You're welcome," Jon said, and bid them a good day.

Laura stopped in to visit Liam later, before she and Jen went to the barn.

"I feel like I'm missing everything," Liam sighed. "Now Jon's off for the day, and you and Jen are going riding, and I get to go to the doctor with Hannah."

"Oh, poor baby. We'll all be together tonight." She kissed him on the cheek. "Please be a good patient. You're almost healed."

"Liam!" Hannah called from down the hall. "We will be late."

He looked at Laura and rolled his eyes. "You girls have fun. Maybe you could take Sky and let Jen ride Rose…"

"Yes, I think that's best. Sky can be a bit of a handful sometimes. We're going to ride with saddles and bridles, like Jen is used to."

Jon was enchanted by the countryside he saw on the way to Limerick. He and Aidan talked about Ireland while Jon looked out the window, enjoying a view of the fields of ever-changing green, dotted with white sheep, grazing contentedly.

"By the way," Aidan said, "I only have a quick errand to run in town, but I thought you would have a particular interest in the more important destination: the music store."

"Wow!" Jon replied. "We're on the same wavelength."

"Well, I thought you could help me pick out a set of drums for the music studio."

"Perfect! My father gave me money to get Liam a gift after his accident, and I know the studio needs a set—and maybe some recording equipment."

"We'll see what the two of us can come up with today."

Along the way, Aidan pointed out Glenstal Abbey. "That's where Liam will be going to school in the fall. St. Andrews, where I would like Laura to go, is a little farther down the road."

"Laura never mentioned going away to school," Jon remarked.

"That's because she's stubborn and refuses to think about it."

"She definitely has a strong will," Jon laughed.

Aidan looked at Jon thoughtfully. "Are you considering going to Trinity?"

Jon, embarrassed, gazed out the window. "I'd love to, Sir, but I have a lot of make-up studying to bring my grades up. I was a real goof-off last year in school. I *am* a good student when I work at it, and my test scores before last year were good. I'm really going to change my ways this year and do some catching up. It's my senior year."

"I can see you are very bright," Aidan smiled. "And you do have the ability to focus on your goals."

Jon felt good that he had Aidan's confidence. "I want to be like Liam."

"Yes, I'm proud of him. He will accomplish whatever he sets his mind to."

The music store had a large selection, and Jon found a beautiful set of used drums very much like the ones Jen had at home. They were blonde maple wood and had a deep, warm sound.

"I'd be happy to buy a brand new set if you want," Aidan said.

"No, but thank you. These are really high quality, and they come complete with the cymbals and hardware. I think my gift to Liam will be some more microphones and stands for the studio." He wandered to the pro audio department, and Aidan followed.

"Now, let's talk about recording equipment," Aidan said, catching Jon's attention. "While you're here, maybe you could help me pick out some things for Laura and Liam. It's a secret, though—for Christmas."

"You're a cool father," Jon smiled. "Don't get me wrong—my father is very generous, and he's actually gone with me to the music store. But he would never plan it."

Aidan found Jon's open and warm personality to be truly enjoyable. He was certain Liam's friendship with Jon was the reason Liam recently began to open up and laugh more. It was also clear that Jen was a great friend to Laura.

Aidan felt determined that their friendship be given every opportunity to grow. The laughter and excitement around the Manor was contagious, and having these young people as guests was refreshing to him. It was a welcome contrast to Hannah's spoiled and moody daughters.

On the way home Jon told amusing stories and jokes, and Aidan could see he was not really the "bad boy" his image sometimes projected, but really just a benevolent rebel who wanted to be his own man.

"Aidan!" Jon suddenly exclaimed. "We just came from Limerick, and you didn't tell me any—limericks, I mean."

"Well," Aidan chuckled, "most of them are only fit for telling in a pub."

"Go ahead, then. We're just two guys in a car—no ladies."

"You've got a fairly sharp wit, laddie, and you'll probably repeat the nasty ones."

"Well, it just so happens that I already know some," Jon said with a devilish grin.

"All right, I guess I can't stop you now—but later I'll be watching you."

"Let's see now…" Jon scratched his chin, and a twinkle came to his eye.

There was a young maid from Madras,

Who had a magnificent ass.

Not rounded and pink,

As you probably think,

It was grey, had long ears, and ate grass.

Aidan laughed heartily. "That's a good one—had me going for a second. How about this—it's a little easier to tell a mixed crowd:

There once were two cats from Kilkenny.
Who each thought there was one cat too many.
So they scratched and they spit,
And they tore and they bit,
Now instead of two cats, there aren't any."
Jon laughed easily as they pulled in the driveway.

Laura and Jen saddled the two horses and rode off to explore the estate. Sky and Rose felt good, and Laura noticed that Jen was quite at ease in the saddle.

"Do you want to gallop?" Laura asked. A big grin came to Jen's face.

"Let's go!" They galloped across the meadows and through the trees, the wind in their faces. Sky and Rose headed for the familiar trail to the cave. Laura had already decided to share the special place with Jen.

"Now, you have to keep this a secret. This is where Liam and I would go to explore when we were little, and now it's our private space." Laura's face saddened. "We spent the night here alone after Liam's father died." Jen squeezed Laura's hand.

"That must have been hard for Liam. I can't imagine losing either of my parents." Jen suddenly fell silent, perhaps remembering that Laura had also lost her mother.

"It's okay, Jen." Laura looked at her wistfully. "My mother died when I was eight. Not long after, I met Liam. He was the one who was really there for me. I don't know what I would have done without him."

Moved that Laura was opening up to her, Jen impulsively hugged her. "I can see the bond between you two. It's very special." Laura smiled.

They walked in silence to the cave, and Jen noticed the inscription on the wall.

"My Friend, My Life, My Love...Liam and Laura." She looked right into Laura's eyes. "That is the most beautiful thing...Liam loves you so deeply. Someday, I want to find a love like you two have..."

"Well, hopefully you won't have to hide yours."

Jen gave Laura a compassionate smile. "You won't have to hide forever."

Laura looked pensively at the carving. "I never knew I would find a love like Liam's—and now it's clear to me that I will never love anyone but Liam."

Jen sighed. "You're very lucky you two have each other. I've had bad luck with guys. Every time I think I might be in love, he turns out to be a jerk. I hope someday I'll find my Liam."

"Oh, I'm sure you will, but please keep your hands off the original." They both laughed, tears coming easily to their eyes.

Laura pointed out the angle of the sunlight in the cave. "Liam always says when the sun shines on the red rock, it's time to go. Speaking of Liam, he'll be wondering what's taking us so long."

Jen took another look around the main room in the cave. "With this great place, it's a wonder you don't stay here for days on end."

"When we're singing and writing songs in here, time stands still."

Liam received a good report from the doctor. His x-rays showed he was almost healed. Although the strength had almost completely returned to his arm, he was still restricted from riding horses. The best news to Liam was that he could start learning to drive. After he and Hannah returned to the Manor he rested, content to read for a while. Later he began to wonder why none of the others had returned.

When Aidan and Jon drove in Liam was waiting at the door, watching as the two laughed out loud, apparently having great fun without him.

"Where have you been?" he asked as they came up the steps.

"Having a grand time!" Jon said with a devilish grin.

Liam gave Jon a suspicious glance. "Well, tell me about it."

Jon told him a limerick and described the city with contagious enthusiasm. Liam was happy his friend was enjoying his trip. Then it was his turn to share his good news from the doctor.

The girls came in through Laura's favorite back entrance to clean up before dinner. Noticing Cook was preparing for the fry, they realized they needed to hurry.

"Follow me," Laura said, leading Jen up a narrow stone stairway.

"How many ways do you have to get upstairs?" Jen asked.

"Lots—but this is my favorite."

Soon the girls joined the others on the patio for the fish fry. Everyone seemed to be enjoying themselves but Danny, who was still uncomfortable around 'the Royals.' Once everyone was seated for dinner Danny soon relaxed, grinning at Jon's animated recounting of their morning at the river. Everyone laughed at how Jon could make a simple fishing experience sound so hilarious.

Jen couldn't take her eyes off Danny, watching his every move. She caught his glance and engaging smile more than once, but wondered why he hadn't actually spoken to her. Finally Jen whispered to Laura.

"Does Danny have a girlfriend?"

"I don't know—but I can ask Chloe later."

"Just don't let her know I'm the one who's asking."

"Don't worry—I won't let on."

Jon stood up from the table. "In honor of this fine meal, I would like to make a toast to..." He looked blankly at Laura. "What is the cook's name?"

Laura shrugged. "I don't know—we just call her Cook." There was an embarrassing silence. Even Aidan couldn't recall the name after eighteen years of employing her. His accountant always made out the employees' checks.

"Fiona—Fiona is my name." A shy voice could be heard from the kitchen.

"Fiona!" Jon proclaimed. "What a beautiful name." The lady appeared at the door with a sheepish grin on her face. "Tell me, Fiona, what does your name mean?"

"Fair," she replied softly. "It means fair."

"Fiona," Jon continued, "I toast you for all the wonderful meals you prepare." Everyone except Hannah lifted their glasses and gave the cook a loud cheer. Aidan noticed Hannah's lack of participation. *I remember how Fey always fussed over the staff.*

Jon walked over to the side table where he picked up a box of chocolates wrapped with a gold bow on top. Unbeknown to Aidan, Jon had bought them in Limerick that day. "This is for you, my Fair Fiona!" She blushed and graciously accepted his gift—and his kindness.

After dessert, Laura asked if they could be excused to go to the studio.

Aidan smiled. "Of course—go ahead and have fun."

Danny was speechless as he entered the studio and saw all the equipment. Jen quickly said, "I'm so happy you're going to play with us, Danny. We really need you—I mean, a bass player."

Danny blushed and tried to hide his embarrassment. "So what instrument do you play?"

"I usually play drums—but we don't have a set here. Instead I'll probably play the Fender electric piano."

"You play drums? And piano?"

"Yes, both—but not at the same time."

Danny laughed. *All that talent...and she's cute, too!* But Danny's nervousness never really subsided while the others got set up.

"Here you are," Jon said, handing Danny's bass back to him. "You're all plugged in and ready to go."

"Are you sure you want to play with an Irish country boy who's only had a few lessons in school?"

"I'm an Irish country boy," Liam proclaimed. "When I was younger, my only music teacher was my mother."

"But you had a song published and recorded," Danny said.

"I was in the right place at the right time—with the right friends." Liam smiled as he glanced at Jon, who grinned back.

"Let's rock 'n roll!" Jon cried. "I'll start off, and you guys can pick it up as we go. This is a new one I just heard on the radio."

Danny was a little hesitant at first, but soon fell into place, once he found the right key. His confidence was boosted when he noticed Jen smiling at him. They worked through several more songs as Danny relaxed, fitting in nicely.

"Not bad," Jon remarked. "We need to pick up the pace a little, though. Let's trade off solos for eight bars each."

They had played for several hours when Laura put up her hand. "I think Liam should call it a night now. He's still healing, you know."

"C'mon, we're just warming up," Liam protested.

"Enough for tonight," Jon agreed. "Let's meet here again tomorrow night. I'll guarantee it's going to be great," he added with a mysterious twinkle in his eye.

"Are you sure you want me back?" Danny asked.

"You bet we do!" Jen answered with a smile. "Can I walk out with you?"

He blushed but agreed.

"Good night, Danny," Jen said sweetly when they got to patio. "I'm looking forward to seeing you tomorrow night."

"Good night, Jen," Danny replied softly and hurried off.

Laura made sure Liam went to bed before retiring to her own room. A few minutes later there was a knock at the door.

"Can I come in and talk to you?" Jen said.

Laura opened the door. "What's on your mind? As if I have to ask…"

"I think Danny is so sweet and so cute. But he doesn't seem interested."

"Irish boys don't move as boldly as your American boys," Laura laughed.

"Did you find out if he has a girlfriend?"

"Chloe told me he was saving all his money for school and doesn't date. She did say he notices the cute girls in the village, but he's quite shy. Danny just moved here from Tipperary, where his family lives. He'll be going to school here this fall. He wants to get a college scholarship playing rugby."

"Does he live with Chloe and Patrick?" Jen asked.

"No. With the baby coming, they don't have the room. Right now he's living above the shop where he works."

"Oh, this is exciting!" Jen cried. "He's so dreamy…"

271

"Jen, you're falling for him pretty fast. What are you going to do? Ireland is a long way to have a boyfriend."

"I don't know," Jen sighed.

ᏫᎬ Chapter Thirty-Two ᎬᎬ

"I think we sounded pretty good last night," Liam remarked at the breakfast table.

Jon smiled. "I think we should have a concert for everyone."

"We're not that good," Liam laughed.

"I would love to hear to you young musicians perform," Aidan said.

"We need more than a week to practice," Liam replied, shaking his head.

"I don't expect perfection," Aidan explained. "I would simply like to see what holds your interest for so many hours. We'll all be traveling to Dublin on Saturday, so why don't you have a performance the night before?"

"Sounds great to me," Jon said. Liam shrugged and the girls agreed. "If it's all right with you," Jon added, "I'd like to invite everyone—including the staff."

"That will not be possible," Hannah replied. "The staff is entirely too busy."

"Nonsense," Aidan argued. "I'll give them the night off."

Hannah shuddered and left the table in a huff.

Jon winced. "Aidan, I'm sorry if I've caused any trouble."

"She'll get over it," Aidan said with a wave of his hand. "Now, what's everyone got planned for today?"

"Patrick said he would give me my first driving lesson today," Liam announced.

"Should we all take the high ground?" Jon teased.

"Very funny. I'll have you know I've had hours behind the wheel of a tractor."

"Oh, I feel much better now," Jon quipped.

"Jon," Laura said, "I've got plans for you: a horseback ride on the estate today."

Jon's smile was replaced by a look of worry. "Only if you give me a very gentle horse to ride, and we don't do anything but walk."

273

"You can ride my horse, Rose," Laura smiled. "I'll ride Sky—Liam's horse."

Hannah had returned to her seat at the table, ignoring looks from the others. "Jennifer, would you like to go to the village with me this morning?"

"That would be nice," Jen replied cheerfully. "I would like to get my mother and father a present from Ireland. Do you think I might find something in the village?"

"Yes, there is a lovely shop that sells Waterford Crystal and Irish linens."

"Excuse me," Iris said to Liam quietly. "Patrick is at the back door wantin' to know if you'd be ready for your lesson." Liam thanked her and excused himself from the table.

Laura turned to Jon. "I see you've already got your jeans and boots on. Let's go."

They started down the path, and Jon said, "I'm not really afraid to ride. I just don't want to do something stupid and get hurt."

She smiled. "I won't let you do anything stupid. Rose is very gentle, and she doesn't get spooked or distracted. She'll follow Sky anywhere."

Laura put saddles and bridles on the horses. Jon took a deep breath, and then mounted Rose cautiously. Rose, as though aware of her insecure passenger, looked at Laura.

"Jon, relax. She's not going to take off with you."

"That's easy for you to say. You ride her every day."

Relieved when they finally reached the cave, Jon quickly dismounted.

"Now that wasn't too bad, was it?" Laura asked.

"It wasn't as bad as I thought it would be," Jon admitted. "I still don't know how you ever talked me into it, though."

"Well, I wanted you to see our special place, and riding is the best way to get here—unless you want to do a lot of walking. Anyway, here it is."

"Laura, this is unbelievable! How did you ever find it?"

"Liam and I just stumbled upon it one day. It's our secret retreat. No one but Patrick knows about it—and now you and Jen."

"I feel honored to be included." He gazed up and then around. "I bet this cave has the best acoustics for music."

"Yes, and Liam says it's the most inspirational place to write songs."

"Oh, I can believe that—I can feel a kind of magic here." He then noticed the inscription on the cave wall. "Wow, this was written by a poet in love."

Laura blushed, but agreed. Then, knowing how long it had taken to get to there, she suggested they go back.

On the return trip, Laura was pleased to see that Jon was far more relaxed.

Patrick drove the pickup to the Manor, where Liam was waiting with great anticipation.

"Liam, I know you'll be wantin' to get your hands on the wheel right away, but I think it would be best if you watch me drive first." Liam agreed and climbed in.

After demonstrating, Patrick downshifted and pulled to a stop on a dirt service road. "Are you ready to give it a try?"

"Oh, I've been ready!" Liam said as he slipped behind the wheel.

After a few tries—and one stall—Liam was smoothly shifting through the gears. "You're catchin' on pretty fast," Patrick remarked. "A lot faster than my first lesson, when I drove the family pickup into a ditch."

Liam laughed, causing him to swerve, but he quickly recovered. As he turned back towards the barn he spotted Laura and Jon walking up the path. He carefully pulled alongside them and stopped.

"Hey Big Guy, look at you driving!" Jon exclaimed.

"Yeah, I'm getting the hang of it. How was your ride?"

"It was great—I didn't fall off," Jon laughed.

"Is it hard to learn how to drive?" Laura asked.

"Only on me, when Liam drove into the ditch!" Patrick teased.

"C'mon," Liam protested. "I stayed on the road. Can I give them a ride home?"

Patrick rubbed his chin. "Only if you keep it under the speed limit."

Laura and Jon jumped into the bed of the pickup. Liam drove carefully all the way, pulling up to the front steps of the Manor and setting the parking brake.

"You're doing great for your first time," Jon said as he jumped out.

Laura flashed Liam a smile. "I'm proud of you!"

"Thank you both, and thank you for the lesson, Patrick. But more than that, thank you for this wonderful truck."

"You're most welcome, lad," Patrick replied. He looked skyward. "He would have wanted you to have it." A bittersweet smile came to Liam's face.

"Look what I bought for Mother and Father!" Jen said to Jon as he came in with the others. She held up an exquisite Waterford crystal vase. It glimmered in the bright sunlight streaming through the living room window.

"It makes my box of chocolates look pretty sad," Jon frowned.

"It's the thought that counts," Laura pointed out.

"Well, in that case, I just had a thought. Maybe I can find something in Dublin."

At dinner, Liam told Aidan about his successful driving lesson.

"It sounds like you're getting the hang of it," Aidan remarked. "Just remember, you can only drive on the estate until you get your license."

"I feel privileged just to be able to drive," Liam replied.

"Excuse me," Iris said. "There's a delivery here—the man's at the front door."

"It seems terribly late to be getting a delivery," Hannah said with a frown.

"Well," Aidan said, "let's all go see what it is." He glanced at Jon, who was grinning. They all went to the entry, where a uniformed delivery man was waiting.

"Liam Delaney?" Liam nodded slowly, and the man passed him a clipboard. "Sign here, please. And where do you want this set of drums?"

"But...I don't understand..."

Jon winked at Liam. "Remember, you were the one who was worried we wouldn't be prepared for the concert."

"You can't have a complete band without a set of drums," Aidan added.

Liam's face lit up. "Now I know what you two were doing in Limerick!"

"Wait!" Jon said. "There's more—microphones and stands, a gift from us."

"I really don't know what to say—except you guys are the greatest. Thank you."

Just then Danny arrived and immediately joined in Liam's excitement. Without hesitation, he volunteered to help take the new equipment to the studio. Naturally they began playing as soon as everything was in place. It didn't take long before the group was in the groove. Danny faced Jen as they played, remarkably in sync with each other. *For such a pretty little thing she sure can keep the beat!*

Liam was inspired and sang powerfully, but after a couple of hours, his fatigue was obvious.

"That should be enough for tonight," Laura announced.

"I have to be at O'Grady's early in the morning anyway," Danny said.

Ignoring Laura's suggestion, Jon and Liam continued working on a new song. She marched over to the amplifiers and turned them off.

Liam smiled. "I guess she means business." Jon, still focused on the song, just picked up the acoustic guitar.

Jen went with Danny downstairs and out to the patio. He was quiet as they walked, and Jen began to worry. He finally spoke.

"Jen, thanks for walking me out."

She moved in closer. "Danny, I really like you. I don't want to be pushy—but I'm leaving in a week. Don't you like me?"

Danny blushed and looked at the ground. "Jen, I do like you. I just didn't think you would be interested in a working-class boy like me."

She impulsively kissed him. Danny ignored his inhibitions and passionately returned her kiss. They held each other in silence for a long moment until Danny spoke.

"I really do have to go, but it's a rush job and I'll be done by noon. Could I see you then?"

"Oh, Danny, I would love to! How about a picnic—just the two of us?"

Danny smiled. "I know the perfect place by the river. Meet me at Chloe's at one."

"I'll be there—you can count on it."

Danny kissed her again, and she let her hand linger in his as he stepped back to leave. He continued walking a few steps backward as she waved sweetly to him.

When Danny turned down the path, Jen watched until he was out of view before returning to the Manor. She felt like she was floating back up the stairs. *I can't wait to tell Laura!* Jen ran back to the music room.

"Well, what's going on here with my little sister?" Jon asked, noticing the dreamy look in her eyes.

She blushed. "Nothing—I just think Danny is a real nice guy."

Jon glanced at Liam. "I think my sister has been bitten by the love bug."

Laura interrupted. "Lights are going off!"

"All right, all right!" Jon complained, placing the guitar back in the stand. He walked out with Liam.

Jen whispered to Laura. "I need to talk to you—I have the most exciting news."

"I'll bet you do—I'll come to your room in a few minutes after I make sure Liam is actually going to bed." Jen agreed.

They left the darkened studio, and Laura followed Liam into his room.

"Checking up on me, Nurse Laura?"

"I just wanted see if you need anything."

He closed the door and gently took her hand. "I have everything I need now."

"Oh, Liam, I miss our time alone. I can't wait until we can ride to the cave."

"I know—I miss you, too." He kissed her on the cheek, and they said goodnight.

Jen answered Laura's first knock, and she eagerly pulled Laura inside.

"I have the most wonderful news! Danny said he likes me, we kissed, and we're going on a picnic tomorrow," she said breathlessly.

Laura gave her a hug. "I'm very happy for you, Jen! But what's going to happen if you fall in love with him?"

Jen's face saddened. "I know—I'll be so far away. But what if I had never met him? That would be worse."

"I can't imagine being without Liam," Laura sighed. "I know we're meant to be."

"I feel like Danny and I are meant to be," Jen said. "And somehow, it will happen."

༼ৡৡ *Chapter Thirty-Three* ৡৡ

F iona set down a large platter of pancakes in front of Jon, who gave her his irresistible smile. "Fiona, you're in my dreams."

She giggled girlishly and patted him on the shoulder, but then looked up to see Hannah's glare of disapproval. The flustered cook quickly retreated to the kitchen.

Aidan ignored his wife's disdain, asking, "So, what do you girls have planned for the day?"

"I think Jen and I will go for a ride and a picnic," Laura said.

"Now, let's see…Liam," Aidan said with a twinkle in his eye. "I suppose you'll be wanting some more time behind the wheel?"

"Jon wants to go with me today," Liam announced.

Aidan raised his eyebrows. "Two teenagers and a set of wheels could be trouble."

"I solemnly swear," Jon proclaimed, "we'll keep it under a hundred."

Aidan chuckled. "Oh—I feel much better now."

Laura and Jen helped Fiona make an elaborate picnic lunch, and then walked down to Chloe's cottage together.

"Jen, promise me you won't do anything foolish."

Jen smiled thoughtfully. "It's too soon to tell if Danny is Mr. Perfect, and that's who I'm saving myself for. Thanks for caring—and covering for me."

Laura was about to respond when Jen's attention was drawn to Danny, who was coming up the driveway. A grin came to his face the moment he caught her eye.

"Hello there, handsome," Jen said cheerfully.

Danny blushed. "I'm so glad you showed up."

"Why wouldn't I show up?"

"Well, another girl might have changed her mind…but then, you're different."

Laura felt like she was invisible. "Hey, I'm still here!" They both laughed.

"Sorry, Laura," Danny apologized. "I was just..."

"Forget it," Laura replied with a wave of the hand. "You two go and have fun."

They thanked her and Laura smiled as she watched them, already immersed in conversation, carrying the picnic basket together.

"My, don't you look thoughtful, young lady," Chloe said cheerfully to Laura as she stepped out to the front porch.

"Hello, Chloe!" Chloe smiled, then squinted as she looked down the path.

"Is that my brother...and Jen? Walkin' together?"

"Yes, they're going on a picnic."

"Ahh...I see—and you're not goin' with them. Okay. Laura, perhaps you'd join me for lunch." She agreed, and the two went inside.

"The truth is," Laura said, "they do want to get to know each other better."

"Well, that sounds nice—especially for Danny, bein' so shy and all."

Laura decided to change the subject. "When's the baby due?"

"Two weeks!" Chloe exclaimed. "Would you like to help me with the nursery?"

"Of course," Laura said with a smile. "And I want to help you with your baby when it comes. I want to have two children—a boy and a girl. "

"That's very sweet, and I appreciate it."

"Chloe, tell me what it's like to be pregnant."

Chloe was surprised at first, but then remembered that Laura was an only child. *Laura was only eight when her mother died—too young to be asking about such things.* She took Laura's hand, placing it on her tummy. Laura's eyes widened as she felt the baby move.

"He must have heard you," Chloe smiled.

"Oh my!" Laura cried. "Does it hurt?"

"Oh no, my dear! 'Tis the most wonderful thing. Patrick and I have wanted a baby ever since we got married. Four years is a long time to wait. It's a true blessin' for us. We have so much love to give to a child."

As they talked some more about family and marriage, Chloe noticed the sparkle in Laura's eyes. "Laura, do you have a certain young man in mind?"

"Did Molly say something to you?"

Chloe smiled knowingly. "She didn't have to. I can see the love in your eyes—not to mention Liam's, when he's lookin' at you."

Laura blushed. "Yes, we do love each other—and someday we will be married."

"Well, Patrick had a talk with Liam about usin' good sense."

"Yes, Molly has talked to me, too, but we haven't done anything! Liam has plans for the future, and we don't want to be foolish. Promise you won't tell Father—Liam doesn't think he would understand just yet."

"Oh, you can count on me. Any time you need to talk about anythin' at all, you can come to Chloe." Laura gave her a big hug.

They spent several hours whiling away the time as they worked on the nursery.

Jen and Danny found the perfect spot to be alone. They talked about everything from music to school, comparing life in America to life in Ireland.

"Danny, will you miss me when I leave?"

He responded with a passionate kiss. "Does that answer your question?"

"What are we going to do? I've never felt this way before."

He held her close. "I don't know, but I've never felt like this either, and I don't want to lose you." They kissed again, but Danny suddenly pulled back. "I really don't know why you're interested in me, Jen. You come from a privileged family. I really don't have anything to offer you."

"Oh, you're so wrong, mister! You've already given me much more happiness than I could ever find from anything material." Jen looked into Danny's soft brown eyes and saw that he, too, felt the connection. *He is Mr. Perfect!*

"I guess we'll have to cherish what we have now," Danny said, kissing her again. "What time do you have to be back?"

Jen looked at her watch. "Oh—I told Laura I'd be back by now!"

Laura had just stepped off the porch when Jen and Danny returned.

"Well, you two must have gotten lost in the woods," Laura teased.

"I'm so sorry," Jen said. "We lost track of time."

"That's all right," Laura smiled. "But your lipstick is smeared—and yours too, Danny!" He blushed and they all laughed. "You are playing music with us tonight?"

"I wouldn't miss it," he replied, smiling at Jen.

Jon teased Liam regularly while they drove around the estate, and then told him limericks and jokes. Liam laughed so hard he had to stop the truck several times just to catch his breath.

"I'll really miss you when you leave, Jon."

"Don't worry—somehow I'll figure out a way for us to come back. But right now we have a lot more important things to worry about—like the lineup of songs I've worked out for Friday's show. We'll go over them tonight." Jon smiled smugly.

"You're definitely the driving force of this band," Liam remarked.

"Thanks, Big Guy. But without your songs, there would be nothing to drive."

"Thank you. I think our energy is pretty strong—like brothers." A warm smile came to Liam's face. "I've always wanted a brother—and I can't imagine a better one."

Jon was quiet for a moment, tears coming to his eyes. "What if I could convince my parents to come to Ireland for Christmas? Of course, Aidan would have to invite us."

"That's a great idea—Laura's going to love it!"

"I know Jen will," Jon chuckled. "In fact, I think it's going to be almost impossible to drag her away from a certain Irish boy."

"Jon, have you ever been in love?"

"I love all women," Jon said with a grin. "But if you mean like you and Laura—I don't think that kind of love happens very often."

"What about your sister and Danny?"

"Liam, she's in love with being in love—she's a hopeless romantic. There's no way the relationship can last. They're too many miles apart."

As soon as he finished dinner, Jon asked if they could be excused. "We have a concert to rehearse for."

"Of course," Aidan answered. "What time do you want us there Friday night?"

"Well, Fiona said she'd be finished in the kitchen by seven. Maybe eight?"

"Now we are scheduling our time around the servants?" Hannah protested.

Aidan darted a look of disapproval at her. "The concert is being put on by this young group, and they can invite the entire village if they want." The room went silent.

Hannah felt a chill go down her spine. She thought it must be the American influence, where the privileged mingle with staff. *When Jon and Jennifer leave, we will return to proper etiquette.*

Laura broke the ice. "We'd better go practice—the concert is tomorrow night."

Jon and the others nodded and got up, welcoming any excuse to leave the table. Laura looked back to see her father, his jaw set, glaring at Hannah. She sat stoically, apparently unaffected by the disagreement.

Danny had just arrived at the studio. He was in a confident mood, and his eyes lit up the moment he saw Jen. "Is everyone ready to rock 'n roll?"

"As a matter of fact we are," Jon answered, looking at the two of them. "We've worked out a great song list, and if we all focus on the music, then we'll be ready." Jen giggled, and Danny shrugged. They got the hint and went right to work.

It took only a couple of hours for the band to play through the song list, and Jon was pleased. "That sounded pretty good, guys. I expected it to take us half the night."

Danny rubbed his chin. "I have an idea for more…showmanship. My little sister Kelly is in Theater Arts at school. She could do the stage lighting for us."

"That sounds great," Jon replied. "Okay, everyone—we need to have a final rehearsal tomorrow afternoon. Danny, can you be here at three o'clock?"

"If we make it four, Kelly and I can both be here. I'm meeting her at the train station." They agreed, and everyone left the rehearsal feeling charged up.

Hannah put a damper on the excitement the next morning at breakfast.

"Now children, remember you must be packed for tomorrow's trip to Dublin—and the trip to London afterwards. Jennifer and Jon, you will be flying home from there."

Aidan felt a pang of sadness as he witnessed the gloom darken the young spirits.

He was determined to shift the focus. "Oh, I'm sure they'll all be ready to go. Tonight we have a concert to attend. Is there anything else you musicians need?"

"Thank you, Aidan," Jon said with a smile. "We appreciate everything you're doing for us."

Later that morning Jen sat on her bed staring at her suitcase, saddened at the thought of leaving her new boyfriend. Laura came in, instantly picking up on Jen's mood. "I talked to my father about inviting you and Jon and your parents for Christmas. He said he thought it would be a brilliant idea."

Jen threw her arms around her. "You're the very best friend anyone could have!"

Laura smiled warmly. "I'll really miss you and our long talks when you're gone," Laura sighed. "I can always talk to Molly and Chloe about things—but it's not the same."

"It's really good that you have them," Jen replied. "Especially Molly. She's young enough to know how we feel. Hannah's from the dark ages!" They laughed.

At four o'clock, Danny and his sister arrived as planned. Kelly was a stunning fifteen-year-old with long, dark red hair and soft brown eyes, petite like Molly, with the same outgoing personality. Kelly took an instant liking to the studio and jumped right in to help. Along with her other talents, Kelly played the violin—and she had brought it.

Unprompted, she pulled it from the case and began playing. Jon, already taken with her beauty, was now delighted with her talent. *Why did Danny wait to bring her around until my last day here?*

The rehearsal began without delay and went so well that Jon gave Kelly a violin part. She set the lighting with a motorized color wheel. When not on stage, she would make custom changes with spotlights. Kelly was enjoying the experience offstage and on, and it was clear to everyone she was going to be an asset.

When the rehearsal was finished Jon held his hands up. "Attention, everyone please. I believe I've got a name for our band: The Siblings."

There were a couple of laughs and they all agreed to the name.

ᔕᗃ *Chapter Thirty-Four* ᔕᗃ

Hannah was surprised—and quite irritated—to see the entire staff marching up the stairs to assemble in the studio. She had assumed they'd have no interest in listening to music she expected to be loud and offensive.

To the contrary, there was great enthusiasm among all the guests, some of whom had never been inside the Manor. The anticipation of hearing Laura and Liam's music was compounded by the prospect of seeing them in a band with "the Americans." The lively conversations and laughter made the studio sound like a full auditorium. Jon tapped on the microphone and the guests began to quiet down and take their seats. "Hello to all the fine friends and family of Montrose Manor. Thank you for coming. I would like to introduce our band, The Siblings!" There were several whoops and hollers, and everyone laughed—except Hannah, who was nearly beside herself.

The group started off with two lively rock 'n roll songs—just right for the mood of the crowd. Jon took the mic again.

"Now we're going to slow things down a bit. We'd like to perform our original version of the song already climbing up the charts in America: *I Remember When*, written by Ireland's own son, Mr. Liam Delaney." Everyone cheered.

Liam sang with the kind of passion that can only come from the heart, where the song was created. The lyrics told of the struggles of a young man tempered by the kinship he felt with his soul mate. Several times during the song, Liam's eyes found Laura's.

By the time the song ended, the crowd was under the spell of The Siblings. Some in the audience were even brought to tears. Everyone applauded elatedly, and Jon gave Liam a hug.

"Thank you so much!" Jon yelled into the mic. "And thank you, Liam, for writing that song! We're going to take short break. Thank you."

Aidan walked right up to Liam. "Son, you are a passionate performer! I think your version of your song is far more touching than the recording I heard of the American band. If you keep this up I'll have to send out for more tissue."

"Thank you, Aidan, you're very kind."

While getting refreshments, the guests mingled and shared their enthusiasm.

"Liam's got such a brilliant voice," Mr. Callahan said. "He can really belt it out."

"And what about Danny and Kelly?" Patrick remarked. "I never knew they were so talented."

"Neither did I," Chloe said. "Danny has always been so shy."

"Jon seems to have brought out the best in everyone," Patrick agreed. "It's a shame he and his sister will be leavin' tomorrow."

"It's lookin' like Danny's goin' to be very sad about it," Molly remarked. "Do you see the way he's lookin' at Jen, now?"

"Indeed I do," Chloe sighed.

After the break, to the delight of all, The Siblings continued to perform for another hour with a unique combination of lively rock, soulful ballads, and traditional Irish songs. When they finished with *Echoes of My Heart,* there was a standing ovation that seemed like it would never end. When the applause finally subsided—and Jon could be heard—he thanked everyone for being such a wonderful audience.

"Jen and I have special thanks to give to Aidan and Hannah and all the fine people of Montrose Manor! We've had a wonderful time here."

Aidan took the microphone. "I'm so very proud of you all! You have great talent, and I hope to see it continue." There was more hollering and applause and Aidan waved his hand to quiet the crowd. "I've got an announcement!" The noise level lowered, and Aidan turned to face The Siblings again. "Jon and Jennifer will be here for Christmas vacation." Everyone clapped heartily, with the exception of Hannah. Aidan continued. "I trust this audience will join me in my request that The Siblings give us another concert at Christmas." More cheers followed, and Laura was elated.

"Thank you, Father! Will Mr. and Mrs. Bianchi be coming, too?"

"They will all be here for two weeks."

Jon and Jen gave Aidan a hug and thanked him. The audience slowly cleared out, and the teens talked about the upcoming holiday as they packed up instruments.

"Jen, I'd like some time alone with you before I have to go home," Danny said.

"We could go for a walk," she replied sweetly.

"Kelly, would you mind?" Danny asked.

"Oh, don't worry about Kelly," Jon replied before she could answer. "I'd be more than happy to keep her company." He flashed Kelly his most charming smile.

"I'll bet you would," Liam whispered, nudging Jon.

Laura smiled. "I think Liam and I will go for a walk, too,"

"See you guys later," Jon said.

Danny and Jen strolled along the river, and then stopped on the arched bridge.

"Jen, I have something for you." He took the gold chain and cross from around his neck and placed it around hers. "I hope it will help you to think of me."

"Danny, it's beautiful! I will always wear it." She gave him a passionate kiss.

"Jen, it's tearing me apart that after tonight I won't see you until Christmas."

She looked at him with tears in her eyes, and placed her hand over the cross. "You'll be in my heart." They embraced.

Danny's thoughts and feelings were stirring as never before. *When she looks at me, problems melt away, and I see the promise of how life could be.*

Laura and Liam walked through the rose garden and sat on a bench overlooking the river. Liam gently kissed her.

"Laura, have you given any thought to going to St Andrews?"

"I can't think about you leaving me." Laura's big brown eyes welled up, and Liam held her face and kissed away the tears.

"I'm not leaving you—I'm trying to get my education so we can be together for the rest of our lives. Please, help me make our dreams come true."

She looked up at him sadly. "So you want me to go to St. Andrews?"

"Yes—we'll be together more if you do. The two schools are only a few miles apart, and we'll be riding the train together."

Just then, Danny and Jen came walking up from the river. Jen ran to Laura to show her the gift from Danny.

"Oh, Jen, it's beautiful!"

Liam shook Danny's hand. "The best to you both."

"I only wish we had more time together," Danny sighed, putting his arm around Jen. "I wish we all had more time together—you're such great friends. And thanks to the band, I'm actually becoming a musician."

"The three of us can still play on the weekends," Laura said. "Liam and I will be home from school." She winked at Liam, and he gave her a hug.

Liam looked at Danny. "The Irish part of the act could continue here, and the Americans can practice at home. We'll join up again in December and do another concert for our favorite audience." Liam's optimism was contagious, and they all hugged.

"We'd better go to the studio," Liam said. "Jon will think we forgot about him."

"Knowing my brother, he doesn't even miss us," Jen laughed.

"Oh, no!" Danny said comically. "My sister! Maybe we should hurry back."

They all laughed and walked leisurely back to the Manor.

"Did you really mean it about school?" Liam quietly asked Laura.

"I'm thinking about it," she replied with a playful smile.

Kelly and Jon were in deep conversation and didn't notice the others had returned.

"Kelly, we need to go home," Danny said. She looked up at him with surprise.

"How long have you been here?"

"Long enough," Danny replied. The others laughed and Jon smiled, knowing Kelly had hung on his every word. *She's so sincere—different from the girls I've known.*

Everyone hated to say goodbye. No tears were spared as each of the young musicians promised to stay in touch. The studio that had been so alive only hours before sounded painfully hollow as Liam closed the door.

Jen felt powerless as she watched Danny disappear down the steps with his sister. She fell onto her brother's shoulder. "Oh Jon, why does this have to happen to me? I have to travel halfway around the world to find the love of my life!"

"It's only a few hours away on the Concorde," he smiled, wiping her tears. "Things have a way of working out. We'll be back before you know it."

"That was really compassionate of Jon," Laura said to Liam as they walked to her door. "He truly loves his sister."

"Beneath that clown suit beats a heart of gold," Liam remarked.

Laura sat up for a while reading the pamphlet from St. Andrews. The pages began to blur as her thoughts kept drifting off. *Should I go? I've never been to a school.*

She finally fell into a restless sleep.

In his room, Jon climbed into bed with bittersweet feelings in his heart. *I've never felt as happy as I am when I'm playing music here—and spending time with Liam.*

Jen's thoughts were not as comforting to her. *I don't know if I'll make it through the next three months without Danny.* It was a long time before she fell asleep.

Liam was reliving their first concert performance in his mind as he lay in bed. He felt truly satisfied, and realized Jon was a great band leader—and a great friend. *He makes me a better musician—and a better person.*

The next morning, the four of them looked like they had been up all night. Very little conversation took place as they sat down for breakfast. Fiona brought out a platter, placing it in front of Jon. His mood suddenly brightened

"Real American bacon!" he cried. "Where did you get it?"

"It is called streaky bacon here," Fiona replied. "I had to order it special. The butcher usually only carries back rashers—our regular Irish bacon. I was afraid I wouldn't get it before you left."

Jon stood up and gave her a big hug. "Fiona, you're the greatest!"

Naturally, Hannah was displeased. *This tawdry display is despicable.* She said, "Children, you only have a few minutes to finish eating. Then you must gather your luggage so we can go to the train station."

Jon tied into his bacon, but not before Liam grabbed a few strips. The four then dragged themselves from the table and went up to get their bags. Jon was the first one to return, and went to the kitchen to say goodbye.

Tears came to Fiona's eyes the moment he walked in. "Jon, you are the sweetest boy! If I were only twenty years younger, I'd be chasin' you." They both laughed until Hannah appeared at the doorway, scowling. Jon looked away and rolled his eyes, causing Fiona to laugh again.

In the grand entry, Aidan couldn't help but notice Jen's long face, and put his hand on her shoulder. "Jennifer, please don't look so sad—we'll have you back as often as we can." She smiled and thanked him.

Once everyone was seated on the train with the journey underway, the beauty of the changing countryside began to lift their spirits.

"Where were all those sheep when I was trying to get to sleep last night?" Jon asked. They all laughed.

A limousine was waiting at Pearse Station in Dublin to take them to the hotel.

"I can't wait to see Trinity," Jon said as they walked through the lobby.

"That's first on the agenda," Aidan replied. "We'll meet back here at noon."

Jon was in awe as they walked through the plaza between the stately buildings that defined the Trinity College campus. He suddenly had a strong feeling he was destined to study here, in the company of respected scholars—and his best friend.

"Jon, I really hope you can go to college here with me," Liam said.

"I have a feeling it's going to happen."

When the tour was complete, Aidan suggested they split up. "You young people will find plenty to do in this city."

"Jon," Hannah said, "that crystal shop is just down Grafton Street on the right."

"Thank you. I should be able to find something nice for my parents there."

"Okay, then," Aidan said. "Hannah and I are going to Dublin House. We haven't stayed there in quite some time, and we need to check on the place. After that, we're going to Meegan Enterprises. We'll see you back at the hotel at four."

Jon found a lovely Waterford crystal candy dish to go with the vase Jen had bought. Liam noticed Laura admiring a stunning crystal heart necklace, and when Jen called her away to look at something else, he seized the opportunity.

"Excuse me," he asked the clerk. "Do you engrave here?"

"That's one of our specialties," she replied.

"I'd like to see this one, please." Liam pointed to the crystal heart. "If you can have it done soon—and keep it a secret from the young lady over there—I'd like to buy it." She agreed, and Liam described the engraving he wanted. He didn't mind the cost—he'd saved money from working in the barn that summer.

The engraving was finished in just a few minutes, and Liam slipped the gift-wrapped box into his pocket, unnoticed by the others.

When they returned to the Grand Hotel, Hannah was waiting for them in the lobby. "Aidan is still in a meeting with Seamus O'Donnell. We're having dinner with them afterwards. I hope you will not mind being on your own for the evening."

"We'll be fine," Laura answered. "We can have dinner here at the hotel and maybe go to a movie."

"Or we could go to the rock concert on the Trinity campus," Jon said. "I saw a poster about it when we were there."

"Well, if you go, please make sure you get safely back to the hotel," Hannah cautioned. "You children stay together, and we will see you for breakfast at nine in the dining room." Hannah rushed off.

"Well, what kind of trouble can we get into?" Jon said with a twinkle in his eye.

Liam shook his head. "Let's just go to the concert."

"Do you know who the band is?" Laura asked.

"No, but they're a new group," Jon replied. "I think they're students here."

"You think we'll ever get to do a concert this size?" Liam asked.

"You can bet on it!" Jon said. "After we're established, we'll do bigger ones."

"Whatever you say," Liam smiled, amused with Jon's confidence. "As long as you don't forget why we're studying at Trinity."

"To study all the hot Irish chicks," Jon replied. Laura and Jen both hit him.

The band turned out to be fairly good—somewhere between rock and punk. The members were from Dublin and all in their early twenties. Liam was intently focused on the lead vocalist, studying his technique and timing.

"We could be playing here—like them," Jon said, "and sooner than you think."

Liam agreed. "We have our own sound—and I like it more as we perfect it."

After the concert the four teenagers walked slowly back to the hotel. With a mixture of inspiration and the melancholy of knowing they would be parting the next day, they all said goodnight.

"Laura, can I talk to you in your room?" Liam asked in the hallway. She nodded and opened the door.

"I've missed our time alone," he sighed. Laura closed the door, and Liam gave her a kiss. He then reached into his pocket and handed her the gift-wrapped box.

"What's this?" she asked.

"It's my heart—for you." With a smile lighting her face, Laura opened it.

"Liam, it's beautiful! And you have my initial engraved on it."

Liam took her closer to the light. "It's actually LLL—for *Liam Loves Laura.*"

She kissed him tenderly, and then Liam gently fastened the necklace in place.

"I will never take it off," Laura vowed. "Your heart will be next to mine, always." She admired the crystal in the mirror. "Liam, I've decided I will go to St Andrews. I know I'll hate being away from home, but if you're not there it won't be the same anyway. And it will make Father happy."

"I think you've made the right decision. We're growing up, and we can't live in the shelter of Montrose forever. I'll do whatever I can to make it easier for you."

Laura smiled sweetly. "Just knowing you will be near gives me comfort."

Liam held her close for a while before speaking again. "I should probably go. Your father might check up on you soon."

Laura looked sadly at him. "I just want to spend the whole night with you, alone."

"Me too—but you know it wouldn't be wise, even if your father wasn't here."

"I know. But it seems like we have to steal moments to be together."

"We'll have a few days at home—I promise."

The next morning in the elevator Laura revealed the necklace to Jen and Jon.

"Laura, you're so lucky to have this guy," Jen sighed, leaning into Liam affectionately. "And be able to see him all the time."

"Well," Laura replied, "I'm going see him less when we both start school. Yes, I'm going to St. Andrews. But I've figured out how we can see each other during the week." Laura had a mischievous gleam in her eye as she looked at Liam.

"How are going to do that?" Jon asked. "A prison break from boarding school?"

"Both our schools offer a dressage class off campus at the Fairmont Stables. And if we just happen to have the same class…" Laura threw her hands up in a show of innocence.

Liam looked at her with surprise. "How long have you been planning this?"

"Ever since I started looking at the pamphlets for both schools."

"Leave it to Laura to figure out how to close the miles between you two," Jon mused. "Or is that kilometers?" They laughed, and Liam gave Laura a quick hug.

"I think it's very romantic," Jen sighed. "You both love riding horses."

"You amaze me, Laura Lye." She flashed Liam *that smile,* and his heart skipped a beat. Their eyes locked for only a moment before the elevator doors opened.

Liam had his plate piled high when Aidan and Hannah joined him in the breakfast buffet line.

"I think Dublin agrees with you, Son."

Jon laughed. "I know it agrees with me. I hope it will be my home next year."

"I have a feeling you'll make it happen," Aidan remarked.

"Thank you," Jon replied. "You know, it's really not necessary for all of you to fly with us to London. We can find our way—we'll just look for the Concorde."

Aidan shook his head. "No, I promised your parents. Besides, Hannah has something planned for us in London today."

Laura rolled her eyes and whispered to Liam, "I can hardly wait."

☙ *Chapter Thirty-Five* ❧

S addened by their friends' departure, Laura and Liam were quiet in the limousine as it made its way through the London traffic. Hannah broke the silence.

"I have a surprise for you children—we are going to visit Emily today and help her with wedding plans." Liam turned pale.

"What do we know about planning a wedding?" Laura frowned.

Hannah ignored the question and rambled on about the upcoming nuptials to be held in the spring at the Fox estate.

Aidan was finally able to get a word in. "Laura, you and Liam are expected to be in the wedding party."

"Why would Emily want us? She has lots of friends."

"You are her family," Aidan insisted. "Elliott's family is all participating—and we will all do our part to support Emily. Do either of you have a problem with that?"

"Oh, no, Sir," Liam answered. *I would do anything Aidan asked me to do—but why does it have to be Emily?*

Laura tried a new angle. "I have decided I should go to St. Andrews—Liam and I will be in school then." Liam smiled.

"Laura, you are not thinking," Hannah corrected. "The wedding will be on a Saturday and you do not have school on the weekends." Liam's smile faded.

"Laura," Aidan said, "I am pleased you've made the right decision about school. Now, I expect your cooperation for Emily's special day."

Laura hung her head. "All right, but what does she want us to do?"

Hannah smiled. "This is why we are here—she can fill us in on all her needs."

Liam cringed. *Oh great...Emily's needs are what I live for.*

Emily was being fitted for her wedding gown. The Harrods store attendant escorted Hannah and the others to the viewing area. Emily, with three attendants in tow, strode out of the dressing room as if she were royalty.

Hannah marveled at her daughter's wedding gown. "Oh, Emily!"

The lunchtime conversation was dominated by Emily as she went over her wedding plans in excruciating detail. Of course everything involved great sums of Aidan's money.

"Aidan," Emily asked sweetly, "I would like you to give me away. With my real father being…dead since I was only twelve, I think of you as my father now."

"I would be honored, dear."

Emily glanced smugly at Laura, who narrowed her eyes. Then Emily flashed a coy smile at Liam. "Liam, Elliott would like you to be a groomsman. And Laura could be…let's see…a flower girl."

"Flower girl?" Laura exclaimed. *How can she be so insulting?*

Hannah intervened. "Laura is a little old to be a flower girl."

Emily sneered at Laura. "Oh, all right—a junior bridesmaid, then."

Mother and daughter chatted endlessly though the rest of lunch about the numerous wedding parties they would be attending.

"Laura, you will, of course, attend all of my bridal showers," Emily said arrogantly.

Aidan spoke up. "Laura will not be able to attend. She will be at school."

"Yes, I forgot she was just a school girl. Well, she is a little young, anyway."

Liam reached for Laura's hand under the table and gave it a squeeze. She smiled at him and touched the crystal heart hidden beneath her blouse.

At last it was time to fly home. Laura and Liam were relieved they could finally talk, seated a few rows behind Aidan and Hannah.

"Can you believe that witch wants us to be part of her wedding?"

Liam shook his head. "I guess this is one of those unpleasant situations you can't get out of."

A mischievous smile came to Laura's face. "Oh, don't give up so easily, my dear. I'm going to come up with a plan."

"You are an angel," Liam said, touching her cheek.

Patrick greeted Laura and Liam as they arrived at the barn the next morning. "Well, there's the world travelers! How are you feelin', lad?"

"Good as new—I think. We'll play it safe, though."

"Okay—you take it easy."

Sky sensed Liam's caution and began walking at a gentle pace.

"I feel all this power beneath me, and I want to unleash it!" A gleam came to Liam's eye. "Let's go!"

Sky took off through the trees at his usual full gallop, with Rose close behind. When they got to the corral at their secret cave, Liam nimbly jumped off. "I think I'm healed."

"That's the best news I've heard in a long time," Laura told him.

Once in the cave, Liam kissed Laura. "I told you we'd have some time alone."

"We'll have to treasure every moment, since we're going to different schools." Not wanting Laura to dwell on that, Liam turned to pick up his guitar.

"I guess we'd better get busy working on my latest song, then."

Laura grabbed her own guitar. They spent several hours laughing, talking, and playing songs. As usual, time got away from them and they had to race back to the barn.

The horses and riders were still breathing deeply as Patrick came around the corner. "Well, I'm glad to see you took it easy." They all laughed.

At dinner Aidan reminded them about school. "We'll be leaving early Monday morning—your classes start Tuesday. That should give you time to settle in."

"Father, did you make the arrangements for the dressage lessons?"

"It's all set up," Aidan smiled. "Your lessons are Wednesdays at three."

❦

Danny came by on Saturday night, and they worked in the studio for several hours.

"It sure is different without Jen and Jon," Danny sighed when they took a break.

Laura patted him on the shoulder. "Have you heard from Jen yet?"

"No—I don't have a phone, so I'll have to wait to get a post."

"Hmm," Laura said with a twinkle in her eye. "It's late afternoon in New York—she should be home. I don't suppose you'd like to talk to her...."

Danny's face lit up. "You're a real sweetheart!"

Laura made the call, and Jon answered. "My little Colleen, how I miss you."

"I miss you too, but there's a certain Irish boy who misses your sister even more."

"Of course," Jon replied. "Put him on."

"Danny, are you there?" Jen said sweetly.

"It's so good to hear your voice." Danny said softly.

They were soon immersed in conversation, oblivious to the rest of the world.

"Liam," Laura sighed, "I couldn't stand it if we were so far apart."

"I will never let that happen."

Before Danny left that evening he thanked Laura again for the call to Jen. "I miss her so much already." He hung his head. "Well, I guess I'll tell you guys some bad news now. I'm not sure if I'll be able to play music with you on weekends anymore."

"Why not?"

"I won't have a place to live here. I was working off my room and board at the garage, but because of school I can't work enough hours now. I'm afraid I'll have to move back to Tipperary with my parents."

"But what about the rugby scholarship for Trinity?" Laura asked.

"That was my plan—but I can't support myself here. Unfortunately, this high school is the only one offering that scholarship."

Laura thought for a moment. "If I found you a place to live—would you stay?"

"Laura, it's very sweet of you to think of me, but I also need a job to support myself. Some things are just not meant to be. I guess college is out of my reach. I do want to finish high school, though, and I can still do that back home."

Laura was determined. "Danny, don't give up your dream. Let us help you."

He smiled. "You're both good friends and I appreciate your support, but I'll be all right. If it's okay with you, I'll come for a visit over Christmas and see Jen."

Liam patted him on the shoulder. "Let's play some music again tomorrow night anyway." Danny agreed, and then left.

"Liam, we have to help him. He can't give up on his dream because of money."

"There are lots of thing you can't do when you have no money," Liam sighed. "I understand what he's going through."

"Well, I intend to help him find a way. We owe it to Danny and to Jen—they're our friends!"

Liam smiled at her. *She's the most compassionate person in the world.*

Liam went to bed, but Laura would not rest until she came up with a solution.

"Father, may I talk to you?" she asked, finding him in the study.

"Yes, my dear. What's on your mind so late in the evening?"

"It's about our friend, Danny—Danny Bailey." Aidan nodded and she explained the whole problem to him.

"What is it you want me to do, Laura?"

"I was thinking that if Danny could help Patrick in the barn on weekends, maybe you could pay him a small wage. And...Chloe and Patrick could feed him his meals."

"I see you have worked out his employment needs, but where will he live?"

She smiled confidently. "What about the Delaney cottage? It's next to Chloe and Patrick, and no one has lived there since Mrs. Delaney...passed."

Aidan smiled. As he sat back in his chair as he looked fondly upon his daughter. He was amused—and proud—that she had thought this all through to help out a friend.

"Laura, my dear, you have your mother's compassion." She beamed. "I will let young Danny move into the Delaney cottage and give him part-time employment. But…I have several conditions."

Laura threw her arms around her father. "Thank you so much!"

"Hold on—you haven't heard my conditions yet."

"I'm not worried. You're always fair. I love you, and you're the best father!"

"I'll need to talk to Danny tomorrow to go over my conditions, and of course, this all has to have his parents' approval."

"He'll be here tomorrow night to play music."

Aidan shook his head. "I think I should talk to him sooner."

"Liam and I will go see him right after church." She kissed her father goodnight and left. Aidan's smiled lingered as he reached for his handkerchief to blot his eyes.

The next morning after early mass Laura and Liam stopped by the garage where Danny was working. "What brings you two here on a Sunday?" he asked, surprised.

"Danny, I have solved your problems. A place to live and a part-time job."

Danny looked at Liam. "Is she for real?"

"Oh, she's better than real."

Laura went on. "I have talked to my father and—"

"I will not take any charity from Lord Meegan!"

"Danny! It's not charity, so forget your foolish Irish pride and hear me out."

Danny took a step back, his eyes wide with surprise.

Liam smiled. "You'd better listen—she's worked hard on this one."

Laura described the proposal, while Danny listened patiently.

When she was finished, he put down his sander, stood up straight, and folded his arms. "I appreciate what you've done, but I can take care of myself."

Liam shook his head. "Danny, you should look at this as an opportunity, not a handout. Besides, with the baby coming, I'm sure Chloe and Patrick will need some extra help, too."

Laura put her hands on her hips and took a step towards Danny. "Trust me—this will not be a handout. My father will make sure of that. He's a good businessman. He said there will be conditions. He wants to discuss those with you today."

"Well, I guess it won't hurt to hear him out," Danny conceded. "I'll have to talk to Chloe—and my parents, too."

"Good," Laura said. "When will you be off work?"

"In an hour. I'll take a shower and be at the Manor about two o'clock."

"That will be just fine," Laura smiled. "Now try to look at the big picture—and your future. Think about Jen…"

Danny smiled at the mere mention of her name.

The look of determination returned to Laura's face as she and Liam walked through the gates of Montrose. "We need to talk to Chloe before Danny does." Liam smiled, knowing there was no stopping her now.

"Well," Chloe remarked after hearing the proposal, "I know my brother has a lot of pride. It's not really foolish pride. He wants to get an education on his own. He would never ask for a helpin' hand. But this seems to be a good opportunity for him, and it would certainly be helpful to Patrick and me to have him here. Plus, Mum would have a place to stay when she comes to help with the baby."

"Perfect!" Laura cried. "It will all work out."

Chloe shook her head once. "Oh, Danny will have to make up his own mind. Patrick and I can point out some of the advantages, but a Bailey always makes up his own mind. Just ask my father." Patrick was walking in and a smile came to his face.

"Are we talkin' about the Bailey pride, now?" He gave Chloe a kiss on the cheek, and Laura told him about the plans. "Well, I sure could use the help around here—and Chloe will need her mum. I think it's a wonderful idea, and I'll encourage Danny all I can."

303

"Thank you, Patrick. I'm going to go tell my father that Danny will be here at two o'clock. I'm also going to ask him to go easy with his conditions."

"On the contrary," Chloe said. "He should make it hard on Danny so it won't seem like a handout."

Curious, Laura looked to Liam, who nodded in agreement. The two left the cottage. Laura sighed. "I just can't understand such foolish pride."

"When you're poor, your pride is all you have," Liam explained. "I can understand Danny's feelings. A man wants to make his own way and hold his head up."

"Liam, you don't feel bad that my father is helping you, do you?"

"Oh, there are times it bothers me, but I'm determined to make something of my life—and I think he knows it. I intend to pay him back for his generosity someday, and then I can really hold my head up and be proud."

"I couldn't be more proud of you than I am right now, Monkey Boy."

ᴄ✓ Chapter Thirty-Six ᴄ✓ᴏ

Fall 1980

Laura looked out the front window for Danny, concerned that he hadn't arrived yet. It was almost two o'clock. She had a sudden realization: Danny had never used the front door. She ran through the dining room and saw him coming up the path.

"Am I late?" he asked as he came up the steps.

"Oh, no—I just wanted to greet you."

"Well, greetings to you, too. But don't feel like you have to escort me."

"Father's in his study, down the hall and to the right."

Danny took a deep breath and knocked on to the partially open door.

"Come in!" Aidan called out. Danny entered the room, and to his surprise, Aidan stood up from his desk to shake his hand. "Have a seat, lad." Danny waited until Aidan was seated before taking his own chair.

"Danny, I have a proposal I think will benefit us both. Laura has told me you're looking for a place to live. The cottage next to Chloe's hasn't been occupied for some time. It's in pretty bad shape. If you'll agree to do the cleanup, repairs, and the yard work, that will be payment for your rent. Also, I'll give you a wage for helping Patrick in the barn on the weekends." Danny started to nod, but Aidan interrupted.

"Before you agree, I have several conditions. First, I do not want you to be employed outside this estate—I'll give you enough work here." Danny was bothered by the statement but held his tongue. Aidan explained. "You see, I feel it is of utmost importance that you keep your grades up. I understand you've applied for a rugby scholarship to Trinity."

"Yes, Sir."

"It won't come to you on a silver platter. There will be practice and games on top of all your studying. If you have a match on the weekend, I'll insist you play. You can make up work for me another time."

Danny realized Laura was right—her father had just made an offer he couldn't pass up. "That sounds fair to me, Sir. I'll work hard at school—and for you."

"Good. Of course, we'll need your parents' approval."

"My parents will be here today for a visit. I'm sure they'll think it's a fine idea. Thank you—and I can get started right away on the cleanup of the cottage."

They shook hands and Danny thanked Aidan again before he left the study, feeling very good about the arrangement.

"Well? How did it go?" Laura asked.

"Brilliantly—you're a genius. Thank you." Danny bowed slightly and Laura's face lit up. "But," he added, "it's not all peaches and cream—I have to work hard. I'm starting right now on the cottage."

"We'll help you," Laura offered.

Liam agreed to help and walked with them down the path. He concealed his reluctance to return to the place that held so many traumatic memories for him. The night Liam's mother was taken to the hospital was the same terrible day the Deacon nearly beat Liam to death. Over a year had passed since, and Liam had not once set foot in the cottage.

The stepping stones leading to the door of the Delaney home were overgrown with weeds, and the front porch was literally falling apart. Danny glanced at Laura in anticipation as he opened the door, breaking through a maze of cobwebs.

With foreboding in his heart, Liam dragged a few paces behind. He waited for Danny to clear the way with the broom before he took a step towards the door. A sudden chill went down his spine and his feet would move no further. He felt the urge to turn and run—as he had so many times from the Deacon.

Laura, unaware of his reaction, marched right through to survey the kitchen. "Oh, this is a mess—but it'll be fun helping you get your new place ready."

Liam forced himself to take a few steps into the living room. From where he stood he could see the filth, and his shame went beyond the neglect that lay before him now. His mother, in her weakened state, had abandoned her very pride in her final days. His mind drifted back to a time from his childhood when she happily sang to him while sweeping

306

and scrubbing. She'd once been the perfect housekeeper. *We may not have much money,* she had explained, *but we can always afford to be clean.*

Liam began to feel nauseous. Suddenly the door opened, and he jumped.

"Liam—it's me, Patrick. Are you all right?"

"I just need some air." Liam turned and rushed outside.

Patrick turned to Laura, who was oblivious to Liam's upset as she busily scrubbed the kitchen counters. He was about to say something when the rest of the cleaning crew arrived: Chloe, Molly, Kelly, and Mrs. Bailey, all of them armed with mops and buckets.

"Thanks for coming to help, everyone," Danny said.

"It'll be great place for you," his mother remarked, "with a wee bit o' scrubbin'. Your father's already gone up to thank Lord Meegan, so let's get busy!"

"Looks like you've got plenty of help," Patrick said as he turned to leave. "I've got to get back to the barn." Outside, he suggested, "Liam, how about you help me bring in the horses."

"I would like that," Liam sighed.

Up at the Manor, Sean Bailey shook Aidan's hand vigorously.

"Lord Meegan, I can't thank you enough for givin' my boy a chance. He wants to go to college so bad, and we just don't have the means to send him. He's a real fine boy."

"I can see that, Aidan said. "I'm happy to help him get a good education." The two men left the study together, drawn to the kitchen by the aroma of Irish stew. Fiona looked up and smiled.

"I've made a big pot to take to the cottage for all the helpers," she announced.

"That's very considerate of you, Fiona," Aidan said cheerfully.

"I was goin' to start dinner for you and the missus in a few minutes, Sir."

Aidan looked thoughtful. "Do you have enough stew to feed all of us?"

"Yes, Sir, I do," she said, beaming.

"Then maybe we should all join the workers, and see how it's coming along."

Hannah had just walked in. "Aidan, may I have a word with you?" Her tone was sharp, and Aidan turned away from her.

"Fiona and Sean, go ahead without me. I'll be along shortly." They grabbed the pot and several pans of soda bread and headed out the back door.

"Aidan Meegan, whatever are you thinking? I go out for a couple of hours, and you are up to your elbows helping the servants. What is going on down at that dirty old cottage anyway? It seems the entire staff is there."

Aidan, a patient man by nature, had just been pushed too far.

"Hannah, these are good, hard-working people who are just trying to make their way. You've always been a lady of privilege, and maybe you can't understand. If you wish not to help, that's your business. But I choose to be involved in what is important to my daughter. And I will no longer tolerate your condescension of the working class. I have made my way through life trying to be a fair-minded person, and I don't intend to stop now.

"I'm going to the cottage to help them get it ready for Danny to move into. Yes—Danny will be living there rent-free, and I don't want to hear a word about it."

With that Aidan marched over to the pantry and grabbed a large bottle of Bushmills. He turned to face Hannah one more time.

"I will be having my dinner with the Bailey family tonight." With that he strode out the back door.

Hannah stood with her mouth open in shock.

Patrick and Liam finished with the horses and walked up the path.

"Lad, I can understand how it must be for you to go back into that cottage. But remember, there were plenty of good times there, too."

"I know you're right—but it's just so hard for me."

Suddenly, Patrick stopped. "Do you hear that? Some good ol' Irish music—sounds like they're havin' fun. What do you say we join them?"

Liam nodded slowly. "Maybe I need to face my demons. I think I'm ready now."

The two arrived in time to see Kelly playing the fiddle, accompanied by her father on the accordion. Fiona was beginning to serve the stew, and Aidan was pouring the drink.

Laura turned to Liam. "I was worried about you. Is everything all right?"

"Everything is just fine."

The evening went on, with Aidan clearly enjoying the music and drink with these down-to-earth people. Sean had just finished telling a humorous story and Aidan laughed heartily, and then turned to see Laura laughing with Chloe and Molly. Aidan put his hand on Danny's shoulder. "When you're ready for lumber and paint—and anything else to fix this place up—please charge your expenses to my account."

"I can't thank you enough, Sir—this is going to be a wonderful place to live."

"You are most welcome," Aidan replied, taking a bow. He stood up and wobbled for a second. "Laura, we should call it a night. We do leave early tomorrow morning."

Everyone thanked Lord Meegan for his generosity. Carrying a small box under one arm, Laura took her father's hand and she and Liam walked him back to the Manor.

"Father, I'm very proud of you for helping." She gave him a hug and his heart melted.

Aidan thought, *I know Fey would have spoken words just like that. Now I have to face Hannah again. What have I gotten myself into?*

Liam followed Laura to her room. "What's in the box, anyway?" he asked.

"Something for you. I found it hidden in the back of a cupboard in the cottage." She pulled out a photo album.

Liam opened it to find pictures of him as a young boy with his father and mother. Tears flooded his eyes.

"There are good memories too, Liam."

"You're an angel." He kissed Laura on the cheek and went into his room, his emotions stirring as he sat down to look through the album.

Each turn of the page brought a fond reminder of the love from his childhood. *I will always remember where I came from and who I am.*

The next morning Molly stopped by Laura's room. "I'm really going to miss having you and Liam around." She had two packages. "I think this might help you and Liam get through school."

Liam had just started down the hallway. "Did someone mention my name?"

"Liam, look! Molly has presents for us." He walked into the room, and Molly handed them the gifts. Laura was pleased to discover they were matching journals.

"Girls sometimes have diaries," Molly remarked, "but these are journals—one for each of you. You can write your thoughts to each other during the week, and exchange them on the weekends."

"Molly, you're so thoughtful," Laura said. "You're always such a help to me."

"You're the greatest," Liam agreed. "Thanks for caring."

"I understand about young love," Molly sighed. "Just promise me you won't be foolish." They nodded and Molly gave them each a hug. "Now go join your father and I'll see you on the weekend."

Laura and Liam arrived at the breakfast table to find Aidan drinking coffee. He'd hardly touched a bite of food. Hannah was nowhere to be seen.

"Father, is Hannah feeling all right?"

Aidan took a moment before looking up from his paper. "It will be just me taking you two to school this morning. Hannah has gone to Dublin on the train." Aidan offered no explanation. Laura and Liam looked at each other quizzically.

On the drive to St. Andrews there was very little conversation. Laura and Liam were silenced by the realization of their imminent separation, and Aidan was lost in his own troubles. They were almost at their destination when Aidan finally spoke.

"We'll go to your school first, Laura. That way Liam will know where to meet you."

Fairmount Riding Academy came into view. Laura said, "Look, Father—this is where we will take our dressage lessons."

Aidan did not respond. Liam glanced at Laura, shaking his head.

A few minutes later Aidan pulled through the gates of St. Andrews Catholic School for Girls. Immaculate grounds surrounded the church, its prominent spire and dome marking the center of the stately campus. One of the nuns greeted the three as they walked through the main courtyard.

"I'm Sister Bridget. Welcome. We've been expecting you, Lord Meegan."

"Thank you," Aidan said. "This is Laura, who is enrolled here, and Liam, who will be attending Glenstal Abbey. Liam will be meeting Laura here on Fridays so they can ride the train home together."

"Yes, Lord Meegan. I will be Laura's counselor. I hope to be able to answer all of your questions today."

"Thank you, Sister," Aidan replied.

Sister Bridget smiled as she shook hands with the young teenagers. "How nice to have a brother to escort you home on the weekends."

"Pleased to meet you, Sister Bridget," Liam answered. "I would like to ask your permission to call Laura from Glenstal to see how she is doing. This is her first time going away to school."

"How thoughtful of you," Sister Bridget remarked. "You may call her sometime after her last class—I would say between three and five would be a good time." The nun invited the three to follow her to the dormitory, and they headed down a long corridor.

"Laura's room is to be shared by two other girls—they will be arriving later today. Ah, here it is." The sister opened the door, gesturing for them to enter.

Laura gulped. It was a far cry from her beautiful suite and private bath at Montrose, but she knew she would have to make the best of it.

"You are the first one here," the nun pointed out, "so you may pick out your bed."

"Thank you—I will take the one by the window." The other two were bunk beds. Laura did not find anything appealing about the idea of having someone sleep on top of her or below her. Liam brought in Laura's bag and she put her belongings away.

"Sister Bridget," Laura asked, "what time do I have to officially be here?"

"We are having orientation at two o'clock today."

Laura looked pleadingly at her father. "Can I go with you and Liam to his school, and then come back before orientation?"

Sister Bridget answered. "That will be fine for today."

They bid the sister a good morning and drove on to Glenstal.

At Glenstal, Headmaster Collins greeted them in the office.

"Liam, we are quite pleased you will be attending our school. We have several fine letters of recommendation on your behalf."

Liam was surprised to hear someone thought enough of him to write a letter, let alone several people.

"May I inquire as to who sent the recommendations?" Aidan asked.

"Why yes, let's see…one was from the tutor, Mrs. O'Brien—she gave a glowing report of Liam's scholastic records. Then there was one from a Father O'Malley on Liam's high moral fiber—and his wonderful voice. And there was another letter from a Robert Bianchi, an American investor. He gave Liam a very high character reference."

Liam blushed, and Aidan spoke for him. "That was very thoughtful of them."

"Well, I'm confident young Mr. Delaney will keep up the good work. Now, one of our escorts will show you and your family to your room."

As they followed another young man out of the office Aidan patted Liam on the back. "Son, everyone is proud of you—especially me."

Liam's dorm room was larger than Laura's and shared by only one other student.

"Your roommate has already checked in," the escort noted, "and has taken the bed by the bathroom. I guess that means the one by the window is yours." That suited Liam just fine—there was a grand view of the lake. The young man bid them a good day. They thanked him, and he left.

"I like your room, Liam—it's very comfortable." Laura tried to force a smile, but Liam could see the uncertainty in her eyes. His own frustration was immense, knowing there was no opportunity to really talk with her, let alone kiss her goodbye.

"I should get Laura back to St. Andrews," Aidan said, looking at his watch. "I'm going to grab a cup of coffee from the cafeteria, and then I'll meet you at the car."

As soon as he was out of sight, Liam took Laura into his arms.

"I love you, Laura Lye. Remember, you have my heart."

She touched her necklace and tears welled up in her eyes. "Liam, I'm scared. I need you to be with me, please."

"Laura," he said tenderly, "I don't want to be away from you either. Remember our dream. This is the difficult part—but we will get through it."

He kissed her and held her for a few moments. Liam's heart was breaking, but he had to be strong.

"Your father is waiting. Do you want to say goodbye here, or do you want me to walk you back?"

She looked up at him, wiping her tears to give him a passionate kiss. "I will always love you, Liam." With that she turned and ran. Liam, alone and powerless, felt only the pain gripping his soul.

Aidan, lost in thought again about Hannah, wasn't even sure how he'd made his way to the car. He was still feeling the sting of the call he'd made to Dublin House early that morning. Josie, the housekeeper, had answered, confirming that Hannah had spent the night.

"Lady Meegan left to meet a friend early this morning," Josie had said. "She instructed me to open the house and to come daily—but she didn't say for how long."

❦ *Chapter Thirty-Seven* ❧

Laura slowly walked into orientation and took a seat in the back, alone. She had not met her roommates yet. In fact the only person she had met was Sister Bridget, who was in front of the hall, standing a little to the side of a tight-lipped lady who appeared to be the one in charge. The older nun aimed a pointer at the chalkboard where there was a long list under the heading, Sister Margot's Rules of Conduct.

"Tardiness will not be tolerated," Sister Margot stated, her jaw set firmly. Laura shrank in her chair. "Your uniforms and shoes are expected to be neat and clean at all times. No accessories, jewelry, or fancy hair clips will be allowed. Your hair must be neatly tied back or cropped short."

Sister Margot went on and on, and Laura's despair took on a new dimension as she realized her very individuality was being revoked. *Oh, who cares anyway? Liam's not here.*

"Miss Meegan, do you care to repeat what I just said?" Sister Margot asked sharply. Laura snapped out of her thoughts, horribly embarrassed while all eyes were upon her.

"I'm sorry—I guess I—didn't hear what you said."

"Miss Meegan, I would think since this is your first day at St. Andrews you might want to know what is expected of you. You are to remain after everyone is dismissed, and we will go over everything again." Laura could hear whispering and stifled giggling.

Sister Margot rapped her wooden pointer on the podium. "Silence!" Laura jumped, knocking her notebook off her lap. The nun narrowed her dark, piercing eyes.

When the others were dismissed Laura remained seated, frozen with humiliation. She could no longer hold back the tears.

Sister Margot marched towards her, carrying the pointer like a riding crop. Laura cringed.

"You will follow me into my office. And stop this childish display—you are far too old to be crying."

Laura looked to Sister Bridget for compassion, but the younger nun seemed intimidated herself. She turned her back to Laura and went about her duties.

Laura continued to whimper, unable to control her emotions while she dutifully tagged behind the head nun. Sister Margot's office was a reflection of her persona—cold and dark. Laura took a seat, nervously wringing her hands.

"Miss Meegan, you must learn to be respectful at this institution. Your life of privilege has no meaning here. Our rules are in place for a reason, and there is no room for a disobedient student."

"I was not being—"

"Miss Meegan—I am speaking. You will not interrupt." Laura's head was spinning and she felt nauseous. The color drained from her face rapidly and the head nun took notice.

"You may go to the restroom down the hall and compose yourself. I will expect you back here shortly."

Laura walked out of the office but ran to the restroom. She splashed cold water on her face and made an attempt to pull her hair back into a braid. *I wish I could run away! I don't even know where I am! I need Liam!* Tears began to flow again. Finally, Laura got control of her emotions and returned.

"It will not happen again, Sister Margot. I promise."

The head nun studied her. "I understand you have signed up for dressage lessons off-campus." Laura nodded cautiously. "And your brother has been given permission to call you in the afternoons. These are privileges which can be taken away when the rules are broken." Laura was horrified. She opened her mouth to respond, but the nun raised her hand. "Not a word, child—or the restrictions will start this afternoon, with your phone call. Do you understand?"

Laura sat up straight in an effort to show respect. "Yes, Sister Margot."

"Fine, then. You are dismissed."

Laura glanced at the clock—Liam would be calling soon. She hurried to the recreation room and took a seat by the phones. The other girls were playing games and talking, but as the minutes slowly passed no one showed any interest in Laura. She looked at the clock—it was already half three. She answered the phone on the first ring.

315

"Hello?"

"Hello, this is Liam Delaney—"

"Liam! It's me!"

"I'm sorry I couldn't call earlier—my orientation took longer—"

"Liam! Please come and get me and take me home!"

"Laura, you know we can't do that. Now tell me what's going on."

Sobbing, Laura struggled to explain.

Liam softened his voice. "Laura, will you do something for me?"

"I'll try."

"Hold on to my heart. Then go to your room and write in your journal—everything you're feeling. Please try to get along with everyone, and do your best to follow the rules. Remember, we see each other tomorrow at Fairmont for the dressage orientation, and again on Wednesday for the first class. I'll write in my journal, too, and we'll exchange them tomorrow."

There was a long silence.

"Liam, I need you. I don't think I can stay here tonight."

"Yes, you can. Do it for me—for us. I love you, and we will get through this together. Remember, my heart is with you all the time."

"I'll try," she sighed. "But I can't wait until I see you at Fairmont tomorrow." Liam said goodbye, and she reluctantly hung up the phone, turning her back to the curious onlookers.

Liam wasted no time—he called the Manor.

"I'm glad to hear from you, Son," Aidan said. "How's everything going?"

"I'm fine—but Laura's not."

"I can't say I'm surprised. What's the problem?"

Liam described her situation. "It may be too much for her to handle—she wanted me to come and get her."

"I'm sure if she gives it time things will work out."

"No, Sir, I think she needs our help—now. I have a feeling she may leave."

"You mean...run away?"

"Yes. I wouldn't put it past her. But I convinced her to stay until I see her at Fairmont tomorrow."

"That's good," Aidan sighed. "You know how dramatic she can be sometimes. Call me right after the dressage lesson and give me an update."

"Thank you, Sir—I will."

"No, thank you for calling. You are a good brother."

Liam sat for a moment after hanging up. *If he knew the way I love his daughter I doubt he would be thanking me.* He went to his room to write in his journal.

Dear Laura,

My angel, I wish I could tell you everything was all right. I feel your pain and wish I was there to take it away. Have the faith I have in you. Trust me—we will find a way for things to get better.

Remember, there is a place where we go to share our souls, where we have shared our hearts, our tears, and our fears. We will be at that place, soon...together.

Always know that I'm right there in your heart.

With all my love,

Liam

Laura walked to her room and opened the door. One girl was sitting on her bed, while another was going through her drawers.

"What are you doing with my things?"

The girl on the bed stood up. She appeared to be the older of the two. "You're the rich girl who got into trouble at orientation," she said. The other girl sneered at Laura and stepped away from the dresser.

Laura straightened her belongings and firmly closed the drawers. She remembered what Liam had said and took a deep breath, turning to face the girls.

"I'm sorry—I'm not having a very good day. My name is Laura Meegan."

"I'm Nola," the older girl said, "and this is Eileen. This is our third year at St. Andrews. We have first choice on the beds."

"I really don't care which bed I sleep in tonight. I'll be leaving soon."

"Too good to stay here, Miss Richey?" Nola sneered, her dark eyes narrowing.

Eileen, the slightly heavy redhead, just laughed.

Laura didn't know how to respond. In an effort to get along—like Liam had said—she smiled. "I just don't think this school is right for me."

"Where have you gone before?" Eileen asked.

"I've always been tutored at home. This is my first time at a school."

"No wonder she thinks she's too good for us," Nola laughed.

Laura could see they were not going to give her any sympathy. In fact, it was clear they intended to make her life miserable.

"Which bed do you want me to take?"

"I will take the bed by the window," Nola announced. "And Eileen will have the top bunk." Laura dutifully moved her shawl and pillow to the lower bunk. Without another word she grabbed her journal and went to the recreation room.

Dear Liam,

As I write, my pen keeps slipping on my tears. Why do I have to feel so much pain? There are some things in the world that don't make sense, and being apart from you is number one. I'm in love with you and always will be. Our separation makes no sense to me, and I can't stay here without you. This is more than I can endure. I know you will come up with some solution for us. No matter where we are, Liam, as long as I'm with you, I'll always be where I belong.

Love, Laura

It was time for dinner. Laura tucked the journal safely under her arm and walked to the cafeteria alone.

Nothing looked appealing to her—all the food was overcooked. Serving herself small portions, she found a seat at a nearly empty table. The girls at the other end appeared to take no notice of her, and Laura made no attempt to speak to them. Returning to her room, she quickly climbed into the lower bunk and held on to Liam's heart necklace. Soon, a fretful sleep overcame her.

318

Aidan tried to relax himself by reading in bed, but it wasn't working. His worries about Laura plagued his thoughts all day. *Have I abandoned my daughter again in her time of need?* He began thinking about the mess he had gotten himself into with Hannah. It only compounded his frustrations.

Aidan drifted off into a restless sleep, and he was soon pulled into a nightmare with rapidly changing images and disturbing scenes. Hannah's stern face came into view, scolding Laura, who was crying and calling for her mother. Fey's image appeared for a split second—and then vanished. Then, suddenly, everything became illuminated, as if the clouds had broken, and before him was the River Maigue in all its splendor, framed by the willow trees and the flowering shrubs. There were two people walking hand in hand on the path along the river. They were Laura and Liam. Aidan awoke in a peaceful frame of mind. *Thank God for Liam.*

Laura awakened to the sounds of Nola and Eileen getting ready in the bathroom. She waited patiently for her turn, but realized morning roll-call was in fifteen minutes. Laura decided she'd better dress and use the public restroom down the hall to wash up.

Breakfast was no better than dinner. Laura picked at a few things and then returned her tray. It was time for her first class, and she certainly didn't want to be late.

The day went by very slowly, full of challenges for the misplaced girl from Montrose. Remembering which class was next—and finding it—was a job in itself. At one point, Laura was completely lost.

"Can I help you?" A soft-spoken girl approached her.

Laura nodded. "I'm very lost. Do you know where the music department is?"

The girl smiled. "Follow me. That's where I'm headed."

"Oh, thank you! My name is Laura—this is my first day."

"I know. I recognize you from orientation," the girl replied with a sympathetic smile. "My name is Susan and this is my second year at St. Andrews." Fifteen years old and pretty, Susan had auburn hair and

319

brown eyes. They walked together down the hall and entered the music class, taking seats next to each other.

"I'm so glad this is my last class of the day," Laura sighed. "I surely would have been late for this one. Nobody has been friendly—except for you. Thank you again."

Susan smiled. "I know how hard it is to be the new girl. I still don't really feel accepted here—I only have a few friends."

"I can't believe the others haven't accepted a nice person like you."

"Oh, it's just their cliques. I guess I don't fit in."

"Then there's no hope for me."

"Well, anyway, you'll like the music teacher, Sister Mary. She's one of the few fun teachers here."

The nun tapped on the podium and began the class by asking students from the year before to sing a song of their choice individually, a cappella.

When Susan's turn came, her shyness disappeared as she sang. She reminded Laura of Liam in that way. The girl's voice was nearly operatic in quality, and Sister Mary praised her when she finished. Susan beamed with pride.

The class almost went by too quickly for Laura, but finally it was time to go to Fairmont Academy. She couldn't wait to see Liam.

The day had been a busy one for him, with a heavy load of classes. The other students were friendly, but rugby was the only thing on their minds. When Liam told them he wouldn't be trying out for the team, they all thought he was crazy.

His last class of the day ended, and soon he was on the path to Fairmont. He was told it would take nearly an hour to walk from Glenstal Abbey, but it would be well worth it to see Laura.

She recognized him from a distance and broke into a run. Tears flooded Laura's eyes as she threw her arms around him.

"Oh Liam, you have to help me!" She told him about her roommates, and he listened to every word before he spoke.

"Laura, is there anything at all good about school?"

She wiped her tears and managed a smile as she told him about her music teacher and Susan.

"Let me think about everything," Liam said, reassuring her. "We'll talk after our class." He gave her a hug, and they walked over to begin orientation at Fairmont.

The head riding master was an accomplished grand prix dressage equestrian. Her name, Una, meaning *united*, described her well. Una was indeed united with her horse as she rode gracefully across the arena to classical music. A very attractive blonde in her early twenties, Una was petite and athletic. She skillfully dismounted and turned to face her eight students. Liam was one of only two boys in the class.

"Welcome to the art of dressage," she said cheerfully with smiling blue eyes.

After Una introduced everyone she had each student take turns riding a basic pattern on one of the other horses. Assessing their skill levels, she assigned each student a horse.

Laura was partnered with a beautiful warmblood named Copper Crown. A bright chestnut with high white stockings, Copper, as Una fondly called him, was big, bold, and very well-trained. Laura loved him right away and she was soon immersed in the pleasure of riding, the last two days' anguish temporarily forgotten.

Liam's horse was a white Lipizzaner. A descendant from the Spanish riding school, General Patton was the largest and most majestic horse at the stable.

"Very few students are allowed to ride The General," Una said. "We save him for our exhibitions. But you have very gentle hands—you're an accomplished rider."

Liam thanked her, feeling privileged, and rode off to the other end of the arena where Laura was.

"Laura, you look grand on Copper Crown. Do you like him?"

"He's wonderful—I feel so much power under me."

"I'm really happy with The General," Liam said with a smile.

After the lesson the two thoroughly groomed their horses before putting them away, and Una took particular notice.

"I am so impressed," she remarked. "No one stays to groom horses after class. Most of my students just hop off and go."

Laura and Liam told Una about their horses back home at Montrose, and she listened with genuine interest. Una's warmth and friendliness allowed Laura to feel at ease, further separating her from her troubles. Liam was pleased.

He turned to Laura thoughtfully as he walked her back to St. Andrews. "Do you think you can stay in school until the weekend, and then we'll talk about everything on the train home? Remember, we have dressage again tomorrow."

She looked at him with sad eyes. "You know it will be difficult for me. But I'll try."

At the school gates, Liam gave her a quick kiss and pulled out his journal. "Here's what I wrote. Did you bring yours?" Laura nodded. "Good. You can write in mine tonight, and we'll trade again tomorrow."

Laura handed him her journal, and then had to run to make it on time for dinner.

Liam returned to the academy, where Una was putting away her horse, Jaromir.

"Hello, Liam—did you forget something?"

"No, I wanted to talk to you about Laura."

"Come inside the office, then. It's starting to get cold."

He explained to her about Laura's melancholy and her thoughts of leaving St. Andrews. "But I could see she really enjoyed her lesson here today."

Una sighed. "I went to St. Andrews myself, and I know how hard it can be. The sisters are tough, and some of the girls can be mean. I think I might be able to help."

"Anything would really be appreciated."

"First thing is that you and Laura should be reassigned to my advanced class. The headmasters require my recommendation for this, and it's safe to say you're both qualified. The best part for Laura is that the class is Tuesdays and Thursdays—it will give her two afternoons a week away from St. Andrews."

"Thank you so much!" Liam exclaimed.

"Ah—but I think I can do more," Una added with a smile. "One of the students in my advanced classes is a real sweetheart—and she goes to St. Andrews. She would be a perfect roommate for Laura—if I can influence Sister Margot. I do have some pull with the school. I will suggest they should be roommates so they can walk to and from dressage class together."

Liam wanted to give the young lady a hug, but decided against it. "You would do all that for us?"

Una gave him a warm smile. "I have two wonderful students with lots of natural ability, and I don't want to lose them."

"Thank you, again," Liam said. "I'd better run or I'll be very late."

"I can give you a ride—I drive right past Glenstal Abbey." Liam thanked her again and helped her close up the barn.

"Come tomorrow for your regular class anyway," Una said as she dropped him off. "It might take a couple of days to work out the transfer to the advanced class."

Liam made it in time for dinner. Afterwards, he called Aidan to report the news.

"Liam, you've gone out of your way to help Laura. I really appreciate everything you've done. I'll call the school and see if I can help to get things moving along."

"Thank you, Sir. This might be just what Laura needs."

"I'll make a nice donation to the Fairmont Riding Academy in Una's name."

After hanging up the phone, Liam went to his room to read Laura's journal. It was heart-wrenching, but he knew things would be looking up. His exhaustion from worrying the night before overtook him in a matter of minutes.

Laura stayed in the recreation room as long as possible, not wanting to return to her room. When the nun finally called lights out, Laura reluctantly gathered her textbooks—and Liam's journal. She headed right for the shower without a word to Nola and Eileen. As Laura dried her hair, she could hear the two laughing and whispering. Laura finished in the bathroom and went to her bunk, only to find they had spilled hot cocoa on her white uniform shirt.

"Oh my," Nola said, "I guess it was in my way—sorry!"

Laura gave her a dirty look but didn't say anything. She grabbed her shirt and tried to rinse off the stain, but it was no use. Fortunately she had one more, but Laura silently cried herself to sleep.

Laura got up early while her roommates slept and actually looked forward to her first class as an escape from them. Knowing her way around the school made the morning easier, and the afternoon brought music class and her new friend Susan. Laura's spirits were boosted as she hurried off the grounds.

Liam was waiting for her just outside Fairmont. She ran to him. "I'm really trying to get along, but my roommates are unbearable!"

"I'm very proud of you." He smiled and gave her a kiss on the cheek. "We will work this out—I promise. Let's get our horses."

The riding lesson went well. Once again, Laura was calmed by the sheer enjoyment of riding Copper Crown.

Liam reassured her again on the walk back to St. Andrews. "Remember, we only have two more days until the weekend. Please try to hang in there for me."

"I'll do my best," she said sadly.

After dinner, Laura was summoned to Sister Margot's office. *Whatever did I do now?* She entered to find the nun sitting behind her mahogany desk. The head nun looked up over the rim of her glasses, her face expressionless as she studied Laura.

"Miss Meegan, Have a seat. How was your riding lesson today?"

"Fine, Sister Margot. I was on time to the class and getting back."

"It is not a question of tardiness. You would do well to not make assumptions."

"Yes, Sister Margot." Laura sat with her hands folded, fearful of what was next.

The head nun eyed her for a moment before she continued. "Do you have the opinion that you are a more accomplished rider than the others in your class?"

Laura gulped. "Oh, no, Sister—I have a lot to learn."

"Indeed you do. However, you have apparently made a good impression on your instructor." Laura looked surprised. "Una Monahan

324

has recommended you transfer to her advanced classes on Tuesday and Thursday." Laura started to protest, but Sister Margot put her hand up. "Your brother has been recommended also."

Laura sighed with relief, but quickly straightened her posture as she realized the nun was not yet finished.

"Miss Monahan also feels there would be some advantage in your rooming with another of her students—something about walking together to and from Fairmont. It seems like much ado about nothing to me—but, nevertheless, you must prepare yourself for sudden changes in life."

"Yes, Sister," Laura answered dutifully

"Fine, then. Now, you must go and pack up your belongings. I will have Sister Bridget come by to take you to your new quarters."

"Thank you, Sister."

Laura hurried to her room and was relieved to find Nola and Eileen out. She packed her things as fast as she could, hoping to be gone before they returned. When Sister Bridget arrived to escort her, Laura was waiting at the open door.

"I see you're all ready to go."

"Yes, Sister." As they left the room they passed Nola.

"Well," she muttered, "you didn't last long, Miss Richey." Laura ignored her and continued to follow Sister Bridget—all the way to another wing of the school.

"Laura, these are your new roommates, Tara and Susan."

"Laura! It's you!" Susan from music class gave her a hug.

Fifteen-year-old Tara greeted Laura with a warm smile. "I understand you will be in my dressage class."

"Yes, I'm riding Copper Crown. Who do you ride?"

"I ride Brigadoon, the big grey warmblood."

"I can see you will all get along just fine," Sister Bridget remarked. "Goodnight." Laura thanked the nun, who bowed slightly and left.

The room was large with three single beds. "Which one is mine?" Laura asked.

"The one by the window," Susan answered. "It has a nice view."

"Are you sure?" Laura asked in disbelief. The girls both nodded.

Laura smiled as she thought of Liam. *He's right—things can change.*

Her new roommates introduced Laura to their friends at breakfast, and Laura felt confident enough to participate in breakfast chatter. The walk to Fairmont that afternoon was fun. Tara was outgoing and made Laura feel like she belonged.

"It's good to see you happy," Liam remarked when they arrived.

"Somehow I think you had a hand in this," Laura remarked. Liam just smiled. "Liam, this is my new roommate, Tara. Tara, this is Liam."

Tara fluffed up her long blonde hair. "Pleased to meet you, Liam. I've heard so much about you."

"Hello, Tara. Pleased to meet you. Let's get our horses."

With the newcomers, there were a total of five students in the advanced class, all equally accomplished riders. Una was pleased to see they all were serious about learning the art of dressage. After the lesson Laura cheerfully put her horse away and thanked Una for recommending her.

"You are quite welcome," Una replied. "You have a great seat and gentle hands. You should go a long way with dressage." Laura beamed.

Liam had just finished grooming The General. Una approached him.

"Liam, the extra care you and Laura take with your horses really helps me. If you want, I can give you a ride to Glenstal most every night."

"Thank you. Would it be all right if I walk Laura and Tara to St. Andrews first?"

"Yes, that gives me time to catch up on paperwork before you return."

Liam joined the two girls. They talked enthusiastically about the horses and were at the gates of St. Andrews before they knew it. Tara said goodbye and ran off to the dorm. Laura hung back for a few moments.

"Liam, I think I'll be all right now. I don't know what you did, but thank you."

"Laura Lye, we can get through anything together."

"Especially since tomorrow is Friday! Meet you right here after school."

Liam returned to Fairmont feeling like the weight of the world was off his shoulders. He laughed easily, helping Una load a couple of saddles into her truck.

Liam knew Una was the instrument of change for Laura and he appreciated it more than the instructor knew. But it was his own determination that brought everything into play in only two days' time. A warm feeling came over him from knowing he could successfully look out after Laura and bring her happiness. He took great pride in being her protector. A satisfied smile came to his face.

☜ *Chapter Thirty-Eight* ☞

L iam was anxiously waiting for Laura at the gates of St. Andrews on Friday afternoon. It pleased him to see her talking and laughing as she walked with another girl. They both came up to greet him.

"Liam, this is my other roommate, Susan."

"Pleased to meet you," Liam said. "Laura told me you have a beautiful voice."

Susan blushed. "I've heard you have a wonderful voice yourself."

"Maybe someday we will get to sing together," Liam said. Susan smiled agreeably at that.

Laura asked, "Where do we get the train, Liam?"

"The bus will pick us up right here and take us to the train station."

"Here it comes," Susan said. "My father will be coming to pick me up after he gets off work. It was nice meeting you, Liam."

Once they were on the train and away from familiar eyes, Liam took Laura into his arms and gave her a very long kiss.

"Wow, Mr. Delaney, you must have really missed me."

"You have no idea, Miss Meegan. You know, I think this is going to work for us. We really have something to look forward to at the end of the week."

"If I always get a reception like that it'll be worth it."

Liam flashed her a mischievous grin. "I have a surprise for you. Tomorrow we can ride to the cave, and I'll show you what it is."

Aidan greeted them with a big hug when they walked in the Manor.

"It's been so lonely here without you." Aidan's face was drawn, but his tone was cheerful. "There's something I want you both to see. Are you up for a walk?"

"Sure," Liam replied as he looked curiously at Laura.

A few minutes later the three were strolling down the path by the river.

"Father, is Hannah still in Dublin?"

Aidan looked away. "Yes. I've made her very mad at me."

"What could you ever do to make someone mad?"

"I'm not perfect, my dear. Hannah has her standards, and I've let her down."

"I can't imagine you ever letting anyone down. You've really helped Danny."

"Yes—and that was a big part of Hannah's upset. She feels I have become too involved with the staff."

"Oh, Father, that's what makes you special. You care about people and give them a chance. I love you for being the person you are. Please don't let Hannah change you."

Liam spoke up. "If you hadn't come to my rescue I'd be in a home for unwanted boys. I'll never forget what you've done for me—I'll carry it in my heart forever."

Aidan stopped walking, his eyes filling with tears. "You two are more important than I can put into words. What you've said means a lot to me."

They continued down the path until Danny's cottage came into view.

Aidan beamed. "Well, what do you think?"

Laura and Liam fixed their gazes on the freshly painted home, not believing their eyes. The yard was weeded and now lined with large flower boxes spilling over with zinnias and limnanthes. The fencing was new, as well as the front porch and railing.

"This is beautiful!" Laura cried. "Thank you, Father."

"Oh, I had very little to do with it. Sean Bailey is a great carpenter, and Danny—well, his talent and energy know no bounds."

Just then Danny opened the front door. "Welcome home! How was school?"

"We'll talk about that later," Liam said. "The cottage looks grand!"

"This is a fine place to call home," Danny replied proudly. "I want to thank you all for making it happen."

Aidan bowed slightly, and Danny invited them in.

Laura looked around in amazement at the freshly painted interior with new curtains and slip covers on the furniture. "Danny—this is incredible! I can't believe all you've done."

"Oh, I can't take credit. Mum is the decorator—and quite the seamstress to boot."

Aidan turned to Laura and Liam. "Don't be fooled by Danny's modesty. He's a jack of all trades in his own right." Danny blushed.

Liam decided to save him. "Hey! Are we going to play music tonight?"

"I'm looking forward to it," Danny replied. "I'm not sure how much I'll be able to play next week when Mum arrives."

"Is Chloe excited about having the baby?" Laura asked.

"That's all she can talk about," Danny said, laughing.

Liam walked solemnly through the cottage, his own mother on his mind. The moment of sadness was slowly replaced by a feeling of completion as he stood tall in the living room. *That was another time and another place.*

Laura noticed his mood and quietly approached him. "Are you all right?"

Liam smiled. "I've got so much to look forward to. I've let the past go."

"I'm very proud of you," Laura said, touching his arm.

At dinner, Laura and Liam tried to keep the conversation lively for Aidan's sake.

"It's so nice to have home cooking again," Laura remarked. "I must tell Fiona how much I appreciate her." Aidan nodded, but just stared at his coffee. "Father, would you like us to keep you company tonight?"

"No, dear, you two go on to the studio with Danny. I have some work to do in my study." Laura could see the sadness in his eyes and knew he wanted to be alone.

"I'm really beat," Danny said after a few hours of working on songs.

"Me too," Liam agreed, "and I miss my comfortable bed." They got no argument from Laura, and they all agreed to pick up where they'd left off the next night.

"I miss my big room and my privacy. I think I'll soak in a hot bubble bath."

"That's my cue to leave," Danny remarked as he waved goodbye.

At breakfast, Laura studied her father. "Did you sleep at all?"

He looked thoughtfully at her. "I need to go to Dublin and speak with Hannah. I have to resolve this matter between us. I'll leave Monday after you go back to school."

"Father, if it's bothering you, go now. We'll be fine with Molly and Fiona."

Aidan rubbed his chin. "Maybe I could go and be back on Sunday afternoon."

"Don't worry about us," Liam assured. "We have plenty to do. We're going to ride our horses today, and we'll be back in the studio tonight."

"Thank you, Son. I think I'll leave right away."

Laura gave her father a hug, and she and Liam headed for the barn.

Patrick greeted them with a big smile. "Boy, has the place been quiet without you two." Kite spotted Liam and walked gingerly over to him. "He's gettin' a little slow these days," Patrick remarked. "It must be the cool weather. He always wants to hang out by the stove in the kitchen."

"How old is Kite now?" Laura asked.

"Well," Patrick said thoughtfully, "Liam has had him almost six years—and the vet thought Kite was old when you found him."

Liam picked up the little dog and hugged him. "I think he's the best dog in the world. I don't care if he is old." Kite licked Liam's face and wiggled in his arms.

"Liam, I have to make a trip to Kildare today and I hope to be back home before dark so Chloe is not alone too long. Would you feed the horses this evenin' for me?"

"Of course—I'd love to."

"We'll also check in on Chloe," Laura added.

Patrick smiled. "You two are the greatest."

Sky and Rose were happy to go for a ride, and they raced through the fields tirelessly.

"Wow!" Liam remarked when they arrived at the cave. "Our Arabians may be small compared to dressage horses, but they sure have big engines."

Laura put her arms around her mare's neck. "I will always love Rose the best."

"And Sky will always be my number one."

Laura was a few steps ahead of Liam walking into the cave. She turned to face him. "I'm ready for my surprise."

Liam gave Laura a tender kiss, which heightened her anticipation, but then he pulled back. "Let's go over here." He led her by the hand to the straw bed. Laura sat down slowly, urging him towards her, but Liam slipped away and turned to pick up his guitar.

"I've been writing a song for you," he announced. "It's called *Hold Me.*" Laura smiled, concealing her disappointment as Liam began to sing a beautiful love ballad.

When Liam finished the song he put his guitar down. "I still have work to do on it, but—"

Laura jumped up and silenced him with a passionate kiss, running her hands down the small of his back. She pushed her body closer, enticing him with her seduction.

Liam forced himself to pull back. He spoke in a weak voice. "I guess you liked the song."

Laura moved in again, wildly kissing him.

"Laura, we need to stop now!"

"Why? We love each other."

"You know why," he answered, backing away.

"Liam, don't you want me as much as I want you?"

"There's nothing I want more at this moment—but we can't be foolish."

Laura ignored his refusal and again moved towards him until Liam's back was literally against the wall. As gently as he could, he pushed her away.

"I mean it, Laura. We need to leave now." To show her how serious he was Liam walked to the corral, grabbing both the horses' rope collars and placing them around their necks. In a few moments he was mounted up, ready to go.

Laura was angry and humiliated, but she went with him. They rode in silence back to the barn. Liam was frustrated by his own actions and tormented by his burning desire for Laura. His sense of honor had prevailed, but now he'd hurt the one he loved.

As they put the horses away in the barn the silence dragged on, chilling Liam more profoundly than the darkening skies. The stillness was broken only by a sudden cloudburst.

In spite of the downpour, Laura took off running for the Manor. Liam got his truck from the tractor shed, and started slowly up the driveway. His eyes straining, he spotted her a short way up the road.

"Laura! Get in—you're getting soaked."

"Why would you even care?"

"Please get in. I'm sorry. Can't we talk about this?" She answered by turning away towards the footpath. She was out of view in seconds.

Liam sped up the driveway, arriving at the Manor before Laura. He had just enough time to run inside and grab a towel before she appeared at the back door. He stepped forward to dry her off.

"Don't touch me!" Laura brushed past him to run up the back stairs.

"You sure have a way with her!" Fiona remarked at the kitchen door.

"Thanks. Very funny."

Molly appeared from the dining room. "It's really pourin' out there. I hope it will let up soon. I have a date with Brent. Will you and Laura be all right?"

"We'll be fine," he answered flatly.

Fiona tried to cheer him up. "I've made you a chocolate cake. And there's a big pot of soup and fresh-baked bread for your dinner. Lord Meegan will not be home, so eat whenever you want." Fiona glanced at the clock and then out the window. "The mister is picking me up—soon, I hope. We have to visit his mother in the hospital. I would rather spend the night here, the way it's comin' down, but we promised her we'd be there tonight."

"Thank you, Fiona. Be careful out there. You too, Molly."

The two ladies donned their foul weather gear, and their respective rides soon arrived. Liam decided to have a piece of cake before returning to the barn to feed the horses. As he sat alone finishing his milk, Liam jumped at the crack of thunder and nearly dropped the glass. Ever since that ill-fated night when his father died in the barn fire, Liam was deeply disturbed by thunder and lightning.

He shook off the fear and the grief. *I'd better get to the barn.*

ᴄ♪ *Chapter Thirty-Nine* ᴄ♪

The wind picked up so fiercely that Liam could barely shut the door of his truck after climbing in. With rain pelting his windshield he made his way towards the barn, more from memory than from what he could see. A sudden cracking sound from behind caused Liam to instinctively duck. It was not thunder, but a huge limb that separated from one of the trees and came crashing to the ground. With its branches brushing against the truck, Liam pushed on.

The horses were agitated from the storm and announced their displeasure loudly when he entered the barn. Softly singing as he fed them, Liam attempted to calm them—and himself. He secured the barn, including the storm doors. Noticing the clock in the tack room, he realized how long the whole process had taken. *I'd better check in on Chloe.*

Watching for Patrick's return, Chloe was standing at the front window.

"Liam! Come in before you get taken away by the wind!" He hurried inside and sat down by the warm fire.

"Thanks, Chloe. How are you doing?"

"I'm fine," she groaned. "Except for this lower back pain that won't go away. But I guess when you're as big as I am, your poor back just can't take it."

Liam stoked the fire, adding the last piece of wood. "I'm going to get more firewood for you. I'll be right back."

"That's very kind—you're always thinkin' of others." Chloe noticed something in Liam's voice and decided to speak up once he returned with the firewood. "Liam, you look sad to me. Where's Laura?"

Liam did not reply right away, and began stacking the wood next to the hearth. He paused and turned to Chloe. "She's mad at me. She locked herself in her room."

"Don't take it hard. Young girls are often moody—it's her changin' hormones."

You got that one right. A crack of thunder saved Liam from having to reply, but it was unsettling to him. "Chloe, maybe I should stay with you until Patrick gets home."

"Oh, that's so sweet, but I'll be fine. Besides, Danny should be here soon. He's been at O'Grady's doin' some work on the hay lorry for Lord Meegan."

"If you're sure, I'll go to the Manor. But if you need anything—please call."

She nodded and smiled. "Now hurry before you get soaked again."

Once inside the Manor, Liam went right to Laura's room and knocked. "Laura, are you all right? Can I come in?"

Taking her silence as a hint that she wasn't ready to talk, Liam went to his room. Just then the lights flickered. Another crack of lightning lit up the night sky and the Manor went dark. Liam heard Laura's door open from across the hall.

"Liam, are you there?"

"Yes—I'm right here. Stay there while I light a candle." Shielding the flickering flame, Liam made his way to her room. "I'm sorry I didn't handle things very well."

"I'm sorry, too," Laura said, touching his arm. "I don't know what got into me. I felt so much passion for you...after you came to my rescue at school...and then the beautiful song..."

Liam gave her a hug. "We both had an emotional week, and we're normal teenagers—with desires. We just have to keep our heads clear."

"Liam, you're the one with the clear head. I'm a hopeless case."

He smiled. "But I love this hopeless case."

"Please don't give up on me. I'm trying to grow up and be more responsible."

He kissed her on the forehead. "Speaking of responsibility...I think we should go and stay with Chloe until Patrick comes home. I checked on her after I fed the horses. She said she would be fine, but I'd feel better if we were there."

"She's all alone in the dark," Laura said. "We should bring her candles and something to eat. But you change into a dry shirt first."

Laura packed up a pot of soup, some candles, and flashlights.

Liam had parked as close to the back patio as possible. As they hurried to the truck, Laura was almost swept off her feet by the wind.

"Wow!" she exclaimed after they climbed in. "Drive carefully, Liam."

"Don't worry. I'm on the lookout for anything, including that big branch."

The cottage was illuminated only by the glow of the fireplace. Liam parked and they carried everything in. Laura's flashlight revealed a pained expression on Chloe's face. When she did not get up from the rocking chair, Laura rushed to her side.

"Are you all right?"

Chloe looked up and shook her head. "This pain in my back is unbearable."

"I'll fix you a hot water bottle for your back," Laura said. "And we brought soup." Liam lit some candles while Laura headed for the kitchen.

"Thank you, dear. I suppose my worryin' is getting' to me. Patrick should be home by now—and Danny, too."

"I'm sure Patrick is just driving very slowly because of the storm," Liam reassured her. "Do you want me to look for Danny?"

"Oh, no, stay here where it's warm and dry. He'll be here as soon as he can. I'm sure he tried to call, but the phone is out."

Laura got the water bottle behind Chloe's back, and then handed her a bowl of soup.

"My, but you are a good nurse. Thanks so much."

A few minutes passed and Chloe said she was feeling better. Laura and Liam looked out the front window for any sign of the others.

"That soup really hit the spot," Chloe remarked as she stood up. "Ohhh!" She winced in pain and dropped the bowl. Following the crash was a sudden gush of liquid.

"Oh, my God! I'm havin' the baby!" She made her way to the daybed next to the fireplace.

"Liam, what do we do?" Laura cried.

"Help Chloe take off her wet clothes. I'll get towels."

Just then the door opened and a gust of wind blew across the room. Danny stepped in, soaked to the bone. "The bridge is flooded—I had to walk down to the—"

"Danny!" Laura cried. "Your sister's having her baby!"

"Now?"

337

"Ooh!" Chloe moaned. "I feel the baby comin'!"

"What are we going to do?" Danny asked, panicked. "She needs a doctor!"

"Chloe has Nurse Laura—and two strong men," Liam said calmly. "The baby's coming now."

Danny quickly nodded and wiped his wet hair away from his brow. "What can I do?" he asked.

"Get a blanket and warm it by the fire," Liam said.

Chloe cried out with every contraction, and Laura soothed her, wiping her forehead as she held her hand. Danny tossed the blanket over a chair by the fire and rushed to his sister's side. "What can I do now?"

"We need scissors and string," Chloe groaned. "To cut and tie off the cord."

Danny went to Patrick's tackle box and got some fishing line. He found scissors and alcohol in the bathroom.

"You'd better hurry!" Chloe cried.

Laura pulled back the covers. "I can see the baby's head now."

Chloe was pushing with all her strength, but it seemed to Laura that she was making no progress.

Laura looked fearfully at Liam. "Why is it taking so long?" she whispered.

"Babies take longer than foals," Liam explained. "She's doing fine."

After a few moments of catching her breath, Chloe gave a final push and the baby was born. Laura placed the newborn on the warm blanket.

"It's a boy!" she announced.

Chloe wept while Danny held his sister's hand.

Liam studied the infant—he did not appear to be breathing. He grabbed the baby, and in one swift motion turned him upside-down and stuck his finger in the tiny mouth.

Chloe was shocked. "Liam! What are you—"

The baby gasped and cried loudly. Laura heaved a sigh of relief, while Liam began rubbing the newborn with a towel.

"This little guy just needed some stimulation to get started," Liam explained. He gently placed the infant on Chloe's tummy. "It's probably time to cut the cord, but I've never done this."

"Tie it off in two places," Chloe explained, "close to the baby—then cut in between." Liam made the knots and the cut.

Suddenly, Chloe let out another yell.

"Oh! I'm sorry!" Liam said. Chloe just shook her head and began to push.

"Do we have another baby coming?" Laura gasped. Chloe shook her head again.

"No," Liam said. "She's passing the placenta."

Danny sat down. "I feel weak…"

Patrick came through the door, shaking off the rain and removing his hat. He turned to the scene before him—a revelation: he was now a father.

Chloe, her newborn son wrapped warmly in her arms, gave her husband a smile that spoke volumes. "We have a son."

Patrick came to his wife's side and kissed her tenderly. He was mesmerized by the miracle of his newborn. Laura handed him a towel for his hands, but his gaze never strayed. He gently placed his hand on the baby, as if blessing both mother and child. "The road was closed. I had to walk in. I—"

"It's okay, dear. I had the best help anyone could ask for." Chloe nodded towards the three, now standing quietly by the kitchen door. "I want to thank you all from the bottom of my heart. I couldn't have done it without you."

Danny patted Liam on the back, and then gave Laura a hug. "These two were the delivery team. All I did was raid Patrick's tackle box for some fishing line." Everyone laughed, relieved at the happy ending.

Liam turned to Laura and Danny. "Should we give them some private time?"

"Absolutely," Danny replied. "I think I've got a soft, dry bed waiting for me."

Laura told Patrick there was soup on the stove for him, and they said goodnight.

Laura was still smiling as Liam drove them back to the Manor. "What a wonderful experience to see the baby being born." She affectionately squeezed Liam's arm. "Someday I want children, too."

At Laura's door, Liam held her in his arms, her flashlight illuminating the hall and the rain still pelting the windows. The day's exhaustion finally began to grip him.

"What a night. I think I'll turn in."

Liam woke up to sunlight streaming into his room. The storm had cleared and he had slept through much of the morning. He dressed and went down to the kitchen where Laura was making hot cocoa. She seemed especially beautiful to him.

"Good morning, Nurse Laura," he said with a big smile.

"Good morning to you! Fiona made breakfast—it's still warm in the oven. Would you like me to fix you a plate?"

"Thank you. I'm starving."

Liam was soon on his second serving while Laura sat with him and suggested, "When you're finished I think we should go see the new baby and Chloe."

"Laura, you were really brave last night."

"Brave? I was terrified! You're the one who took charge and saved the baby when the rest of us thought he was fine."

Liam shrugged. "Well, I guess my experience with foaling mares paid off."

"You underestimate yourself. You did everything right—including cutting the cord. You didn't get that from foaling mares."

"I guess I was running on instinct. I'm just glad we were there to help Chloe."

"You were the one to check up on her…while I was sulking in my room."

"Don't be so hard on yourself," he said, squeezing her shoulder. "We've had a very intense week. Now, shall we go and see the little O'Brogan?"

Chloe saw Laura and Liam through the window and motioned for them to come into the house. They stepped inside to find her in the rocking chair nursing her son. Liam blushed.

"Oh, Liam," Chloe teased. "After what you saw of me last night, this is nothin'!"

Liam quickly changed the subject. "You did a great job last night, Chloe."

"Thank you, Liam. So did you. Would you like to hold the baby?"

Liam hesitated. In the bright light of day, he realized how tiny the newborn really was. "I'd better not."

"What? Do you think you'll drop him? I sincerely doubt that, the way you took charge of him last night and all."

Liam carefully reached for the child. Tears came to his eyes as he held the tiny little life in his hands. "Oh Chloe, he's so perfect—a real gift from God."

The baby opened his eyes and looked at Liam.

"Philip Liam O'Brogan," Patrick said, appearing from the bedroom. "Meet your Godfather—if he'll accept."

"You want me to be his Godfather?"

"And Laura to be his Godmother," Chloe answered.

"We'd be honored," Liam said, looking at Laura, who was beaming. "Laura, do you want to hold him?" he asked, already knowing the answer.

"I'd love to," she replied. "But look at you—you're such a natural."

Liam placed the baby in Laura's waiting arms. She soon had the infant asleep, as she rocked him gently while singing a lullaby.

Chloe gave Liam a nudge. "Isn't that a pretty picture?" He smiled and nodded.

Patrick gave Liam a pat on the back. "You were a real hero last night. I will always be in your debt."

"I only did what was needed. I'm grateful Danny and Laura were here, too. Besides, Chloe's the one who did all the work."

"You'll always be the hero in my book," Patrick insisted.

"I'll agree to that," Danny said as he walked in. "Liam was a hero."

"All right, you guys—enough," Liam said modestly. "I think we should let Chloe and the baby rest."

"We should ride to the bridge to see how much damage the storm caused."

Laura agreed to Liam's plan, and it wasn't long before the two had Sky and Rose at the front gates of Montrose. Just then Aidan drove in.

"Everyone all right?" Aidan asked. "I saw the lorry pulled off the road before the bridge back there."

"We're all fine," Liam answered. "I'll tell Patrick they've opened the road again."

Laura laughed. "Patrick has had other things on his mind the last few hours." Aidan looked at her quizzically. "We delivered Chloe's baby last night," she announced.

"Oh, my God!" Aidan exclaimed. "How are they?"

"Mother and son are healthy and happy. We'll fill you in on all the details later."

"Thank God it all turned out well. See you in a while. I may check in on Chloe and Patrick later."

Before dinner that evening, Aidan pulled Laura into an embrace. "I can't begin to tell you how worried I was when I couldn't get through to you on the phone. We had our share of rain in Dublin, but we still had power. It seems every time I'm away there's an emergency here at the Manor."

"It all turned out well," Liam remarked, "thanks to Nurse Laura."

Aidan shook his head while he looked at Liam. "Chloe and Patrick had high praises for you as well when I saw them today. She told me about your fast thinking when the baby wasn't breathing. I'm very proud of you, Son."

"Thank you," Liam said humbly.

"From what I heard," Aidan continued, "the two of you have earned the title of Godparents. And I like the name Philip Liam. I plan to open an account for the baby's college fund. I'll do it in your names."

"Oh Father, that's very thoughtful of you," Laura exclaimed.

Aidan smiled, but then looked away.

Hesitantly, Laura asked, "Father, how did things go in Dublin?"

Aidan sighed. "I don't know. Hannah wants me to be someone I just can't be."

"I know you'll do what's right. But please be true to yourself."

⫷ *Chapter Forty* ⫸

At Glenstal, Liam was adapting quickly to the rigors of a demanding class schedule. His natural thirst for knowledge was the key driving force, but he also wanted to avoid the embarrassment of being unprepared. Two years younger than any of the other students, Liam did not want to be singled out for any reason—including his age—although his large stature helped to conceal it.

Liam's only true relaxation was riding The General during his dressage lessons, and—of course—seeing Laura during the class.

Laura's classes were easier than she had feared, and to her surprise she was doing well. Her new friends were helping to give her a more positive attitude, and conforming to the strict policies set by the nuns was less of a daily challenge.

On the other hand, Laura's ex-roommate Nola was becoming her number one adversary. Nola hated the fact that Laura was attractive and wealthy, and she would humiliate Laura at every opportunity. Laura was able to avoid the jealous girl everywhere except math, the one class they shared—which was Nola's best subject. Whenever the students were called on to answer aloud, Nola was always swift with her response while Laura needed a moment to work out the answer. Nola could be counted on to sigh or yawn, resulting in the other girls giggling—until they were silenced by the teacher.

Laura's prime inspiration in overcoming the various obstacles was, of course, Liam. She lived for the twice-weekly dressage lessons with him, and for Friday afternoons when he waited for her at the gates of St. Andrews. His love revived her, particularly on that day when they would leave the week behind.

The weekends at Montrose were filled with playing music with Danny and riding Sky and Rose. Laura always managed to find time to help Chloe with Little Philip.

Laura and Liam made a point of having dinner with Aidan as often as possible, but he spent much of his time alone in the study. Laura was worried, not really knowing what she could do to help him. Finally the day of Philip Liam's christening arrived, and she was certain her father's participation would brighten his spirits—until she found him in his study.

343

"Father, you're not dressed. Aren't you going to the christening?"

"No dear, you and Liam go ahead. I've got some work to do here."

Laura was disappointed but could tell he'd made up his mind.

Philip Liam O'Brogan, now two months old, was as good as gold during the ceremony. In the Irish tradition, Chloe had taken her magic hankie from the wedding and stitched it into a christening bonnet for the baby.

After the ceremony there was a small celebratory gathering at the O'Brogan cottage. Chloe and Patrick opened a card from Aidan which contained a generous check to open an account for the baby's college fund. They asked Laura to thank him.

Laura's pace was slow as they walked home from the party. She sighed. "I wish I could do something to help Father—he's so sad. Maybe I should call Hannah."

"Oh, Laura," Liam cautioned, "I don't think you should interfere."

"Well, someone has to make a move. I can't stand to see Father like this."

As they rounded the last bend in the path, they could see Aidan's Mercedes going down the driveway until it was out of view.

"I wonder where he's going," Laura said with surprise. Liam just shrugged.

In the kitchen, Fiona shook her head when Laura asked. "He didn't want dinner—said he would get some stew at the village pub."

Laura didn't know quite how to respond.

"I know, dear," Fiona remarked with compassion. "I thought it odd myself."

"That's enough," Laura announced. "I'm calling Hannah."

Fiona glanced at Liam, who threw up his hands and followed Laura to the study.

"Laura, dear, it is good to hear from you," Hannah said. "How are you and Liam doing in your new schools?" Hannah's tone was cheerful, and Laura was encouraged.

344

"Things are fine at school. We're both very busy and learning a lot."

"That is wonderful, dear."

"But Hannah, I'm worried about Father. He's been very unhappy with the situation between you two."

There was a pause before Hannah spoke. "I love your father, and I know he loves me. We just have different standards."

"So you're going to let your differences keep you apart?" Laura asked pointedly.

"Child, it is more complicated than that."

"All right then," Laura said. "You will each have your standards to keep you warm at night." Hannah gasped, but Laura continued before she could speak. "Hannah, I admit I don't know the facts, but what I do know is my father loves you. That tells me he sees a good person in you. Don't you see the good person in him?"

"Of course I do—I love your father. But we have had words. I said some fairly harsh things to him. I fear he may not forgive me."

"At least talk to him—you can't just leave it unsettled."

"Laura, your boldness is a bit unnerving, but I can see it may turn out to be a good quality in you. I will think about everything you have said. Thank you for calling."

Laura hung up with a triumphant smile on her face. Liam shook his head.

"You're amazing. I'm proud of you."

The next morning when the phone rang, Laura jumped to answer it.

"Good morning, Montrose Manor...Oh! I'm so glad it's you...Father, it's for you, and you'll definitely want to take it in your study."

Aidan put his paper down and looked at his daughter quizzically. "Who is it?"

"It's your wife calling from Dublin."

Aidan jumped up and did exactly as his daughter suggested.

Laura waited with her hand still over the phone. She rolled her eyes as she looked at Liam. "I hope I don't regret this someday," she whispered, before hanging up, hearing her father pick up the extension in his study.

Aidan looked excited a few minutes later when he reappeared in the dining room. "I'm leaving for Dublin—hopefully to work things out with Hannah. If all goes well you'll see her next weekend when you come home. I trust you two can get yourselves to school tomorrow morning?"

"Of course, Father. And we wish you the best."

"Thank you both—especially you, young lady. Apparently you had some very bold, but very wise words for Hannah." He gave Laura a big hug and she beamed.

Laura was always relatively quiet during the Monday trip back to school, knowing she would be saying goodbye to Liam. This morning she was particularly subdued, her look of worry clearly visible to him.

"I'm guessing that look of concern has nothing to do with your father. It's about Copper Crown, isn't it?" She sadly nodded. During the Thursday class the horse had pulled up lame, and Laura was unable to complete her lesson.

"Remember," Liam assured, "Una was going to have the veterinarian look at him Friday and take x-rays. It could be something simple—like a stone bruise."

"I guess we'll find out tomorrow," Laura said solemnly.

Laura couldn't wait for the bell to ring Tuesday afternoon.

As the girls approached the academy they could see Liam—he had a sober look on his face. Laura's heart sank.

"They can't use Copper anymore for lessons," he said sadly. "The veterinarian said he's developing arthritis and dressage is too hard on him."

"Oh no! What will happen to him now?"

Una walked up and answered Laura's question. "I hope to find him a home. It will be hard, though. Who wants a huge horse that costs a fortune to feed and nobody can ride? I hate the thought of…putting him down."

"No!" Laura cried. "He can go to Montrose Manor and retire to green pastures."

Una cautiously smiled. "Do you really think your father would take him?"

"My old pony Lilly has arthritis, and she's in pasture, doing just fine. I'll call my father right away and ask him about Copper. Father's got a big heart and would never let a horse be put down just because he was no longer useful."

"That would be wonderful," Una sighed. "Copper deserves the best. I hope it works out. Well, let's get class started." She walked with the three over to the arena.

"Today we will ride our patterns to music," Una announced to the students. "Laura, you can ride my horse, Jaromir."

Laura felt privileged. Majestic and proud like The General, Jaromir was also a white Lipizzaner. She approached him with great anticipation and stroked his shoulder. "Hello, Jaromir," she said kindly. "I am honored to ride you today."

The regal steed lowered his head, giving Laura a look of approval with his soulful eye. Laura mounted him carefully and assumed her natural seat, to which he responded by standing in readiness for the first command. She sat up straight and picked up her reins, and the gelding moved forward into a walk.

Laura was impressed with Jaromir's smoothness and grace, feeling as though he was drawing her into the rhythm of the dance. Her focus shifted to the particular way he flowed with the music. At that moment, Laura understood the world's love of Lipizzaners. *They are truly bred for dressage.*

After class Laura made the phone call to Montrose Manor from Una's office.

"I'm sorry, Miss Laura," Iris informed her. "Your father's still in Dublin—I'm not sure when he'll return. When I hear from him I'll be sure to tell him you called."

"Thank you, Iris," Laura replied.

Una had gathered her students for a meeting. She waved at Laura to join them.

"I have an announcement to make: we have been invited by the Spanish Riding School in Vienna to tour and see a special performance. The trip will be during the Easter vacation. I will need to get a commitment from ten students to be able to plan the trip." Laura, Liam, and Tara said they wanted to go, along with two of the others.

Laura returned to the phone and called Dublin House, but there was no answer—even after several tries. She hung up, disappointed.

"Una, I can't seem to reach my father. Please promise me nothing will happen to Copper until I talk to him."

"I'll speak to the owner of the academy," Una replied.

Two days passed, and Laura had still not heard from her father.

"This is not like him," Laura said to Liam before the Thursday lesson. "He should at least be checking in at the Manor."

"Remember, he's still trying to resolve his problems with Hannah. I'm sure he'll get the message from Iris and call you soon."

Class began, and Laura did her best not to worry so she could concentrate on riding. While she finished grooming Jaromir, Una approached her.

"I'm afraid the owner of the academy does not want to keep Copper any longer if he's not paying his way."

Laura began to cry, and Liam intervened. "It won't be long until we hear. I'm sure the owner can give Copper a few days after everything he's done for Fairmont."

"If it was up to me, he would have a home here for life," Una said. "But I just work here—it's not my decision."

"I understand," Liam said. "But please express to the owner that Lord Meegan has been out of town." He turned to Laura. "Don't be upset—it'll all work out."

"I just don't understand how anyone could be so cruel," Laura sobbed.

"It's a matter of finances for some people," Una explained.

"Father, where have you been?" Laura exclaimed when she finally got the call the next day. She didn't give him a chance to answer before blurting out the story.

"Laura, calm down. I was away with Hannah for a few days, and we're back at the Manor now. We can discuss this matter when you come home this weekend."

"No, Father—please! They are going to put Copper down."

"I'll call the owner of the academy right now," Aidan said. "They will not do anything with your Copper—I promise."

"Thank you Father. I love you. I'll see you tomorrow night."

On the train, Laura's spirits were renewed. "Liam, do you think Father and Hannah worked everything out?"

"I think we should stay out of it now."

"I know. You're right. I just want to make sure they're happy."

"I have really missed you two children," Hannah said, greeting them in the entry with a smile. "Although I guess I should think of you now as young adults."

Laura gave her a hug. "Welcome home."

"Thank you—I am happy to be here."

"Where's Father?"

"I am not really sure. But I do know Patrick asked to see both of you as soon as you got home. You may find him in the barn."

"We'll go right now," Liam said, setting his books on the table.

When they entered the barn Aidan suddenly appeared from the tack room, a gleam in his eye. The clip-clop of hooves could be heard from further down the aisle. Laura and Liam turned to see Patrick leading Copper Crown towards them.

"Oh, Father! You're the greatest!" Laura dove into Aidan's arms, and then turned to stroke the big chestnut's neck.

Patrick was beaming. "I picked him up this mornin'. He's a grand gentleman—walked right into the lorry like he knew he was comin' home."

Laura rubbed Copper's forehead. "We'll take good care of you."

Patrick bent over and slowly felt along the length of Copper's leg. "You know I've worked with horses with arthritis before. Some of them responded well—they even came up perfectly sound."

"My father used to make a liniment and sweat wrap for the joints," Liam said.

"I know the one—I'll give it a try."

"Whatever it takes to make him comfortable," Aidan said.

A glow of contentment radiated from Laura's face as she sat down to dinner. She carried a sense of fulfillment which could be read by anyone in the family with no explanation. Because of Laura's natural persistence, those close to her found renewed strength and conviction in overcoming nearly impossible odds. In turn, they fueled her, sustained her, and loved her. It was all she needed to move on to the next challenge or nurture the next soul, whether family or friend, two-legged or four. Her father felt the warmth of her gaze at that moment and reflected it right back to her.

"My dear Laura," he said softly. "You're determined to save the world, aren't you?" Laura beamed and even blushed a little. Aidan winked at Hannah, and then turned back to his daughter.

"We think you're pretty good at it."

Liam shook his head, but found no reason to stifle a smile. An easy laughter broke out between them that seemed like it could last forever.

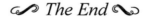 *The End*

ᗆ*About the Author* ᗑ

C arol Carpentier's interest in horses came from her maternal grandfather, who was a coachman for Lady Buxton in England during the late 1800s. She was fascinated with his stories of her rail travel throughout the U.K., which required him to load the team of horses onto a railcar along with the ornate carriage, and to care for them along the way.

Carol's sense of the equine spirit led to a successful career as an Arabian horse breeder for over forty years in Santa Cruz County, California. During that time, she also worked as an equine veterinary assistant, and the combined careers allowed her to interact with a diverse complement of trainers, riders, and breeders from all over the world.

She was born on Mare Island, California, to a U.S. Navy officer and his wife. The relocation of their small family every few years instilled in her a fondness for travel which she has shared with her husband, Bob, for 35 years. Her three grown children like to journey with them when they can, and all members of the family reside in California.

Who's to Say Where the Wind Will Blow began as a seed planted by her grandson, Brent, who at age ten, accompanied them to Ireland. The magnificence of the castle where they stayed in County Limerick prompted Brent to say, "What a wonderful place for children to grow up."

Who's to Say Where the Storm Will Pass

Part Two of the *Who's to Say* Trilogy

A idan Meegan feels a growing pride in his extended family of Montrose Manor, as it has broadened to include the Baileys of County Limerick and the Bianchis of New York. But their collective strength is soon to be challenged, as a guest at the manor brings unforeseen peril that will threaten their very lives. Laura Meegan, plagued by feelings of vulnerability, clings ever closer to Liam Delaney, who, as her adopted step-brother, must be vigilant in concealing their love for one another. Controlling his urges for her, Liam affirms his scholastic and musical pursuits, looking to a future in which he is worthy of Laura in her father's eyes.

As best friends and confidants, Jon and Jen Bianchi accompany Laura and Liam with dressage students on a trip to the Spanish Riding School in Vienna. Romance does blossom there—but it is in the hearts of Jon and an equestrienne who risks her career for his charms.

During a Christmas ski holiday in the Italian Alps, thrill turns to terror as two among the families become lost in a snowstorm so severe that the nighttime search is called off by the rescue team.

The respite of Montrose becomes the backdrop for the inevitable discovery of Laura and Liam's secret, leading to the unfolding of their worst fear: separation from each other.

From the winner's circle at a Kildare racecourse to a hospital ER in Tuscany, the hallowed halls of Trinity to a police raid in St. Moritz, the families of Laura, Liam, Jon, Jen, and Danny are put to the test as they share the joys and brave the elements in *Who's to Say Where the Storm Will Pass.*

CPSIA information can be obtained at www.ICGtesting.com
Printed in the USA
LVOW100315240712

291101LV00006B/3/P